I0649905

Penumbra

A Journal of Weird Fiction and Criticism

No. 2 ☾ 2021

Edited by S. T. Joshi

"A man must make his own penumbra . . ."—Angela Carter

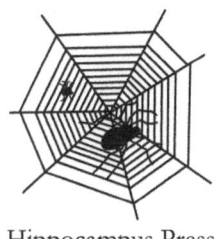

Hippocampus Press

New York

Published by Hippocampus Press
P.O. Box 641
New York, NY 10156
www.hippocampuspress.com

Cover art by George Cotronis. Cover design by Daniel V. Sauer,
dansauerdesign.com.
Hippocampus Press logo designed by Anastasia Damianakos.

PENUMBRA is published once a year, in Summer. Articles and letters
should be sent to the editor, S. T. Joshi, ℅ Hippocampus Press. Literary rights for articles will reside with PENUMBRA for one year after
publication, whereupon they will revert to their respective authors.

ISBN 978-1-61498-349-1 paperback
ISBN 978-1-61498-350-7 ebook

Contents

Fiction

Nonfiction

Classic Reprints

Poetry

Notes on Contributors

Lost for Words

Ramsey Campbell

"I'll tell you what to write."

My neighbour at the table full of writers lifts a blink to the man who's holding out a copy of our book. "Nobody does that," she lets him know.

"Your editor must love you." When Liz Cheung only gazes at him he says "I mean I'll give you the inscription."

"Not even that, sorry. Real writers don't use other people's words."

This amuses him, though not much. "Just sign your story if you can be arsed."

Liz signs in kanji and an elegantly florid English hand. She's first in line, and now the man moves in front of me. "Are you going to play hard to get too?"

"What did you want in your book?"

"Roy Stafford." It sounds as if he means to put me in, but he's reading my name from the cardboard strip propped up in front of me. "To Charles Vane," he says. "From one writing soul to another."

"You're a writer too."

"More than some," he says as if I've insulted him. "You'll be seeing my name."

How much does he look like a writer? You could say his broad flat whitish face resembles a page on which his features have left plenty of space for information. His small thin mouth gives nothing much away, and maybe wariness has shrunk his eyes, while his dinky nose renders his big nostrils comical. I'd note all this on my phone to use somewhere, but I don't want him to see. Instead I say "I can write what you said."

He splays his copy of *Vampiric Visions* so wide at my tale about

Barney the vampire that I hear the spine crack. As soon as I've inscribed the book he snatches it and sticks out his free hand for a shake. It's so loose and spongy that I could imagine it absorbs anything it finds to assimilate, another image I should store for future use. He caresses my inscription before licking his fingertips, which have picked up ink. "Thanks for the words," he says. "I'll take care of them."

I've attended plenty of signings at conventions like this one—ContraryWise—but this is the first time I've participated. Everyone who brings a book makes me feel more like a writer—the woman who's stuck a yellow nametag on the first page of each story, the man who lends a different coloured pen to each contributor, even the fellow who piles dogeared volumes in front of every author except me. Perhaps because of how Vane fingered my inscription, nobody else lets him dictate theirs. When he reaches the far end of the table he glowers at everyone behind it and mutters something his mouth shrinks. Once we've all dealt with the queue Asha Kumar brings us books to sign for Perdition Editions, the dealer who's hosting our event. I'm signing the last one—my signature has begun to look as if the final syllable has been stretched thin for easier consumption—when Asha leans over my shoulder like a teacher observing a pupil at work. "Roy, let's have a word."

"I didn't do anything too wrong, did I? I signed that writer's book the way he asked."

"You did more than your duty for Mr Vane. Now come along with me."

She leads the way out of the dealers' room, where a few tables still display books—not Venomous Videos, though, or Shirts Don't Hurt or Ornament Yourself. At the bookshop where I work I can find anything customers want if they give me just a hint what it is. Asha's determination makes me nervous even when I see we're heading for the bar. "What will you drink?" she says.

"Anything except what Barney does." When her smooth dark oval face yields a patient smile I say "Can I have a pint of Fan's Fancy?"

It's the ale the hotel has put on for the convention—renamed, at any rate. When Asha orders a glass of white wine for herself I wish I'd taken the chance to seem sophisticated. I trail her to a table in a side room, which is empty except for us. "Here's to Barney," she says and clinks her glass against my tankard, which offers her a duller note. "I'd like to see more of him."

"You mean you'll be editing another vampire book."

"That could happen, but I was wondering if he has one in him."

For more than a moment I feel lost for words. "Are you asking me to write one?"

"Or possibly a series if you think you could. I really think you've found a winning formula. I'm sure a lot of readers would like to know more about Barney and his family."

"Anything in particular?"

An idiot asks that—an amateur who sounds as if he's already run out of ideas—but his editor is too professional to treat him like one. "All the men who have to work down the mines where it's dark," she says. "The cousin and her sex shop with the blacked-out windows. I liked his uncle's butcher's shop with the sign that says 'You're pudding' that the ordinary customers think is mispunctuated. And Barney having to cycle off to yet another village every night to feed."

"I didn't have much room to write about his night shift at the slaughterhouse."

I'm hoping to inspire her so that I'll be inspired, but she says "I wouldn't see a novel in that by itself."

"I did have a bigger idea," I say, only to feel as if someone has stolen too many of the words that make it up. My head is growing brittle as a hollow egg by the time I manage to add "The sun never touches their side of the valley, but someone could build a new estate on the other side, and all the new people would be a temptation. Maybe Barney's family could campaign against it and try to stop all the building work so nobody finds out what they are."

Asha lifts her glass, but not to tap my tankard, and I'm afraid I've used too many words to shore up an idea that won't support a comment. She takes a sip of wine before saying "Might you have time to write up a synopsis before I leave on Sunday? Then I could pitch it next week."

The drink I take is larger than her glass. "You want to publish it."

"I'd say it has legs, maybe as many as a spider. Just give me enough to show my colleagues." She repeats her sip and stands up, leaving her glass half full. "Have fun with it," she says, "and I'll see you on our panel."

I gulp the rest of my pint and head for my room, where the dressing-table provides barely enough space to work. I scribble on the pad of hotel notepaper, but the demands of the synopsis and tomorrow's panel seem determined to outshout each other. I'm supposed to be meeting friends at Die For Thai—we've dined together at conventions for years—but straining to piece thoughts together leaves me no time and very little appetite, and I phone Shaun, pretending I'm ill. I end up with half a sheet of points to make on the panel but nothing for the book beyond a title. All this feels as if it has scooped out my cranium, and I crawl into bed.

Vampiric Visions is the morning's first panel, and the first I've ever been on. I find a table to myself at breakfast in case I'm visited by any new ideas. I'm halfway through a plateful loaded from the buffet when my intake grows lively in my guts, and I barely make it to my bathroom. A pill to some extent quells the burbling of my innards just a few minutes short of the panel, and I venture down to the main auditorium, bearing my cardboard name. Asha and several of her other writers are already seated onstage, and Charles Vane is on the front row. I'm hoping Asha will introduce the panellists, but she simply describes the anthology. "Now tell us about yourselves," she says and leans forward to send me an encouraging look.

"I don't need to tell anyone who I am." This sounds insufferably pompous, and I rush to add "I mean, you can all see my name, that's unless you're sitting too far back or you can't see anyway if you've got some trouble with your eyes or you're blind, except you couldn't be or you wouldn't be able to read our book. So for anyone who can't make me out, I'm Roy Stafford."

I've generated several titters, not the reaction I was trying to produce. Perhaps people think I meant to be funny, but my babbling was caused by Vane's relentless stare, which looks hungry for words and satisfied with none of mine so far. "I wrote the one about Barney the vampire," I drone doggedly on and am wondering how to stop when Asha intervenes. "We'll come to everybody's stories," she says. "Just let me assure anyone who's visually impaired that we've brought out an audiobook of the anthology. Your turn now, Liz."

All this sounds like a series of rebukes for my performance, and so do everyone's opening speeches, far more professional than mine. At least they postpone the questions Asha sends along the panel. Why are vampires still valid? What can they tell us about ourselves and contemporary society? What have we each brought to the theme that gives it relevance? My microphone screeches at most of my answers, which ramble unless they falter, and Liz Cheung keeps moving it away from me as though I'm not worth hearing. Since I don't feel remotely relevant I can only claim to have added humour with my story—Asha seemed to think so when we had our drink—but Vane stares as if I've laboured over telling an unfunny joke. I'm pathetically grateful when Asha shuts me up by suggesting comedy can be relevant and says she thinks mine is. A ContraryWise helper brandishes a placard that gives the panel five more minutes, and Asha invites questions from the audience. At once Vane demands "What was wrong with the story I sent you?"

"I told you in my email," Asha says. "I don't think this is quite—"

"Too original for you, was it?" He throws his head back, poking his larynx at her, while he tells the audience "It's about a vampire who feeds on language."

"I said I liked the idea, and the same with your novel. I did suggest how you might fix them."

"By writing like somebody I'm not," Vane says and glares at me.

"Or like yourself but better," Asha says. "Yes, lady in the crinoline, you had a question."

"You've still got mine." As Vane stalks out of the auditorium he declares "I got what I came for."

The costumed woman wants to know what future we think vampires have, and I come up with the idea of putting one in the crew of a spaceship. Does that earn me any of the applause at the end of the session? As we vacate the stage Asha accosts me. "I'm sorry I was such a," I say so hastily I outdistance words. "You know, what you could have done without. Not much use."

"You contributed, Roy. It was your debut, after all. Any progress on what we discussed?"

"I've got a name now, I mean a name for it. A title." All this feels like a delay in owning up to *"Barney's Barney with the Builders."*

"A little wordy, do you think? Perhaps *Barney's Builder Barney.* No, that doesn't work either. Don't panic. I'll be here till noon tomorrow."

That doesn't feel like much time once I start to work on the synopsis. Surely summarising shouldn't be as hard as writing a novel—it doesn't need so many words—but once I'm in my room I struggle to compose a single sentence. It feels like trying to assemble an item only to discover you've lost some parts. Suppose I can't write it until we've agreed on a title? I spend hours straining to piece one together, and more of those looking for Asha. She's sharing a bottle of wine with a writer in a bar opposite the hotel, and greets me with a neutral glance. "How about *Barney and the Builders?*" I plead.

"It needs to tell the public what kind of book we're offering. Try and relax with it, Roy. Perhaps your synopsis will suggest a title."

How can I relax until I've succeeded? Someone has tidied my room, and I lock myself in. I won't risk eating much after the effect breakfast had. I don't even finish the biscuits that come with the coffee I gulp in the hope of setting off thoughts. Barney, I write on the pad, and when I can't think what should come next I crumple the sheet and scrawl his name on the next page. That doesn't release any words, and it feels as though he and I can't act until I find him some. I haven't by the time I lie down to rest my throbbing head, and when I wake it's dawn.

I can't think in the room with the bath in. Once I've finished in there I make coffee, hoping it will sting my brain awake, and sit at the desk, the piece of furniture like one with paper to write on. Barney's name is waiting on the top page, but it's as dead as a name on a stone. Where's my writing soul? Even Charles Vane says I have one. Barney tries, Barney doesn't want, Barney thinks, Barney goes to . . . Every start I make feels like losing yet another sentence. I'm crossing out the latest useless clump of words, digging the ballpoint so hard into the page that it blots the sheet beneath, when the phone rings by the bed. I'm afraid the caller may be Asha, and it is. "Just checked out, Roy," she says. "Don't worry any more if you've nothing for me."

A harsh taste of coffee lurches up my throat. "Don't you want it now?"

"I always want what I ask for. I may have been a little hasty, though."

"How do you mean?"

"I should have given you more time. Do you think a week will help?"

Going home should, and I say so. "I'll be looking for your ideas," she says.

I'm doing that with no success. When I take the train home the wheels mock me by clacking like a keyboard. Can my phone give me words? The potential sentences it puts together lead nowhere useful. Barney tries to be happy, Barney doesn't want to be happy, Barney thinks I'm the best . . . I wish I could believe him. Barney goes to the best place, but that isn't where I am, and I only hope that's home.

You could think the main room of my flat is walled with books. A girl I had round did—she said they made her feel shut in—which is why I don't have girls round any more. The books are even on the television screen, dim ones that look as if someone tried to rub them out. I'm hoping all the books will lend me words or wake up some I've read in them. I sit at my window facing rooms with no books in and switch on my computer, but it's no more help than the phone was. Asha told me to relax, and she's supposed to know what's best for writers. I microwave a curry out of the freezer, and it's muttering in my stomach when I go to bed.

Who said "I always want what I ask for"? Asha did, but I don't know whose voice I dream of hearing. Maybe Barney could say it, which feels like an inspiration until I'm at my desk, where my head grows emptier than all the rooms opposite. Searching for my writing soul only reminds me of the words Vane made me write, which seem to have formed a barrier that won't let any others through. All the books have grown remote from me, though they remind me of the libraries I spent so much of my childhood in, where my parents worked. Maybe going back to work tomorrow will unblock my mind.

I'm on the late shift. The branch of Texts is the only place you'll see books in the shopping mall. It's between the ABSolute Power gym and Corset Is, the vintage lingerie emporium. When I leave the staffroom, Terry Henderson is waiting for me at the counter. He's the manager, whose torso and bald head are so close to round that he looks like a figure 8 stuffed into a suit. "Here's our expert," he tells a pair of customers. "I guarantee he'll identify the book. He's better than any computer. Never crashes either."

"You're my last hope." The taller woman leans on her stick to bring her face down to my level. "I read it when I wasn't even half your age," she says. "All I can remember is a chappie who wanted to blow up a bridge."

"He sounds like Alec Guinness," her dumpy companion contributes, "but it's not that bridge."

I've recognised the book. My parents used to ask me questions like this when they realised how much about books stayed in my head. The cover of the edition the shop sells is in there, but I can never think of an author until I've come up with the title. I smile at the woman and open my mouth, which produces an empty sound too much like a belch. "It's, I know it, just thinking of the word," I mumble. "It goes, you know, ding. A thing that rings."

Terry and the women stare at me as if they're watching a performer fail onstage. "A bell," the dumpy woman suggests.

"That's it, a bell. The one that rings for somebody."

"For Whom the Bell Tolls," Terry says like the punch line of a joke he's heard.

"By Ernest Hemingway," I want to prove I know.

Since I'm facing him, it looks as if I'm telling him. "Now I've got one for you," the dumpy customer says.

I'm still thinking of Hemingway—of how that book fell back on awkward words because it couldn't use the real ones. "It's a romance, this one," the woman is saying. "About sisters getting married and one catches a cold in the rain."

I know it, and I don't see how she can't. Who's the author? Why does my brain need the title first? I feel as if I'm spitting out the few words I can find in the dark inside my head. "It's you thinking you're better than everyone else."

The stooped woman raps the floor with her stick. "What are you saying about her?"

"I'm not. I wasn't. It's the first word of the name," I say and have to add "And you take against people for no reason."

"You don't know the first thing about me, young man. I assure you I always have plenty of reason."

I feel as if she's trying to shove my words back into my mouth. "That's the other part of it, of the name. They're what it's supposed to be about."

"Verity," her dumpy friend says, "I think he's trying to tell us it's *Pride and Prejudice*."

"See, you did know." This sounds accusing, and I try to make up for it by saying "I expect you know who wrote it too."

"Jane Austen," Verity says before her friend can speak. "Would it be too much trouble for you to escort us to the books?"

I'm afraid my struggles with language may blind me to the order on the shelves, but I manage to lead the women where they need to go. I hope the sales will placate Terry, but once the customers have limped and plodded off he says "What kind of joke was that supposed to be?"

"No kind for me. My brain seized up, that's all."

"Let's see it stays with us if it went off." As if this is related Terry says "Have a successful weekend?"

"I think I've sold a book I'm going to write."

"Try keeping your mind on real ones while you're at work."

"Writing's work too." Since he doesn't look convinced I say "And I'm in a real book."

"You're in nobody's book now except their bad ones, so you'd better start working on that."

He thinks he's being clever with his words. I won't waste any more on him – I already feel I've got too few. When I go home I try to put the day out of my mind, but this doesn't help me work on what my book will be about, it simply leaves more room for words that won't let any others in. From one writing soul to another, from one writing soul to another . . . I feel as if I won't be rid of this until I understand it, but that's staying out of reach. At last I can only slump into bed.

I've got no ideas when I wake up, but I'd have no time to write them before leaving for work. I'm first there except for Terry. "I hope your mind's clearer today," he says as he lets me in.

"Clear as, you know, the thing I said yesterday."

He stares as if he thinks I'm joking, but there aren't as many words in my head as I need. It feels like being lost in one of those big stone places with no light. What's Terry telling me? To put out new stock. I can do that—I still know which letters come before which. I'm putting the old books off the bits of wood they're lined up on, the planks, onto the thing you push along when two men come over. One has no hair on top and his friend has some round his mouth. "Just ask him," hairy mouth says. "He'll know."

They both look like they want to laugh. "What?" I have to ask.

"He's after a book he saw the film of but he can't remember the name."

I think Terry's put them up to this. "Why are you asking me?"

"I heard the guys you work with giving you a quiz. They just had to say anything about a book and you'd know what it was."

That was weeks back. It feels so long ago I might as well be someone else. "You're wanting to buy it, are you?" I say to skin top man.

"If you've got it I'll have it or I wouldn't be here." As Terry frowns at me across the shop the man says "All I can tell you is a woman weds her doctor but he wants someone else and ends up an alcoholic."

This sounds like a joke about the story. I can see the book with no words on it in my head. Trying to think who wrote it makes my head go thin. I have to say the book's name, but all I can get out is "It hurts."

"What does?" hairy mouth says like he doesn't care.

I could say my head. Instead I say "That's like the first bit. It hurts."

Both men stare at me, and skin top says "We didn't come to play a game."

I wonder, but I say "I'm trying to help you. It's like hurting in the dark, the name." That's still more like my head, but it doesn't mean anything to the men, so I go louder. "Hurting when it's dark, that's what it's like."

A woman who's been finding books near us makes a noise like a stopped cough. "I believe the gentleman may have *Tender Is the Night* in mind."

"That's the one," skin top says, "and thanks."

He isn't thanking me. He should. "Scott Fitzgerald," I tell him, maybe too loud.

"I knew that. No need to holler at me."

I keep on at my job while he gets the book and goes to the pay place. Once the men have gone Terry comes over. "What was the noise about?"

"The thing like a cough, you mean."

"Don't be clever, Roy," he says, though I didn't mean to and don't feel it. "What were you yelling about?"

"Just finding that man his book." Terry's stare won't go away, and I want to know "Did you send him?"

"I didn't, and I won't be sending you anyone while you're like you are. If you were saying just now you're feeling ill, you'd better tell me how."

I can't let anybody know what's happening to me. It could lose me my job. "Don't need to," I tell him, but he watches me over the pay place, the shelf with the tills on. I finish getting books to wheel away and bring ones to put where they were. I'm putting when people start going for lunch. Soon me and Terry are the only ones on the bottom floor. A woman and a little girl come in, and I see they want to ask a thing. Terry tries to get them, but they've seen me. "Excuse me," the woman says, "are you available?"

I don't seem to know the word. "Am I what?"

"Could you help? My daughter has been searching for a book."

"What's it called?"

"That's what we're here to ascertain. Betsy, tell the gentleman what you know about it."

"Some friends go to the seaside and there's a fairy in the sand who grants them wishes."

I know the book. I can get the name from my mind. "I see a gang like her," I tell the woman, "and the thing that comes along."

"What on earth are you saying about us?"

"Not you. Like her." I poke a finger at the girl. "Her," I say louder. "Some of them."

"I assure you she would go nowhere near a gang. Kindly make yourself plain."

"I'm trying, you stupid—" More words come out and get louder. There's quite a lot of them, just not ones children are supposed to hear. The woman pulls the girl away from me as Terry gets here.

She's going to talk to him, but he's quicker. "Go home, Roy," he says. "Go now and wait till you hear from me."

Maybe he doesn't mean leave the thing I was pushing along, but he can have it. I get my coat from the room with all ours in, and I'm off out when the girl says "Look, mummy, there's the book." I see her run to get *Five Children and It* off a table. It's not her fault her mother's all the things I said. She can have her book, and I can do mine now, because I'm not at work.

Except I can't. When I try to think about it all I get is what I wrote in Charles Vane's book. No use going home yet, so I go to the trains. Going, I talk to Asha. "How's it developing?" she says.

"It'll come." I mustn't run out of words till I know "What's Charles Vane's, the place he lives in?"

"Why do you need his address, Roy?"

"Got something for him."

A quiet bit and then "Let me find it for you."

I need to say another thing. "Was his book about words being magic?"

"What makes you think that?"

"I got close to him."

"I shouldn't get too close, Roy." Stops and says "It was more about words being vampiric, stealing all their victim's thoughts and everything that makes them human. It didn't really work."

"Oh yes it did."

Shouldn't have said. Don't use up words arguing. She doesn't, just says "Here's his address if you're sure you'd like it."

"Sure."

She gives and says "Shall I be hearing more from you this week, then?"

"You'll hear." Don't know what yet. Must stop Vane's words, put them out. Won't need words to get ticket from thing you put card in. Maybe won't have any when I see him. Doesn't matter, even good. If words gone, kill.

Borrowed Time

Ngo Binh Anh Khoa

She came amid a blizzard
That froze my being whole,
With eyes like glacial oceans
That drowned my captured soul.

Beneath her binding presence,
I felt her lips on mine,
Whose chilling touch ignited
Lust—sinful yet sublime.

Fear turned into fierce yearnings
That blazed within my core
Till reason all but fled me,
Replaced by thirst for more.

Then, through our carnal sessions,
She stole my warmth from me
So she could taste the feeling
Of "living"—fleetingly.

Now here I am, discarded,
A voiceless earthbound shade,
While she's moved on with her "life"
And on another preyed.

Spooky Action across Time: Caitlín R. Kiernan's Fiction Disturbs Noël Carroll's *Philosophy of Horror*

James Goho

Caitlín R. Kiernan entangles fact and fiction and the past and the present in "As Red as Red" (2010). The story introduces iconic horror monsters, only to dismiss them as unnecessary for horror literature. Kiernan camouflages Abby Gladding as a "vampire" to reanimate the history of "vampirism" in Rhode Island. She pictures the image of the werewolf as smoke drifting across Benefit Street in Providence from a story by H. P. Lovecraft. And she mourns the suffering of the falsely accused witches in 1692 in Salem, Massachusetts. In "As Red as Red," Ms. Howard is alone in a haunted landscape. Abby Gladding, the imaginary vampire, is not a Noël Carroll type of monster but a sympathetic character who helps Ms. Howard to navigate her transitions between fantasy and reality and between estrangement and acceptance. Ms. Howard sees "nothing malevolent, or hungry, or feral" in Abby's smile (*AR* 255).

Kiernan's story and others are counter-examples to Carroll's theory of horror fiction and film. In this essay, I sketch Carroll's hypothesis, identify criticisms of his theory, offer counter-examples to his notion of monsters, and discuss in detail how "As Red as Red" unsettles his theory.

A Sketch of Nöel Carroll's Theory of Horror

In *The Philosophy of Horror; or, Paradoxes of the Heart* (1990), Noël Carroll argues that the presence of a monster is the defining characteristic of horror literature (*PH* 15), or what he calls "art-horror" literature to distinguish its fictionality from "natural horror" (*PH* 12). He breaks horror literature away from what he calls "tales of terror," such as the work of Edgar Allan Poe (1809–1849). Carroll notes that "most of Poe's work does not fit into the genre of horror" (*PH* 215n10). But he extends his definition to science fiction. This is a category mistake, as S. T. Joshi points out in his *Unutterable Horror: A History of Supernatural Fiction* (8). Science fiction is a separate and distinct genre of literature with its own academic disputes on a proper definition.[1] Carroll goes on to suggest that art-horror does not include the originating Gothic texts, including the American Gothic texts of Charles Brockden Brown (1771–1810), early twentieth-century texts published in pulp magazines such as *Weird Tales,* and more (*PH* 15). Carroll's definition excludes many of the most significant examples of supernatural and non-supernatural horror, according to Joshi. Not only that, Joshi and others identify further problematic aspects with Carroll's theory.

Carroll defines a monster as "any being not believed to exist now by contemporary science" (*PH* 27). Moreover, these monsters are "impure and unclean. They are putrid or moldering things, or they hail from oozing places or they are made of dead or rotting flesh [. . .] or are associated with vermin, disease" (*PH* 23). These "unclean and disgusting" things provoke not only fear in characters but also "revulsion, nausea, and disgust" (*PH* 21–22). According to Carroll monsters are meant to frighten readers and viewers because they are threatening and loathsome.

Furthermore, these monsters violate our sense of the world as they fail to fit into real-world conceptual categories. Carroll names

---

1. Darko Suvin defines science fiction as a "literary genre whose necessary and sufficient conditions are the presence and interaction of estrangement and cognition" realized through an imagined space differing from an author's empirical environment (7–8). This imagined space must be scientifically conceivable. Such science fiction exhibits a "novum" which is a cognitively possible innovation. China Miéville, John Rieder, and others have challenged Suvin's definition.

this their "interstitiality" (*PH* 43). They are disgusting and impossible, according to Carroll. The human characters in horror stories or films directly experience that fear and disgust (in a fictional sense they feel real horror), while readers of such fiction experience "art-horror" revulsion and disgust. Readers are also repulsed by the monsters, as are the characters. That is, readers and audiences identify with and mimic the reactions of characters confronting horror monsters. The monsters horrify us, although we know them to be impossible. However, horror literature works to overcome the unpleasant emotions of disgust and revulsion through well-made narratives, according to Carroll. He argues that the enjoyment of horror literature is not with the monster, but with how the "presentation of the monster is staged" (*PH* 181). Consequently, the key source of interest and pleasure in horror literature resides in the "processes of discovery, proof and confirmation that horror fictions often employ" (*PH* 184) that resolves the anxiety induced by the presence of monsters. This is Carroll's solution to the "paradox of horror," that is, the answer to the question: how can there be an enjoyment of unpleasant or painful emotions like disgust and fear that horror is meant to produce? Notably, Carroll admits he did not conduct any empirical research with audiences or readers of horror to help form or test his theory (*PH* 30).

Aaron Smuts calls Carroll's solution a "compensatory cognitive pleasure" that arises from our "pleasure of discovery" in the resolution of the horror story or film's plot (47). But Smuts suggests that Carroll's hypothesis leaves out the possibility of readers' pleasure from monsters or identification with monsters. A simple explanation of the fact that there is so much interest in horror literature would be that we enjoy the fear that fiction produces. Berys Gaut says there is no paradox of horror because fear may not be an inherently unpleasant state. Gaut goes on to argue the negativity of the emotion can be explained as meaning the object of the emotion is negatively assessed; it is not the emotion itself that is unpleasant. Also, Gaut says the issue is a matter for empirical investigation, because "there is no a priori, conceptual problem about the enjoyment of negative emotions in real life, or in fiction" (344). He goes on to say it is not true that all horror narratives involve monsters in the sense of impossible beings, defined as beings not believed to exist according to contemporary science, for example, in "slasher" movies. Brigid Cheery adds that Carroll's definition of monster precludes from "art-horror" many horror films with monsters who could exist and others where the monster is sympathetic and does not frighten the human characters (161–62).

Brian Laetz challenges Carroll's hypothesis on two grounds. Firstly, he denies Carroll's claim that "[h]orror appears to be one of those genres in which the emotive responses of the audience, ideally, run parallel to the emotions of characters" (*PH* 17). This means that if a monster frightens human characters, it will frighten audiences. It may be empirically true that readers or viewers react differently from the human characters depicted in the genre. And it may be true that readers react differently from one another. Secondly, Laetz disputes Carroll's claim that horrific monsters disgust audiences or readers because of their impurity. In some horror narratives, a character may have the same impurity as the horrifying monster. Laetz suggests the film *Scanners* (1981) as an example. Daniel Shaw argues that horror fictions are often enjoyable because they allow audiences to identify with a powerful monster and with the victims who are often ultimately triumphant. Additionally, he says audiences may sympathize with the monster. Shaw's principal example is Hannibal Lecter in *The Silence of the Lambs* (1991), whose intellect, wit, and assistance in an investigation of a serial killer may bring him sympathy or admiration from an audience. Lecter is called a monster in the film. Carroll has replied to most of the criticisms of his theory.[2]

---

2. For example, Carroll argues that nominally actual creatures in horror literature become fantastical beings outside of contemporary science because of the outsized manner in which they are portrayed in fiction and film. And human psychopaths become impure because they resemble, act akin to, and are called such in texts and films.

Carroll's book extensively reviews the horror literature and he provides an array of examples to support his argument. His book includes an insightful chapter detailing various plots that work in horror to produce the "pleasure" that readers and viewers experience from the narratives. And the depth of his analysis reflects his extensive research in the field. He bases his work in the Anglo-American Analytic Philosophy tradition, especially Ordinary Language Philosophy. My sketch of Carroll's thesis here does not do complete justice to his depth of thought or the full complexity of his theory of horror.

Carroll's objects of study are horror stories and films; these are the phenomena he strives to explain with his theory. As with any theory, if it fails to account for the objects of its study, the theory is problematic. My argument is that not all horror stories and films have a monster in Carroll's definition. Some have monsters that are not loathsome and do not cause disgust. In some stories, readers identify with the monster, not the human characters. And some horror stories have no monsters at all. My main examples come from Caitlín R. Kiernan's fiction along with a close reading of one of her short stories. It is not clear to me how many counter-examples would cause Carroll to shift his thinking. I suspect that Carroll would say my examples come from stories that are not part of art-horror literature; this, of course, is meant to end all debate on the nature of horror literature, generally understood. I think he would argue that Kiernan's work should be classified as tales of dread where weird events create a sense of "unease and awe" and "anxiety and foreboding" in readers and audiences (*PH* 42).

Problematic "Horror" Literature for Carroll's Theory

As already noted, critics have pointed out problems with Carroll's thesis on readers' reaction to the presence of monsters. There are many "horror" stories where readers may identify with the monsters, not the human characters. And the "monsters" in some stories may elicit sympathetic responses from readers, for example, in Laura

Mauro's recent story "Sun Dogs" (2017), where the human character Sadie flees with a female were-coyote to escape from violent men with guns. In addition, readers may identify with a monster who has Carroll's prescribed characteristics, for example, the outsider in Lovecraft's story "The Outsider" (1921). Carroll references this story as an example of a loathsome monster, yet the narrator (the outsider) is a sympathetic monster. Readers may identify with the anguish and pain of the protagonist's discovery about himself. That is the point of the story. It is told from the monster's point of view. And there are stories where the only "character" is the so-called monster. Belicia Rhea's short-short story "Door Skin" (2020) in the first issue of *Penumbra* has no human character. "[T]he thing that lives in the forest" (264), that is, the monster, is the narrative voice and only character. Michael Griffin's weird novella *Armageddon House* (2020) features four human characters and no monsters, unless you count their underground, labyrinthine concrete bunker as one.

In other stories, readers will identify with, or admire the monster, for example, in Kiernan's "The Wolf Who Cried Girl" (2007). In that story, the wolf/girl, who falls between ontological categories as Carroll argues, represents people with mental health challenges who end up abandoned on urban streets. Her "savior" uses her for sex. The wolf/girl evokes sympathy, not revulsion, which falls instead on the human character. Another example is Kiernan's "For One Who Has Lost Herself" (2006). That story also features a being between categories, a selkie. Nevertheless, she does not cause revulsion; rather, the human who stole her skin and took her away from her home in the sea is the repulsive one. In Kiernan's "Unter den Augen des Mondes" (2008) ["Under the Eyes of the Moon"], an angry male character repeatedly beats a fearful, caged female werewolf who longs to see the shine of her mother, the moon, fall on her cage floor. In these and other tales, Kiernan writes from the perspective of the monsters, so to speak, to show us their fears, their night terrors, and their despairs. She also writes of human characters turning into the "monsters" in such stories as "Rappaccini's Dragon (Murder Ballad No.

5)" (2008), where Daniel transforms himself into a deadly poison to avenge the killing of his twin. These examples illustrate the limitations of Carroll's theory surrounding the notion of "monster."

There are many other counter-examples in Kiernan's work. In "To This Water (Johnstown, Pennsylvania 1889)" (1996), a group of men brutally rape Magda, a daughter of a Hungarian immigrant. Subsequently, she commits suicide. Her suicide is inextricably linked to the failure of a dam that engulfs Johnstown, killing hundreds. Tom Givens, a witness to the rape who failed to help Magda, sees her riding the front wave of the torrent crushing over the city. Readers abhor the human rapists and Tom Givens, not the specter of Magda, who is the supernatural element. "Tall Bodies" (2012) features creatures that are outside of current science but are wonderful. The creatures "move slowly and with an exquisite grace" (*Ape's Wife* 126); they are "oh so beautifully tall" (*Ape's Wife* 129). Kiernan's musical "The Ammonite Violin (Murder Ballad No. 4)" (2006) includes three characters, a serial killer (called the Collector), Ellen who plays the violin for the Collector, and Ellen's sister whom the Collector murdered. The unnamed sister is a sympathetic ghost who speaks through the violin that Ellen plays. The human "monster" in the story, the Collector, is not outside current science and could exist. He is not depicted as loathsome; rather, he is a pathetic, contemptible, psychopathic killer who ends by killing himself. Beyond that, the supernatural element, the dead sister, elicits love and sympathy, not disgust.

A Case Study of Monsters in "As Red as Red"

Horror literature, broadly understood, does not need a Carroll-type monster. The "monster" in Kiernan's story "As Red as Red" (2010) could be the character, Abby Gladding, who may be a vampire, but she also has hints of a witch and perhaps a werewolf, or a ghost—an entangled icon of horror writing—or none of these. Kiernan's story writes about "monsters" from the horror archives in a much different way from what Carroll envisions. The main character, Ms. Howard, a folklore student, is working on her master's thesis on the so-called New England vampires, or more correctly the exhumations related to the consumption epidemic in New England from the late seventeenth into the eighteenth century. Another character in the story is the supernatural atmosphere of Newport and Providence, Rhode Island, which seems to affect Ms. Howard more and more as the story progresses. This combined with her research on exhumation sparks Ms. Howard's sensitivity to unusual events, associated with her sightings of Abby Gladding. Ms. Howard first spies Abby drenched with rain, her long black hair haloing her pale face on Bowen Wharf in Newport. Then she speaks with her in a café on Thames Street in Newport while Abby draws a circle within a circle on a window. On another day, she thinks she sees Abby outside a library window where Ms. Howard finds circles on the glass. Abby also appears in Ms. Howard's dreams.

Kiernan weaves fiction and fact together into a haunting first-person narrative of Ms. Howard while she struggles with her thesis, the haunted landscape of Rhode Island, and her loneliness. These surface traumatically in her dreams. The factual elements of the story include real locations in Newport and Providence.[3] One example is the Redwood Library and Athenaeum (founded in 1757) in Newport. There Howard rifles through old newspaper clippings, microfiche, and ancient, yellowed books on the history of vampirism and consumption in Newport. Kiernan also places scenes in the Common Burying Ground in Newport and on Benefit Street in Providence.

In addition, Kiernan references actual reports on Rhode Island "vampire" incidents in the late seventeenth and eighteenth centuries. These include Nancy Kinder's "The 'Vampires' of Rhode Island," from *Yankee* (October 1970); Paul F. Eno's "They Burned Her Heart ... Was Mercy Brown a Vampire?" from the *Narragansett Times* (25 October 1979); and Eugene C. Emery Jr.'s article "Did

---

3. Kiernan walked the locations presented in her story (*Beneath an Oil-Dark Sea* 271).

They Hear the Vampire Whisper?" from an October 1979 issue of the *Providence Sunday Journal*. The authors' names appear in Michael E. Bell's *Food for the Dead: On the Trail of New England's Vampires* (2001), not in Kiernan's story. She also quotes from the historic article "The Animistic Vampire in New England" by George R. Stetson, published in *American Anthropologist* in 1896.

Kiernan goes on to name several Rhode Island women who were erroneously reported as vampires, most of whom were consumption victims. Kiernan mentions Mercy Brown, Sarah Tillinghast, Nellie Vaughn, Nancy Young, and Ruth Ellen Rose. The Mercy Brown (1872–1892) exhumation incident occurred in Exeter, Rhode Island, in 1892, and is the most thoroughly documented exhumation occurrence.[4] She died from consumption. Her heart and liver were burned on a rock (Holly and Cordy 337). Sarah Tillinghast, who was born in 1777, is buried in an unnamed cemetery near Exeter, c. 1799. Her father exhumed her body. Her heart was burned (Holly and Cordy 339). Bell also identifies the facts in these cases and the other so-called "vampire" incidents. One of these "vampires," Nellie Vaughn, died from pneumonia when she was nineteen and was buried at first on the family farm and then moved to a public cemetery in West Greenwich, Rhode Island, in 1889. Her reburial probably led to her becoming associated with the New England "vampire craze."[5] Nancy

---

4. Bell traces the relationships among families beset by consumption in Exeter. Mercy Brown's father, George Brown, was a member of Exeter Grange, where William Rose was a Worthy Master. Rose exhumed his daughter, Ruth Ellen Rose, in 1872. Rose's wife, Mary Tillinghast Rose, was the great-granddaughter of Stukeley Tillinghast (1741–1826), who had several of his children exhumed in 1799 (Bell, "Vampires and Death" 135). Pardon Tillinghast (1622?–1718), mentioned in Lovecraft's "The Shunned House" (*CF* 1.465), was probably the great-great-great-grandfather of Stukeley Tillinghast. Pardon was a common name in the Tillinghast family.

5. Nellie Vaughn's tombstone displayed the phrase "I Am Waiting and Watching For You," which may have contributed to the false legend of her vampirism.

Young died in 1827 from consumption when she was nineteen in Foster, Rhode Island. Her remains were exhumed in that year and burned, while the family inhaled the smoke in hope of a cure for consumption. Ruth Ellen Rose was born in 1859 and died in 1874. Her father reportedly exhumed her the same year.

In their 1994 article, Paul S. Sledzik and Nicholas Bellantoni identify twelve documented "vampire" activities in the eighteenth and nineteenth centuries in New England, with six in Rhode Island. Eleven of those deaths were associated with tuberculosis. Bell's more recent research unearthed more than twenty documented cases of exhumation ("Vampires and Death" 125). At that time a tuberculosis (then called consumption) epidemic ravaged New England. Consumption meant a wasting death for those so inflicted. It was one of the main causes of death in the Eastern United States in the nineteenth century. The scourge affected large parts of the population and its causes and treatments were unknown. To combat the disease, people sought and found a "folk remedy."

Ms. Howard's research focuses on this folk remedy, manifested as vampirism for some. Yet the "vampires" she studies are not disgusting and loathsome; rather, they evoke sympathy from her and readers. That is because they were mistakenly identified as vampires in newspapers or popular accounts. They were victims of a wasting disease, not villains. And they suffered in death through exhumation from their graves and being labeled as monsters in popular accounts.

New England communities carried out the folk practice to face the real horror of consumption. The originating local documentation generally does not refer to "vampirism." Rather, outsiders first used that word (Bell, "Vampires and Death"). The practice of exhumation expressed families' commitment to their community. It was an act of solidarity to help stop the spread of the wasting disease. And it provided a sense of limited control against an unstoppable disease. The folk medicine prescribed exhuming people who had died from consumption and then burning their hearts and possibly their livers and lungs. The smoke was considered a preventive against consumption. As bizarre as this may seem, it was an accepted social response to grief, fear, and hope to save the living in those communities.

The fictitious "vampire" in the story is Abby Gladding. She is not loathsome, impure, or repulsive. Indeed, the human character Ms. Howard may love her, or at least yearns to see her, to date her. Abby Gladding does not cause disgust, although throughout the story there are hints that she takes on various attributes of a vampire, a werewolf, or even a witch, for there was "back-fence talk that Abby had practiced witchcraft in the woods" (*AR* 269), in other words, malicious gossip accusing someone of being a witch. All these attributes are ascribed to her by others. Kiernan's Abby represents monster icons. But they all turn out to be wrong for Abby, as it was for the New England female "vampires" and the so-called witches of Salem, Massachusetts, in 1692, when a witch hysteria engulfed the town. Nineteen were executed, most of whom were women.[6]

Abby appears as a spooky return from time past in Rhode Island. Abby's then becomes Ms. Howard's now. Ms. Howard is afraid at times, but she does not fear Abby. Entangled in the dark New England past, Abby distorts space and time into a haunted present in Rhode Island. Ms. Howard's attraction to Abby fuses with a fear of unexplainable events in her life.

Fear is at the core of horror literature. In "As Red as Red" that fear manifests itself as a "strange *disquietude*" for Ms. Howard (Ruskin 37). Abby is the supernatural element in the story. Her recurring images carry Ms. Howard's imagination into regions of spooky entanglements of her research, her loneliness, and the haunting past of

---

6. Carol F. Karlsen describes the community erupting with false witch accusations, forced confessions, denials, trials, and death. Close to two hundred people were accused, fifty-five tried, and nineteen murdered. The great majority were women. Francis Hill documents how the innocents were imprisoned in foul and stinking cells. Some were chained to walls; others were tied neck to heels. Dorcas Good, a four-year-old girl, was put in iron manacles and chained to the wall of a cold, dark cell, where she went mad. These women suffered real horror.

New England. It is a past that H. P. Lovecraft often called upon in his fictions.

Situated in Rhode Island, Kiernan's story recalls Lovecraft's "The Shunned House,"[7] which also mixes the fictive with fact, including similar historic material. Lovecraft's story traces the heroic efforts of an unnamed narrator and Elihu Whipple, his uncle, to remove an evil presence in the basement of the "Babbitt" house on Benefit Street in Providence.[8] William Harris, his wife Rhoby (Dexter) Harris, and their four children were the first to live in the house. While residing there, family members suffered from a strange wasting disease. Of interest for Kiernan's story is that Lovecraft alludes to the Mercy Brown vampire incident,[9] noting that in "1892 an Exeter community exhumed a dead body and ceremoniously burnt its heart to prevent certain alleged visitations injurious to the public health and peace" (*CF* 458–59). Lovecraft hid the name "Mercy Brown" in his characters. After the death of her husband, Rhoby Harris's sister arrived to help her. Lovecraft named her Mercy Dexter. She in turn brought in extra help with an Ann White from Exeter. Ann is the character who says there is a vampire in the house. Lovecraft had a quiet sense of humor.[10]

Another connection between Lovecraft's story and Kiernan's may be William Harris's child Abigail. Born in 1757, she was one of the first to die in the house. Perhaps she is the source for Kiernan's Abby. Or the source may lie in the Common Burying Ground in Newport. At least two Abby Gladdings are buried there, as well as

---

7. "The Shunned House" was published in *Weird Tales* in 1937, but it was written in 1924.

8. The story is based at an actual house in Providence that was built c. 1763 (Joshi, "Explanatory Notes" 416).

9. Joshi identifies the source of Lovecraft's information on the Exeter incident as Charles M. Skinner's 1896 *Myths and Legends of Our Own Land* ("Explanatory Notes" 417 n7).

10. In *Food for the Dead*, Bell suggests that Lovecraft may have had a "playful smile" when he invented the names (185).

many other Gladdings.[11] Or the source for Kiernan's Abby may be the young (b. 1773) Abigail Staples, whose father, Stephen Staples, petitioned the Cumberland Rhode Island Town Council on 8 February 1796 to exhume her body. It was approved (Bell, *Food for the Dead* 301–2).

A more curious connection to Lovecraft's story is that Ms. Howard rents an apartment on Prospect[12] Street in Providence, not far from the house at 135 Benefit Street. In Kiernan's story, Howard walks past that shunned house and spots part of one of four signs nailed on the house's gatepost: *Oubliez le Chien* (Forget the Dog). There were such signs that Kiernan probably saw on one of her walks in Providence. Bell reports them: *"Attention Chien Bizarre; Chien Fort Méchant et Pou Nourit; Chien Lunatique; Oubliez le Chien Attention au Maitre."* The signs tell passersby to beware of the mad, strong, underfed, lunatic dog, but the last sign says, forget the dog, beware of the master (Bell, *Food for the Dead* 178–79).

The use of French alludes to Lovecraft tracing the evil of the house back to a fictitious French inhabitant of the house, named Etienne Roulet, and then to his "ancestor," Jacques Roulet of France, who is reported as factual and appears to have been a human behaving akin to a wolf. When Ms. Howard walks away from that house, she faintly glimpses a dark blur of something large and black rushing across the street. This recalls the "wolfish shapes taken by smoke from the great chimney" of the house in Lovecraft's story (*CF* 455). Late in Kiernan's story, the French connection arises again

---

11 They are Abby W. Gladding and Abby Cranston Gladding. Kiernan's character's full name is Abby Mary Gladding on her grave stone. Gladding is an old family name in Rhode Island traced back to the 1600s. John Gladding (1640–1727) was one of the Founders of Bristol, Rhode Island. George W. Gladding (1787–1839) partnered with Matthew Watson to establish Watson & Gladding in Providence. The business continued under different names for over 200 years.

12. Perhaps this is the Thomas Lloyd Halsey house at 140 Prospect Street, where Lovecraft situated the home of Charles Dexter Ward in his short novel *The Case of Charles Dexter Ward*.

when Ms. Howard finds the phrase "*Je-rouge*, or 'red eyes'" (*AR* 270) scrawled on a margin of the newspaper page containing the story about the exhumation of Abby Gladding. These eyes may also reflect the "wolfish" (*CF* 475) eyes of the monstrous thing with dripping claws in the basement of the house on Benefit Street—the thing that once was Elihu Whipple.

Lovecraft's "The Shunned House" includes a Carroll-type monster, a "cloud of fungous loathsomeness" (*CF* 475), a "filthy thing," a thing with a skin "fishy and glassy—a kind of semi-putrid congealed jelly" (*CF* 478). Kiernan's story references Lovecraft's but does not imagine such a Carroll-type monster. Rather, her story evokes fear, unease, and apprehension that pervade the entire landscape and timescape, as the past slowly inundates Howard's day and night experiences. Kiernan's work in fiction builds on the weird fiction of Lovecraft, as Lovecraft's is connected to his predecessors, such as Poe, in the tradition. This tradition suggests that typologies and theories of "horror" need to attend to the evolutionary character of supernatural horror literature.

Kiernan's story also reflects on common horror literature techniques, as if discarding them along with the monsters. Early in "As Red as Red" (2010) she addresses an expectation of horror stories when she writes that Abby's smile gives "no foreshadowing, not even in hindsight. It surely isn't a predatory smile" (*AR* 255). Abby is not a Carroll-type monster. Somewhat later, Kiernan writes that Abby's "eyes seem somehow brighter than they should in the dim light of the coffeehouse, so there's your foreshadowing, I suppose, if you're the sort who needs it" (*AR* 256), as if to mock the conventions of some dark fictions or the expectations of literary theorists on standard horror literature plot techniques.

However, Kiernan deploys dreams as plot techniques. That is because fear and illumination appear in Ms. Howard's dreams. Kiernan writes two key dream scenes in her story. In the first, Ms. Howard sees Abby under a tree playing the violin in the North Burying Ground in Newport. The music seems to shape the night.

Something clatters behind Ms. Howard and when she turns back to the window, Abby is gone. In the second dream Ms. Howard hears Abby telling her to open her eyes. Ms. Howard rests in "a liminal state" (*AR* 265) between waking and sleep. This alludes to Poe's thoughts on that interstice between wakefulness and sleep when the "confines of the waking world blend with those of the world of dreams" that is at "the very brink of sleep" (1383). It is a time of visions and awe rich with intense creativity and insight. Ms. Howard sees Abby standing in a green pool with her long black hair draping her naked body. Her violin bow falls, sending circular ripples across the pond. Abby says, "I wear this rough garment to deceive" (Zechariah 13:4). Later in the story, Ms. Howard finds the phrase etched on the gravestone of Abby Gladding. In the King James Version of the Bible, "prophets shall be ashamed every one of his vision, when he hath prophesied" precedes that phrase. Abby also tells Ms. Howard "inwardly, they were ravening wolves" (*AR* 266). But this phrase is preceded in Mathew 7:15 with the warning to beware of false prophets. Both references seem to warn Ms. Howard about the false claims made against the young exhumed women. The biblical phrase may mean that there is a time for truth and liberating oneself from falsehoods. In Kiernan's story, the phrases mean that the vampires and werewolves are illusions. The genuine core of supernatural horror is more disturbing, dangerous, and insightful than mere "monster" stories.

Ms. Howard awakes disoriented from her second dream with her chest aching; she had suffocated as if she "was drowning[13] and h[ad] only just been pulled to safety" (*AR* 267). Seemingly awake, she thinks she sees the head and shoulders of a young woman with the muzzle and sharp ears of a wolf. Still, she feels no fear.

In part, the dream clinically describes "sleep paralysis." This is the temporary paralysis of one's body while passing between stages of wakefulness and sleep. During that time one feels conscious but is unable to move. It often happens that one suffers pressure or feels as

---

13. Ms. Howard in her dream mirrors the fate of Abby Gladding.

if one is suffocating during that paralysis. Nicholas D. Kristof says that reports suggest a person may also experience a sense of dread and terror. This reads like an account of the Sarah Tillinghast "vampire" incident by Sidney S. Rider[14] (1833–1917). In "The Belief in Vampires in Rhode Island" (1888) he claims that Sarah Tillinghast "came every night and sat upon a portion of the body, causing great pain and misery. So it went on" (38) to the members of her family. These may have been instances of sleep paralysis. Equally interesting, Lovecraft in "The Shunned House" depicts a similar experience. When Whipple awakes from a dream while in the basement of the shunned house, he exclaims, "My breath, my breath!" (*CF* 472). During the dream, he says he felt a "personal sensation of choking" (*CF* 473). Kiernan may have had this incident in mind when writing the dream sequence in "As Red as Red." Thus, Kiernan connects her dream sequence to an actual account of a purported visitation by an alleged "vampire" and a fictional account. Again, Ms. Howard thinks that there is nothing to fear. This second dream performs in a manner akin to a folklore dream that foretells the future. For Abby Gladding died from drowning, as etched on her headstone in the Newport Common Burying Ground in Kiernan's tale. In the dream, Abby tells Ms. Howard, "You've seen all that you need to see, and probably more, I'd wager" (*AR* 266).

After that dream Ms. Howard travels to Abby Gladding's gravesite in Newport as if guided. At the tombstone Ms. Howard thinks, "[t]here's no fear in me, no shock or stubborn disbelief at what I've discovered or at its impossible ramifications" (*AR* 268). That is because Abby is not a monster. Later Ms. Howard discovers an article in the Redwood Library and Athenaeum from the *Newport Mercury*[15] telling of Abby's exhumation, which was followed by the usual folk

---

14. Lovecraft mentions Rider in "The Shunned House" (*CF* 456).

15. The *Newport Mercury* was published in various incarnations from 1759 to 1928. The article that Ms. Howard discovers would have appeared when Solomon Southwick (1731–1797) was a contributor/editor. Abby Gladding's father's name is Solomon Gladding.

remedy. But Abby had died from drowning; she did not have consumption. Ms. Howard thinks she has discovered documentation of the first purported vampirism in New England in 1785.[16]

The second dream sequence acts as such dreams often do in folk tales. I am not sure if this was deliberate. The key pivot toward story closure arises from the second dream. Dreams are often used in folk tales to move the plot along, as they allow access to information by the protagonist that would not normally arise during their waking state. Judit Gulyás says the dream narrative tells or hints at the existence of something or somebody that provokes a sense of purpose and action. Kiernan integrates the dream scene into the overall narrative as a way to move the plot forward toward a denouncement. This plot pivot suggests the intrusion of the supernatural or the unexplainable or fantastic or impossible event into the story. And yet again Ms. Howard shows no disgust or revulsion. She sets off to Abby Gladding's grave. She does feel fear in the story; it is an ambiguous fear. She feels an unease in the face of something dismayingly impossible, something that stresses the ontology of her world. It does not come from a monster but from an accumulation of strange and troubling events in Ms. Howard's life.

Surfaces abound in "As Red as Red." There are windows in libraries, in cafés, and in a bedroom, where a window looks over a burying ground in a dream. A pond ripples in circles akin to those found on windows. The body of Abby Gladding is found in the cold waters of Newport Bay. And there is the earth into which bodies are buried only to be exhumed. These boundaries are breached repeatedly as Ms. Howard, with Abby as her guide, travels between the

---

16. The actual first reported instance of a "vampire" incident occurred in 1784 in Willington, Connecticut. An article in the October 2012 *Smithsonian Magazine* (printed after the publication of Kiernan's story) quotes a letter from Councilman Moses Holmes to the *Connecticut Courant and Weekly Intelligencer* in June 1784 that warned people about a "Quack Doctor" who was convincing families to dig up and burn the bodies of their dead relatives to cure their consumption. Of course, Abigail Tucker wrote the article.

real and the impossible, the past and the present. Kiernan's story evokes the complex emotional states of Ms. Howard in these shifting, unnerving environments. Readers sense that unease, which does not arise from monsters. It arises from the way Kiernan conveys the past and present environs of Providence and Newport through the emotional responses of Ms. Howard, which express her loneliness, loss, and trauma as she researches disease, dissolution, and death in Rhode Island. Her estrangement in an unnerving environment is part of the human condition that horror fiction, at its best, works to unveil and bring to light in all its strangeness.

The erotic and eerie tension between Ms. Howard and Abby Gladding drives the story. That is because it embodies the tension between the real and the impossible. Readers may experience the shudder of disorientation that Ms. Howard feels in that unnerving environment. I think they will not feel repulsed by Abby Gladding. She represents the terror, grief, and despair of all those women falsely accused of being monsters. Abby helps Ms. Howard to navigate through her inchoate experiences and dreams arising from a cultural memory of disease, mourning, and death as if she is the voice for all those exhumed young women calling out to leave them in peace. And there is closure for Ms. Howard because she buries her discovery about Abby Gladding. She refuses to exhume Abby Gladding once again for an academic thesis. That is because Abby is not a monster, as the other so-called New England vampires and witches were not monsters. In this "horror" story ghosts are finally allowed to rest in peace.

Concluding Thoughts

Kiernan's folkloric supernatural tale "As Red as Red" entangles fact and fantasy, past and present. She establishes a sense of realism in Rhode Island by locating the story in existing settings and citing historic people and documents. To this she adds Rhode Island legends and folklore, allusions to weird literature, along with fictional characters and events to create an ambiguity between the real and the impossible. And Kiernan's "gift of fantasy" works the transformations from one frame of space and time to another, so that Abby and Ms. Howard move uniformly toward each other for brief periods. This allows events long in the past that were once in the future to reappear in Ms. Howard's present in a distorted form, perhaps resulting from the supernatural field characteristics of the Rhode Island environs. In the story Ms. Howard and Abby Gladding are linked inextricably to each other despite their separation in time. They are entangled to such an extent that Abby's impossible appearances impact Ms. Howard's actions; that is, supernatural events cause "realistic" actions.

Kiernan writes this story in her signature rhythmic, graceful prose, allowing readers to experience the inner and outer life of Ms. Howard in all its beauty, unease, and trauma. Kiernan enriches her imaginative craft through her careful historical research on Rhode Island and her embedding the story in the supernatural horror tradition. The story expresses the inquisitiveness and care of a folklorist alongside the loneliness of a young woman beset by disturbing events, which elude explanation through physical phenomena, yet who perseveres against confounding experiences in a haunted environment.

Although the story uses the figures of impossible, iconic horror monsters, they are not loathsome monsters. Abby Gladding does not disgust Ms. Howard. In fact, readers may identify and sympathize with Abby, or Ms. Howard, or both. Readers probably react differently to the overall story. I suspect that it is not empirically true that all readers react in similar ways to horror literature. Mark Valentine in "With Whispering and Murmuring: Walter de la Mare's 'Seaton's Aunt'" (2014) summarizes several different readers' reactions to de la Mare's story over many years. They composed significantly different assessments on the role of the three characters in the story. They also reported varying personal reactions to the story.

Kiernan's fiction disrupts Noël Carroll's thesis that monsters define horror literature through their loathsomeness and repulsion.

Carroll also claims that readers and viewers respond to the depiction of monsters with disgust in the same way as do the human characters (whom they identify with) in that fiction. I suggest that a) not all "monsters" in "horror literature" must engender disgust or are repulsive, b) not all readers will view the "monsters" as loathsome, impure, repulsive, and disgusting, c) not all readers will identify with the human characters in "horror literature," rather they may identify with the "monsters," and d) not all forms of "horror literature" need "monsters" in Carroll's definition of such. Of course, I am using "horror literature" in a broader sense than Carroll's "art-horror." I refer to a broad range of supernatural horror literature. There are many labels applied to fiction and film in that general sense of horror, including "strange," "weird," "dark," "supernatural," "ghost," or "Gothic." David Punter says that the "Gothic" is also a contested site and arguments abound on a correct definition. "Horror" is similar. My limited intent here is to point out a flaw in Carroll's thesis, by citing some of the research showing such a flaw, to expand this with further examples, and with a close reading of Kiernan's story "As Red as Red."

Carroll has been criticized for not encompassing what are generally considered to be singular examples of the literature (not encompassing Poe is almost enough to disqualify the generality of his theory in my mind). However, Carroll does identity some important aspects of the literature in the field. He is to be recognized for his attempt to understand the field and to place it within a comprehensive philosophical framework. I think that Carroll's reliance on ordinary language fails to account for the evolution of the language of "horror literature" over time from the original Gothic to the modern weird and dark fantasy. There are alternative strategies to identify the key elements or commonalities of the broadly thought of field of horror literature that will help us understand the impact and the continuing allure of the literature.

Carroll says his philosophical strategy uses an analysis of "ordinary language." Ordinary Language Philosophy (OLP) is a recognized approach within the Anglo-American Analytic Philosophy tradition that was pioneered by Gilbert Ryle (1900–1976) and others at Oxford University from 1945 to 1970. However, OLP is not a universally accepted method for understanding phenomena in the world. It is criticized as an inadequate philosophical methodology to understand actuality because it is limited by its sole focus on the use and interpretation of current "ordinary" language. OLP is overly conservative in that it fails to appreciate the variation of uses in language and the evolution of language and thus fails to appreciate the variation and diversity of voices in horror fiction and its adaptation and change over a long time. Bertrand Russell (1872–1970) was an early critic of OLP, and there have been many others, such as Ernest Gellner and Wilfred Sellars.

I suspect philosophical generalization and definitional regimentation are not the most fruitful ways to characterize and understand horror literature. A historical view may be more useful, as it allows for an appreciation of the shifting and evolutionary nature of the practices and products of horror literature. A more flexible approach to definitional issues is likely to prove more revelatory about the continuing power of Gothic horror literature.

John Rieder disputes Darko Suvin's prescriptive definition of science fiction. Rieder suggests that the genre consists of works that have a "family resemblance" rather than specific defining characteristics (*Colonialism* 16). "Family resemblance" is a notion from Ludwig Wittgenstein's *Philosophical Investigations* (1953). He explored "family resemblance" as a means to connect particular uses of the same concept. In many cases there may not be one common thing, but rather "similarities, relationships and a whole series of them at that" (66) make up a word or concept. He suggests there is no reason to look for one essential core in which the meaning of a word resides. Wittgenstein says we should journey with a word through its "complicated network of similarities overlapping and criss-crossing" (66) to understand fully its genuine meaning. A family resemblance eschews the exactness Carroll appears to say is essential for understanding and appreciating horror literature. A family resemblance suggests no one defining characteristic for every member of that family; rather, they are connected by a series of overlapping similarities, where no one feature is common to all things. This strikes me as a more fruitful strategy to understand the wide reach of "horror literature." Moreover, a nuanced view of the literature over its long history would allow for a greater appreciation of and insight into the shifting nature of the practice and outcomes of horror literature. It is a literary genre of conflicting critical views that typify a vibrant and evolving literature.

Works Cited

Bell, Michael E. *Food for the Dead: On the Trail of New England Vampires*. New York: Carroll & Graf Publishers, 2001.

———. "Vampires and Death in New England, 1784 to 1892." *Anthropology and Humanism* 31 (2006): 124–40.

Carroll, Nöel. *The Philosophy of Horror; or, Paradoxes of the Heart*. New York: Routledge, 1990. [Abbreviated in text as *PH*.]

Cherry, Brigid. *Horror*. New York: Routledge, 2009.

Gaut, Berys. "The Paradox of Horror." *British Journal of Aesthetics* 33 (1993): 333–45.

Gellner, Ernest. *Words and Things: An Examination of, and an Attack on, Linguistic Philosophy*. 1959. New York: Routledge, 2005.

Griffin, Michael. *Armageddon House*. Pickering, ON: Undertow Publications, 2020.

Gulyás, Judit. "A Function of Dream Narratives in Fairy Tales." *Folklore: Electronic Journal of Folklore* 36 (2007): 129–40.

Hill, Francis. *A Delusion of Satan: The Full Story of the Salem Witch Trials*. Boston: Da Capo Press, 2002.

Holly, Donald H., Jr., and Casey E. Cordy "What's in a Coin? Reading the Material Culture of Legend Tripping and Other Activities." *Journal of American Folklore* 120 (2007): 335–54.

Joshi, S. T. "Explanatory Notes." In H. P. Lovecraft, *The Dreams in the Witch House and Other Weird Tales*. Ed. S. T. Joshi. New York: Penguin, 2004. 397–453.

———. *Unutterable Horror: A History of Supernatural Fiction.* 2012. New York: Hippocampus Press, 2014. 2 vols.

Karlsen, Carol F. *The Devil in the Shape of a Woman: Witchcraft in Colonial New England.* New York: W. W. Norton, 1987.

Kiernan, Caitlín R. *The Ape's Wife and Other Stories.* Burton, MI: Subterranean Press, 2013.

———. "As Red as Red." In *Beneath an Oil-Dark Sea: The Best of Caitlín R. Kiernan, Volume 2.* Burton, MI: Subterranean Press, 2015. 255–70. [Abbreviated in text as *AR*.]

Kristof, Nicholas D. "Alien Abduction? Science Calls It Sleep Paralysis." *New York Times* (6 July 1999): 1. www.nytimes.com/1999/07/06/science/alien-abduction-science-calls-it- sleep-paralysis.html?pagewanted=all&src=pm. Accessed 20 November 2020.

Laetz, Brian. "Still Two Problematic Theses in Carroll's Account of Horror: A Response to 'Monsters and the Moving Image.'" *American Society for Aesthetics Graduate E-journal* 2, No. 1 (Fall 2009/Winter 2010). asageorg.files.wordpress.com/2019/03/brian-laetz-still-two-problematic-theses-in-carrolls-account-of-horror-a-response-to-monsters-and-the-moving-image.pdf. Accessed 30 November 2020.

Lovecraft, H. P. *Collected Fiction: A Variorum Edition, Volume 1: 1905–1925.* Ed. S. T. Joshi. New York: Hippocampus Press, 2015. [Abbreviated in text as *CF*.]

Mauro, Laura. *Sing Your Sadness Deep.* Pickering ON: Undertow Publications, 2019.

Miéville, China. "Afterword: Cognition as Ideology." In Mark Bould and China Miéville, ed. *Red Planets: Marxism and Science Fiction.* Middletown, CT: Wesleyan University Press, 2009. 231–48.

Poe, Edgar Allan. *Essays and Reviews.* New York: Library of America, 1984.

Punter, David. "Introduction: The Ghost of a History." In David Punter, ed. *A New Companion to the Gothic.* Oxford: Blackwell, 2012. 1–9.

Rhea, Belicia. "Door Skin." *Penumbra* No. 1 (2020): 263–65.

Rider, Sidney S. "The Belief in Vampires in Rhode Island." *Book Notes* 5 (31 March 1888): 37–39.

Rieder, John. *Colonialism and the Emergence of Science Fiction*. Middletown, CT: Wesleyan University Press, 2008.

———. *Science Fiction and the Mass Cultural Genre System*. Middletown, CT: Wesleyan University Press, 2017.

Ruskin, John. *Selected Writings*. Ed. Peter Quennell. London: Falcon Press, 1952.

Russell, Bertrand. "The Cult of 'Common Usage.'" *British Journal for the Philosophy of Science* 3 (February 1953): 303–7.

———. "Foreword." In Ernest Gellner. *Words and Things: An Examination of, and an Attack on, Linguistic Philosophy*. 1959. London: Routledge, 2005. xi–xiv.

Sellars, Wilfred. *Science, Perception and Reality*. London: Routledge & Kegan Paul, 1963.

Shaw, Daniel. "A Humean Definition of Horror." *Film-Philosophy* 1, No. 4 (1997). www.film-philosophy.com/vol1-1997/n4shaw. Accessed 30 November 2020.

Sledzik, Paul S., and Nicholas Bellantoni. "Bioarcheological and Biocultural Evidence for the New England Vampire Folk Belief." *American Journal of Physical Anthropology* 2 (1994): 269–74.

Smuts, Aaron. "Art and Negative Affect." *Philosophy Compass* 4 (2009): 39–55.

Suvin, Darko. *Metamorphoses of Science Fiction: On the Poetics and History of a Literary Genre*. New Haven, CT: Yale University Press, 1979.

Tucker, Abigail. "The Great New England Vampire Panic." *Smithsonian Magazine* (October 2012). www.smithsonianmag.com/history/the-great-new-england-vampire-panic-36482878/. Accessed 21 November 2020.

Valentine, Mark. *Haunted by Books*. Leyburn, UK: Tartarus Press, 2020.

Wittgenstein, Ludwig. *Philosophical Investigations*. Tr. G. E. M. Anscombe. Oxford: Blackwell, 2001.

When Old Gods Rattle Chains

Adam Bolivar

Come hear the wand'ring balladress,
    Whose tattered cloak is red,
With sun-browned skin and wild of tress,
    By elf-roads she is led.

She strums her father's oaken lyre,
    And deftly fingers strings,
To sow her lays across the shire,
    The ballads that she sings.

Folk shun her in the wary town,
    Her and her devil's song,
Which makes the parson fret and frown,
    And rail of right and wrong.

And yet they come, a hooded few,
    Still yearning for the days,
When witches in the country knew
    To keep ancestral ways.

They come to listen by the stones,
    Which kindred blood still stains,
And feel the stirring in their bones,
    When old gods rattle chains.

A Green Shade

Geoffrey Reiter

> "And in þis he shewed me a lytil thyng þe quantite of a hasyl nott. lyeng in þe pawme of my hand as it had semed. and it was as rownde as eny ball. I loked þer upon wt þe eye of my vnderstondyng. and I þought what may þis be. and it was answered generally thus. It is all þat is made."
>
> —Julian of Norwich

> "Annihilating all that's made
> To a green Thought in a green Shade."
>
> —Andrew Marvell

Isabella and Abigail checked their coordinates, looking for the witch's house. The trails were far behind them now, and they were wending through a maze of scabrous-skinned birch trees. The sun was bright but arcing westward, and they saw its rays only in the shreds of light that clawed through the dense foliage above. The tattered sunlight mixed eerily across Abigail's blue eyes with the reflection of the GPS image glowing from her phone. Isabella was a step or two behind her friend, but her nut-brown eyes were directed ahead of her, toward Abigail and the trees and Magus, their German Shepherd.

"Are we any closer to the spot?" Isabella asked. Magus had begun tugging obstinately at his leash.

"I mean, I think so," Abigail replied, still staring into the screen. She pointed to the map, and Isabella peered over her shoulder. If their calculations were accurate, Rachel Bourne's residence would be within a mile of this place.

If they were accurate. The two women knew there were countless variables, which meant innumerable ways they could be wrong—three and a half centuries was a long time. Yet they also felt an inexorable desire to identify this destination, a yearning as though they were on a pilgrimage and not just an indulgence of curiosity. Some recess of their souls felt a longing to discover what had become of Rachel Bourne.

They had learned about her by accident. Abigail was scrolling through university archives for her thesis, investigating Puritan expatriates to New Hampshire, when she started catching references to "that foule witch Goody Rachel Bourne, who hath made sundry and divers couvenantes with the Devil." Intrigued, she began ignoring the tedium of her thesis, hunting instead for any snatch of seventeenth-century gossip about this "foule witch." The hunt was slow going—it seemed no one *wanted* to speak of her, and she was scarcely the only Rachel Bourne of her day. But Abigail gradually tracked her movements and her history—or at least the skeleton of her history.

Rachel Mayhew came as a child of the great migration in the 1630s, granddaughter of a minister, and her family settled in the Connecticut River Valley. She married local boy Forthright Bourne in 1642, seemingly as an ordinary churchgoing young woman. How she went from Puritan wife to scorned sorceress remained unclear. Forthright disappeared from the record by 1647, and the next references to Rachel were depositions accusing her of calling down profane curses on the local livestock. To Abigail it fit a familiar pattern: the townsfolk spurning a woman isolated, on the fringes of the community. When another local couple died, presumably of smallpox, suspicion fell on Rachel, who apparently fled (or was cast out). She was next heard from in Portsmouth, where she seemed to dispense herbal remedies for a few years and may have served as a midwife.

But by 1654 she had once more become estranged from a community. The records now broke the pattern; whatever circumstances turned the town against Rachel, they were never mentioned overtly. Oh, there were still the references to her pacts with demonic forces, but no allusions to hexes and neighborly strife. A few documents seemed to suggest odd happenings during a particular week early in the year, the "heavens' deformation." Then she was gone.

This was where Isabella had come in. Knocking down mochas past midnight at The Magic Bean, she and Abigail started doing what graduate students do: talking about their theses. And Abigail realized that Isabella—with her background in IT and her obsession with geocaching—would be the perfect partner. So together, they followed every scrap of remaining evidence to identify the last known location in which Rachel Bourne was sighted. Finding clues from this point was almost impossible; but fur traders and Abenaki at that time occasionally talked about a woman living alone in a small cabin up in the northwest section of the state.

After months spent poring over algorithms and digitized manuscripts, the two had extrapolated a plausible location, a little patch of earth that apparently survived unvisited even in twenty-first-century New England, one that would have been almost inconceivably isolated in the seventeenth century. What could have drawn Rachel, barely in her thirties at the time, beyond the reach of English or French or even Indian settlement? Abigail couldn't say for certain, but one line of Rachel's deposition stood out to her, the officials asserting that she "claims she hath on sundry occasions summoned forth a great green power."

What secrets lay hidden in that phrase, this "great green power"? Who could say? But for a woman, a widow, alone in a wild frontier, the pursuit and prospect of such a power was surely tantalizing— tantalizing enough, it appeared, that she would forsake all human bounds to seek it.

And so they hiked, Abigail in blue jeans with a red flannel shirt hanging loosely over her church camp tee, Isabella in merino wool and jogger pants. They were well past paths and the painted markings of the formal trails at which they had begun, beyond even the seemingly ubiquitous signs of human presence, the granola wrappers and plastic water bottles and old condoms. Aside from their shoes on the dirt snapping sticks, the explorers heard only natural sounds—the phrases and trills of sparrows, the quack of waking wood frogs in vernal pools, the bellowing of a waterfall like a distant dragon of the prime. It seemed to them pristine, unspoilt, nature untarnished by the malices of man.

They had parked the car about two-thirds of the way up the mountainside, and at first they had continued to ascend. Now, though, they mounted an acclivity, and then their course sloped down, somewhat sharply. It was no mean feat to navigate through the tangle of creepers and roots, dodging spiderwebs thick as linen. Even as Abigail followed the route proffered by her device, she increasingly began to feel she was descending into a maze, an Escheresque convolution of impossible geometries, a labyrinth populated with the denizens one would expect of a labyrinth. *Where's my thread?* she thought to herself, meaning it as a joke, though she didn't laugh.

Magus began barking abruptly, causing Abigail to gasp in surprise and shift her attention to Isabella. The dog was straining at his leash, bared teeth and black-brown eyes fixed at a thicket to their west, not far from the gradually sinking sun. Abigail caught a glimpse of movement amid the hawthorn.

"Who's there?"

The voice came from the thicket, and a figure emerged. He was perhaps forty, with a bronze-blond hedge of beard leading up to a green visored cap. An orange vest blazed out over his wine-dark flannel shirt, and at his side was a bolt-action rifle. He regarded the two women quizzically with faded blue eyes.

"Didn't expect to see anyone else around," he added after a pause. "You ladies should probably be careful out here."

Isabella's eyes narrowed as she stared at him. She made no attempt to soothe Magus as she responded, "Why is that?"

The man shrugged. "I just figured. We're a hell of a way from town here."

"I think we know that," Abigail replied as levelly as she could.

Shrugging again, the man said, "Sure. I just meant be careful.

Even I don't usually come out this far, but I imagine there could be other hunters around." He scratched at his beard. "I wouldn't want anyone to get . . . hurt."

The man straightened his posture, keeping his gaze on Abigail and Isabella. Then he turned away, heading north through the thicket. Abigail looked nervously at her phone. "It looks like we may be headed in the same direction," the man stated without turning back. "I'll let you know if there are any problems."

"We'll be all right," Isabella shot back through half-clenched teeth. The man didn't answer, and soon his large strides took him out of their view as he was swallowed up by the wood ahead.

Isabella exchanged a glance with Abigail. Magus had stopped barking, but his leash was taut. She could feel the pulsing of her heart, the tightness of her trembling muscles, and she could see the same in Abigail.

"Do you want to keep going?" Abigail inquired.

Isabella squinted incredulously. "Hell, yes," she confirmed.

Abigail nodded. "Right. I don't want to stop when we're this close. Just . . . keep your pepper spray handy."

They resumed their hiking, even more attuned now to the environment around them. But because of this renewed awareness, they noticed an odd feature of their surroundings: the forest grew strangely quiet as they advanced. A true wilderness is never silent; life is boisterous, noisy, carefree, and away from human populations, scampering feet, sudden wings, and plaintive mating cries ride the breeze. The odd unnaturalness of the stillness wasn't exactly reverent, as though some awe pervaded the wood. It felt—though neither could say how she knew this—like a stifled, strangled, choked reticence.

So silent was it that Isabella actually cringed at an abrupt cracking sound, one so unobtrusive she scarcely would have heard it on a normal hike. Looking down at her feet, she saw she had stepped on a dried hazelnut. Ahead of them, deeper in the valley, were several hazelnut shrubs, their catkins dangling like narrow coffins, and little

❧

magenta blooms like blood bursting. Their V-veined leaves hadn't begun growing in the nascent warmth of spring; the branches looked gaunt as pietàs in the midst of the surrounding verdancy. But the ground ahead was covered in nuts, which puzzled Isabella. These hazelnuts must have dropped last summer; yet how could there be so many strewn about the ground? The fauna of this region ought to have devoured such a feast months ago.

Magus had stopped barking as well, but he was moving erratically, his legs juddering, his tail curled under his belly, more like an ill-trained beagle puppy than his usual sturdy self. Isabella glanced up at Abigail, who was looking back at her phone, following its lead.

"We've got to be close," Abigail mumbled.

"I hope so," Isabella grunted. "This place is . . . I don't know, a bit weird, yeah?"

Abigail paused and looked up from her device, glassy eyes glinting as she turned back to her friend. "Isabella, that dude is way ahead of us now. And the dog would warn us if we were in any trouble."

Isabella shook her head. "It's not that. Don't you feel it? Like something was nearby? Not a man or anything, but . . . something. *Diablo,* girl, I thought you were the one who believed in shit like that."

Abigail laughed, lightly but not unnervously. "I believe in God, not ghosts, Izzy. Not somethings. If you want, you can come to church with me on Sunday."

Isabella scowled. "Twelve years of mass didn't exactly make me a choir girl, and a walk in the woods sure as hell isn't going to."

Abigail shrugged. "Fine. Then let's go find us a witch."

They resumed their course, emerging into a thick realm of maple, beech, and the ubiquitous bone-white birch, interspersed with ridges of coarse quartzite. Isabella's vision seemed to grow indistinct for a moment amid the crowd of tree trunks. She looked back the way she thought they had come, but she could no longer see the hazelnut shrubs.

"We're almost there!" Abigail shouted excitedly. Her voice burst into the stillness so starkly that Isabella nearly cried out. She bit her tongue and castigated herself. Abigail was happy; why shouldn't she be? It was a beautiful spring day, and they were nearing their destination, the culmination of months of work.

But this place did not look like nature as she knew it, not like the parks she and her *abuela* had visited on the outskirts of town, not even like the trails she used to hike with her ex-boyfriend, when she would leave him half a mile behind her amid the groves and the copses. Every detail of growth here seemed sickeningly, uncannily clear, as though she were aware of the rustling of maggots in rotten bark, though still she heard nothing. That stump lying prone at her feet: it looked horribly like a terrified rabbit, as though some small creature had been swallowed by the bark and transmogrified while writhing to escape. Yet if she looked at the same stump from a different angle, it once again appeared to be only a dead, diseased slab of maple, as one might find in any forest.

Then there was the scream. It was a human scream, sharp and short, and soon replaced by a guttering gurgle, and then once more by quietude. The woods weren't dark, but the canopy kept out a clear view of the sun, and Isabella couldn't tell what direction it came from, any more than she could now tell where they were.

"Abby, what the hell was that?"

"I don't know," Abigail replied tersely. She pointed ahead of her. "It came from there . . . I think?"

"Where's there? And where are *we?*"

"I don't know," Abigail repeated, snapping at Isabella because she was angry with herself. "My phone's not working."

"You told me we'd have no problems!" Isabella growled. "There are supposed to be towers nearby. Did you charge . . . ?"

"Yes, damn it, of *course* I charged the stupid thing." Abigail pried her eyes from her screen's dark glass, which now showed only her panicked reflection, and cast her gaze about their surroundings. "This way," she beckoned, striding ahead with all the boldness she knew she did not have. Isabella followed behind her, and for a time, they began to walk together in feigned purpose.

Suddenly, though, Magus bolted, with so little warning that he pulled his leash free from Isabella's hand. The dog bounded ahead of them about ten feet and stopped for a few seconds, his teeth bared, his body spinning uncertainly. Then he started up again, racing over a rise. Isabella didn't hesitate, running past Abigail toward the little slope where he had disappeared. Abigail was hardly so sanguine about chasing the dog, but she had no desire to find herself alone in the wood, and she pursued them. Even as she did, though, she felt as though *she* were the one pursued. The darkening green of the wood that surrounded her looked unreal—symbolic, yet a symbol that stood for nothing living, like the painted face on an ancient coffin.

So they ran. On the other side of the rise, the ground sloped deeper into the valley, shadows tessellated like netting on the earth. Dodging trees, the friends' momentum carried them farther and farther down, until Isabella stopped without warning. Abigail quickly came to a halt beside her.

"What?" she asked.

Isabella didn't answer; she didn't need to. Abigail could see what she saw.

"Oh my God," Abigail whispered, her throat dry, but with bile threatening deeper in.

It was the man they had seen . . . or it had been. His beard and cap were unmistakable. But his body was encased in a birch trunk, had become melded there. The outlines of his vest were visible but had been made the same mottled, dry white as the bark, and Abigail couldn't say where he ended and the tree began. Every detail they could see looked preserved, down to the hairs around his chapped lips, which were slightly parted, making a hollow of his empty throat. It might have been a sculpture of a man, expertly whittled down from a log, but his body protruded in a way no tree could extend.

And just fifteen feet farther on, they saw the remains of Magus.

They found him at the bole of a white ash, and his body was entangled with its roots, so that much of his lower half was indistinguishable from the vertical creasing of the tree's gray bark. His mouth was twisted into a howl he had never had the chance to utter. One of the front paws twitched slightly, as though it remembered what it had been like to be a dog, bounding free across open earth. But that was the only sign of life—except, of course, for the empire-slow sap-life of the vegetation that Magus had become.

Abigail could barely breathe for fear, and this only increased the horror—was she to be next? She whirled around shuffling away from trees as much as she could, while Isabella stood beside her, sobbing, teeth clenched.

"Why?" Isabella whispered with ferocity. It was all she could say; only questions remained.

Abigail grabbed her hand. "Let's go, Izzy."

"Go where?"

"Anywhere but here."

Abigail tugged, and Isabella acquiesced, so the two of them ran once more, though they could not say where; beneath the canopy of green that filled the dimming sky, all geography seemed to vanish. Nothing looked familiar in the sporadic shards of sun that broke through the leaves like glass splinters about the peaty ground. But Abigail was right, of course; whatever else, they had to move.

It was thus that they stumbled into a glade, a little hollow in the thick press of forest, where one sight was visible with appalling clarity. It was a fireplace, an old stone hearth and chimney, standing alone within a ring of trees; the work of centuries had torn away the rest of the house, and only that narrow, mortared tower of the home remained. Isabella knew what it was in an instant; they had come at last to the site they sought.

It was not the lonely, denuded hearth itself that caused her stomach to churn, however, but what was within it. Isabella saw *her*, Rachel Bourne, for she stood, like Magus, like the hunter, engulfed inside the very stone of the erect, desiccated chimney. There she had remained, for three hundred years and more. In some ways, time and the elements had done their work; fingers were missing, small patches of shale worn down. Yet her image endured in ghastly familiarity. Isabella could see the coarse texture of her wool frock, even what looked like a berry stain on the left sleeve. Frozen fringes of once-flaxen hair spilled from beneath her bonnet and framed her face. It was a young-looking face, slightly plump and speckled by pimples, with close-set eyes and a little nose and large lips—lips that had been screaming in an ecstasy of terror since before America was a nation.

And here, Isabella truly felt *its* presence. Past faith or doubt or science or any knowing that might track through her synapses, deeper than blood or marrow, Isabella now knew the nearness of the thing that Rachel Bourne had summoned. It was the great green power for which she had been cast out, and Isabella had always understood why Rachel, a woman alone in a dark society, would seek out a power, but now she understood why the people had sent her away. For what Rachel had brought forth in her quest for strength was a darkness beyond all human reckoning—beyond space, beyond gender, beyond nature yet embedded in it, a parasite of matter and spirit, a green that grew from the earth like the wasp from the caterpillar. Isabella knew too that it did not seek her annihilation, but its unfathomable intelligence had its own alien ends. It hadn't sought to destroy Rachel either, or Magus, or the hunter, but it had moved inside its little sphere of creation, and it *had* destroyed them, and another such movement might destroy Isabella or Abigail too. And they would find themselves absorbed into the landscape, like monuments shrouded in mosses, their consciousnesses dwindled to the unminding existence of the vegetable or the desolate coldness of rock, and their screams too would be drowned out by the silence of the shade.

"Aunque pase por valle tenebroso," she murmured by an ancient instinct, "ningún mal temeré, porque tú vas conmigo." This time, she grabbed hold of Abigail. Her friend's arm was still, so still that

Isabella feared that it would break off and crumble, that Abigail too had been transmogrified into the hellish ecosystem. But her resistance was only the stiffness of nightmare, and in a moment, her sky-blue eyes caught Isabella's.

"Abby, come," Isabella said, and sparing a tear for Rachel as she ran, she led Abigail away from the grisly glade.

They still didn't know where they were going, though, and who knew what were the boundaries of the green power? Isabella could still sense its inhuman thoughts oppressing her soul and her viscera, like the pressures of a deep abysm. Abigail was no help; she went along unresistingly, but her countenance was glazed with a sheen of dread. All around them, the tree trunks still rose skyward like stakes, and the burning green of the leaves above occluded more than ever the rays of the westering sun. If she could *see* the sun, Isabella might know where they were. But when they ran, she felt like they were locked in an endless track, like tracing the perimeter of a compass when she wanted to be following a point on the rose.

And then, she heard the crunch, the tiny sound of a splintering shell. She looked down at her feet and saw the hazelnuts. Beside her and Abigail stood the little row of shrubs. Isabella picked up the shell she had stepped on, regarding it for the briefest of moments, and then she knew where they were. Pulling Abigail along, she ran, with the same urgency as before, but now with direction. Beneath her tight pants her thighs burned, but at this she rejoiced, for now they were climbing, ascending from out the valley. Her grip on Abigail slackened, for Abigail too was striding with purpose, and the pain in her legs was a pain that *meant* something. Her chest heaved with the force of it all, and yet she breathed freely, for the weight of the green shade was lifting. They were emerging from its dominion.

So it was that some minutes later, the two women found themselves on an outcropping en route to their parking space. They sat on rocks in a clearing, trembling, inhaling and exhaling, never speaking, for words seemed absurdly inadequate for what they had seen, what they had known, and it all made them weep as they never thought they could. They embraced each other in their exhausted relief, and Isabella could feel her friend's heart against her own and exult, because a tree or a stone has no heart to beat. When they released each other, she looked back down the way they had come. The sun had dropped beneath the horizon, but a roseate glow suffused the west, illumining in red and pink all manner of things above the shadows. She held between her fingers the untimely but ripe hazelnut, and carefully she raised it up into the light of the sky, where it glowed like a round little world in the night.

The Almost-Nonhuman: Life and Death in Kelly Link, Carmen Maria Machado, and George Saunders

Mairead Drake

In many slipstream texts, characters appear who blur the distinction between what is human and what is not. These almost-nonhuman characters (ghosts, zombies, or other human-appearing, but not always feeling, entities) are often used by slipstream authors to explore the concept of humanity by breaking it. They are not human fully, but in the way they are portrayed they are not quite nonhuman either. Authors such as George Saunders, Kelly Link, and Carmen Maria Machado provide characters and concepts that push against the definition of humanity from the inside, leaving their readers to decide when they have broken through and their subject is no longer human.

The questions of how big of a box humanity fits into, whether it is a more malleable definition than we have been led to believe, and what factors lead to dehumanization are raised by these writers. Many of the almost-nonhuman characters are impacted by issues of communication, representations of themselves, capitalist systems, and violence, all things that might affect the lives of those reading as well. In including almost-nonhuman entities in ways that both humanize and dehumanize them, authors of slipstream fiction attempt to define humanity and look at how contemporary discourses might contribute to more than just the dehumanization of characters on a page, but to those who currently exist under the definition of human. In doing so, they wrestle with the idea of whether humanity is something inherent or whether it can be impacted by outside forces, such as changing modes of communication, damaging portrayal of bodies in the media, the reduction of individuals to participants of capitalism, and the rationalization of violence.

Ghosts are one of the more commonly used examples of the almost-nonhuman, pushing against the definition of human by their very nature, having once been considered human without argument, but with complications arising from their incorporeal nature and lack of traditionally defined life. Despite these factors, they are often humanized by slipstream authors, and one of the ways that seems to be most effective in doing so is by portraying them as able to form connections and relationships with one another and with the living. This mode of humanization is the main focus of Kelly Link's "The Great Divorce," which follows the managing of a number of relationships between the living and the dead by mediums, the central story focusing on Alan Robley, a living man, and Lavvie Tyler, a dead woman, who are getting a divorce. Humans are naturally interconnected beings and social creatures, and by allowing dead individuals to continue or create relationships, authors such as Link let the dead continue to exist as something almost human, rather than something completely separate. In "The Great Divorce," these relationships are not simply a holdover from when they were living: they can be formed after death, as seen with Alan and Lavvie, who meet after Lavvie is dead (Link 199). The dead are not being grandfathered in with the ability to keep relationships; they have the ability to create new ones just like the rest of humanity. In a similar but distinct point, the dead also retain their agency to surrender these connections and are not locked into the relationships they had when they were living as simply an echo that is acting out old habits: for example, the fact that Sam Callahan's wife chooses to leave him after she passes (Link 206). Relationships, whatever their nature, are often seen as a part of an individual's humanity, and Link's giving the ghosts in her story the ability both to create and to dissolve relationships humanizes them.

In "The Great Divorce," the dead are not truly separate from the living: a character in the text, Sarah Parminter, even has occasional difficulty remembering which people are dead and which are alive, highlighting this lack of separation between them (Link 212). If one can be mistaken for the other, the dead and the living must at least be similar. However, Link makes it clear that, although the dead might be indistinguishable from the living while they retain relationships, losing their connection to others is what makes them separate (Link 199, 203). If connections are what make something human, the implication becomes that without connection to others we may lose our own humanity. Death is not what stops one from being human, but a lack of relating to others. There are a number of implications resulting from this idea, the most significant of which being that people can begin to lose their humanity before they become one of the dead, if they are isolated from others and do not maintain some relationships.

The relationships in this story are maintained by communication that, when occurring between a member of the dead and a member of the living, must be filtered through a third party in the form of a medium or ouija board (Link 200). While ouija boards and mediums are examples of filtered communication, this term can be applied to any form of communication in which information isn't being passed directly between parties. More mundane examples might be things such as letters or text messages, where the communication can be deliberately altered or, perhaps more likely, lose meaning accidentally due to lack of context or tone. Over the course of the story, Link demonstrates that issues of filtered communication often lead to misunderstandings that cause relationships to be ended, thus making the growth of filtered communication a factor that might dehumanize.

The idea of filtered communication being a dehumanizing factor might make more sense when you consider that the collection that includes "The Great Divorce," *Magic for Beginners*, was published in 2005, three years after the creation of Friendster, two years after LinkedIn, and one year after Facebook. Cell phones were becoming popular. Fears of how the Internet and technology would change the way humans related to one another were common at the time, common enough that many editorials were written on the subject of the progress of social media and technology and how they might impact social interactions between humans. One such article arguing against these fears, by anthropologist and ethnographer Jordan Kraemer, was written to convince people that this progress would not "inevitably lead to social alienation" and was published the same year as *Magic for Beginners..* How these new forms of communication might impact relationships between individuals was a common fear, and it would make sense for authors writing at the time to explore this issue. Cell phones and social media, especially at their advent, might seem very much like a ouija board or medium, a third party through which communication was now being filtered, that might have a large impact on the way humans related to one another.

This filtered communication leads to a number of difficulties in the text, as seen when Alan and Lavvie discuss their divorce through a medium. There are clearly differences between what both individuals believe to be true, and the fact that their primary communication is through a third party increases the disconnect between them. Sarah, the medium, explains to Alan that "You don't understand her [Lavvie], but she still loves you" (Link 201). This lack of understanding, presumably due to their lack of ability to communicate directly, is the root of the problem between the partners, each believing very different things about their relationship. Because their communication is filtered, Lavvie and Alan have developed different perspectives and understandings, both loving the other but not being able to understand each other. For example, Alan sometimes does not "even feel like the kids are [his]," while Lavvie is reminded of him whenever she looks at them (Link 202–3). Likewise, while Lavvie assumes he is jealous of her friends and "only married a dead woman because [he liked] the people at [his] work to think [he is] trendy," Alan spends his time wondering what his wife might look like (Link 202). If they could speak directly to each other, these issues might have been solved earlier, but instead they are allowed to fester. Since none of these things were discussed directly between the two, they are only able to be voiced by Sarah, which effectively disconnects them from each other even more. Like a digital message that often lacks tone and context, information passed through another is bound to lose some of its meaning.

Despite the struggles we see them facing, the reader is led to believe that Alan and Lavvie are an example of a couple truly trying, as divorce is uncommon among the dead and the living (Link 199). The most common way a living person might deal with irreconcilable issues with a dead partner is to "no longer [acknowledge] the admittedly tenuous presence of his spouse," to simply stop recognizing them as a human presence (Link 199). The severing of people from human connections is how they are dehumanized, and the need for filtered communication is how they end up there. The act of simply not acknowledging someone's presence is also something that is far more possible through means of modern filtered communication, such as social media, whether it be through ignoring a message or blocking someone, and much easier than ignoring an actual person. Not only can filtered communication lead to the breakdown of relationships, it can also arguably provide easier methods of breaking them off. If connections to others are what humanize, and a lack of connections and relationships can be what marks someone as separate from the human world (even when death does not, as in the case of the world Link has created), a sense of apprehension around emerging forms of communication is understandable.

Filtered communication between individuals is not the only impact of social media that slipstream authors seem to be gesturing toward as causing feelings of dehumanization. Carmen Maria Machado's "Real Women Have Bodies" depicts women whose physical bodies fade from reality. While they are different from Link's ghosts, given that it is unclear whether they are living or not, they share a similar incorporeal nature that alludes to what is dehumanizing them, the portrayal of their bodies (Machado 127, 134). Communication is not simply something that occurs between individuals, but also something that can occur between entities, or between an entity and individuals, and technology has made this easier than it ever was. Advertisements and public figures create images for individuals of the public that portray an ideal, which can then be internalized by the recipient. When the collection *Her Body and Other Parties*, containing "Real Women Have Bodies," was published in 2017, digital media had progressed far beyond what it was in 2005, allowing for more specific issues with it to be realized, such as the portrayal of women's bodies. Many reviews of Machado's collection commented on her handling of this topic. Jen Corrigan's review in *The Coil* notes that the collection as a whole feels connected because of the emphasis in each of the stories on "exploring the experiences of women . . . and their bodies," bodies that have been subjected to violence, "collectively or individually." The portrayal of women's bodies is an example of the collective violence that Machado explores. While the portrayal of women's bodies has been an issue for much longer than the Internet, digital media has amplified the critical lens that was placed on an individual's form, and a common issue in this lens is the expectation of thin bodies, which might explain why the women in the text fade, taking up less space than has been projected onto them. A report published the same year as Machado's *Her Body and Other Parties* created by researchers at the University of Technology Sydney and the University of West England discovered that the use of Instagram, specifically if users followed health or celebrity accounts, was "significantly positively correlated with thin-ideal internalisation and drive for thinness" (Cohen et al. 185).

The fading of women into nothingness represents an extreme that highlights this phenomenon. When the women in "Real Women Have Bodies" begin to fade, it seems that they develop a need to become part of an object. We see women purposely allowing themselves to be sewn into dresses, and later the narrator wonders what other objects women have been placed inside (Machado 134):

> I wonder about the merchandise I pass. Who's in there? The
> wooden picture frame samples arranged in descending v's down a

felt display case look askew, as if they've been invaded. The glass-and-steel chess set in the window of the game store--are those reflections of passersby in the fat curve of the queen and the pawns, or faces peering out? There's an ancient Pac-Man machine that takes everyone's quarters, seemingly on purpose. I walk past the heavily scented entrance of a JCPenney cosmetics counter, and imagine customers uncapping tubes of lipstick and twisting the color free, and faded women squeezing up around the makeup, thumbs first. (Machado 136).

While Machado is technically personifying the objects, almost making these inanimate things more human, the fact that the reader knows they are personified because they might actually contain human women complicates this idea, which means that the personification of these objects is a way to dehumanize the women inside them. The women are quite literally becoming objectified, and subsequently dehumanized as well. Again, by using extreme visuals Machado highlights a very real consequence of the portrayal of women in the media.

Another factor that dehumanizes in this particular text is the capitalist system within which the women exist. Blame is initially placed on the fashion industry, which given its history of how women are portrayed is not unreasonable, but is explained away by the fact that women who do not have bodies cannot be sold to, as they cannot wear clothes, though they admit to trying (Machado 128). The women are now simply entities that cannot participate in the process of labor and purchasing that generates revenue for the fashion industry, among others. This idea is highlighted in the fact that the "first reports [of women disappearing] at the height of the recession," a time when participation in the labor system would have been particularly stressed (Machado 127). Thus, after it is discovered that the faded women can no longer be sold to, their problem is mostly ignored, and still "no one knows what causes [them to fade]" (Machado 128). Capitalism has no use for those who cannot produce or consume, and thus under a capitalist system those without exploitable bodies are held with little regard. Those who can participate are reduced to just a part of the system, while those who cannot are ignored.

The reduction of an individual to a participant in this system as a method of dehumanization is not exclusive to Machado; it also appears in the way Kelly Link uses zombies in *Magic for Beginners,* specifically in the stories "The Hortlak" and "Some Zombie Contingency Plans." In the former, the zombies are portrayed as inhabiting a town that seems as if it might be indistinguishable from American suburbia, including places of commerce such as movie theaters and bars (Link 38). The zombies themselves are usually portrayed as completing pointless tasks or trying to purchase objects they themselves brought into the store (Link 39, 47). Living in a town so similar to a place humanity might reside in and attempting to try and purchase things might have been a means of humanizing zombies in a different portrayal; but since the zombies appear to do nothing but labor and purchase, and because both seem to be done in a way that is pointless, they seem distinctly inhuman. Existing as a mechanism for commerce, even though it seems like such a human thing, dehumanizes; it is what we are able to do besides such things that marks an individual as more human.

George Saunders also demonstrates how living simply to survive within a capitalist structure can dehumanize in "Offloading for Mrs. Schwartz," in which the narrator strips both the titular Mrs. Schwartz and eventually himself of memories, in order to make enough money to keep Mrs. Schwartz's bills paid. Selling her parts of themselves may keep her alive, but at the loss of who they both were as people. Mrs. Schwartz herself becomes disoriented with the changes that occur to her body without her realizing it (Saunders 76). The story culminates with the narrator having to leave himself a note to tell himself what to do, but he seems to be aware that the body left behind is separate from himself, as the language he uses identifies it as a different individual, a "you" instead of "I" (Saunders 77). In trying to stay afloat within the system, both Mrs. Schwartz and the narrator lose what makes them who they are. What is left behind, a human that is no longer itself, is not quite human any-more as it has no personal identity, but likely would not be considered a fully nonhuman entity either, much like the zombies and ghosts discussed earlier. The loss of personal identity through the demands of capitalism to stay alive illustrates that the reduction of individuals to only what they can contribute to such a system as dehumanizing.

Saunders also presents the presence of violence and the process of rationalizing it as a dehumanizing factor. Like Link, he uses ghosts as an almost-nonhuman entity, but instead of highlighting relationships and connections as the way to portray the human side of them, Saunders humanizes his ghosts by showcasing their agency, emotion, and capacity for thought. For example, the ghosts of the McKinnons in "CivilWarLand in Bad Decline." Their agency seems present yet limited: they are able to interact with the world around them far more than might be expected of something that is dead, yet they are forced to repeat their past (Saunders 24). Despite their death, the Mrs. shows grief for the fate of her husband and Maribeth wishes for love (Saunders 12). Likewise, when the Mr. is forced to re-enact his attack on his family, he regrets his actions and wishes to explain (Saunders 25). Regret, desire, and grief are all things that are considered human emotions and serve to humanize the ghosts. Yet, once Saunders has built a level of humanity, he takes it away by subjecting the ghosts to violence.

The backdrop of the story that features the McKinnons is CivilWarLand, an amusement park inspired by one of the bloodiest periods of American history. To create such an amusement park is to normalize the violence that both occurred during the war itself and also the violence that preceded and caused it. This normalization of violence by those running CivilWarLand and those attending it can be seen throughout the story, perhaps most notably when Samuel, the hired security for the park, kills the teenage gang members who attempted to kidnap the niece of a family of visitors. Not only is there is very little reaction to the display of violence within the park, but a complete acceptance and thankfulness for it. The family even joins in, "kicking and upbraiding the six gang corpses" (Saunders 16). After their brutal murder the corpses are treated as objects, less than human; and thus, the normalization of violence effectively dehumanizes them.

A study on collective violence by researchers at Princeton University found that individuals are "more likely to recommend harsh treatment for dehumanized others" (Littman and Paluck 92). To normalize and rationalize violence in this way, it is necessary to lessen the humanity perceived in the victim, the offenders seeing themselves as human acting out violence against a less-than-human entity. The moment the McKinnons seem the least human is when they are forced to re-enact the moment of their death. The family is violently murdered by the father before he kills himself. In this moment they lose the agency that Saunders previously used to humanize them, instead just becoming an echo of the past repeating itself. It's something they are "compelled to act out," rather than being able to act and react of their own volition (Saunders 24). The moment of their reduced agency overlaps with the moment of extreme violence that ends their life, highlighting the dehumanizing factors of both.

While all these authors take different approaches and focus on different aspects, they all attempt to accomplish a similar goal of defining humanity through what it is not, asking what traits are necessary to make something that might be considered nonhuman human again, or for the first time, and what traits or experiences often associated with it have no bearing on an individual's humanity. By engaging specifically with current discourses but through the lens of the almost-nonhuman, Saunders, Link, and Machado are able to explore the fears of modern humanity and what impact they might have. Though they all tackle different features of what it means to be human, what they have discovered collectively is that humanity is malleable and can be impacted by the environment it is placed in, but also that humanity is not as tied to the systems that many of us live under. The authors mentioned in this essay are not the only authors doing so; examples include David Wong's protagonist in *John Dies at the End*, who discovers that he is not as human as he thought he was, but rather a creation that had replaced the real him, and Jonathan Sims's personified fear, The Stranger, in *The Magnus Archives*, who is representative of that which is so close to being human it is frightening. External forces, like new technology relating to how we communicate with one another, the portrayal of not just women's but all bodies in the media, and how individuals are affected by economic systems and violence, impact all our lives; and being able to explore their impact through fiction allows authors and readers to think about possible consequences. The use of the almost non-human is a way for us to do so.

Works Cited

Cohen, Rachel, et al. "The Relationship between Facebook and Instagram Appearance-Focused Activities and Body Image Concerns in Young Women." *Body Image* 23 (December 2017): 183–87.

Corrigan, Jen. "Speculative Feminism: On Carmen Maria Machado's 'Her Body and Other Parties.'" *The Coil* (28 April 2018). medium.com/the-coil/book-review-carmen-maria-machado-her-body-and-other-parties-jen-corrigan-237ead82e6bc

Kraemer, Jordan. "The Myth of Tech Gadgets and Social Alienation." *SFGate* (16 November 2005). www.sfgate.com/opinion/openforum/article/Culture-and-Technology-The-myth-of-tech-gadgets-2595020.php

Link, Kelly. *Magic for Beginners*. New York: Random House, 2005.

Littman, Rebecca, and Elizabeth Levy Paluck. "The Cycle of Violence: Understanding Individual Participation in Collective Violence." *Political Psychology* 26 (February 2015): 79–99.

Machado, Carmen Maria. *Her Bodies and Other Parties*. Minneapolis, MN: Graywolf Press, 2017.

Saunders, George. *CivilWarLand in Bad Decline*. New York: Random House, 1996.

Night Hags

Wade German

O dreamful sleeper
     At the door
Of dreamland's steeper
     Untold lore,
Now what reaper
     To abhor
On Nightmare to you rides?
       In she glides

From nether, needing
     Nascent dreams
For outré feeding—
     So it seems;
Amid the pleading,
     Evil screams
As thought and psyche change,
      Turning strange

To mind unwoven,
     Undermined,
By horrors cloven:
     Now a mind
One with coven
     Of her kind,
That knows not dreams, nor light,
      Only night.

The Interminable Abomination

Mark Samuels

> "He asked me if I had read the stories of a certain Edgar Poe. I
> told him I knew them better than anyone and had good reason for
> doing so. Then he asked me, in a very emphatic tone, if I believed
> that this Edgar Poe existed. *I* of course asked him who he thought
> wrote all the stories. He answered: "*A club of very clever, very pow-
> erful writers, who know everything that's going on.*"
> —Charles Baudelaire to Auguste Poulet-Malassis,
> 8 January 1860

> "I became *insane,* with long periods of *horrible sanity.*"
> —Edgar A. Poe, 4 January 1848

It is a curious thing, but despite a thirty-year career in the trade, of
handling books, reading them, and selling them on at a small profit,
I cannot say that my occupation ever inspired in me the desire to
write anything by way of a narrative—whether fictional or autobiographical. I confined my writing activities to business correspond-
ence, to my *Secondhand Bookshops Gazetteer,* and to my quarterly
mail-order catalogue, *Vathek's Book-List.* If I were to mention that
my principal London "rival" in the trade was Aloysius Condor
Books—a long-established firm and member of the ABA and currently run by its founder's even more unscrupulous nephew Nicholas
Condor—then the genre of literature which I bought and sold will
be immediately obvious to its aficionados. How horrible, then, that I
am now *under a compulsion* to write what follows hereafter and to do
so in that very genre.

But I must not get ahead of myself. Let me, then, try to arrange
events in their proper chronological order and reveal them as they
were themselves revealed to me.

I had, for the last few years, become semi-retired in the
bookselling trade: the increasing domination of the Internet pushed

up prices everywhere (even in high-street "charity"—a gross misnomer—shops) so that not only were fewer bargains to be found but also the traditional bricks-and-mortar secondhand bookshops began closing down. They were the prey of increasingly fiendish local business rates as London streets previously thought of as "downmarket" were gentrified and diversified by the ruling Islington tyranny. My own *Secondhand Bookshops Gazetteer* halved in content as the closures gathered pace. It was becoming more difficult to obtain stock cheaply for my quarterly book-list. Although I could still rely on the occasional sale of an individual's personal library (often sold by a next-of-kin with no interest in reading, let alone an interest in books), the physical labour involved in carting hundreds of volumes by myself over uneven pavements aggravated my lower back to the extent that my occupation became akin to medieval racking.

And it was in this sad twilight of my career as a bookdealer when I received a query from a customer with whom I had not communicated for a couple of years—Colonel Archibald Dowson. Once he had been a valued, lucrative client of mine (though we had never spoken over the telephone, let alone met face-to-face, and his typed letters were always curiously unidiomatic). Another of my customers had told me this lucrative client had once been a colonel in the British Army—stationed somewhere out in Burma during the Second World War. He was notorious for his obsession with horrors, the ghastlier the better. It seemed he could not get enough of them on the printed page: even after his experiences with nightmarish, real-life horrors committed out in the Far East. And there were also strong rumours that his own military career had ended in disgrace. He had, it was said, perfected acts of hideously refined cruelty against captured soldiers of the Imperial Japanese Army. But—rather oddly in light of the above—he had, it was said, married some Oriental widow twenty years after the end of the war.

I had sold dozens upon dozens of extremely rare and expensive volumes to him (volumes which now, I had no doubt, would fetch an even greater sum when advertised and sold via *Vathek's Book-*

List). In his latest typed communication, as unidiomatic as ever, he made it clear that he wished to offer for sale his entire library, since he was in dire need of funds because of his impending move to a bungalow situated out in Gallows Langley in Hertfordshire. The thought of what items he might still have in his possession (and of how cheaply they might now be obtained) flashed through my mind; I had delicious visions of row after row of shelving filled with well-kept volumes, of hundreds of choice items issued by the likes of Derleth and Wandrei's Arkham House.

It is common practice with me to insist upon a list of at least fifty or so of the titles contained in a private library before I commit myself to making a personal visit to view and to make an offer (I loathe all time-wasting). However, the colonel had bought dozens of individual titles of the highly collectible, expensive type from me in the past in order—as he, then, ungrammatically, put it—to "gaps fill up some in our library."

Would that I had followed my own tried-and-tested precautions!

We had arranged, over the telephone, for me to visit late in the morning; and I was struck by the breathless, wheezing quality of his speech and by his curt manner. He did not seem able to talk much at length, and so I had not insisted upon his giving me some verbal idea as to the current state of his book collection. I wondered if he had been a heavy smoker: and if the edges of the books in his possession were irrevocably browned by the tarry patina of decades of pipe or cigarette smoke. Sometimes even the tobacco stench takes months to dissipate from books contaminated in this inexcusable fashion.

Colonel Dowson still lived in the same flat on the second floor of one of those steep six-storied Victorian buildings on the Muswell Hill Broadway (the address, of course, was familiar to me), and once I located his bell on the outside intercom in the porch (it read simply "The Colonel" in all upper-case letters but with the additional words "& Mrs." crossed out), he buzzed me in through the main front door following a brief exchange of words. It had been extremely difficult to find a spot to park my van within reasonable walking distance, and I thought—with some trepidation for the state of my lower spine—of the effort which might well lie in store for me: viz., the carrying of boxes of heavy books to my vehicle. I had already decided upon my maximum financial outlay: two thousand pounds in banknotes and another two thousand by cheque; the latter only if absolutely necessary. I had no doubt that in a month or two I would recoup the investment and, eventually, make a reasonable profit on my bulk purchase.

As I climbed the winding staircase with its ornate wrought iron balustrade and marble steps, I wondered how long Colonel Dowson had been confined to this place and whether he would have adopted all the suspicious reserve which is supposed to be characteristic of the hermit. There seemed to be no lift in the building, and it did not appear possible—if his breathlessness over the telephone were a true indication of his health—that Colonel Dowson would have been capable even of descending the stairs, let alone of ascending them! He must have made arrangements for all provisions and so forth to be delivered and then carried up to him.

On the second-floor landing, I saw that the door to his flat had been left slightly ajar, but nevertheless I paused on the threshold, knocked upon the peeling black paint of its panelled wood, and called out "Colonel?" through the gap. I heard the sound of something like a rusty bicycle approach the other side of the door, but there was no spoken reply to my query. Eventually, however, the door swung inwards and, beyond it, in the hallway, seated in a rickety wheelchair, was an emaciated ancient whom I supposed to be in his early eighties. A pure-white toothbrush moustache bristled above his upper lip, and his bald pate was heavily liver-spotted. He wore a pair of black-rimmed NHS-issue spectacles, and the lenses were of such thickness that the eyes behind them were weirdly distorted. He must have been virtually blind. The unpleasantness of his wrinkled features was complemented by an expression of acute impatience. A long, slightly askew, hooked nose and obscenely age-enlarged ears provided the finishing touches to this ghastly portrait of death-defying decrepitude.

He was wheezing in a highly alarming manner.

"Ah, you must be the colonel," I said. "How nice to see you in the flesh. We arranged for me to come over today, just before lunchtime, so I might make an offer for your books."

Colonel Dowson did not reply, but looked me up and down with unconcealed distaste. He put a gnarled, arthritic forefinger to his lips, bumped the wheelchair around until it faced in the opposite direction, and hand-propelled his little chariot along the brown linoleum of the hallway towards the dark interior of his second-floor hermitage.

I followed after him, murmuring vapid pleasantries about the awfulness of this cold weather for the time of year. He made no response. Perhaps, I speculated, his brain was as infirm as his body and I might obtain the collection at a considerably reduced price.

I found myself in a dingy parlour with flock-red-velvet wallpaper and little furniture: always a terrible omen. There were no bookshelves in sight; nor were there any books. On a corner desk squatted an old, battered manual typewriter. There was a lingering, persistent smell, though not born of tobacco—but as of something organic and rotten concealed close by. Two central-heating radiators continually gurgled as the hot water circulated inside them.

Colonel Dowson had positioned himself alongside an oxygen cylinder and was inhaling weakly from behind the clear plastic mask which he had placed over his nose and mouth. I heard the increased hissing of the gas whilst he adjusted a pressure valve. Finally, apparently refreshed—or replenished—he discovered there was now enough oxygen inside his lungs to speak to me.

"You are uncommonly tardy," he said. "I expected you ten minutes ago. You have caused me to delay my luncheon."

His speech had that peculiar combination of tone—wheedling

and menacing at the same time—which is often characteristic of the strong-willed when they are enfeebled by old age.

"I can only apologise," I said. "It was very difficult to find somewhere to park. I wonder if I might sit down? My back is playing me up."

"BLAST YOU AND YOUR STUPID BACK!" he shouted, although the rather shocking initial effect of this outburst was mitigated by its trailing off into a wheeze after the "stupid."

He coughed weakly and swallowed twice before absently waving his hand towards a frayed easy chair to his right, impatiently motioning at me to be seated.

"Again, I apologise, Colonel," I said. "I don't wish to intrude or to take up more of your time than is necessary, so perhaps I might just see the books? I assure you I'll offer a fair price."

He utilised the oxygen cylinder again, on this occasion for a longer period. He seemed to be preparing himself for a short soliloquy, and it was finally delivered with little of the cultivation he had previously evinced. He was, I supposed, consciously getting down to business.

"A fair price? A fair price!? I should think so! It was my late wife who built up the collection. That's how she learnt our lingo. You probably don't realise what widows—or Oriental ones at least—are like. She was an obsessive: and cruelly devious. Anyway, obsession was what killed her in the end. She read those books to me once my eyes were buggered up—that was thirty years ago—they started to go bad just after I married her. I should have expected it all along. Anyway, don't think I don't know about those books and their subject-matter. I demand that horror stories be realistic—and the more *informative*, the better. What I want are the facts, not imagination. I understand what real horror is, and I won't be fobbed off with the usual artsy and bohemian fictional claptrap which passes for it these days."

"Ah . . . well . . . yes . . . quite," I replied, intermittently, as he expounded his personal philosophy of the horror genre. I wondered how long he had been cooped up in these rooms alone. His vapid loquaciousness indicated he had possibly not spoken to another living human being for weeks.

From what he had said I surmised that the purchases he had made in the past from *Vathek's Book-List* were made on behalf of his wife (probably, I supposed, as wedding anniversary or as birthday presents). I doubted that a man like Colonel Dowson would have let his spouse anywhere near a chequebook. He probably gave her a weekly allowance which was sufficient for basic housekeeping and no more. Still, he was practically blind, so doubtless she'd managed to arrange things to her own liking on occasions.

Eventually I managed to turn matters back to the business in hand.

"And where," I said, "do you store the library now?"

"The collection's all in the 'book-room.' I have to warn you, though, I'll want the whole amount in cash in advance. I can't be going along to the bank to cash cheques at my age and with my handicap," he said. "Too many bl—um—muggers around these days."

His head swivelled vaguely towards a doorway on the far side of the parlour, which I had assumed contained a kitchen area. The interior of this great beyond was obscured by one of those hanging screens of bead-strips which keep out flying insects, and which went out of fashion sometime in the late 1970s. Its gaudy design depicted a tropical jungle, and the idyllic scene (doubtless now unappreciated by the colonel himself) undulated gently in his overheated but draughty flat.

"It's the doorway on the left, *not* the one on the right. That one's my late wife's room," he said. It was closed off by white, heavy drapes hanging from a rail. There were several large black beetles crawling along the folds of the material.

I still harboured the hope that the 'book-room' on the left would be a bibliophile's Aladdin's Cave.

The colonel took several further deep inhalations from his oxygen cylinder and then wheeled himself in the direction of the tropical barrier. I followed close behind and was soon within the *sanctum sanctorum.*

It was not a large room; scarcely more than an oversized larder, but the walls were lined on three sides with shelving—and what awaited me therein was bitter dregs and the disappointment of my recently raised hopes. A bare lightbulb, suspended from a cord in the ceiling, revealed the degree of despoliation to which the 'bookroom' had been subjected by an earlier raider. A strong whiff of musty, decaying old books still remained to taunt me; that odour which, to the non-reading public, is as unwelcome as halitosis at close quarters, and yet which, to a book-lover, is akin to the fragrance of roses in a summer garden.

"Nicholas Condor—perhaps you've heard of him?—came the other day," the colonel wheezed. "Still, I'm certain there's enough good stuff left to make your journey worthwhile. He assured me he didn't take very much of real worth away with him."

I tried to articulate a coherent response but managed only a half-stifled gurgle.

"Anyway, I'll leave you alone to make an estimate," he said, bumping his wheelchair around before disappearing behind the fake tropical jungle.

I grimly surveyed what little remained upon the denuded shelves: a ratty and dusty complete set of Dornford Yates hardbacks, a few audiobook cassette editions of 'Sapper,' a wide selection of titles on Second World War military campaigns in the Far East, and an extensive variety of large-print biographies or memoirs, mostly of former servicemen.

Nicholas Condor had been extremely thorough.

On only the half-concealed bottom shelf was there anything of the slightest interest to me in my line of business, and these were all just extremely well-thumbed paperbacks. There were a handful of Panther editions from the 1970s by "Lovecraft & Derleth" [*sic*], Clark Ashton Smith, and Arthur Machen, also a few Tandem collections by Charles Birkin and by R. Chetwynd-Hayes, two Sphere-issued titles by William Hope Hodgson, an inevitable early-1980s Corgi paperback reprint of Robert Bloch's *Psycho,* and half-a-dozen battered Fontana or Faber paperback horror and ghost story anthologies, including two edited by Robert Aickman and one edited by Basil Davenport. Lastly, however, there was an anthology edited by Victor Armstrong. At sight of the spine my breath came a little quicker. This final book bore the title *Unknown Nightmares.*

It appeared Condor had not been as thorough as I had first thought.

I fairly snatched this thick, yellowing-edged paperback off the shelves to take a closer look at it. Published in 1996 by Maelström Books (an imprint of Jackson Publishing Ltd), it was an item for which I had received several enquiries. The entire edition had been cancelled before it had gone to print and only a few advance reading copies had leaked into general circulation. I could not recall the exact reason for its sudden withdrawal, but it was certainly the sole item of any real value left in what remained of Colonel Dowson's—or, rather, his and Mrs Dowson's—collection. I was still rather staggered that Condor had overlooked it. The cover (an uncredited piece of art heavily influenced by the style of Richard Powers in his paintings for the Ballantine Horror series) depicted the rotting face of a corpse with an interpenetrating background of dotted starlight in dissolving, surreal, technicolour.

I turned to the contents page. It listed rarities such as "The Corpse-Brotherhood" by Edmund F. Bertrand, "The Mind of Midnight" by Ivan Gilman, "The Hideous Pleasures" by Henri Nisard, "Ego et Mater Tenebrarum Unum Sumus" by Veronica Plunkett, "The Dybbuk Pyramid" by Trefusis Vrolyck, "Teeth of White Static" by Joanna Wolski, and a tale entitled "The Interminable Abomination" by 'X.'

I flicked through the volume at random and arrived exactly at the page where "The Interminable Abomination" story began.

I glanced at the first line and then the next line, and then the one after that; and the words, which themselves seemed grotesquely disordered and unidiomatic, rapidly began working on my mind like an incantation. By the time I was only halfway through the initial paragraph, the page became the sole object of existence in the entire universe, blotting out all else. Reading the text was akin to falling into a night-black well of inconceivable depth—with one's own thoughts disintegrating the further one descended into its mystery.

The narrator told of being dead and buried but of slowly regaining self-awareness—and of the dreams a rotting brain is forced to dream. The tale gradually unveiled what really happens to sentience after one dies; that death is not always the end at all, but can be a doorway to the beginning of stupendously greater terrors undreamt of by the still-living. There were terrifying references to labyrinthine nests of necrophagous larvae infesting night-black coffins in the subterranean depths of cemeteries right across the globe. Here were unveiled the terrors of a larvae-riddled brain as it deliquesced in an eternal nightmare: destined, *post mortem*, to become a hopelessly insane, nightmare-tortured carcass. And the hellish cycle went on indefinitely via metempsychosis: the larvae pupated into beetles, carrying the cumulatively festering dreams inside them, emerged from underground and mated, and then burrowed back down, depositing their eggs in newly-dead human brains, creating more and more larvae, and . . .

Suddenly I was dimly aware of the Colonel wresting the book out from my hands and then his raised voice.

"YOU'LL PAY FOR THAT PARTICULAR BOOK BEFORE READING IT!"

I was dumbfounded and still in shock after reading even that small portion of "The Interminable Abomination." My knees felt like water and a sheen of ice-cold sweat soaked my forehead. A wave of nausea swept over me and I felt a strong urge to vomit.

"Get a grip on yourself, man!" the colonel barked, indifferent to, or unaware of, my distress. "You daydream as much as an old sergeant-major of mine did—that is, until I arranged to have him chased for two miles by a saltwater crocodile through a swamp on Ramree Island!"

I staggered through into the parlour and then slumped into an armchair. My head lolled against a white lace antimacassar. The oppressive heat in the flat was overwhelming.

The colonel followed after me, apparently unsure how to react to my now-obvious distress. Getting no answer to his barked queries, he disappeared into another room.

A few moments later he reappeared with a dusty bottle of Hankey Bannister in his lap and fumblingly poured out a finger into a chipped, bone-china cup.

"Drink some of this," he said. "Works wonders."

After I'd drunk it there was a long pause. He took the opportunity to use his oxygen cylinder again, but his distorted, useless eyes were fixed on me the whole time. I had the distinct impression he thought I might be putting on an act.

"I must have given you quite a scare just now," he said, when he could breathe more easily again, "but the truth of the matter is that you've been daydreaming in there for well over half an hour. Couldn't make out what the devil was taking you so long. Anyway, let's get down to brass tacks. How much for the lot?"

It was still difficult to concentrate on what he was saying, however I did feel myself recovering, at least partially. I wanted nothing more than to get out of his flat as soon as possible. My mind was in revolt against my experience in the 'book-room' and I wondered whether I might, in fact, have been the victim of some kind of epileptic seizure. Even the thought of the value of that copy of *Unknown Nightmares* had been thrust to the back of my mind.

"I'm still not feeling well, Colonel," I said. "I'm going to have to leave now. I'll write to you about the books when I can think straight. I need to see a doctor."

"WHAT'S THAT? LEAVE? LEAVE! Don't talk rot. You haven't even made an offer yet," he replied. The wheedling-cum-menacing tone was back in his voice. "Nothing wrong with you, damn it: just had a funny turn is all—a touch of the vapours. Don't be such a bloody fool. Stay and read the rest of that book if you like."

"Yet again, I can only apologise," I said. "I really must go. I'm feeling very ill."

I shakily got to my feet and wandered along the hallway towards the landing, keeping one hand against the wall to provide some support. Behind me, I could hear the colonel alternately wheezing and cursing.

"Come back here you damn swindler! CROOK! SCOUN-DREL! Don't you walk away from me while I'm talking to you! GET BACK HERE! THAT'S AN ORDER!"

I inadvertently slammed the front door behind me.

That afternoon I spent several hours in the Accident and Emergency ward of the nearest hospital—the Whittington on Highgate Hill. When I explained what had happened to me at the front desk, they seemed to think it quite possible I had suffered a kind of minor stroke, and a battery of tests was immediately performed upon me. In the end, however, they could find no evidence of brain haemorrhaging nor any kind of microbe infection, and I was sent home with the recommendation I should have a further series of tests in a week or so to examine other possible physical or organic causes.

These further tests yielded no solutions to the mystery.

During this period I expected to be the recipient of irate, typed communications from the colonel, but he did not contact me at all.

I dismissed the sudden effect the story had had upon my health as some bizarre coincidence. But, as time passed, I was haunted each night by those dreams I was convinced a rotting, larvae-infested brain is forced to dream.

I was driven to discuss these events face-to-face, in confidence, with a young psychiatrist friend of mine (and subscriber to *Vathek's Book-List*), a certain Doctor Arnold, who recommended I start on a course of anti-depressants. He also made the following observations:

"Don't take this the wrong way," he said, "but I think it would actually be beneficial if you could locate another copy of that story. It appears to have acted as some kind of psychological trigger-mechanism. Best not to read it again of course, at this point, but I'd like to take a look at it myself, as a preliminary measure. I might well be able to connect it, through psychoanalysis, with suppressed mental trauma from your childhood lurking deep in your unconscious mind. It should aid me in determining the exact nature of any complex. Eventually, when properly understood, the story will be divested of whatever hold you imagine it possesses over you. Tell me, were you ever locked in a cupboard under the stairs for bad behaviour, as a boy?"

His last query seemed asinine and I was reluctant to follow his other advice. But what else could I do?

Was what I had read in "The Interminable Abomination" really just a fictional account of larvae-infested corpses made aware, over and over again, *and in different bodies,* of their own dissolution—a *post-mortem* insanity raising the infernal curtain to infinitely greater horrors? Did the dream spawn reality or did reality spawn the dream?

I simply had to dispel all such debilitating obsessions. No piece of fiction can have an effect like that on a reader in real life. But still I continued to ask myself the same question: *who was its author? Unknown Nightmares* had listed the tale only as being by 'X.,' and I decided to contact the book's editor, Victor Armstrong.

Tracing Victor Armstrong proved to be no simple task. Maelström Books (and indeed Jackson Publishing Ltd.) had closed down almost a decade previously after its premises had mysteriously burnt to the ground following the (hastily withdrawn) publication of *Unknown Nightmares,* but I did manage to contact the publisher of Armstrong's last anthology (called *Blind Nightmares,* appropriately enough) issued merely half-a-dozen years ago by JAW Books. The publisher, Jacob Andrew Whitemoor, was extremely sympathetic (and happened to be a subscriber to *Vathek's Book-List*), but he told me the last he had heard of Armstrong was that he had decamped permanently to Mexico a few years ago and had now given up editing anthologies; furthermore, Armstrong expressly wished to have nothing further to do with weird and horror fiction, in all its various guises. Whitemoor, however, did—finally—give me the name of the hotel on La Calle de Bucareli in Mexico City which was Armstrong's last known contact address.

After three telephone calls to the hotel I finally managed to track him down to another place—the Café la Habana—which, apparently, he had made his regular haunt during afternoons and early evenings.

"Victor Armstrong?" I said.

A muffled pause, then a cry of:

"¡Señor Ingles, el telefono!"

"¿Quien es?" came the distant-sounding reply. "¿Lopez?"

"Perdón pero no lo sé señor. Un otro Ingles."

"Who is this?" a voice slightly slurred by excessive drinking eventually enquired in English.

In as concise a fashion as I was able, I explained why I wished to speak with him. After digesting the information he replied:

"No, I don't know who actually wrote the story. It was listed as being by 'X.' and therefore anonymous. Anyway it must have been long out of copyright. The elderly woman who sent it to me at claimed she found it in some obscure Victorian periodical dating from the 1890s and transcribed it herself. Rather haphazardly."

"Who was the woman?" I asked.

"*What was* her name?—um—Dawson, I think."

"Not Dowson?"

"Yes, you're right, it was Dowson, not Dawson. Originally her surname was—apparently—'Mleen,' though. Some ex-pat Oriental lady. The wife of a half-mad, blind old sod of an English colonel, so I gather. He certainly was a character all right. Kept getting her to pass on complaints that my anthologies weren't gruesome or realistic enough."

"Did you read the story yourself?"

There was a pause. I heard him swallowing a drink filled with chinking ice-cubes.

"Of course I read it—well, some of it: despite the fact she'd banged it out on an old manual typewriter. I don't publish stories without reading them first. Not unless they're written by Steve King."

The line was breaking up. I had another question:

"What did you make of what you'd read?"

"I was already over-budget, had a pressing deadline, desperately needed a royalty-free filler for the anthology, and I thought the idea, despite its deficiencies, was a pretty interesting one: that central conceit of a game of chess played in a nightmare between the author and the reader which—"

The line dropped out, but was re-established.

"—but anyway, publication of the book was taken out of my hands."

"That doesn't sound like the same story, the one I read was more *ghoulish* and, well, much more—I suppose—*Lovecraftian*."

I heard a distinctly audible groan down the line at my citing that particular adjective.

Then the line abruptly went dead.

Thereafter, despite numerous attempts on my part, Armstrong could never be persuaded to come back to the telephone to speak to me.

It proved impossible to obtain another copy of *Unknown Nightmares* on the open market. After making enquiries amongst all my other competitors in the book trade who specialised in weird/horror/fantasy/speculative fiction (which enquiries were met either with baffled amusement, pleas of ignorance, or a kind of 'in-the-know' disgust), I concluded that what few—if any—extant copies there were remaining of the anthology were now secreted away in private collections. I even put out a rushed "special supplement" of *Vathek's Book-List* featuring a front-page advertisement making it known I would pay the best price for a copy housed in any of the personal libraries of my subscribers. I also consulted ABE Books and the other online book retailers, but, similarly, to no avail. Finally I turned to the British Library in the hope that a file copy had been deposited (as was customary with reputable publishers) for the purposes of establishing copyright. After much to-and-froing I was advised their copy had been stolen several years earlier (or, rather, was suspected of having been stolen) by a notoriously light-fingered scholar, one they would not identify—but since insane and then deceased—who was rumoured to have had sordid connections to another older person they would not name, a sometime contributor to *The Necrophile*—that infamous, banned magazine published briefly in the United States during the 1950s.

The younger, nameless, light-fingered scholar's private library had been left to the Sternburg Institute Library in Bloomsbury. I made an appointment there on the basis of undertaking some research, but found, whilst on the premises, that they disavowed being in possession of *Unknown Nightmares*. Instead a security guard was summoned and ushered me out after I mentioned to a librarian the likelihood that any copy of the anthology in their possession had actually been stolen from the British Library and was not, therefore, legally, their property.

Since my own nightmarish experiences in reading only a fraction of the story "The Interminable Abomination," it was not difficult for me to understand how a tangled web of intrigue, evasion, denial, secrecy, and even outright fear had been weaved around the anthology in which it had last appeared.

Readers may wonder about the very first publication of the story, but my efforts to track it down via this method proved equally frustrating—though in a more prosaic fashion. Of the innumerable journals and periodicals containing fiction published during the 1890s only a percentage have survived into the modern era, and of that number an even smaller proportion has been transferred to microfilm or digitised. The tale's having been published pseudonymously as 'X.' was a further barrier (since it was often used by printers in lieu of "Anonymous"), as was the possibility that "The Interminable Abomination" may not even have been the story's original title. Certainly, I could find no trace of its existence at the Colindale Newspaper Archives or in any other such records offices.

The nightmares were getting worse. I frequently had to resort to a mixture of morphine and Dexedrine in order to keep myself going. My health, both physical and mental, was deteriorating at an alarming rate. Doctor Arnold wanted me to check into his private "psychiatric welfare centre," The Glanville Home, for observation and treatment, but I declined his offer.

There was nothing for it but to approach the colonel again. Now I knew his late wife had been instrumental in bringing "The Interminable Abomination" to Victor Armstrong's attention in the first place, it seemed logical that it was actually the colonel who knew more about this whole ghastly affair than anyone else. He was also the only person who was still definitely in possession of a copy of *Unknown Nightmares*. Perhaps he even owned a copy of the original 1890s periodical in which "The Interminable Abomination" had first appeared. After all, Armstrong had told me it was the colonel's Oriental wife who had "haphazardly" transcribed the thing from its first publication.

I could trace no telephone number and therefore, in desperation, wrote him a letter of grovelling apology, asking for another opportunity to examine what remained of his book collection. This time, so I assured him, I could make a definite commitment to pay him very handsomely indeed—in cash—on the spot. I would even make an extra reimbursement to him for my "unforgivably rude behaviour" on the last occasion we had met. I hoped that a kindly friend or neighbour would read it aloud to the blind old fascist swine.

My letter must have been forwarded on by Royal Mail to the colonel, who, it transpired, had already quit his Muswell Hill eyrie in order to relocate to sheltered accommodation in Hertfordshire. The perfunctory, scarcely legible, handwritten reply contained no more than instructions detailing how to find (on foot from the nearest railway station) the bungalow in which he now dwelt and the time and date at which it would be convenient to him for me to make my visit. Doubtless he had dictated the reply and had someone write it down on his behalf, as I'd hoped he would.

Two days later, just after 11 A.M., following a train journey of half-an-hour or so, I disembarked from the stopping service I had caught at London Euston and stepped out onto the platform of Gallows Langley station in the south Hertfordshire countryside. It had been continuously pouring with rain all morning in London's endless brick-and-concrete labyrinth. And now, as if the deluge had followed me here, I saw, in the western distance, lushly green, open fields rising up along the side of a valley, and Hertfordshire's wider, rural skies also churning with a Stygian mass of seething black-and-grey storm clouds. Dotted here and there one could spot flocks of dirty sheep grazing, all seemingly utterly oblivious to the elements.

I was feverish and running a temperature. I could not face the prospect of trekking on foot through dripping arcades of trees and uphill lanes, as the written directions demanded, in order to reach the colonel's bungalow.

Just outside the railway station's entrance porch and halfway up a grassy bank was a small wooden cabin. Above a front window-cum-hatch was a cheaply-printed commercial sign reading "Gallows Taxies [sic]: We Won't Hang About." I went up to the hatch and knocked on the raindrop-splattered glass. A blurry face momentarily appeared behind the pane on which a handwritten note had been stuck up on the other side saying "back in 5 mins." Then a side door opened and the owner emerged, wearing a sou'-wester, mackintosh, and wellington boots, all of them a matching shade of truly garish yellow.

"Down there!" he said, pointing to the rusting pile of metal parked up on the kerb—which deathtrap he appeared to be indicating was the taxi. The thing was some sort of model surviving from the 1970s (I have no interest in the make of motorcars), but I wondered if he was still running this antique wreck in order to save paying the full road-tax.

Once I was ensconced in the back seat, I felt even clammier than before, and my fever had appreciably worsened. I had also developed a hideous migraine.

"Where to, mate?" the driver said, without turning around.

I wordlessly passed to him, over his shoulder, the written directions which the colonel had sent to me.

He studied them briefly and then said:

"These directions are all wrong. Whoever wrote these would have sent you on foot round the long way. But righto, I'll get you there in a jiffy."

The bungalow proved to be at the end of an unmarked but gated side-turning off a meandering country lane hemmed in on both sides by rows of dripping hornbeam trees. The lane had snaked up the entire side of the valley, and rivulets of rainwater ran down ditches on both sides of the slightly raised, puddle-pitted surface of the tarmac. The taxi had struggled to make the steep ascent, but my driver evinced not a word of protest about the hazardous driving conditions. Perhaps driving a deathtrap makes one indifferent to such lesser dangers. I dreaded to imagine the consequences had I attempted to make the journey myself on foot as the colonel had instructed. When the taxi driver dropped me off I provided a generous tip along with his stated fare, although he merely tipped his sou'-wester without ever turning around, let alone expressing thanks, and seemed eager to be on his way.

Such was my confused state of mind that I quite forgot to tell him to return in half-an-hour and wait here to collect me.

As I have said, the bungalow was situated at the end of a gated side-turning; and a single stile along the path prevented anything other than pedestrian access. There was no sign to indicate ownership or even the address.

The bungalow itself was a red-brick construction of no great distinctiveness, save for an enormous mass of ivy which had been allowed to engulf almost the whole of the exterior apart from the windows. Dotted around on the vast, overgrown front lawn were a multitude of stone objects which, in the gloom, and at first glance, I took to be the remaining foundations of a former, extensive, construction, one imperfectly razed at ground-level.

My feverishness was turning into a palsy. My head seemed to be splitting.

I looked for a doorbell or knocker and discovered instead an old handbell fixed and mounted vertically on the adjacent right-hand wall, with a length of string attached to the clapper.

I rang the bell several times, the noise piercing through the background hiss of the heavy rain which still continued to fall.

The door to the bungalow swung open and I nearly fell through it, staggering inside.

When next I was fully conscious of my surroundings I found myself slumped in the same armchair—with its white lace antimacassar—from the colonel's flat in Muswell Hill. So, too, the same oppressive heat and foul background smell; as of something rotten having been concealed somewhere close at hand. I momentarily wondered if I might actually be back in his previous residence, and if all the intervening events since had been nothing but a nightmare brought on by "The Interminable Abomination." But I *was* inside a bungalow—of that there could be no doubt. The colonel was sat in his wheelchair facing me, drawing heavily from the oxygen mask on his face and adjusting the pressure valve on the cylinder. Behind him was a door to another room. It was closed off by the familiar white drapes hanging from a rail—and the black beetles which I had seen upon it the last time had now considerably multiplied in number. The interior of the bungalow had become dark and the colonel had lit table lamps on opposite sides of his living quarters; for my benefit rather than his, I supposed. There were a number of cardboard boxes still unpacked, a couple of bulky, unpacked tea-chests and, atop a small corner desk, there lurked the same old manual typewriter with a sheet of blank paper already inserted.

"Awake, are you?" he said, after taking off the mask. "But still feeling poorly, I suppose? Don't have another attack of the vapours. We've yet to conclude our unfinished business. I know why you're here—and it's not to buy my remaining books; it's because you want that particular story. And I want you to have it."

I felt worse than ever at the realisation that he knew, as well as I, the cause of my physical and mental deterioration.

"I'll give you six thousand pounds. Cash," I said, taking out a hefty, somewhat damp, quarto-sized packet from my raincoat. "For both *Unknown Terrors* and for the magazine in which the original version appeared."

He rolled his wheelchair across the carpet, paused at one of the tea-chests, fumbled around inside, and drew out from its depths a mouldering Victorian periodical enclosed in a bright-yellow plastic folder and the bulky copy of *Unknown Nightmares*.

We exchanged goods.

He really couldn't tell the difference. What I had given him was not six thousand pounds; it was fake—Monopoly money.

But then, one by one, he began tearing up the false banknotes with his arthritic and gnarled fingers, chuckling obscenely as he did so.

"I imagine that you'd like to sit here and read through both of those things, but—all in good time," he said.

His words seemed to be coming from a great distance away. His voice was little more than a dim echo. And had the room become appreciably darker? It could not still be early afternoon; it must now be the middle of the night.

"Yes, it was the missus who rediscovered that damned thing by 'X.' in that old Victorian magazine, and, yes, she sent it to Armstrong after 'transcribing' it herself. But it's never the same story when read twice: it changes constantly and takes more and more of the life from its readers. You know, by the end the doctors told me her brain was so rotted and so acidic that parts of it actually began leaking from her skull, dribbling in a yellow putrescence out of her ears and her nostrils. Nevertheless, it was amazing how lucid she appeared to be at the very end. The doctors said that's often the way in the final hours before death with patients who've suffered massive brain damage and the like—terminal lucidity, they call it. Finally, I told them to turn off the damn life-support: and that was the only thing still keeping her alive. Not that that was the end of it. Not by a long chalk."

"But *who* was the original author, this 'X.'?" I managed to gasp. "Someone struck entirely from the records?"

"How the devil would I know? Maybe it's 'The Interminable Abomination' that's the author—*or the authors.* The last thing my wife would say to me on that point—though she must have gone insane by then, despite her apparent lucidity—was to babble some fanciful rot about *an irresistibly horrible, aeons-old continuum.* And she still babbles on about it even now. Useless."

The following phrase came back to haunt me: *"he was notorious for his obsession with horrors; the ghastlier the better. It seemed he could not get enough of them."*

Had he himself been mentally and physically damaged after hearing the story read aloud and yet had escaped the worst of its effects through not being able to read it for himself? Although the room was beginning to turn on its axis, my thoughts felt clearer than they had ever been; as if I had finally recovered my sanity—but a sanity which was now infinitely horrible.

Something warm and slimy began oozing out of my nose and ears, and I found myself looking over at the corner desk to the manual typewriter with its waiting sheet of blank paper. I felt compelled towards the machine in order to write.

"Read the stuff I've given you first. That's what you came for. Then whisper to me, one page at a time, as you write your own version," he said. "Start at the beginning. Type it up just as it really happened. First-person singular is always best. And you must give me only the facts. I don't want any products of your imagination. It's cowardice to create a horror which avoids stark reality."

"Music in the Blood": Greg Bear and the Gothic Imagination

John C. Tibbetts

> "I can take so much supernatural in its place, but now things were spilling over, smudging the clean-drawn line between my work and the World."
>
> —Greg Bear, "Dead Run" (*Tangents* 131)

Although Greg Bear[1] fearlessly treads the spaceways in his galaxy-devouring epics of science, hardware, and apocalyptic events, his allegiance to the core tropes of the Gothic narrative never wavers. Faustian pacts, hungry ghosts, quests for forbidden knowledge—even the transformative powers of music—are just as much at home in the haunted house next door as in a galaxy-hopping spaceship. He numbers among his colleagues microbiologists and astrophysicists as well as his fantasy and Gothic forbears, Mary Shelley, Edgar Allan Poe, George MacDonald, William Hope Hodgson, H. P. Lovecraft, and H. G. Wells. "He's out to effectively erase the boundaries of SF and fantasy," writes critical commentator Gary K. Wolfe, "including supernatural horror" (Review of *The City at the End of Time*). It's an unholy alliance as much as it is a mind-bending experience for his loyal readers.

"I try to extend the range of discovery," Bear writes in the preface to his first collection of stories, *The Wind from a Burning Woman* (x). To what result? That is for his characters and for us to decide.

---

1. Greg Bear (b. 1951) is the author of nearly fifty books of science fiction, gothic horror, and epic fantasy and has won both the prestigious Nebula and Hugo Awards. He has served on political and scientific action committees and has advised Microsoft Corporation, the U.S. Army, the CIA, Sandia National Laboratories, Callison Architecture, Inc., Homeland Security, and other groups and agencies.

Literary Dialogues

To begin with, much of Bear's work may be considered as conversations or dialogues with past works of fantasy. In *Dinosaur Summer,* for example, he proposes an alternate universe wherein Conan Doyle's *The Lost World* is a chronicle of real events—and real dinosaurs. The short story "Sleepside Story," for all its enigmas, seems ultimately a new twist on the fairy tale tradition, with sly references to "Beauty and the Beast." Likewise, "Richie by the Sea," from the *Sleepside* collection, imagines a shape-shifting sea creature like the Selkie of Celtic mythology that feeds off children in a coastal village. Bear frequently evokes the transcendental visions of the Victorian master fantasist George MacDonald, as in "The Visitation," also from *Sleepside,* wherein the Trinity—a lion, a lamb, a dove—that comes to call upon a young woman is revealed to be a "wild beast," a "thing beyond ugliness or beauty," that toys with humanity (134). MacDonald again peers between the pages of Bear's most recent novel, *The Unfinished Land,* a Quest narrative, wherein a young boy discovers the magic within him that will ultimately touch with Genius those whom he encounters.

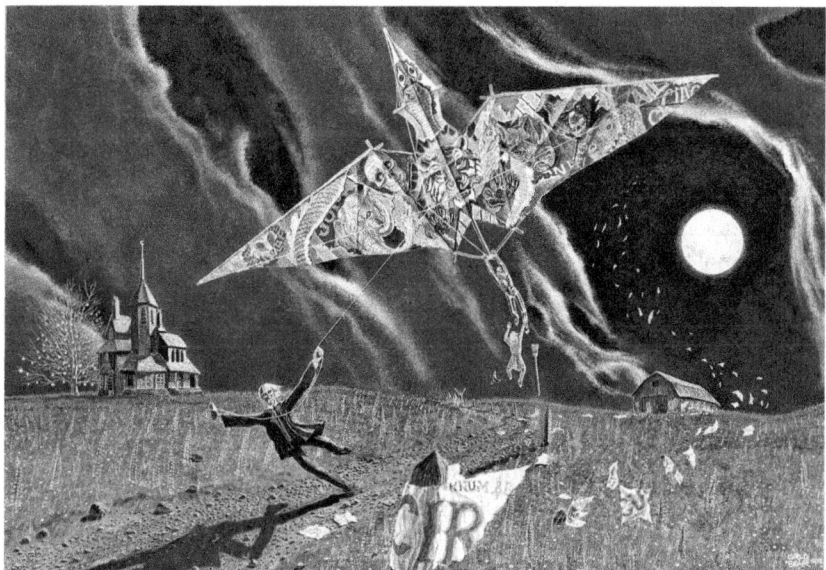

"Halloween Kite," painting by Greg Bear (by permission)

Closer to the Gothic tradition, many of Bear's stories—and I dare to suggest the same of his contemporary, Brian Aldiss[2]—bear a respectful kinship with the works of Poe, Mary Shelley, William Hope Hodgson, and H. G. Wells. References to Poe abound in the wickedly titled "The Fall of the House of Escher." The example of William Hope Hodgson hovers over one of his most complex novels, *The City at the End of Time*. Critic Gary K. Wolfe claims it borrows elements of both style and imagery from Hodgson's 1912 masterpiece, *The Night Land*, "whose pyramid-shaped Last Redoubt, shadowy monstrosities and impenetrable surrounding darkness Bear appropriates to remarkable effect." In addition, Bear himself points out, "some of the visions in *The Night Land* I actually incorporated into a novella set in the Eon universe called *The Way of All Ghosts* and dedicated it to Hodgson. Moreover, his *The House on the Borderland* has got to be one of the great visionary novels of all time. And it's compellingly readable."[3]

Shelley and Wells are here, too, which brings me to my own first encounter with Bear's work with my discovery at a young age of a book that stood out on my father's Arkham House bookshelf, *The Wind from a Burning Woman* (1983). The imprimatur, Arkham House, itself promised encounters with Gothic worlds, mingled among more overtly science fictional stories. I was hooked with "Petra." And so have many others who have read this multiple-award winning story. "Petra" is as close to pure Gothic as Bear has ever come. It fairly reeks with Mary Shelley's *Frankenstein* with a

---

2. I refer particularly to Aldiss's trilogy of novels derived from and expanding upon Mary Shelley's *Frankenstein*, Bram Stoker's *Dracula*, and H. G. Wells's *The Island of Dr. Moreau*—respectively, *Frankenstein Unbound* (1973), *Dracula Unbound* (1991), and *An Island Called Moreau* (1980). They stand as classics in the postmodern interrogation of the Gothic tradition.

3. My interview with Greg Bear, quoted throughout these pages, transpired in Lawrence, Kansas on 10 July 2004. Portions of it appear in my *The Gothic Imagination* (Palgrave Macmillan, 2011), 359–84. Hodgson's *The Night Land* was first published in 1912 and subsequently reworked by Hodgson himself in a shortened version, *The Dream of X*. See the essay by Sam Moskowitz in *The Dream of X* (West Kingston, RI: Donald Grant, 1977), 9–12.

setting akin to Mervyn Peake's *Gormenghast* trilogy. Petra, like Dr. Frankenstein's creature, is an orphan, a hybrid (in this case, of flesh and stone). "An ugly, beaked, half-winged thing," he lives in a vast, claustrophobic cathedral, not unlike *Gormenghast*'s gigantic castle, the House of Groan. Nothing less than the Death of God has turned the cathedral inside out: the stony gargoyles and saints have come alive; they live high in the rafters, strictly segregated from the beings of pure flesh below. In his search for a holy calling, Petra seeks the Stone Christ. "We must remake the world ourselves now," he is told; "what an opportunity, to be the architect of an entire universe!" (88–89). Revolution is brewing. He throws aside the great drapes and lets light into the darkened reaches of the cathedral. "Flesh and stone," he promises, "become something much stronger" (89).

"Petra" propelled me on my search for more Gothic elements in Bear's works. "Dead Run," for example, from Bear's second story collection, *Tangents,* is again mindful of George MacDonald's Christian humanism—Bear calls it "Christian Surrealism"—in its fable of the protagonist's confrontation with life, death, and salvation. John is an over-the-road truck driver who, Charon-like, ferries the zombie-like bodies of the "living" dead to their ultimate destination. "There aren't many hitchhikers on the road to Hell," he wryly remarks (121). These days the dead are growing restless. Signs of rebellion are everywhere. Some are escaping the cattle cars and "are wandering around with no idea what to do or where to go" (135). Corporate mismanagement and corruption have arbitrarily been determining which bodies return to the Earth, which take the Low Road to hell, and which take the unmarked path to an unknown salvation. John takes matters into his own hands. His search for any signs of moral clarity among the dead determines his decisions about which ones to save: "I don't want to let everybody loose," he decides, "but I want to know who's ending up on the Low Road who shouldn't be" (146). There's a risk to all this, of course: "If I get caught, I'll be riding in the back." In the final lines John turns to the reader with a warning: "And if you're reading this, you'll be there, too."

Breaking the Seal

Many of Bear's protagonists pursue a dangerous quest in that hoariest of Gothic tropes, the lure of forbidden knowledge and Immortality. Like Goethe's Faust, they declare:

> I'll discern what forces bind
> The world together, and I'll find
> What forces move the stirring seed,
> And from spinning words be freed! (ll. 378–83)

And like Dr. Moreau, in H. G. Wells's eponymous novel, they fearlessly seek "the symbiosis and transformation" of the human species:

> "It's not simply the outward form of an animal I can change" [declares Moreau]; the physiology, the chemical rhythm of the creature may also be made to undergo an enduring modification, of which vaccination and other methods of inoculation with living or dead matter are examples that will, no doubt, be familiar to you." (113)

Again, like Moreau, Bear's protagonists are driven by their egomania and consumed by madness as they tinker with accelerated evolutionary processes and viral mutations. *Vitals* is a case in point. It takes on the quest for eternal life, a topic as old as Prester John and William Godwin's *St. Leon,* and as recent as Jack Vance's *To Live Forever* and Poul Anderson's *Boat of a Million Years.* Hal Cousins is an ambitious young scientist whose quest for immortality rejects several options: the promises of a Deity; the uploading the mind into cyberspace; living in a computer or robot brain; utilizing nano-technology that would send nano-machines to clean up an ageing body. The real problem, Hal insists, is that we breathe, respire, and accumulate poisons over time because of the way we burn fuel. "We're part of a vast biological conspiracy, billions of years old, and we have to shake ourselves loose and grab the reins" (29). Nothing short of something called *mitochondrial chromosome adjustment* is necessary. But to do so incurs risks: "What beasts will you unleash when you cut all the strings?" he wonders (342). Hal injects himself with virus shells that deliver gene modifications.

Vitals is, at heart, a cautionary tale. As one scientist warns Hal: "If we, as individuals, strive to live past our natural lifetimes, what do we contribute to the whole of humanity? Are we smarter at one hundred and fifty than we were at forty? What if we stand in the way of the young? What if we demand all the available resources and starve our society, or go off on eccentric quests that ignore a larger wisdom?" Moreover, continues Bear, "There's the spectre of corporate control: Only the rich and privileged can benefit from immortality . . . The government can render illegal such research, but only to make it available for a privileged few" (103).

In one of his earliest, most celebrated short stories, "Blood Music"—which was subsequently expanded into novel length—Vergil Ulam has developed complicated biochips that have their own intelligence. Interacting with his blood, they have transformed him from within. His spine, his musculature, and now his skin is changing. But now Vergil's afraid that "they" will jump the blood-brain barrier and penetrate and *understand* his brain. "They will find out about *me*," he says, "about the brain's real function" (*Tangents* 20). Later, as this "infection" continues to develop, Vergil claims he can "hear" all the operations inside his blood, a kind of internal "music." He says, "I'm their universe" (24). When the renegade biotechnologist injects himself with his own experimental biochips—organic computers—the results are the horrific transformation of not just his body but that of others and, ultimately, the world itself.

In *The Forge of God* a virus has "invaded" Earth from an extraterrestrial origin. Midwifed by H. G. Wells's *The War of the Worlds* and Lovecraft's "The Colour out of Space," *The Forge of God* is one of Bear's most spectacular "alien invasion" stories. An unknown alien life force of planet-eating machines, hybrids of biology and robotics, is targeting Earth for destruction. It is a mindless, self-replicating, virus-like intelligence that absorbs planets to produce copies of itself that fly off to eat more life-bearing planets. Before Earth is annihilated, a contingent of survivors escape into interstellar space, determined to seek out and destroy the Planet-Eaters.

Bear declares *The Forge of God* is a cautionary tale warning of man's insistence in reaching out to other worlds and assuming that life forms are driven by ethical and religious systems comparable to our own. In short, it's a variant of a Gothic trope: "You see it a lot in writers from Mary Shelley to Lovecraft—man's hubris, you know, risking disaster by courting unknown monsters." Moreover—

> There's always been this question, why aren't the Aliens here yet? You know, here we are sending out signals, but we don't hear any signals coming back. And my one answer that came back to me loud and clear was, Well, you're birds cheeping in the forest from the nest, and there are snakes out there, and they're going to crawl up the tree and eat you if you keep chirping your little heart out! I mean, why are you announcing your presence when you're weak? And if you think there's no life out there, then, okay, we're safe. But if there is life out there, then you have to run with what you know about life, which is that life has both predators and partners.

Part of the problem is our own hubris: "We've tried to isolate ourselves as angelic intelligences, apart from biology. But what about those damned *urges,* which just can't be overcome? And then we get all this persiflage about good and evil and cruelty and all that stuff. It's all part of a natural system. There may indeed be teleological and intelligently directed evolution, but we don't need to blame it on God. . . . Why is the universe not catering to us? This is the scientific principle: the universe does not cater to you" (interview).[4]

---

4. Elsewhere, Bear addresses the role a "God" may or may not play in these evolutionary jumps. "I fundamentally reject creationism or intelligent design by God. I offer a solution that is never heard in either scientific or religious circles: the mystery of God allows for free will in both human behavior and in natural evolution. Nature is thoughtful and creative and even willful—one might say soulful—top to bottom, but even that doesn't begin to describe the reality." See "An Interview with Greg Bear," www.bookbrowse. com/author_interviews/full/index.cfm/author_number/401/greg-bear

Unearthly Music

The terrors that music embodies and unleashes—from the *diabolus in musica* tritone that was once banned by the Church to the Faustian music that concludes Mozart's *Don Giovanni*—the transformative power of music is a frequent theme in Bear's stories. "Music is a kind of magical incantation," he declares; "performing it can risk apocalypse; music is a bridge that melds worlds" (interview). And nowhere is this more apparent than in Bear's stories, "Blood Music," "Tangents," and in his remarkable novel-length *Songs of Earth and Power*. Bear takes his cue from the visionaries Wackenroder, Novalis, and E. T. A. Hoffmann, for whom music is a bridge to other worlds. That transformative power may be exalting, as in Novalis, or infernally disturbing, as in Hoffmann's story "Der Freund": "Music then, is the means by which the incalculable demonic forces of the universe burst in on the calculated life of man, setting up tremendous and destructive upheavals in his personality" (quoted in Schafer 143).

In the aforementioned "Blood Music" we recall that the transformation of the scientist's body is itself a kind of music: "There was a rhythm in my arms, my legs. With each pulse of blood, a kind of sound welled up within me, like an orchestra thousands strong, but not playing in unison; playing whole seasons of symphonies at once. Music in the blood" (33).

"Tangents" is an amusing fable whose musician, a young man named Pal, is Bear's own version of Hoffmann's mad musician, Johannes Kreisler. Moreover, Lovecraft's "The Music of Erich Zann" also comes to mind.[5] Pal sits at his keyboard hookup and plays the

---

5. Lovecraft's description of Zann's violin music evokes Hoffmann's accounts of Kreisler's performances: "Then one night as I listened at the door, I heard the shrieking viol swell into a chaotic babel of sound; a pandemonium which would have led me to doubt my own shaking sanity" (1.286). Lunatic and lover, madman and genius, the musician Johannes Kreisler not only appears in many of Hoffmann's stories but is personified by Robert Schumann in his own writings and music, notably in the piano cycle *Kreisleriana*, Opus 16.

"music" he thinks connects him with the Fourth Dimension. It may just sound like squeaks and squawks to us, but sure enough, it calls forth some creatures who crash through from the fourth dimension. Chunks of three-dimensional space are torn away, and portions of vari-colored, weirdly shaped creatures come and go. "I think they liked the music," grins Pal (183). But the creatures wreak havoc and Pal has to pull the plug on the keyboard. There is an arresting image as the keyboard and Pal are pulled into the fourth dimension. They are literally *peeled* away, like stick-on labels removed from a flat surface. They disappear.

Songs of Earth and Power is a personal favorite and a "must read" for classical music lovers. This epic fantasy of the conjoined worlds of Earth and Faerie, acknowledges Bear, "is a kind of extended combination of George MacDonald and Jorge Borges" (interview). Bear has stitched together two separate early works, *The Infinity Concerto* and *The Serpent Mage,* into a tightly integrated whole. The protagonist, sixteen-year old Michael Perrin, befriends a composer named Arno Waltiri, whose *Infinity Concerto* is reputed to drive its listeners mad and, subsequently, vanish them from the Earth. Perrin indeed falls victim to the music and is translated into the Realm of the Sidhe, a race of elves in an oppressive, cruel world drawn out of Celtic mythology. They are products of a *musical evolution,* as it were, a veritable Wagnerian *unendliche melodie,* from "small songs" to "more complex and more involved" songs; and now "that progress has come down to us. There was no beginning. There shall be no end. Only variations on a theme, never repeating, always improving" (425). After many hardships, Michael is finally released and returns to Earth, although the Sidhe are drawn in after him. Now the care-taker of Waltiri's music, he organizes a performance of the *Infinity Concerto,* which results in uniting the world of Faerie with Earth.

It is by no means incidental that we find many composers, in-cluding Mozart and Gustav Mahler, dwelling in the world of the Sidhe. (Doubtless Johannes Kreisler is there too, although Bear fails to mention it!) Indeed, recalls Bear, their music played a part in the novel's first inspiration.[6] While on Earth their music had come too close to achieving "songs of power" and had had to be thwarted. Hence, their banishment to the Realm of the Sidhe. "They did not die," explains Bear; "their deaths have been *delayed*, you could say—

> Consider: Mahler never finished his Tenth Symphony. I asked myself . . . *Why???* Because when you reach the Tenth Symphony, like Mahler, you've acquired a level of wisdom that creates a song of power. But in my book the elves—I call them the Sidhe—don't want humans to achieve that kind of power. There's forces that will come in to thwart that. I mean, it's a very paranoid vision, the whole gothic thing, like Lovecraft's monsters out to get us. Think what happened with Mozart's unfinished Requiem: the 'Man in Gray' shows up. Who was the man in gray? Salieri? A mysterious patron? A 'Person from Porlock'? Well, I *do* have a Person from Porlock in my book! Literally. Remember him?—he's the person who 'interrupted' Coleridge's poem 'Kubla Khan' . . . and I say that maybe he's the person who also blocked the finish of Mozart's Requiem.

It's a fanciful conceit, admits Bear: "There are so many instances in poetry and music and literature like this that are *really* interesting, because man is blocked from achieving a higher being. And you could take six or seven of those instances and string them into a story; and I did. I'm not sure if Borges actually wrote an essay on the mystery of *interruption*, but he could have."[7]

---

6. In the afterword, Bear reveals that as a youth, while listening to the Adagio of Mahler's unfinished *Tenth Symphony*, "I had an epiphany of life and death as intense as anything I have felt before or since" (554).

7. I can find no references in Borges to this theme. In his two-volume biography of Coleridge, Richard Holmes examines at length Coleridge's possibly apocryphal account of the most famous "interruption" in literary history: "[Coleridge's] account is teasingly circumstantial," writes Holmes, "particularly about the number of elapsed hours and missing lines involved, and with the famously mundane detail of the 'person on business from Porlock.' Yet the effect is to produce a much larger allegory of creativity and its fatal interruption" (435).

Ghostly Horrors

Two novels, *Psychlone* (1979) and *Dead Lines* (2004), are Bear's most ambitious attempts to reimagine the traditional ghost story in a more scientific context. As much fun as the assortment of poltergeists and vengeful spirits is in the former, I give the palm to *Dead Lines*. Indulge me while I examine this remarkable novel at some length. Bear wears his Gothic-loving heart on his sleeve in its dedication page to Lovecraft, Arthur Machen, Sheridan Le Fanu, M. R. James, Ramsey Campbell, Peter Straub, Shirley Jackson, et al. There's something disarming about this overt tribute. "What he shows us most effectively," writes critic Gary K. Wolfe, "is not so much that he's a born teller of ghost tales, or that he wants to do with them much that's particularly new, but that he's an attentive and sympathetic *reader* of them" (Review of *Dead Lines*).

"Now, I love all of those writers," admits Bear. "I just think they're very interesting spiritual writers. But it's a skewed spirituality, sort of a *dire* spirituality.

> What I want to do is use a scientific theory to give you experiences you've never had before, but in a familiar way, and what is that but the ghost story? But it's ghosts like you've never seen before, in contexts that you've never really experienced, but there's enough of an underpinning and a mythos to what you're seeing that it almost makes sense, and that's what provides the scare. You can tie this into experiences you or someone in your family may actually have had. You can say, Oh, I see that. 'Cause I borrowed it not just from ghost stories but from people who have actually seen ghosts.

And about Dead Lines?

> Science is not usually thought to cross over into fantasy because it's constrained from it by cultural prejudices. But I do admit that *Dead Lines* is also the kind of ghost story I love. In the story, the world is running out of bandwidth, and there's a new source of forbidden information channels that reach into the regions of the Dead and release all kinds of dreadful things. It's a Gothic story,

in the sense that you blur the lines between life and death, don't you? For me, the ghost stories aren't scary so much as they are almost a spiritual experience. You're getting access to what could be a view of reality beyond what you could possibly know now, and to me. And science fiction in its extreme metaphysical forms does that to you. It exalts you. And a good ghost story can do that, too. (Interview)

What if, Bear suggests, there will come a technological change enabling us actually to study the phenomena of ghosts? *Dead Lines* proposes that the proliferation of a new line of wireless phones opens the gateway not only to ghostly apparitions of the dearly departed, but to the shadows of hungrily devouring fiends. The commercial boast of the product acquires an ominous tone: "So easy to talk anymore, wherever you were, whatever you might be" (202). A warning is sounded: a warning of the "side effects" of this new technology.

Synopsis: Peter Russell is not having a good time these days. His daughter, Daniella, has been dead for two years. Her bloodied body had been found in some brush, the killer never identified. And his best friend, Phil, has just died. Already a problem drinker, Peter's alcoholism continues to be a problem. His ex-wife, Helen, is wary and reluctant to grant him visitation rights to Daniella's twin sister, Lindsey. Peter's own career has been spotty: sometime photographer, producer of soft-porn films, gopher for a wealthy industrialist named Joseph Benoliel.

Another project on Peter's mind is his contact through Benoliel with a new technology called *Trans*. This is a company that is developing a new line of wireless phones. Peter is curious about this new operation. For one thing, its central plant is located in the now-abandoned San Andreas Prison; and its transponder is placed in the very gas chamber of the cell block where prisoners were executed. But Kreisler boasts that the future is bright. He claims that by 2030 three billion people will own wireless phones:

> "Houses, cars, refrigerators, televisions, wristwatches, eyeglasses, earrings, all will talk to information centers and receive news,

guidance, entertainment, and upgrades for essential services. Companies will whole-body sensors that transmit data to doctors and hospitals around the world. No one will ever need to be alone and in danger again." (84–85)

But there is a downside to all this: "In less than twenty years, the world will run out of bandwidth. Radio, TV, cell phones, wireless, all will halt screeching growth" (86). Kreisler claims also to have solved this potential problem:

> "I discovered a new source of bandwidth, forbidden information channels, not truly radiation at all, unknown until now. Channels in what I call Bell continuum, after John Bell. . . . Trans is like the way photons and electrons and atoms, everything tiny, sing to each other all day, every day, tell each other where and who they are, to balance the books and obey the laws and keep everything real. We send our messages along similar channels. That means you can use Trans anywhere. No degradation to huge distance. . . . Trans reaches below our world, lower than networks used by atoms or subatomic particles, to where it is very quiet. Down there is a deeper silence than we can know, a great emptiness. Huge bandwidth, perhaps infinite capacity. It can handle all our noise, all our talk, anything we have to say, throughout all eternity." (85–86)

Through the woof and weave of incidents that accompany Peter for the next few weeks, Peter begins to suffer strange visions, of ghostly presences or wraiths (the projections of a living being). Some of Bear's finest prose here is worthy of the delicacy of James and Wharton. One apparition is described as "a shaded hesitation of empty air" (195). One female wraith is described: "He saw that the woman's face was like a flat sheet of mother-of-pearl. Her eyes opened to quizzical hollows. Less than solid, she resembles a paper doll frayed by careless snipping. Peter could actually see her edges ripple." And when it disappears, "it unraveled drastically, peeling and dissolving in shreds like a tissue-paper cutout dipped in a bowl of water" (46). Hallucinatory or not, they *seem* real, like the image of his dead daughter, Daniella, a semi-transparent crystalline form that reveals the bones and muscles beneath the skin: "He could see deeper, through the wisps of what might have been an afterthought of clothing; deeper still, below the skin, into lightly sketched outlines of bones and organs, kept in place by some slavery to mortal form, but no longer functional, certainly" (140).

Others are seeing ghosts of their own. All around the world come reports of hauntings: Benoliel and his mistress, Michelle; hordes of phantoms crawling around during a movie shoot in Prague; reports of sightings of the dead Daniella. And all of these apparitions seem to have been triggered by the use of the Trans phones.

The book is filled with passages that hint that death is only the beginning of a *second* death, where the remaining essence of the dead can only gradually pull away from the memories and sense of the living. An ageing character named Schelling muses:

> "Death is more like being born. It's a long, hard giving up of warmth for something you don't know. There's a desperate glamour that surrounds the living, and for a time, the dead think they are still in the game. They cling to any memory of their life—the sharper and stronger, the better. . . . Their mournful need holds them to the Earth. And so they must be shaken loose, like flakes of old skin." (173)

Assisting in this separation, perhaps, are shadowy forms that eat that dead skin, as it were. They could be regarded as either scavengers or friends in disguise.

The use of the Trans phones may be responsible. Schelling notes: "I am convinced that these instruments of communication are highlighting the dead and their supernatural entourage, perhaps even blocking the pathways of our final liberation" (175). And all the while, the individual phones are filling with an evil, thick black goo, the residue of all the awful things released in the course of their use.

Peter feels helpless. All he can do is begin to destroy every one of the Trans he can find. In the final forty pages or so, he is involved in a succession of horrific adventures and confrontations. Benoliel owns several houses, all shadowed by gruesome atrocities in the past, and all connected by an underground trolley track. After finding the murdered Benoliel, he enters the underground regions where Michelle had conducted tortures and murders, including the death of Daniella. Peter tracks her down and finally, confronted by her wizened, suddenly aged and ravaged form, watches in terror as she is devoured by one of those predatory shadowy devouring forms.

The final confrontation features Peter invading the precincts of the Trans headquarters in San Andreas Prison. He has known for some time that he is doomed. And sure enough, penetrating the Death Chamber, where the transponder is located, he encounters the central cell of haunts and shadowy predators. The scene fades before the final destruction is described.

Epilogue. Peter is now dead. But remnants of his self remain, playing chess with his dead friend, Phil. Soon it will be time for Peter and Phil to depart. "So many ties, so many things to protect. The pain comes back to him now, and that's the final goad—the pain of awareness that he is diminished. There is so much he cannot recall. Already he is half-lost and ragged at the edges" (245).

"I've long believed that coming into this world and going out of this world are the two hardest things you'll ever do," declares Bear—

> You get your ticket stamped going in, you get your ticket stamped going out. It's just miserable. It's traumatic, it's miserable. And the question is at that point, why is there faith, why is there a need for faith? Because of these two truths. So the people say there must have been something before and there must be something after. Interestingly enough, we don't talk about what comes before. I think it's perfectly legitimate, even in a science fiction story to say, *'What if there is something beyond our ken?'* . . . It's a *discovery* of a new realm in a way that's very frightening. In *Dead Lines* I want to give you the impression that death is a process that has rules and is very, very moving and confusing and also strips away from you the things that you no longer need.

For John!
WHO DRAWS
GOOD
7/9/04

Portrait of Greg Bear by John C. Tibbetts

How Do We Separate the Teller from the Tale?

I conclude with two stories, "Webster" (*Tangents*) and "The White Horse Child" (*The Wind from a Burning Woman*). Like the meta-texts of E. T. A. Hoffmann's *Kater Murr* and George MacDonald's *Lilith*, both are books about books, stories about stories, writers about writing, and readers about reading.[8] Miss Abigail Coates is a latter-day Dr. Frankenstein. She will make a man—not in the charnel house of a laboratory but from the pages of a Webster's Dictionary. Not from body parts but from words. Creator and created are inseparable but divided. Writer and stories, perhaps, connected, but alienated from each other? What mutual destructive forces are unleashed?

In her middle years Miss Abigail Coates hungers for intercourse with a man she has denied herself all these years. She takes down a dictionary and from the words on the page conjures a man she dubs, appropriately enough, "Webster." "Help me," she pleads to the open book, "Everything I can feel can be expressed through the words you hold. Lives exist in you, people and places I've never seen, things dead and things unborn. Haven of ghosts and the preternatural, home of tyrants and saints. Surely you can make a man for me. Small word, little work. You can even *tell* me how to make a man from you" (87). Sure enough, the man now stands before her. His breath fills the house "with the odor of printer's ink" (90). They spend their days in happy concourse: *"Creating men from dictionaries, making love until the bed is damp—at my age! He still smells like ink, not flesh. He doesn't sweat and he refuses to go outside. Nobody sees him but me. Me. Who am I to judge whether he's really there?"* (96). Miss Abigail wonders what baby might come from their intercourse: "All she could imagine was a doctor holding up a damp bloody thing in his

---

8. Hoffmann's *Kater Murr* interweaves two separate narratives—one a biography of Johannes Kreisler and the other an autobiographical narrative by the tomcat Murr—in a seemingly arbitrarily, random manner (see Daemmrich 39–46). MacDonald's *Lilith* proposes that books are like the world, each containing "riddles trying to get out" (see Gills 880–85).

hands and saying, 'Miss Coates, you're the proud mother of an eight-pound . . . dictionary.'" She sallies back, wickedly: "Abridged" (95).

It's only a matter of time before he stirs with an independent will of his own: "Webster was becoming a generator. Kept in the apartment, his substance was reacting with itself; shut away from experience, he was making up his own patterns and organizations, subtle as smoke" (93). He accuses her: "'Why can't you find a human being for yourself? I'm not even a human being . . . I'm nothing but a dream . . . Do you know what I'm good for, what I can do? No. You'd be afraid if you did. You keep me here like some commodity . . . You cannot love the real. The here. You must change the thing you love to please yourself, and damn it should it echo what hides within. Within *you*'" (97–98). Abashed, and a little fearful, she wonders, "*Is he mine, or am I his?*" (94). Worse, she realizes he will create from the dictionary a rival, a woman. She wills him dead. "The smell of printer's ink became briefly more intense, then faded on the warm breeze passing through the apartment. She kicked the dictionary shut" (98).

In the second story, "The White Horse Child," a seven-year-old boy meets two elderly people who tell him stories and who coax stories out of him. One of the stories they tell him is about children who produce nightmares that even adults cannot rival. And what stories they are!

> Yarns about ghosts and dead things, and live things that shouldn't have been, and things that were neither. They talked about death and about monsters that suck blood, about things that live way deep in the earth and long, thin things that sneak through cracks indoors to lean over the beds at night and speak in tongues no one could understand. They talked about eyes without heads, and vice versa, and little blue shoes that walk across a cold empty white room, with no one in them, and a bunk bed that creaks when it's empty, and a printing press that produces newspapers from a city that never was. (53)

Against his parents' wishes, the boy creates stories of his own. His two friends warn him of the consequences all storytellers face, when the storyteller can't be separated from the story:

> "You've taken the fire, and it glows bright. You're only a boy, but you're just like a pregnant woman now. For the rest of your life you'll be cursed with the worst affliction known to humans. Your skin will twitch at night. Your eyes will see things in the dark. Beasts will come to you and beg to be ridden. You'll never know one truth from another. You might starve because few will want to encourage you. And if you do make good in this world, you might lose the gift and search forever after, in vain. Some will say the gift isn't special. Beware them. Some will say it is special, and beware them, too." (60)

His parents are alarmed. They call upon Auntie Danser. She confronts the storytellers: "You plague us with thoughts no decent person wants to think. ... Your very breath is tainted ... [You] question the way we think. Condemn our deepest prides. Pull out our mistakes and amplify them beyond all truth. What right do you have to take young children and twist their minds?" (63). She takes a breath and concludes: "I know where you come from, don't forget that! Out of the ground! Out of the bones of old wicked Indians! Shamans and pagan dances and worshiping dirt and filth!" (63). She will be the one, she admits, who takes them off the school shelves and burns them "for junk."

The boy protests to the enchanted air around him. A sudden gust of wind advises him to go with his aunt. However, years from now, he is further directed, "Send your children this way" (64).

"The White Horse Child" is one of my personal favorites. Bear regards it as close to his personal testament as a storyteller.

Only Human?

Beyond the outer reaches of the spaceways and within the depths of the human heart, Greg Bear is, for all his technologies and biosciences, a storyteller in the most traditional sense. "Stories are people," he declares, "people who are doing things, doing interesting things. That's what it's all about. And we might have a literature of ideas—but *who* has ideas? People have ideas. They don't come out of the void. People have to act on them and to respond to the consequences" (interview). In sum, assesses critic Gary K. Wolfe, Bear always attempts "to valorize the simple value of being human in a universe of almost in comprehensible complexity and indifference" (Review of *Collected Stories*).

I wish to thank Mr. Wolfe for his assistance in the preparation of this article.

Works Cited

Bear, Greg. *City at the End of Time.* New York: Ballantine, 2008.

———. *Darwin's Radio.* New York: Ballantine, 1999.

———. *Dead Lines.* New York: Ballantine, 2004.

———. *The Forge of God.* New York: Tor, 1987.

———. *Sleepside: The Collected Fantasies.* New York: Open Road, 2004.

———. *Songs of Earth & Power.* New York: Tor, 1994.

———. *Tangents.* New York: Warner Books, 1989.

———. *The Unfinished Land.* New York: Houghton Mifflin Harcourt, 2021.

———. *The Wind from a Burning Woman.* Sauk City: Arkham House, 1983.

Daemmrich, Horst S. *The Shattered Self: E. T. A. Hoffmann's Tragic Vision.* Detroit: Wayne State University Press, 1973.

McGillis, Roderick. *"Lilith."* in Frank N. Magill, ed. *Survey of Modern Fantasy Literature.* Englewood Cliffs, NJ: Salem Press, 1983. 880–85.

Goethe, Johann Wolfgang von. *Faust.* Tr. Walter Arndt. New York: Norton, 2001.

Holmes, Richard. *Coleridge: Darker Reflections, 1804–1834.* New York: Pantheon, 1998.

Lovecraft, H. P. *Collected Fiction: A Variorum Edition.* Ed. S. T. Joshi. New York: Hippocampus Press, 2015–17. 4 vols.

Schafer, R. Murray. *E. T. A. Hoffmann and Music.* Toronto: University of Toronto Press, 1975.

Wells, H. G. *The Island of Dr. Moreau.* In *Seven Famous Novels.* New York: Knopf, 1934.

Wolfe, Gary K. Review of *City at the End of Time. Locus* No. 569 (June 2008): 15–16.

———. Review of *The Collected Stories of Greg Bear. Locus* No. 501 (October 2002): 17–19.

———. Review of *Dead Lines. Locus* No. 520 (May 2004): 19.

The Dream of a Dead Poet

Manuel Arenas

First there was blackness; a profound nothingness, where I was not cognizant of my surroundings or the passage of time. Then a faint tick or tapping sound in the wooden walls behind my head brought me to my senses. I emerged from my dreamless slumber with a gasp, like a drowning man surfacing from inky depths, to find myself lying, clothed in a coal-colored suit, atop an ebon-posted bed of sable sheets and canopy, surrounded by candles and incense censers. As my eyes adjusted to the dim light of the room, I discerned a tall, lean, bespectacled young man in shirtsleeves who stood in the shadows just beyond the foot of my bed. As he drew nearer, I saw that his hair was parted in the middle, in Edwardian style; cradled in his left arm was a high hat about which was fastened a black sash. His spectacles were tinted black, of the four-lensed variety that covers both the peripheral and frontal perspectives.

I made motion to hail him but found that my limbs were torpid and would not obey me. Unruffled by my predicament, he reached out his chill, wan hand to me, and at the moment of contact I rose. He then led me from the somber premises and into a black carriage that awaited, a grim sentinel, outside the chamber door. The shadowy coachman, slumped in his perch, hung his pate so low that it was lost beyond his shoulders. As my companion guided me onto the footplate of the carriage, I noted the coachman was flanked by human skulls in place of lamps, their nullified sockets exuding an eldritch luminescence.

As we drove on at a funereal pace, I peered from my window to see, silhouetted against the pallid moon, a procession led down a lich path by pallbearers carrying their mortal load into a desolate and drear mort-house. I felt a vague twinge of dismay as the coach turned to join the cortège. Alighting to enter the edifice, I saw the coachman, his mazzard conspicuously still wanting, spur on his horse with a whip of human vertebrae. Startled, I lost my footing but was caught by my companion and escorted inside.

To my surprise, I found that the decedent had been unceremoniously tossed aside to a corner of the dank room. The coterie of counterfeit mourners filed into a narrow passageway secreted behind a false wall, like a priest hole. Staring incredulously at the desecration before me, I froze, but my companion woke me from my reverie with a touch on the shoulder and bade me follow as he seized the closing aperture.

Down we went on a musty stone stairway into a cavernous room, dimly lit with a series of sconces. The floor was strewn with bridewort, the stifling air redolent with incense and putrefaction, causing me to choke, but my companion and the blackguards we'd shadowed seemed undaunted by the stench. Close to retching, I covered my mouth and nose with my sable pocket square kerchief and ventured unsteadily forward toward the coterie, which had gathered, genuflecting, in front of an ornate bier supported by life-sized pleurants, represented as hooded pallbearers, as in the manner of the Tomb of Philippe Pot, presumably made from limestone and painted to give them a semblance of life. Lying atop a black satin pall were the livid remains of what was once a ravishing woman, swathed in a sable shroud. Her hair was black and luxurious beneath a diadem of platinum, studded with black obsidian. Her purpled lips seemed painted, and indeed they had been rendered so by the ruinous stroke of Death, her once-sightly mien turned by the taint of corruption. Her devotees groveled and laid offerings at her feet, which all bore the conspicuous aspect of being the same color as her habiliments.

As I stared agog at this macabre tableau, my companion stepped up to the bier and, brandishing a book made of jade plates, in the Oriental fashion, commenced to declaim in a voice, strained with a passion hitherto unseen, the contents of said book. His recitation seemed to agitate the idolaters, who moaned and writhed prostrate on the floor. As I heeded his words, my mind filled with a phantasmagoria of grewsome images: cadavers in various states of corruption rising from their plutonian slumbers to frolic haltingly in a danse macabre as their bodies oozed and dripped putrefaction about their crumbling feet.

At the point of collapse, my eyes then registered a sight that my addled brain could not at first comprehend: the pleurants upholding the bier, hitherto motionless, had begun to crouch, lowering the front end so that the recumbent occupant was now positioned upright. Between the wisps of flambeau smoke and incense I saw the dead woman open her jetty eyes, ringed in fire like the Sol niger of the alchemists. She was a chthonic deity peering from across Stygian shores, her cold fathomless gaze drawing mine into the black hole of her caliginous quintessence. She unraveled her sable winding sheet to reveal her moldering figure, wriggling with worms, a medieval transi come to unnatural life. Then came her voice, insinuating itself into my brain with serpentine slipperiness, polluting my mind with foul and profane whispers intimating charnel pleasures were I to follow her into her tenebrous realm. My mind was numb and tractable, her icy words wheedling my will into submission.

As I took my first step toward perdition, an ardent devotee lunged at the revenant daemoness, causing her to turn away and break her thrall. Like fruit withering on a vine, an abrupt necrosis spread throughout the zealot's frame, reducing him to a blackened husk. His comrades followed in frenzied suit, overwhelming the object of their desire, their frenetic orisons becoming their swansong as they plunged into the arms of extinction. Released from my trance, I turned to run but, as I ascended the stairs, my flight was impeded by my companion, whose stultifying clutch stopped me in my tracks. I turned to face him, inadvertently throwing him off-balance, which caused him to tumble backward. In his fall the dark lenses were knocked off of his bloodless face, revealing hollow eye sockets laced with cobwebs, from which disgorged a hatch of pearlish black spiderlings.

My head spinning with the noxious atmosphere and the execrable scenes to which I had just borne witness, I covered my face entirely with my kerchief and resumed my retreat from that wretched chamber. Vision obstructed, I ran blindly toward the doorway of the mort-house when my footstep snagged in the sable winding sheet of the previously discarded remains, causing me to tumble onto the cold stone floor. Attempting to disengage my foot from the sheet, I only became more entangled; the sheet wound its way up my legs, then my waist, to my torso, eventually merging with my kerchief to cover my face and crown. Like the prey in a predator's maw, I acquiesced anon, surrendering to my fate, to be swallowed into the pitchy blackness of the nethermost sleep in a never-ending night.

The Absence

Geoffrey Reiter

She haunts me in her absences. The breath
I once felt warm upon my nape is frozen
Without her bright noonlight white smile, the loosing
Of grinning pale teeth through her lips (a wreath
Of mistletoe). I miss the low sweet wrath
Her trembling voice could breathe, the acid poison
That turned to healing honey when we'd chosen
To calm all rages, salve all harms beneath

The sallow cold decorum of the moon.
She sits not in her wicker chair. She stands
No longer by the garden trellis. She
Has faded to a mem'ry-hole, a tune
Whose verses flee my thought, a gown whose strands
Unthread until the tear is all I see.

Vampire Poetry

Kyla Lee Ward

> The fairy lives on their life, and they waste away. Death is no escape
> from her. She is the Gaelic muse, for she gives inspiration to those
> she persecutes. The Gaelic poets die young, for she is restless, and
> will not let them remain long on earth—this malignant phantom.
> —William Butler Yeats,
> *Fairy and Folktales of the Irish Peasantry* (1888)

If there was ever a monster suited to poetry, that monster is the vampire. The myth of the Leannan Sidhe, as recorded by Yeats (himself a Gaelic poet), is a potent harbinger. The combination of sex and death, the conflicting emotions of fear and desire, the trappings of darkness, antiquity, and superstition, all mark out the vampire as a kind of portmanteau of the Romantic movement—at least, for future generations. Critics such as Christopher Frayling and Nina Auerbach, among others, have noted how works by Coleridge and Christina Rossetti, while not directly concerned with life-draining revenants, nonetheless contains motifs and behaviors that would come to be associated with the same. Poe himself wrote, in "The Philosophy of Composition" (1846): "The death of a beautiful woman is, unquestionably, the most poetical topic in the world." But it is the prospect of her return that draws "The Raven"'s narrator to the door.

This article treats the use of the vampire in poetry. It does not pretend to be comprehensive, restricting its range to a period from the eighteenth century to the present day, and to poems either written or translated into English. Within that range, it focuses on works deemed most interesting or illustrative. It also adopts a definition of "vampire" based on European folklore.

In this folklore, the vampire figure is a repository of sins. The *first* vampire of any epidemic may be the result of any number of faults, such as being born with features—such as red hair and blue eyes, or six fingers on a hand—that are an outlier in the community and therefore potentially the result of adultery, incest, or the presence of an incubus. There may have been a suicide concealed by the family, the deceased may have practiced witchcraft or been otherwise wicked in life, or died excommunicate from the Greek Orthodox Church. Subsequent transmission may be by infection, but even this is implicitly the result of flouting some law, be it omitting the standard precautions or desiring the return of a loved one when such has "gone to God." The Leeanan Sidhe (literally "faerie sweetheart") strikes a more pagan note, but her victims must likewise *accept* her advances: if they remain strong, she cannot harm them. There is reason to consider the Leeanan Sidhe just as much a revenant as the walking corpses of Serbia and Romania: a convincing connection between faerie folk and the ancient dead, the "dwellers in the mound," has been made by anthropologists such as Claude Lecouteux.

Vampire poetry from the past three centuries can usefully be read through the same lens, of sin committed and sin implicit. But, as we shall see, the actual transgressions involved reflect both changing societal mores and traumatic global events.

The oldest known poem that actually mentions a vampire, "Der Vampire" by Heinrich August Ossenfelder, is a perfect example. Rumors persist of an Anglo-Saxon ballad known as "The Vampire of the Fens." However, not only does no one seem to possess the text, research suggests the writer who first mentioned it was actually referring to *Beowulf*. Ossenfelder was a German poet, and "Der Vampire" appeared in 1748. An English translation was made by one Aloysius Gibson, date unknown. In this piece, a man whose virtuous sweetheart refuses his advances imagines himself (after a glass or two) playing the vampire, how he will creep into her bedroom by night and "thy life's blood drain away." Especially interesting is the narrator's insistence that people in his town do truly believe in vampires, just as the young Christine believes in the standards of behavior inculcated by her mother.

As that thoroughly modern vampire, Lestat de Lioncourt, opines with distaste, such vampires were rapists. It took a good sixty years for the first poems of substance to appear in English—during which Johann Ludwig Tieck wrote "Wake Not the Dead," E. T. A. Hoffmann penned "Aurelia"—both contenders for first vampire short story—and a fashion emerged for fiction "from the German." Among British writers, the vampire was an exotic foreigner endangering the purity of British youth, rather than Ossenfelder's comparatively sophisticated metaphor. But in John Stagg's "The Vampire" (1810), there comes the frisson of another kind of sin.

> Young Sigismund, my once dear friend,
> But lately he resign'd his breath;
> With others I did him attend
> Unto the silent house of death.
> For him I wept, for him I mourn'd,
> Paid all to friendship that was due;
> But sadly friendship is return'd,
> Thy Herman he must follow too!
> . . .
> From the drear mansion of the tomb,
> From the low regions of the dead,
> The ghost of Sigismund doth roam,
> And dreadful haunts me in my bed!
> There, vested in infernal guise,
> (By means to me not understood,)
> Close to my side the goblin lies,
> And drinks away my vital blood!

Watching over Herman's deathbed, his wife confirms the awful truth. A council is convened, agreeing that "shudd'ring nature" must be freed from "pests like these," through the classical means of a sharpened stake. In the end, Sigismund and Herman lie together in one tomb.

This is what Stagg's contemporary, George Gordon, Lord Byron, has to say about the consequences of a double transgression: in *The Giaour* (1813), the protagonist is a Christian knight, received as guest in a Saracen castle, who murders his host after seducing the man's wife.

> But first, on earth as vampire sent,
> Thy corse shall from its tomb be rent,
> Then ghastly haunt thy native place,
> And suck the blood of all thy race.
> There from thy daughter, sister, wife,
> At midnight drain the stream of life,
> Yet loathe the banquet which perforce
> Must feed thy livid living corse.
> Thy victims ere they yet expire
> Shall know the demon for their sire,
> As cursing thee, thou cursing them,
> Thy flowers are withered on the stem.

Thus adding a dash of incest to the brew. *The Giaour* was published in 1813, six years before the novella *The Vampyre*, written by Byron's sometime companion John Polidori. "Lord Ruthven" was widely understood to be based on Byron, which led to considerable bad blood.

But in "The Vampire Bride" by Henry Thomas Liddle (1833), it is a woman who returns from the grave, specifically to be revenged upon the man who abandoned her.

> "I am come—I am come! once again from the tomb,
> In return for the ring which you gave;
> That I am thine, and that thou art mine,
> This nuptial pledge receive."
> He lay like a corse 'neath the Demon's force,
> And she wrapp'd him in a shround;
> And she fixed her teeth his heart beneath,
> And she drank of the warm life-blood!

Such a return was prefigured in Robert Southey's epic *Thalaba the Destroyer* (1801), where the hero banishes the demon possessing his wife's corpse in a peculiar test of manly virtue. But it was the image of a beautiful woman draining a man's vital fluids, while he is *completely helpless* and could *never* have asked for this, which really took off both in poetry and prose. Théophile Gautier, a Frenchman, published the novella *La Morte Amoureuse* in 1836. Once Clarimonde, the undead courtesan, draws the narrator into her world, he lives like a Venetian nobleman, with extensive wardrobe and a manor full of servants, including a poet on retainer. This is the first reference I have found to a vampire enjoying poetry, though not, as shall be seen, the last.

Some count Keats's sonnet "La Belle Dame Sans Merci" (1820) as a vampire poem: although the lady's habits are implied rather than stated, she is certainly "a faerie's child." In "The Vampyre" (1845), James Clerk Maxwell recounts his tale of a lover's revenge in an exotic Scots dialect. In 1853, the German literary titan Johann Wolfgang von Goethe recast the legend of "The Bride of Corinth" in ballad form as an overt vampire tale. There are some excellent English translations, including that made by William E. Aytoun and Theodore Martin in 1859. But special mention must be made of the French poet Charles Pierre Baudelaire. In his 1857 collection *Le Fleurs du mal* are two poems, "Le Metamorphoses du Vampire" and "Le Vampire." Here, the vampire is again a metaphor, deployed with consummate skill, if with scant respect for women. The poet first sees his lover as an irresistible force of darkness, writhing like a serpent, overpowering his will and draining his life. But, his passion spent, he realizes he lies with something worse than a corpse, a vessel leathern and full of foulness. In "Le Vampire," a man fantasizes about killing his lover, who enslaves him as drink does the alcoholic or the dice a gambler. However, he concludes that even should he do so, it would make no difference. "Thy kisses would resuscitate, Thy vampire's corpse for thy delight" (translation by Jacques LeClercq, 1857).

Back in Britain, a coterie of poets fought to keep Romanticism or at least decadence alive in the face of Victorian prudery and the rank materialism of industry and empire, and vampires were included in their arsenal. In *Chastelard: A Tragedy* (1869), Algernon Charles Swinburne puts some astonishing words into the mouth of Mary, Queen of Scots.

"When I had kissed him by the faded eyes
And either thin cheek beating with faint blood,
Well, he was sure to die soon; I do not think
He would have given his body to be slain,
Having embraced my body. Now, God knows,
I have no man to do as much for me
As give me but a little of his blood
To fill my beauty from, though I go down
Pale to my grave for want—I think now. Pale—
I am too pale surely . . ."

I note in passing that Sabine Baring-Gould's *The Book of Were-wolves* was published in 1865. This collection of continental folklore does appear to be the vector by which the legend of Erzsebet Bathory reached English-speakers.

The narrator of Madison Julius Cawein's "The Vampire" (1896) seems to have had a thoroughly enjoyable time and calls his lover a fiend with very little provocation. Likewise, both Rudyard Kipling's "The Vampire" (1897) and Thomas Hardy's "The Vampirine Fair" (1910) reduce their encounters with the undead to mere bad relationships. But 1897 also saw the publication of Bram Stoker's *Dracula*, which, while drawing on all that had gone before, would change the way in which these images were perceived, to the point of the Dracula figure becoming a kind of shorthand for all vampires in popular culture.

Dracula, though indisputably an exotic foreigner, is more seducer than rapist (taking notes, perhaps, from his three brides). He shows no particular poetic leanings, but at the sight of Dracula's coach one of Harker's fellow travelers quotes a classic piece of Germanic macabre. "Die Todten reiten schnell"—the dead travel fast—is from Gottfried August Burger's "Lenore" of 1774. "Lenore" is sometimes considered a vampire poem, although the titular heroine's demon lover is explicitly Death itself (and thus a throwback to the medieval danse macabre).

Across the Atlantic, 1897 also saw the publication of "Luke Havergal" in Edwin Arlington Robinson's collection *Children of the*

Night. The title, shared with the opening poem, is more likely to be a reference to William Blake's *Auguries of Innocence* than Stoker's newly released novel. But "Luke Havergal" is also sometimes considered a vampire poem: like the work of the early Romantics, it shares atmosphere and motif, including that of the irresistible woman waiting in the dark. Less ambiguous is "El Vampiro" ("The Female Vampire") (1910) by Delmira Agustini, a Uruguayan poet writing in Spanish. This quotation is taken from the English translation by Allejandro Carceres:

> "Why was I your vampire of bitterness?
> Am I a flower or a breed of an obscure species
> That devours sores and gulps tears?"

Here the irresistible woman is finally given an opportunity to state her own case, in one of the few poems since Ossenfelder to grant the vampire a voice.

It is hard to imagine that a literary landmark such as *Dracula* might not have impacted poetry as immediately as it did the nascent art of film. But the poetic response does seem to have been delayed . . . unless you count *Gatsby* author F. Scott Fitzgerald's "The Vampires Won't Vampire for Me" (1917), in which he bemoans the lack of "vamps" in his own life. Of course, 1914 brought a catastrophe beside which even Dracula's appetite seemed inconsequential.

> What shape was this who came to us,
> With basilisk eyes so ominous,
> With mouth so sweet, so poisonous,
> And tortured hands so pale?
> We saw her wavering to and fro,
> Through dark and wind we saw her go;
> Yet what her name was did not know;
> And felt our spirits fail...

Composed in 1924, Conrad Aiken's "The Vampire: 1914" granted a sinister red mouth and hypnotic allure to the First World War. As both scholar and writer, he was no stranger to the vampire tradition, as demonstrated by the delightful "La Belle Morte" (1916). But in this work, he walks the figure of the irresistible woman beyond personal tragedy to that of an entire generation and finds it equal to the task. The sin here is humanity's inexplicable willingness to embrace the wanton destruction of war.

The twentieth century created vampires from a much greater variety of transgressions. Yeats's own poem "Oil and Blood" appeared in 1933 in his collection *The Spiral Stair*. In distinguishing, with supreme elegance, between the corpses of saints and vampires ("Their shrouds are bloody and their lips are wet"), it speaks of religious hypocrisy and class injustice.

Somewhat blunter is Arthur Kramer's "Vampire," published in the American journal *Poetry* (June 1940). Although the Second World War was now underway, it speaks more of the Great Depression.

> Though men load the earth with plenty, in dismay
> They find themselves homeless, hungry, on the town—
> Confused and helpless, hear their masters say
> "We cannot help it, you can starve or drown."
> I suspect vampires are abroad today.
> Let's go among the graves and hunt them down.

Other disasters followed. But so too did work using more traditional vampire imagery. George Sterling may have slipped a blue-eyed vampire into "A Wine of Wizardry" (1907), but in 1929 another American, Bertrande Harry Snell, contributed an entire ballad to the June issue of *Weird Tales*. In "Vampire," the hapless hero knows what he's courting . . . and considers it worth the risk. Felix Stefanile's narrator compares his iteration of "The Vampire Bride" (in Derleth) to everything from Medusa to Eve, and only daylight can part them. So too the narrator of Roger Johnson's "To His Mistress, Dead and Darkly Return'd" (*Arkham Collector*, Winter 1971), who makes a lovely sonnet of his confession, "I love thee now, thy beauties move me yet."

But consider now "The Vampire's Love Song" by Jeanne Youngson and Margaret Keyes:

> Spiders crawling up the wall,
> Cobwebs everywhere.
> Dust and dirt are piled up high
> On every crypt and chair.
> Bats go winging overhead,
> Round and round the room,
> Come, my dear, oh *do* come in,
> And join me in my tomb.

Another vampire speaks, this time to list the benefits of succumbing to his wiles, provoking Keyes's coy reply. It is a tongue-in-fangs riff on Marlowe's "The Passionate Shepherd to His Love," with Dracula cast as the hero. In "To Dracula, Who Might Possibly Be Standing on the Other Side of the Room," Youngson not only riffs Joyce Kilmer's "Trees" but addresses her subject with obvious affection.

The figure of Dracula, as it turned out, proved particularly attractive to American poets, even those working in free verse. In the prose poem "Dracula" (*Wormwood Review*, 1974), Steve Kowitt reduces him to a primal fear, to which even moderns like himself respond in primal ways. In Peter Fiore's "Dracula's Bolero" (*American Poetry Review*, 1978), Dracula appears as a shuffling anachronism in New York City, before finding redemption in the subway. He could even be applied to a new disaster, in Michael Hulse's "The Death of Dracula (a song from *AIDS: The Musical*), as printed in *Quadrant* (June 1992). "His last words (says the nurse) were: *Damn Bram Stoker.*" Judging by the track list, this was *not* in fact featured in *AIDS: The Musical*, which was produced in Los Angeles in 1995.

A fatal disease that could be transmitted both by sexual activity and by mingled blood provided an obvious context for vampire imagery. But consider the ghoulish ingenuity of Frederick Seidel's "A Vampire in the Age of AIDS." Or the ghastly supposition of his fellow American, Denise Dumars, in "Deathfeed" (*Bloodsongs*, June 1994), that infected vampires lose all Dracula's dignity, reduced once more to animated corpses.

Dracula continued to inspire work of a more romantic cast, ingenious in its reworking of the myth and inventive in its forms. Michael R. Collings's "Three Songs from Dracula: A Threnody of Wolves, Renfield's Litany as Overheard by Professor Van Helsing and The Bloofer Lady" appeared in *Space & Time* (Summer 1983). An entire volume devoted to the subject—*The Dracula Poems: A Poetic Encounter with the Lord of the Vampires*—was released by Robin Spriggs and Brent L. Glenn (Circle Myth Press, 1992), containing a piece from the point of view of a besotted coffin and another from a foul-mouthed wooden stake. But the 1990s and 2000s saw a true renaissance in vampire poetry, triggered by another literary landmark.

"All the old poetry makes sense when you look at one whom you have loved." These are the words of Lestat de Lioncourt, both a lover of poetry and a poet himself, who first appeared in the 1976 novel *Interview with the Vampire,* by American author Anne Rice. Introduced as an antagonist to Louis, the despondent subject of the interview, he took over the narration entirely in *The Vampire Lestat* (1985) (whence the previous quotation) and *The Queen of the Damned* (1988). Over the course of these books, Lestat engages in lengthy self-examination as well as indulgence, and various literary experiments. *The Queen of the Damned* contains lines from his "Requiem for a Marquise."

> In my dreams, I hold her still,
> Angel, lover, Mother.
> And in my dreams, I kiss her lips,
> Mistress, Muse, Daughter.
>
> She gave me life
> I gave her death
> My beautiful Marquise . . .

Lestat has clearly embraced the free verse movement along with contemporary mores.

Signs are that the impact of Rice's work will equal that of Stoker's—if not in terms of broad cultural penetration, then in the creation of both subculture and subgenre. People costume as Dracula for

Halloween: Lestat's devotees wear waistcoats and lace shirts to specially devised nightclubs. His example, alongside Rice's own literary chops, inspired many New Romantics to rediscover the sins of the past and work up a few of their own.

Marge Simon revisits the vampire as addict in the Parkeresque "Vampires Trying to Lick the Habit" (*Prisoners of the Night*, 1993). By kind permission of the author and the publisher, I present the quatrain in its entirety.

> Joining hands, we meditated.
> Afterwards, drank tea;
> Boris swore off caffeine
> And partook of me.

The victims, male and female, of these vampire grooms seek their persecutor's embrace with unashamed fervor, in the likes of David Shipton's "Ode to a Vampire" (*Bloodsongs*, 1994). Some aspire to become vampires themselves. In "Supplication" (*Dreams of Decadence*, Spring/Summer 2000), Dawn R. Cotter considers this a lesser sin than embracing the hypocrisy of contemporary life. With all this going on, the narrator of Angela Kessler's "Lifestyles of the Undead" (*Dreams of Decadence*, Spring/Summer 1996) sees no reason why her existence should not be as comfortable, to say convenient as possible, even if others suffer ("When you want a steak, do you kill a cow?"). But Singaporean poet Christina Sng's "Prey" (*Blood Rose Magazine*, Winter Solstice 2003) posits an entire future society ruled by vampires who breed humans for the hunt. Or is it the other way around?

These liberated vampires can also embrace modernity in less catastrophic, if still uniquely twisted ways. Again, by the kind permission of the author and the publisher, I reproduce here the entirety of Ann K. Schwader's *Sanguine Taggers*, first published in *HUNGUR* #6 (Walpurgisnacht 2008).

> Those first hundred years
> are the worst:
> alchemical

symbols, illegible
sigils of demons,
quotations from Baudelaire
dripping off
the underpass,
befouling fences,
defacing exquisitely
snug mausoleums

& oh, their empties
just dumped anywhere
like spray cans
or beer cans
but stinking by sunrise

sheer hooligan waste
(say the elders' papyrus
whisperings,
leather wings
furled against the dawn)
a deplorable post-modern
fad, but there's
no reasoning with
young blood.

When vampires speak, they reflect on their needs and desires, often with considerable maturity, and make observations on the society that turns these desires into sins. They contemplate the harm they cause and was caused to them, that first sin of intolerance. They may rejoice in the freedom they gain through turning their backs on conventional lifestyles. Sometimes they draw cheeky parallels between their existence and the lives of more typical citizens. In all cases, they explore what it means to be a creature of the night in their time and place.

None of this invalidates the use of the vampire figure as a literal monster or symbol of a parasitic wealthy class. It is in this flexibility that the vampire trope's longevity may lie. But I posit that even the old man listening to the cockpit recordings from doomed aircraft, in

Seidel's luxurious room, holds an utterly perverse appeal, no matter how firmly it is "staked" back into place.

The vampire is still sought out, as the Gaelic poets were wont to seek out the Leeanan Sidhe, by those wishing to penetrate just that little deeper into human experience. If anything, the poets of this most recent decade are more conscious of the way they draw on what has gone before. Thus, Bruce Boston conjures "The Music of Vampires" from the prospect of perverse fulfilment and the stock props of capes and darkness (*HUNGUR* #12, Walpurgisnacht 2011). Ashley Dioses eulogises Erzsebet Bathory with such traditionally formed works as "Castle Csejthe" and "Bathory in Red" (*Weirdbook* #31 & 33, published in 2015 and 2016 respectively). Dracula may himself be seduced and undertake a dangerous journey for the sake of his beloved, inspiring yet another volume in Marge Simon and Bryan D. Dietrich's *The Demeter Diaries*. But, as Frank Coffman declaims in his mega-sonnet sequence, "The Vampire Ball," even a superficial interest in vampires can lead to strange and wondrous encounters.

> Just a fetish—of course—was all it could be.
> The subject—though her passion—could not be true:
> The stuff of the deep fears of benighted races.
> And, though she longed to see the storied places:
> Count Dracul's castle or the England Stoker knew.
> The nightmares Schreck and Bela had made her see
> Were just that—Images, luscious and dark,
> That tempted her wild spirit with their Sin,
> With weird, forbidden rituals of lust.
> She'd meet some new friends in whom she could trust
> Who shared her cravings. A new world would begin . . .

Perhaps conducting such explorations through poetry is safer, perhaps it is not. For it is well known that poetry itself possesses the capacity to drain writers, consuming both their days and nights and leaving them mere revenants on the fringes of literary life.

Works Cited

Agustini, Delmira. *Selected Poetry of Delmira Agustini: Poetics of Eros.* Tr. Alejandro Caceres. Carbondale: Southern Illinois University Press, 2003.

Auerbach, Nina. *Our Vampires, Ourselves.* Chicago: University of Chicago Press, 1995.

Balmori, Stephanie E. "The Vampire in the Poetry of Delmira Agustini." M.A. thesis: Florida State University, 2009.

Barber, Paul. *Vampires, Burial and Death: Folklore and Reality.* New Haven, CT: Yale University Press, 1988.

Barnstone, Tony, and Michelle Mitchell-Foust, ed. *Poems Dead and Undead.* New York: Everyman's Library of Pocket Poets/Alfred A. Knopf, 2014.

Boston, Bruce. *Resonance Dark and Light.* San Antonio, TX: Eldritch Press, 2015.

Bunson, Matthew. *Vampire: The Encyclopedia.* London: Thames & Hudson, 1993.

Coffman, Frank. *Black Flames and Gleaming Shadows.* Sunrise, FL: Bold Venture Press, 2020.

Derleth, August, ed. *Fire and Sleet and Candlelight.* Sauk City, WI: Arkham House, 1961.

Dioses, Ashley. *Diary of a Sorceress.* New York: Hippocampus Press, 2017.

Frayling, Christopher. *Vampyres: Lord Byron to Count Dracula.* London: Faber & Faber, 1991.

Frost, Brian J. *The Monster with a Thousand Faces: Guises of the Vampire in Myth and Literature.* Bowling Green, OH: Bowling Green State University Popular Press, 1989.

Kessler, Angela, ed. *The Best of Dreams of Decadence: Vampire Stories and Poems to Keep You Up Till Dawn.* New York: Roc, 2003.

Lecouteux, Claude. *The Secret History of Vampires: Their Multiple Forms and Hidden Purposes.* Tr. Jon E. Graham. Rochester, VT: Inner Traditions, 2010.

Melton, J. Gordon. *The Vampire Book.* 2nd ed. Canton, MI: Visible Ink Press, 2011.

Moore, Steven, ed. *The Vampire in Verse: An Anthology.* n.p.: Dracula Press, 1985.

Ramsland, Katherine. *Piercing the Darkness: Undercover with Vampires in America Today.* New York: HarperPrism, 1998.

Rice, Anne. *The Queen of the Damned.* New York: Alfred A. Knopf, 1988.

———. *The Vampire Lestat.* New York: Alfred A. Knopf, 1985.

Schwader, Ann K. *Twisted in Dream: The Collected Poems of Ann K. Schwader.* New York: Hippocampus Press, 2011.

Seidel, Frederick. *Going Fast: Poems.* New York: Farrar, Straus & Giroux, 1998.

Simon, Marge, and Bryan D. Dietrich, *The Demeter Diaries.* n.p.: Independent Legions Publishing, 2019.

Weissenberger, Crystal. "Christina Rossetti's 'Goblin Market': A Vampire in the Making?" Auburn University, 2014 (www.academia. edu/10870705/Christina_Rossetti_s_Goblin_Market_A_Vampire _in_the_Making).

Youngson, Jeanne. *The Further Perils of Dracula.* n.p.: Adams Press, 1979.

Some of the concepts and material in this essay were first aired during the Vampire Poetry panel hosted by the author and Val Toh at Conflux 13—Grimm Tales, 2017. The author further thanks Leigh Blackmore, Frank Coffman, Alayne Gelfand, Charles "Danny" Lovecraft, Terrie Leigh Relf and Angela Yuriko Smith for their vital assistance with her research.

The following websites were also of material assistance:
www.isfdb.org
literaryvampire.tumblr.com
poets.org
www.vampires.com

Quiet

Shawn Phelps

Even out in the field, far from the house, Grandmother whispered as she read the Bible to Mary. Every night they walked far out into the field and sat on the bench that had been made long ago from stones found in the field. Its top was flat, roughly troweled cement. They came out to read at sunset so their voices would not disturb Grandfather's studies. Grandmother always reminded her of that. Even though they were far from the house, they must whisper. They must be quiet.

Mary held her hand up to shield her eyes from the setting sun. Its rays made the tips of the grass glow with orange fire. She looked behind her at the house, at its windows that were like shining bronze reflecting the rays, and its gray boards aglow with yellow light.

Tonight, Grandmother was reading about Abraham and Isaac. Mary had to lean close to hear her soft words. Occasionally, Grandmother looked nervously over her shoulder at the house, after which she would give Mary a tight smile and continue reading.

"Finally, they reached the place the true God had indicated to him, and Abraham built an altar there and arranged the wood on it. He bound his son Isaac hand and foot and put him on the altar on top of the wood. Then Abraham reached out his hand and took the knife to kill his son."

"But why would God want Abraham to kill his own son, Grandmother?" Mary interrupted, "I don't like this story. It's bad."

Grandmother stopped reading and stared at Mary. "*Nothing* in this book is bad. *Nothing*. You sound like your mother now."

Grandmother began to read about Noah and the Great Flood. She said it was Grandfather's favorite part of the Bible. He was fascinated with the Nephilim, the children of fallen angels who had come to earth and married human women. Their children were giants who had roved the world tormenting normal men. Grandfather thought that God had sent the Nephilim to punish the wicked.

Before they went inside, Grandmother warned her again that Grandfather needed silence for his studies. He was angry when he was disturbed and he was not well at all to begin with. Grandmother worried that he would exhaust himself with his prayers and fasting. Being a part of God's plan was difficult work.

"We must not interrupt his work," Grandmother whispered to Mary. Grandmother always whispered.

Ever since Mother had left Mary at the farm, she had tried hard to be quiet and well behaved. Grandmother told her how important it was that she move about silently, but it was hard in the creaky old house.

It was especially difficult when going up the stairs. The stairway was narrow and dark, with wood-paneled walls that were scuffed and scraped by the passage of countless hands along its surface. The steps themselves were painted a muddy brown. When she closed the stairway door behind her, it became entirely dark except for a weak glow from a window at the top.

The stairway frightened Mary. In the dark it seemed as though the walls had vanished; if she stumbled, she might fall off into a bottomless void. There was also the danger of the wood creaking under her feet. Mary always put on her heavy wool socks before the climb to further muffle her steps, and she found that by placing her feet close to the wall much of the noise could be avoided.

To get to her room she had to pass Grandfather's door, and it was there that she felt most vulnerable. The door was poorly hung and there were gaps along its edges. Through these spaces she could see a dark shape moving about the room. Back and forth it went, making a sound like a rough broom sweeping across the floor.

When she passed the door, the movement would stop as if Grandfather had paused to listen to her passing.

The thought frightened her terribly. Could Grandfather hear her? She stood quite still, but she was worried he could hear her breathing. She held her breath and slid her feet along the floor, not daring to lift them. She stopped when she had moved beyond the door. Again she saw the change from dark to light along the doors edges that signaled the resumption of Grandfather's pacing about the room.

Safely past Grandfather's door, Mary slipped into her room and slowly, *slowly,* shut the door. She held the knob, not allowing it to click into place. She carefully released it so that it came to rest silently.

Later when she went downstairs, she still heard the whispering through the door. A rhyming, sing-song combination of words was repeated over and over again. Slowly sliding her feet, Mary moved closer to the door. The words were becoming louder and clearer, as if Grandfather was moving toward the door. Then came silence.

Mary began to edge away from the door, and the whispering began again.

She ran down the stairs, unconcerned about the noise she was making as she ran out of the house and into the cornfield. The ground there was dry; clouds of dust puffed up as her feet struck the ground. The corn was pale yellow green, its leaves frayed and brown at the ends. Ragged edges of it scratched at her arms and raised red welts.

Mary ran until she was out of breath and covered with dust. The corn seemed to get closer together as she ran, and the rows became thinner, as if the plants themselves wanted to slow her flight. She began to run, agitating the stalks as she plunged down the row. The dry, jagged leaves slashed at her. Her movement through them made a shaky, chattering sound in which Mary thought she could hear words.

She heard voices coming from the corn, voices that said bad words like the ones naughty boys used to yell at her on the playground. Her old teacher Miss June had taken Joey Brill by the arm and shaken him for saying *those* kinds of words.

The row narrowed to the point that she could go no further. She was surrounded and the path behind her was gone.

The field had swallowed her up. Only the trembling of the stalks behind her gave any hint of where she had come from. The corn was thicker here and bowed over her so that even the sky was partially obscured.

Out of breath, she fell to the ground. The dust covered her sweaty arms and made them itch. The voices stopped when she sat down. It must have been her imagination. The corn stalks rustled and shuddered with a soft breeze. She noticed that their roots were exposed. They looked like the legs of some crazy spider, as if the corn could wrench itself free of the earth and march away if it chose to leave the field. Mary pictured it walking about the farm at night: tall stalks creeping up the stairs and into her room. She imagined them circling her bed while she slept, swaying as they watched her sleep.

She sat hugging her knees, trying to pull away from the corn. The stalks pressed closer, the jagged leaves cutting at her face and arms. They pressed tighter and tighter until she thought she would choke. The sandpapery leaves scoured across her face.

She was lost and had no idea which direction to go to return to the house. It was clear that she could not escape through the corn.

The plants relaxed, falling back away from her. The corn fell away in waves and a long corridor appeared in the field. In the distance she could see the house. It was just like in the Bible when God parted the Red Sea so the Israelites could walk on dry land.

There was only one way to go; the corn had woven itself into solid walls on either side of her. Slowly she began to walk toward the house, the corn springing back into place behind her, sealing off any retreat. Grandmother stood rigidly on the porch watching Mary approach. She said nothing as she climbed up the porch steps in defeat.

Grandmother put a finger to her lips and with her other hand motioned for Mary to go up to her room. After silently climbing the stairs, she darted past Grandfather's door and into her room. There was no sound coming from Grandfather now.

Mary was unhappy at the farm and missed her friends in the city. She wished her mother would come for her and take her home. She remembered the night of the phone call before she came to the farm, when Mother had been crying and asking over and over, "How did you find me?" Mary had heard her saying "I won't do it" and "Just leave us alone." The argument went on for a long time. Mary could only hear parts of the conversation, but could tell Mother was frightened and angry.

The next morning Mother woke her very early and said they must take a trip to visit her grandparents. Mary had never known she had any family but her mother. She had never seen a picture or heard Mother speak of them before. Mother had a peculiar smile that morning and her face was red and shiny. She told her that they were going to the farm for a visit. In fact, Mary would be staying the entire *summer* with her grandparents.

It had been a long drive and Mary had slept on the back seat of the car. When she woke the car seat was hot and sticky beneath her. Her mother was outside the car talking with an old woman.

The two women talked loudly, but Mary could not make out what was being said. Her mother's shrill and brittle voice frightened her. It was like that when she was angry or afraid. The old woman kept shaking her head in disagreement and motioning to the upstairs windows of an old farmhouse. She made a gesture to her lips, as if to quiet her mother.

Mary cried at the thought of her mother. Why had she left her in this horrible place? At last she fell asleep.

The next morning Grandmother said that she had to work in the garden. She sat Mary down in the parlor and gave her a Bible to read. Grandmother told her to keep very still and read from God's word.

Mary tried to do as Grandmother had asked, but soon grew bored with reading. It was still and dim in the living room. Mary could faintly hear the swish-swish of Grandfather's movement upstairs.

The furniture in the room was old and in disrepair. Knitted doilies were thrown over the arms of the chairs and the back of the sofa. An upright piano sat in one corner.

Mary could not imagine Grandmother playing such a thing. She thought of her teacher in music class happily playing songs for them and wished she was back home.

Mary carefully slid the cover back to reveal the piano keys. They had yellowed over the years and some had chipped ends, looking like broken nails on pale fingers. She could see Grandmother through the window, crouching in the garden and pulling weeds. Grandmother would never know if she played softly on the keys.

As Mary struck the first key, she realized her mistake. In the silence the note rang out with unnatural clarity. The sound was like flicking a finger on a crystal glass. Mary wanted to take the sound back, but it was too late. The house gave a shudder, as if the ground under it had settled. A fine shower of plaster dust fell from the ceiling onto Mary. Then there was silence again.

Grandmother appeared in the doorway. She did not look at Mary. As if preparing to ward off a blow, she became hunched and twisted. Her eyes were so round that white showed all the way around them. She stared up at the ceiling, her mouth quivering and working as if she couldn't think of what to say. "It's too soon. Too early to wake him," she mumbled at last.

There came a creaking from upstairs. It was the agonized sound of a great hinge, unhappy to move, but ripped open by overwhelming force. Grandmother's eyes fell upon Mary; her bonnet had come loose and her hair was in wild disarray. She got control of her unruly lips and hissed one word.

"Run," was all she said.

The house shuddered again, and this time Mary was jostled from her seat on the piano bench. As she attempted to stop her fall her hand violently struck the piano keys again.

Mary exploded out of the house, the screen door rebounding from its wooden siding. She could hear a screeching, grinding sound from the stairway. Something was popping like wood in a campfire. Reaching the barn, she scrambled up into the hayloft. Through a knothole she could see the house shuddering. The living room windows blew out and showered flecks of bright glass into the yard.

Light came through knotholes in the barn siding and cut through the shadows like lasers. Each beam illuminated whirling motes of dust, winking and sparkling like miniature galaxies of stars.

Mary sat very still in the hay. She could hear the scurrying of mice and occasionally caught sight of them racing across the floor. Pigeons roosted in the beams, safe under the tin roof. Cats crept in and out of a gap in the barn doors. The heat had made them too listless to pursue either mice or pigeons. One made its way up to Mary's hiding spot and rubbed its head against her until she scratched its ears.

The sun was setting when Mary crept down from the hayloft. She walked back to the house and peeked over the sill of a broken window.

The living room had been destroyed. The piano looked as if a boulder had fallen on it. Each end stood crookedly upright, but the center had been smashed and compacted down so that the whole instrument formed a U-shape, its interior workings sticking out in all directions. Black and white keys lay scattered about the floor; some had even flown up to land on the bookshelves. The piano bench had been flattened as well; its legs had disintegrated into splinters.

Mary tiptoed around the side of the house toward the front door. All the windows were broken and heaps of glass shimmered in the grass. There was silence except for squeaking of the screen door as it moved in the breeze.

The stairway door was missing and Mary noticed fragments of it littering the dining room. Grandmother had already tacked a blanket over the doorway, but it was too small to cover the new opening. Something *too big* had forced its way through the open doorway and had enlarged it. Jagged shards of wood and plasterboard gaped in what was now an almost circular passage.

She found Grandmother sitting on the stone bench, staring at the sunset. When Mary sat beside her, she just kept looking straight ahead. Her face and hands were deeply scratched, but she was otherwise unharmed. Mary had done her best to be quiet. If only she hadn't touched the piano.

"He doesn't mean to act this way . . . but he has to play his part to the end. It is a bitter cup sometimes . . . to be a part of Gods' plan," Grandmother said.

"But Grandmother," Mary asked, "what *is* God's plan?"

"That's not for us to know, child. We mustn't question. We must just accept our part in the great mystery as it unfolds. But Grandfather has learned some of it. The world has become wicked again. Like the days before the great flood. Grandfather thinks God will call some of the faithful to act like the Nephilim and punish his enemies. But there will have to be sacrifices, as in the days of old, to prove our faithfulness and resolve."

"Well, I don't know how I can do my part if I don't know what the plan is," Mary said.

Grandmother turned to face Mary. Tiny beads of blood dotted her face like sweat. She reached out and patted Mary's knee.

"Don't fret about it. Your part is coming soon and it's an important one. When the time comes, you'll know and you must do your best then."

Mary climbed up on the stone bench beside her Grandmother. They both stared at the setting sun, their faces glowing with the orange light.

"I tried to be good, Grandmother," she said. "I tried to be quiet."

Grandmother kept looking straight ahead. She reached out and clasped Mary's hand.

"Hush, child," Grandmother said. "I know you did your best. But that time is past now. Things are coming, and try as you might you won't be able to keep silent. But it doesn't matter a bit now."

From behind them, Mary heard an awful rending sound of wood being bent beyond what it could tolerate. She turned to face the house. The roof was swelling slowly and rhythmically as if the house were taking deep breaths.

As the roof puffed outward, nails shot out like bullets, zinging across the field. Shingles broke loose and fluttered to the earth. The beams complained with great shrieks until they finally gave way with frightful sounds like rifle shots. The roof exploded outward and Grandfather began to emerge, his terrible eyes locked on Mary.

Mary could not move in the extremity of her terror. It was all right, though, because Grandmother took her legs and swung her up on to the bench. She stroked Mary's head and pushed her back so that she was reclining. It was then, as Grandfather moved across the field to meet them, that Mary realized it was not a bench that she lay on.

Guy de Maupassant: Women, Madness, and the Horla

S. T. Joshi

The weird work of Guy de Maupassant (1850–1893) constitutes a relatively small proportion of his total output, but is of supreme interest because it highlights the complex intertwining of his life, psychological makeup, and literary theory in ways that his more mainstream writing does not. Maupassant emerged at a time when weird fiction in France, England, and the United States was at a relatively low ebb, and he revitalized the genre in such an innovative manner that his tales remain touchstones for the intense, artful crafting of weirdness in literature in all its multiplicity of forms.

Maupassant's family was intimately connected with the leading French writers of the period, and Maupassant himself became one of the bestselling authors of the later nineteenth century, although largely on the basis of his mainstream work. His uncle, Alfred Le Poittevin (1816–1848), was a minor French poet and close friend of Gustave Flaubert, who was devastated at Le Poittevin's early death. Alfred's sister, Laure, married her sister-in-law's brother, Gustave de Maupassant, in 1846 in Rouen. Henri-René-Albert-Guy de Maupassant was born on 5 August 1850, at the Château de Miromesnil, near the village of Tourville-sur-Argus, in Normandy. Later the family—augmented by the birth of another son, Hervé, in 1856—moved to the Château Blanc near Étretat, a farming village in Normandy facing the English Channel.

Maupassant's parents struggled to maintain their marriage, and in 1861 Laure had had enough of Gustave's many affairs and separated from him; she retained custody of her two boys. In 1863, in spite of her own religious skepticism, she enrolled Guy in the Institution Ecclésiastique in the nearby town of Yvetot, chiefly so that

Guy could cultivate friendships with the many members of the aristocracy and gentry who attended the school; but Guy, who was himself already rejecting religion, was not happy there and was expelled. Laure then enrolled him in the Lycée in Rouen. There he fell under the influence of the poet and playwright Louis Bouilhet (1822–1869), who lived in Rouen. Bouilhet was, like Maupassant's parents, acquainted with Flaubert, and Maupassant first met the great writer in 1867, ten years after he had created a scandal with the publication of *Madame Bovary*. Both Bouilhet and Flaubert inculcated in Maupassant—who was already writing some poetry at this time—a devotion to aesthetic integrity all apart from commercial considerations. It is not entirely clear that Maupassant, when he became a bestselling novelist, fully adhered to these strictures.

Maupassant graduated from the Lycée in 1870 and was to have begun his law studies in Paris in the fall; but the outbreak of the Franco-Prussian War (1870–71) confounded the plans. The war resulted in a disastrous and humiliating defeat for France that affected the nation's political and cultural outlook for more than a generation. Maupassant himself served in the army. His experiences were not pleasant, as he relates in a letter to his mother recounting the army's retreat from Rouen:

> I fled with our army in retreat. I was almost captured. I went from the front to the rear to carry an order from the commissariat to the General. I did *fifteen leagues on foot*. After having marched and run all the preceding night delivering the orders, I slept on the stones in an icy cellar. If I had not had a good pair of legs, they would have captured me. I ran very well. (Boyd 17)

After the war, Maupassant returned to Étretat to live with his mother. There he renewed his acquaintance with Flaubert and also met other luminaries—Émile Zola, Alphonse Daudet, Edmond de Goncourt, and the Russian writer Ivan Turgenev (1818–1883), who was a fixture in the Paris of the 1870s. During that entire decade Maupassant met regularly with Flaubert and his circle, and the great writer carefully criticized the younger man's early tales, poems, and sketches; he came to regard Maupassant as a kind of adopted son.

But because Maupassant's family suffered some financial setbacks at this time, he could no longer maintain the life of a "gentleman of leisure." In 1872, through Flaubert's influence, he was hired as a clerk in the Naval Ministry, a job he dutifully maintained for seven years in spite of his distaste for the tedious and repetitive tasks he was assigned. In 1879 he moved to the Ministry of Public Instruction, but didn't like that job much better than its predecessor. In spite of some health issues that emerged during this decade, Maupassant also became a devotee of rowing and other energetic activities, much to the amusement of the sedentary Flaubert. But he occasionally lapsed into depression from the monotony of his employment, as he wrote to Flaubert:

> My mind is sterile and tired by the figures I add up from morning until night. At times I feel so sharply the futility of everything, the blind cruelty of life, the emptiness of the future (whatever it may be), that I am filled with a melancholy indifference to all things, and I want nothing better than to remain quiet, quietly in a corner, without hopes or troubles.
>
> I am living all alone, because people bore me, and I bore myself because I cannot work. My thoughts are mediocre and monotonous, and my mind is so stiff that I cannot express them. (Boyd 29)

Such expressions of ennui were uttered throughout Maupassant's life.

Flaubert urged Maupassant to write short stories, which were becoming popular at this time, as an increasing number of magazines were featuring them. Even in the 1870s Maupassant was (as Zola has recounted) telling the Flaubert circle "dumbfounding stories about women, amorous swaggerings that sent Flaubert into roars of laughter" (Steegmuller 64). Some early apprentice work appeared around this time, including the story "En canot" (In a Rowboat), published in the *Bulletin Français* for March 1876. And yet, Maupassant's first literary triumph was not a story but a play, *His-*

toire du vieux temps (A Story of Old Times), put on with some success at the Théâtre Français on 9 February 1879.

At this time Maupassant assembled his first volume, the poetry collection *Des Vers* (1880). One of the poems in the volume had previously appeared in a newspaper and had caused Maupassant to be threatened with prosecution for obscenity; but he rounded up his cadre of impressive literary figures to defend the free expression of literary work, and the case never came to trial.

The same year that *Des Vers* appeared, Maupassant—who had by now developed friendships with Joris-Karl Huysmans and other young littérateurs—published the long story "Boule de Suif" (loosely translated as "Ball of Fat") in an anthology with four other young writers; the book created a sensation, and Maupassant's career as a storyteller was launched.

It was at this time that the French literary world was consumed in a battle between the Naturalists and the Parnassians. The Naturalists—of whom Zola was the paragon—emphasized gritty realism, especially the exhibition of the lives of "lower-class" characters, from manual laborers to prostitutes, and a purportedly "scientific" approach to literature that embraced determinism (the notion that all human action is rigidly determined by the relentless working of cause and effect, and that free will is an illusion) and a coldly impersonal, morally neutral stance that eschews facile judgments on human behavior. The Parnassians, led by such poets as Leconte de Lisle and José Maria de Heredia, sought elegant refinement at all costs, purging their work of anything that smacked of "low" characters or actions but also eschewing objectivity for a lush, emotional approach to life, especially to love and eroticism. Maupassant, like his mentor Flaubert, steered clear of either school, although both writers were more inclined toward Naturalism than Parnassianism. Both schools expressed disdain for popular writers like Alexandre Dumas, who they believed (rightly, as it happened) to be catering to the crude tastes of a wide and indiscriminate public. Some of Maupassant's fellow writers looked down upon him when he himself became popular, although it could be maintained that he almost never buckled down to providing potboilers for the masses except in some of his later work.

The thrill that Maupassant experienced from his early publications was marred by the unexpected death of Gustave Flaubert on 8 May 1880. Having by now retired from the civil service, Maupassant prepared the manuscript of his mentor's unfinished novel *Bouvard et Pécuchet* for publication; but otherwise he plunged into his own writing. He was hired by a weekly magazine, *Le Gaulois,* to write an article for each issue; he also published many of his short stories in that periodical. Soon thereafter he began writing for another magazine, *Gil Blas,* which had been founded in 1879 and developed a reputation for publishing "obscene" literature by Zola and others. It had the appearance of a newspaper, but in fact published stories, sketches, and articles, with little or no current news. Maupassant's first collection, *La Maison Tellier* (1881), created yet another scandal because its long title story was a blandly sympathetic account of the prostitutes who worked in a bordello. The volume was both a critical and commercial success. It contained Maupassant's earliest tale that could be considered weird—"Sur l'eau" (On the River), a rewriting of "En canot."

Maupassant was continuing to suffer from health problems (for which see below) and took trips to Algeria and Corsica, both of which were French colonies at this time. Nevertheless, he continued his prodigious output of fiction: from 1880 to 1890 he published a total of twelve short story collections as well as six novels, beginning with *Une Vie* (1883; A Woman's Life). None of his novels are weird, but nearly every one of his story collections features one or more tales that are within the realms of supernatural or psychological terror. He continued to travel widely, going to Cannes and Monte Carlo in 1883, Italy, Sicily, and the Auvergne region of southern France in 1885, and England in 1886.

During 1887 and 1888 Maupassant's productivity declined sharply as a result of his ongoing health problems. He took another trip to north Africa and subsequently wrote a series of travel essays, "Sur l'eau" (not to be confused with the short story of 1881), in which he continued to express a weariness with life:

> Alas, I have desired all things and enjoyed nothing. . . . How I wish, at times, that I could stop thinking and feeling, that I could live like an animal in a bright, warm country, in a yellow land without crude and brutal greens, in an Oriental country, where sleep is joyful and one awakes without sorrow . . . where love is not fraught with anguish. (Boyd 211)

That final sentence is significant, for by this time it was clear that Maupassant was afflicted with syphilis. But because the etiology of syphilis was not known at this time, no effective treatment was possible. His brother Hervé died in November 1889 of "general paralysis," a euphemism for syphilis. Maupassant's mental and physical condition continued to deteriorate, and in early 1892 he unsuccessfully attempted suicide by various methods. On 7 January 1892 he was taken to the asylum at Passy, where he spent the remainder of his life. He died on 6 July 1893.[1] Although his mother, to whom he remained devoted for the whole of his life, arranged for the posthumous publication of some of his work, she also destroyed many documents relating to his life. She herself died in 1903.

Maupassant's early death from syphilis requires an examination of his attitude toward and relations with women during the entire course of his life. His mother claimed that he first had sex when he was sixteen, with a girl whom Laure denoted only as "the lovely E——"; she goes on to say that "their love was followed by a friendly affection which lasted a long time. He sought only high-class liaisons, and, like his brother, always respected his mother's house" (Steegmuller 30). What this means is that Maupassant did not engage with "peasant girls" or streetwalkers and also did not bring

---

1. It is a curious coincidence that Winfield Scott Lovecraft (1853–1898), the father of H. P. Lovecraft and also a victim of syphilis, almost exactly matched the span of Maupassant's life.

these women into the house.

But that he frequented many prostitutes from this point onward is abundantly clear, and he probably contracted syphilis from one of them. Flaubert himself, hardly a prude in such matters, bluntly ticked off to his young friend some of his derelictions, as he saw them: "Too many whores! Too much rowing! Too much exercise!" (Steegmuller 87–88). It was at this very time that Maupassant was diagnosed with a "herpetic condition, which manifested itself last year in internal, especially cardiac, symptoms, a month ago in loss of hair on head and body, and at present in herpetic eruptions and numerous symptoms which indicate that M. de Maupassant is still under the influence of the same diathesis" (Steegmuller 85). He complained of headaches and insomnia, and took ether to relieve the pain.

After the publication of *Une Vie*, he frequented many prostitutes, both at his home and in brothels. He may have visited several hundred over his lifetime. He also had affairs with married women. Of course, we must understand the nature of French culture at this time, especially among the intellectual and social aristocracy, which tolerated the dalliance of both husbands and wives so long as it was done discreetly. Maupassant, however, indulged in sexual congress to excess. His 1885 trip to Auvergne was made in the company of two whores and his father (his first encounter with his parent since 1872).

Maupassant's activities were fueled by a generally disdainful attitude toward women that could verge on misogyny—while at the same time, in much of his writing, he exhibited both a keen insight into female psychology and, in some of his weird tales, searingly portrayed his male narrators' obsession with the "eternal feminine." The contempt for the institution of marriage and the thirst for an endless succession of physical liaisons expressed by the narrator of "He?" probably reflect Maupassant's own views:

> I look upon all legalized co-habitation as utterly stupid, for I am
> certain that nine husbands out of ten are cuckolds; and they get no
> more than their deserts for having been idiotic enough to fetter
> their lives and renounce their freedom in love, the only happy and

good thing in the world, and for having clipped the wings of fancy which continually drives us on toward all women. You know what I mean. More than ever I feel that I am incapable of loving one woman alone, because I shall always adore all the others too much. I should like to have a thousand arms, a thousand mouths, and a thousand—temperaments, to be able to strain an army of these charming creatures in my embrace at the same moment. (*Sisters Rondoli* 77)

But it is to Maupassant's weird fiction, rather than to any personal failings, that we now turn.

The earliest known work by Maupassant that even approaches the weird is the curious novelette "Le Docteur Héraclius Gloss" (Doctor Heraclius Gloss), a humorous piece that was written in the latter part of 1875 but not published until 1921; an English translation appeared in 1923. The underlying theme of this rather grotesque work is metempsychosis—the transmigration of souls from animals to humans and vice versa. While this theme has indeed been utilized in weird fiction—there are hints of it in Poe's "Metzengerstein" (1832) and "The Black Cat" (1843)—the conception here is tied specifically to the philosophy of Pythagoras. But it is used only for comic effect: the doctor of the title, finding a manuscript dating to 184 C.E., believes for a time that a monkey he has obtained was, in a former life, the author of the treatise, and still later that he himself was the author. But the narrative plainly pokes fun at the hapless doctor, who descends into madness and is confined to a sanitarium. Although Ernest Boyd maintains that the tale constitutes "evidence—the earliest manifestation—of that morbid dread of insanity which was to show, ever more and more insistently, through *Le Horla, Lui?, Qui sait?*" (Boyd 95), the relationship of this tale to Maupassant's later works is tangential.

It is of interest to trace literary influences on Maupassant's weird work. He speaks of Poe as early as 1868 (Steegmuller 31), and in the brief essay "Le Fantastique" (The Fantastic; *Le Gaulois*, 7 October 1883), he links the names of Poe and E. T. A. Hoffmann. Poe's emphasis on the psychological effects of fear, and his literary theory of the "unity of effect" (whereby every word, sentence, paragraph, and episode in a tale must be intimately related to the overall outcome), clearly influenced Maupassant. Hoffmann represented an earlier tradition, deriving from the Gothic novels of the late eighteenth and early nineteenth centuries, and it does not appear that Maupassant was markedly influenced by them. By the 1880s the Gothic novels had long been out of favor, and Poe's approach—whereby terror was confined to the short story and was set either in the present day or in a never-never land of the imagination—had eclipsed the Gothic writers' focus on medieval castles, women in peril, and other themes that were now regarded as hopelessly outmoded.

Indeed, the essay "Le Fantastique" makes the curious assertion that belief in the supernatural is on the verge of extinction because of the advance of modern science. He maintains that the only way to evoke fear today is to remain "within the limits of the possible," and in presenting an exquisite balance between supernatural and natural explanations of the given phenomena. He concludes: "The extraordinarily terrifying power of Hoffmann and Edgar Poe derives from this skill, this specific manner of bringing us into contact with the fantastic, of disturbing us with natural events in which, nevertheless, there is something inexplicable and close to impossible."[2] Much of Maupassant's work is an instantiation of this principle.

The poem "Terreur" (usually translated as "Horror"), appearing in *Des Vers* (1880), is perhaps Maupassant's first authentic contribution to weird fiction. This brief but intense poem displays a protagonist undergoing mental disturbance at the presence of some shadowy entity, and doubt remains to the end whether the protagonist's perceptions are based on reality or are merely the result of hallucination or even incipient madness.

This ambiguity as to the presence of supernatural forces in the world—and the terror and psychological trauma they cause—is at

---

2. The essay is printed elsewhere in this issue.

the heart of the great bulk of Maupassant's weird fiction, early and late. His first genuine weird tale, "Sur l'eau" (1881; On the River), exhibits a boatman who detects hints of the supernatural on the Seine; his impressions are enhanced by night, a mist emerging from the river, and other phenomena. Maupassant creates a powerful atmosphere of weirdness, but ultimately we are told that the bizarre events in the tale can in fact be explained naturally.

The madness theme enters Maupassant's work in his very next weird tale, "Fou?" (1882; Mad?). In this tale of a man whose madness is inspired by love of a woman, we see the protagonist degenerate from paranoia (he becomes jealous of his lover's horse) to murderous vengeance. There is something of the atmosphere of Poe's "The Telltale Heart" here, in the man's repeated assurances that he is not in fact insane when his very narration proves that he is.

"Un Fou?" (1882; A Madman?) exhibits a man afraid of himself—and who also believes that he has hypnotic powers. He appears to demonstrate his abilities by making a knife move solely by the actions of his mind. Whether we are to consider this a supernatural event or merely an actual exhibition of hypnosis is unclear. "La Nuit" (1882; Night) once again engenders a nightmarish atmosphere as the narrator wanders at night through Paris. The loss of his watch seems to symbolize the stoppage of time as he roams a city that seems suddenly deserted.

Other early tales by Maupassant venture into the realm of the physically—or, perhaps, the morally—gruesome. "Le Loup" (1882; The Wolf) is the grim tale of a hunter who seeks revenge by killing the huge white wolf he blames for the death of his brother. "Auprès d'un Mort" (1883; Beside a Dead Man) purportedly recounts a tale about the German philosopher Arthur Schopenhauer—or, rather, of what happened to his corpse after his death. The tale is little more than a macabre (and non-supernatural) joke, but the influence of Schopenhauer's pessimism upon Maupassant's thought is undeniable. "En Mer" (1883; At Sea) is a grisly tale of body horror on board a commercial sailing vessel.

Both of Maupassant's two tales entitled "La Peur" (Fear) reveal interesting features that tie them to the essay "Le Fantastique." The first tale (1882) is one of several where the characters metafictionally discuss the very nature of fear, terror, horror, and other related emotions. In repudiating the notion that mere physical danger is tantamount to fear, the teller of the tale maintains that "Real fear is like a reminiscence of the fantastic terrors of past ages. A man who believes in ghosts and who imagines that he sees one, must experience the sensation of fear in all its atrocious horror" (*Mademoiselle Fifi* 212). The narrator (in defiance of Poe's theory of the "unity of effect") goes on to relate two different episodes he himself experienced, in which at least the suggestion of the supernatural is broached. In the other story entitled "La Peur" (1884), the narrator, echoing the sentiment in "Le Fantastic" by stating that "the supernatural sinks like a lake emptied by a canal" (*Horla and Other Stories* 233) goes on to tell two different tales, one purportedly told to him by Turgenev, and the other speaking of a cholera outbreak in Toulouse. The latter tale, in which the disease is personified, brings Poe's "The Masque of the Red Death" to mind.

"La Main" (1883; The Hand) deliberately sets up a quasi-supernatural scenario only to deflate it at the end. While making a distinction between the "supernatural" and the "inexplicable," the story explains away the apparent actions of a severed hand in a naturalistic manner.

Maupassant's first unequivocally supernatural tale appears to be "L'Apparition" (1883; An Apparition), where a man goes to a friend's abandoned chateau and sees the ghost of the friend's dead wife. Up to this point the tale can be interpreted naturalistically, in that the man might be merely suffering the effects of the sinister atmosphere of the deserted chateau (here, for once, reminiscent of the Gothic castles of the older weird tradition); but when the woman's hairs are actually found on the man's waistcoat, we know that the ghost's manifestation was real.

An entire series of tales focus on women—almost universally

from a male perspective. In Maupassant's stories, women are either objects of fascination or of revulsion—or both at the same time. "La Mère aux monstres" (1883; The Mother of Monsters) is a hideous tale of depravity whereby a peasant woman repeatedly deforms her children in the womb so as to sell them to circuses as freaks. And yet, the tale ends with a bitter twist, whereby a woman in high society in effect does the same thing, as she continues to wear a corset to preserve her shapeliness in spite of the serious injury she causes to her unborn child. In "Une Vendetta" (1883; A Vendetta) a woman in Sardinia, influenced by the long tradition of the vendetta in that island and in neighboring Corsica, trains her dog to exact vengeance for the murder of her son.

But man's unwholesome obsession with woman is stressed in "Le Chevelure" (1884; A Tress of Hair), where a man falls in love with women of prior ages and becomes mesmerized by a lock of hair from such a woman. This is purely a tale of psychological aberration, as is "Le Tic" (1884; The Spasm), a tale of a woman buried alive clearly derived from Poe's "The Premature Burial" and other of his tales (Poe is mentioned at the beginning of the story). "La Tombe" (1884; The Tomb) exhibits yet another man obsessed with women—this time a living one, who had died young, and whose body he madly exhumes. "La Morte" (1887; usually translated as "Was It a Dream?") portrays another man whose beloved has died unexpectedly; but in this case, when he goes to her gravesite, he visualizes a succession of corpses emerging from their graves and rewriting their tombstones to reflect the truth about themselves, rather than the bland and deceitful pieties that have been carved on those headstones. In a bitter twist, the man's beloved recasts her headstone to indicate that she had died while going out to meet another man.

Several non-supernatural tales tread the borderline between crime, gruesomeness, and moral degradation. "Un Fou" (1885; usually translated as "The Diary of a Madman") tells of a judge who, in an insidiously gradual manner, becomes convinced that killing is a law of nature and then himself engages in it, even going to the length of sentencing another man to death for a murder he committed. "Moiron" (1887) similarly tells of a universally beloved schoolteacher who admits to having murdered several of his charges. Interestingly, in a deathbed confession he claims that he did so as vengeance against a God whom he blames for the death of his own children. Contrast this story with "Conte de Noël" (1882; A Christmas Tale), where a woman's madness is cured by a Christian ceremony. The latter is a highly anomalous tale for a freethinker like Maupassant to have written.

"L'Auberge" (1886; The Inn) grimly portrays the death of a man while tending to a vacant hotel in the Alps during winter; but the focus is on the man's friend, who in searching for his colleague believes he hears his ghost calling to him. Maupassant imperishably etches the decay of the man's mind through isolation and fear. In "Le Diable" (1886; The Devil), both the son of an old woman who is on her deathbed and a woman in the village who is the designated watcher of the dead argue in an unseemly manner over how much money she should be paid for her services.

"La Petite Roque" (1885; The Little Roque Girl) is Maupassant's most exhaustive rumination on crime and its psychological ramifications. On the surface, the tale is merely one of the horrible rape and murder of a twelve-year-old girl and the increasing guilt and remorse felt by the killer, the mayor of the small town where the girl resided. In this sense the novelette anticipates the work of Patricia Highsmith and other suspense writers. But because the mayor begins to see visions of the dead girl on numerous occasions, the story comes close to the weird, although there is never any doubt that these visions are hallucinations engendered by the killer's own mind.

We now come to "Le Horla" (The Horla). The final version of this tale is unquestionably Maupassant's greatest contribution to weird fiction, and it is highly instructive to see how he fashioned this novelette by reworking not one but two earlier versions of it. The first, "Lettre d'un fou" (1885; Letter from a Madman), seems, when compared to the final version, scarcely more than the sketch of a story—or, conversely, a kind of philosophical analysis of the limitations of human sense-perception, followed by a brief account of the "supernatural passersby" (*The Horla* 55) the narrator detects in his bedroom, which leads him to believe he has gone mad. There is virtually no portrayal of the apparently invisible entity itself, nor its goals and purposes.

The second version, entitled "Le Horla" but lacking its significant subtitle, appeared in a magazine in 1886. This version opens as many of Maupassant's other tales do—as a narrative by someone else (in this case a physician who was treating a patient who believed himself mad) who recounts the actions and mental tribulations of the protagonist. In the course of the tale the physician does allow his patient to tell his own story, and Maupassant repeats several scenes from the earlier version, especially the invisible entity's consumption of milk and water. There are some conjectures by the patient that the entity is the vanguard of a race of similar creatures destined to overwhelm humanity, but not a great deal is made of this, and the focus is still on the patient's apparent insanity.

It is clear that Maupassant did not feel he had fully exhausted the aesthetic potential of the overall conception in either of these two drafts, and so he wrote a vastly expanded version, which appeared as a small book in 1887. Here he has wisely adopted (as he had done in the non-supernatural tale "Un Fou") the technique of the diary to lend immediacy to the narrator's account and also to depict the gradual decay of the man's mental state over the course of months. But what separates this final version from its predecessors is the slow, painstaking way in which the narrator's gradual certainty of the actual existence of the invisible entity creates terror, the fear of madness, and at the end a frantic desire to kill the entity if he can.

The seemingly irrelevant digression where the narrator is given a display of hypnotism (his female cousin is the subject) sets the stage for his realization that he himself has come under the hypnotic influence of the entity. It is only then that he begins to suspect that the creature is not solitary but one of a legion of entities who will become rulers of this earth in the future.

It is worth discussing the very term *horla*—a word coined by Maupassant. There is a strong likelihood that he intended to convey the notion that the creature was *hors là* ("from out there"), i.e., that the entity comes from outside, not from the narrator's diseased mentality. Indeed, the narrator's mind degenerates precisely because of his increasingly clear awareness that there is such a creature lurking in his presence, largely undetected. As such, the tale becomes authentically supernatural and weird.

The invisible monster entered weird fiction no later than Fitz-James O'Brien's story "What Was It?" (1859), but it is unlikely that Maupassant read that tale. It is more instructive to gauge the influence of "The Horla" upon two celebrated successors, Ambrose Bierce's "The Damned Thing" (1893) and H. P. Lovecraft's "The Call of Cthulhu" (1926).

"The Damned Thing" is a compelling tale of an invisible creature that manifests itself to two men on a hunting expedition. Like Maupassant's protagonist, the narrator of Bierce's tale emphasizes the limitations of human senses as the reason why we cannot perceive the creature; as the protagonist memorably states at the end: "'I am not mad; there are colors that we cannot see. [¶] And, God help me! the Damned Thing is of such a color!'" (Bierce, *Short Fiction* 2.863). Whether this element alone is sufficient to indicate a literary influence is to be doubted. In 1894 Bierce had already denied the influence of O'Brien's tale on his own (Bierce, "Prattle" [*San Francisco Examiner*, 27 May 1894], in *Short Fiction* 1183–84), and although "The Horla" had appeared in English no later than George William Curtis's anthology *Modern Ghosts* (1890), it is not at all clear that Bierce read it or was affected by it.

We can have no doubt, however, as to the story's influence on Lovecraft. In a memorable passage in "Supernatural Horror in Literature" (1927) he states:

. . . Relating the advent to France of an invisible being who lives on water and milk, sways the minds of others, and seems to be the vanguard of a horde of extra-terrestrial organisms arrived on earth to subjugate and overwhelm mankind, this tense narrative is perhaps without a peer in its particular department . . . (Lovecraft, *Annotated Supernatural Horror* 52)

From this description alone we can see that Lovecraft—who read "The Horla" in Julian Hawthorne's multi-volume anthology *The Lock and Key Library* (1909), which he obtained in New York in 1922—found the story highly suggestive in his own evolving conception of Cthulhu. Cthulhu clearly "sways the minds of others" (through dreams rather than any kind of hypnosis), and also is clearly the vanguard of a race of creatures that will clearly overwhelm mankind, as the mestizo Castro tells Inspector Legrasse:

There had been aeons when other Things ruled on the earth, and They had had great cities. . . . They had, indeed, come themselves from the stars, and brought Their images with Them.

These Great Old Ones, Castro continued, were not composed altogether of flesh and blood. They had shape—for did not this star-fashioned image prove it?—but that shape was not made of matter. . . .

Then, whispered Castro, those first men formed the cult around small idols which the Great Ones shewed them; idols brought in dim aeras from dark stars. That cult would never die till the stars came right again, and the secret priests would take great Cthulhu from His tomb to revive His subjects and resume His rule of earth. (Lovecraft, *Collected Fiction* 2.38–39)

These and other passages in Lovecraft's story make clear how central "The Horla" was in the conception and execution of "The Call of Cthulhu" and, consequently, in the elaboration of the entire Cthulhu Mythos.

"Le Voyage du *Horla*" (1887; The Trip of *Le Horla*) is a curiosity, as it bears no relation whatever to "The Horla" except in its title. This is apparently a lightly fictionalized account of an actual balloon ride that Maupassant took on 8 July 1887. The trip became part of the publicity campaign by Maupassant's publisher, Paul Ollendorff, for the book version of *The Horla;* it was he who titled the balloon *Le Horla* (Steegmuller 257–59). For all that the narrative seems largely factual, there are elements of fantasy, terror, and even something of the cosmic in the recounting of this "fantastic voyage" that justify its inclusion in a collection of Maupassant's weird work.

Maupassant's final weird tale, and final story altogether prior to the onset of his madness, is "Qui sait?" (1890; Who Knows?). In many ways it sums up the totality of his weird work. This unnerving account of a misanthropic recluse who believes that his furniture walked out of his house of its own accord, then finds the furniture in an antique shop (the owner, and the furniture itself, subsequently disappear), only to discover that the furniture has returned to his house, is the epitome of Maupassant's tales of mental trauma—and it is exquisitely balanced between supernatural and psychological terror.

One final issue relating to Maupassant's weird fiction needs to be addressed. It has commonly been believed that most of his tales of madness were written toward the end of his career, when he himself was descending into paranoia as a result of his syphilis. But a careful study of the entirety of Maupassant's work reveals both that the weird can be found throughout the chronological range of his oeuvre, and that his intense interest—which perhaps could be said to amount to an obsession—in the multifaceted ways in which the human mind can become deranged emerged at an early stage in his career, and there is a systematic continuity between his early and his later tales, whether on this issue or on others to which he repeatedly returned. The aesthetic control he exercised to the very end, especially in the final version of "The Horla," militates against any facile conjecture that his own impending insanity was somehow the inspiration or catalyst of even his later stories.

Guy de Maupassant's weird output is impressive in scope, and it strongly influenced the subsequent tradition of weird writing. He definitively demonstrated the soundness of Poe's focus on the short story as the ideal vehicle for the weird tale, and his fusion of the supernatural with psychological aberration was pioneering. The subtitle of "The Horla" ("or, Modern Ghosts") encapsulates the entirety of Maupassant's weird writing, in that he emphasized the immediacy of a present-day setting, whether in the bustling city of Paris or in a poignantly evocative countryside, as the ideal venue for the conveyance of terror to a contemporary audience. The cynicism he displayed in regard to human motives may have had its influence upon such writers as Bierce, L. P. Hartley, Shirley Jackson, Roald Dahl, and other writers of satirical horror, while his rigorous focus on the shifting mental states of his narrators probably left its mark on such writers as Oliver Onions, Walter de la Mare, and other practitioners of the psychological ghost story. His tales cannot be fully appreciated except when read in French; but even in English they abundantly convey the dread, horror, and physical gruesomeness he unflinchingly portrayed in dozens of tales long and short.

Bibliography of Guy de Maupassant's Weird Tales

I here provide information on the short story collections by Maupassant in French that appeared in his lifetime, whether they contain any weird tales or not. I then provide information on the original publications in magazines or newspapers of the individual tales.

As Francis Steegmuller has recounted in an appendix to *Maupassant: A Lion in the Path* (353–60), the 1903 English translation of *The Life Work of Henri René Guy de Maupassant* included more than sixty stories that are not by Maupassant. Many of these tales have subsequently appeared in collections of Maupassant's tales, including his weird tales. Steegmuller himself maintained that it is "unlikely" that the actual authors of these stories would ever be found, but the authorship of these stories has in fact been subsequently determined and can be found on a website, *Which short stories are falsely attributed to Guy de Maupassant, and why?* (literature.stackexchange.com/ questions/14259/ which-short-stories-are-falsely-attributed-to-guy-de-maupassant-and-why).

I. Short Story Collections by Maupassant

La Maison Tellier. Paris: Victor-Havard, 1881. Paris: Ollendorff, 1891. [*Contains:* "La Maison Tellier"; "Sur l'eau" (first version); "Histoire d'une fille de ferme"; "En famille"; "Le Papa de Simon"; "Une Partie de champagne"; "Au printemps"; "La Femme de Paul." (The 1891 edition adds "Les Tombales.")]

Mademoiselle Fifi. Brussels: Kistemackers, 1882. Paris: Havard, 1883. [*Contains* (1883 edition): "Mademoiselle Fifi"; "Madame Baptiste"; "La Rouille"; "Marroca"; "La Bûche"; "La Relique"; "Le Lit"; "Fou?"; "Réveil"; "Une Ruse"; "A Cheval"; "Un Réveillon"; "Mots d'Amour"; "Une Aventure parisienne"; "Deux Amis"; "Le Voleur"; "Nuit de Noël"; "Le Remplaçant."]

Contes de la bécasse. Paris: Rouveyre et G. Blond, 1883. Paris: Victor-Havard, 1887. [*Contains:* "La Bécasse"; "Ce Cochon de Morin"; "La Folle"; "Pierrot"; "Menuet"; "La Peur"; "Farce normande"; "Les Sabots"; "La Rampailleuse"; "En mer"; "Un Normand"; "La Testament"; "Aux champs"; "Un Coq chanta"; "Un Fils"; "Saint-Antoine"; "L'Aventure de Walter Schnaffs."]

Miss Harriet. Paris: Victor-Havard, 1884. [*Contains:* "Miss Harriet"; "L'Héritage"; "Denis"; "L'Ane"; "Idylle"; "La Ficelle"; "Garçon, un bock! . . ."; "Le Baptême"; "Regret"; "Mon Oncle Jules"; "En Voyage"; "La Mère Sauvage."]

Les Soeurs Rondoli. Paris: Ollendorff, 1884. [*Contains:* "Les Soeurs Rondoli"; "La Patronne"; "Le Petit Fût"; "Lui?"; "Mon Oncle Sosthène"; "Le Mal d'André"; "Le Pain maudit"; "Le Cas de Mme. Luneau"; "Un Sage"; "Le Parapluie"; "Le Verrou"; "Rencontre"; "Suicides"; "Décorét"; "Châli."]

Claire de lune. Paris: Ollendorff, 1884, 1888. [*Contains:* "Claire de lune"; "Un Coup d'état"; "Le Loup"; "L'Enfant"; "Conte de Noël"; "La Reine Hortense"; "Le Pardon"; "La Légende du Mont Saint-Michel"; "Une Veuve"; "Mademoiselle Cocotte"; "Les Bijoux"; "Apparition." (The 1888 edition adds "La Porte"; "Le Père"; "Moiron"; "Nos Lettres"; "La Nuit (Cauchemar).")]

Yvette. Paris: Victor-Havard, 1885. [*Contains:* "Yvette"; "Le Retour"; "L'Abondonné: Les Idées du colonel"; "Promenade"; "Fripouille"; "Le Garde"; "Berthe."]

Toine. Paris: C. Marpon et E. Flammarion, 1885. [*Contains:* "Toine"; "L'Ami Patience"; "La Dot"; "Rencontre"; "Le Lit 29"; "Le Protecteur"; "Bombard"; "La Chevelure"; "Le Père Mongilet"; "L'Armoire"; "La Chambre 11"; "Les Prisonniers"; "Nos Anglais"; "Le Moyen de Roger"; "La Confession"; "La Mère aux monstres"; "La Confession de Théodule Sabot."]

Contes du jour et de la nuit. Paris: C. Marpon et E. Flammarion, 1885. [*Contains:* "Le Crime au père Boniface"; "Rose"; "L'Aveu"; "La Parure"; "Le Bonheur"; "Le Vieux"; "Un Lâche"; "L'Ivrogne"; "Une Vendetta"; "Coco"; "La Main"; "Le Gueux"; "Un Parricide"; "Le Petit"; "La Roche aux Guillemots"; "Tombouctou"; "Histoire vraie"; "Adieu"; "Souvenir"; "La Confession."]

Monsieur Parent. Paris: Ollendorff, 1886. [*Contains:* "Monsieur Parent"; "La Bête à maît' Belhomme"; "A vendre"; "L'Inconnue"; "La Confidence"; "Le Baptême"; "Imprudence"; "Tribuneaux rustiques"; "L'Épingle"; "Les Bécasses"; "En Wagon"; "Ça ira"; "Découverte"; "Solitude"; "Au bord du lit"; "Petit Soldat."]

La Petite Roque. Paris: Victor-Havard, 1886. [*Contains:* "La Petite Roque"; "L'Épave"; "L'Ermite"; "Mademoiselle Perle"; "Rosalie Prudent"; "Sur les chats"; "Sauvée"; "Madame Parisse"; "Julie Romain"; "Le Père Amable."]

La Main gauche. Paris: Ollendorff, 1889. [*Contains:* "Allouma"; "Hautot père et fils"; "Boitelle"; "L'Ordonnance"; "Le Lapin"; "Un Soir"; "Les Pingles"; "Douchoux"; "Le Rendezvous"; "Le Porte"; "La Morte."]

L'Inutile Beauté. Paris: Victor-Havard, 1890. [*Contains:* "L'Inutile Beauté"; "Le Champ d'oliviers"; "Mouche"; "Le Noyé"; "L'Épreuve"; "Le Masque"; "Un Portrait"; "L'Infirme"; "Les 25 francs de la Supérieure"; "Un Cas de divorce"; "Qui sait?"]

II. Publications of Individual Stories

"L'Apparition" (An Apparition). *Le Gaulois* (4 April 1883). In *Claire de lune*.

"L'Auberge" (The Inn). *Les Lettres et les Arts* (1 September 1886).

"Auprès d'un Mort" (Beside a Dead Man). *Gil Blas* (30 January 1883).

"Le Chevelure" (A Tress of Hair). *Gil Blas* (13 May 1884). In *Toine*.

"Conte de Noël" (A Christmas Tale). *Le Gaulois* (25 December 1882). In *Claire de lune*.

"Le Diable" (The Devil). *Le Gaulois* (5 August 1886).

"Le Docteur Héraclius Gloss" (Doctor Heraclius Gloss). *Revue de Paris* (15 November and 1 December 1921).

"En Mer" (At Sea). *Gil Blas* (12 February 1883). In *Contes de la bécasse*.

"Fou?" (Mad?). *Gil Blas* (23 August 1882). In *Mademoiselle Fifi*.

"Un Fou" (The Diary of a Madman). *Le Gaulois* (10 September 1885).

"Un Fou?" (A Madman?). *Figaro* (23 August 1882).

"Le Horla" (The Horla [short version]). *Gil Blas* (26 October 1886). *Le Horla* [long version]. Paris: Ollendorff, 1887.

"L'Horrible" (The Horrible). *Le Gaulois* (18 May 1884).

"Lettre d'un fou" (Letter from a Madman). *Gil Blas* (17 February 1885).

"Le Loup" (The Wolf). *Le Gaulois* (14 November 1882). In *Claire de lune*.

"Lui?" (He?). *Gil Blas* (3 July 1883). In *Les Soeurs Rondoli*.

"La Main" (The Hand). *Le Gaulois* (23 December 1883). In *Contes du jour et de la nuit*.

"La Mère aux monstres" (The Mother of Monsters). *Gil Blas* (12 June 1883). In *Toine*.

"Moiron." *Gil Blas* (27 September 1887). In *Claire de lune*.

"La Morte" (Was It a Dream?). *Gil Blas* (31 May 1887). In *La Main gauche*.

"La Nuit (Cauchemar)" (Night: A Nightmare). *Gil Blas* (26 December 1882). In *Claire de lune*.

"La Petite Roque" (The Little Roque Girl). *Gil Blas* (18–23 December 1885). In *La Petite Roque*.

"La Peur" [I] (Fear). *Le Gaulois* (23 October 1882). In *Contes de la bécasse*.

"La Peur" [II] (Fear). *Figaro* (25 July 1884).

"Qui sait?" (Who Knows?). *Echo de Paris* (6 April 1890). In *L'Inutile Beauté*.

"Sur l'eau" (On the River). In *La Maison Tellier*.

"Terreur" ("Horror") [poem]. In Maupassant's *Des Vers*. Paris: Charpentier, 1880.

"Le Tic" (The Spasm). *Le Gaulois* (14 July 1884).

"La Tombe" (The Tomb). *Gil Blas* (29 July 1884).

"Le Voyage du *Horla*" (The Trip of *Le Horla)*. *Figaro* (16 July 1887).

"Une Vendetta" (A Vendetta). *Le Gaulois* (14 October 1883). In *Contes du jour et de la nuit*.

Works Cited

Bierce, Ambrose. *The Short Fiction of Ambrose Bierce: A Comprehensive Edition,* ed. S. T. Joshi, Lawrence I. Berkove, and David E. Schultz. (Knoxville: University of Tennessee Press, 2006. 3 vols.

Boyd, Ernest. *Guy de Maupassant: A Biographical Study.* Boston: Little, Brown, 1926,

Lovecraft, H. P. *The Annotated Supernatural Horror in Literature.* Ed. S. T. Joshi. New York: Hippocampus Press, 2nd ed. 2012.

———. *Collected Fiction: A Variorum Edition.* Ed. S. T. Joshi. New York: Hippocampus Press, 2015–17. 4 vols.

Maupassant, Guy de. *The Horla.* Tr. Charlotte Mandell. Hoboken, NJ: Melville House, 2005.

———. *Horla and Other Stories.* Tr. and ed. Ernest Boyd. New York: Random House, 1925.

———. *Mademoiselle Fifi and Other Stories.* Tr. and ed. Ernest Boyd. New York: Random House, 1922.

———. *The Sisters Rondoli and Other Stories.* Tr. and ed. Ernest Boyd. New York: Random House, 1923.

Steegmuller, Francis. *Maupassant: A Lion in the Path.* New York: Random House, 1949.

The Fantastic

Guy de Maupassant

Translated by S. T. Joshi

[First published in *Le Gaulois* (7 October 1883).—Ed.]

Slowly, over the past twenty years, the supernatural has departed from our souls. It has evaporated the way a perfume evaporates when the bottle is uncorked. Placing the opening to our nostrils and taking a deep, deep breath, we detect no more than a vague scent. It's finished.

Our grandchildren will be amazed at their fathers' naïve beliefs about things so absurd and implausible. They will never know what was once, at night, the fear of the mysterious, the fear of the supernatural. Only a few hundred people still inclined to believe in spirits, in the influence of certain creatures or certain things, in lucid somnambulism, and fake ghosts. It's finished.

Our poor, restless, powerless, limited minds, frightened by effects of whose cause we are ignorant, terrified by the ceaseless and incomprehensible spectacle of the world, have trembled for centuries under the strange and infantile beliefs which have served to explain the unknown. Today, we sense that we were mistaken, and we seek to understand without real knowledge. The first great step has been taken. We have rejected the mysterious, which for us is no more than the unexplored.

In twenty years, fear of the unreal will no longer exist even among country folk. It seems that Creation has taken another aspect, another shape, another significance than before. And the end result will certainly be the end of fantastic literature.

This literature occurred in very diverse eras and manners, from the chivalric romance, the *Arabian Nights,* the heroic poem, up to fairy tales and the disturbing stories of Hoffmann and Edgar Poe.

When humanity unhesitatingly believed [in such things], fantastic writers took no trouble at all in spinning their astonishing stories. From the beginning they thrust us into the impossible and kept us there, creating an infinite variety of implausible combinations and apparitions, all the terrifying mechanisms to create terror.

But, when scepticism at last entered into our minds, the art [of the fantastic] became more subtle. The writer searched for nuances, prowling around the supernatural rather than penetrating it. He created chilling effects while remaining within the limits of the possible, hurling our souls into hesitation and bewilderment. The uncertain reader, remaining ignorant, lost his footing as if on a body of water whose depths he could not see; he clung desperately to reality only to plunge even deeper, struggling anew in an arduous and feverish confusion as in a nightmare.

The extraordinarily terrifying power of Hoffmann and Edgar Poe derives from this skill, this specific manner of bringing us into contact with the fantastic, of disturbing us with natural events in which, nevertheless, there is something inexplicable and close to impossible.

[The balance of the essay consists of a personal reminiscence of the Russian writer Ivan Turgenev.]

Waiting in Carcosa

Ann K. Schwader

A pallid mask awaits us all
in token of the coming king
while soft as sorrow, black stars fall.

When truth turns phantom, does its call
diminish into whispering?
A pallid mask awaits us all

becomes another rumor scrawled
to pass the time—an idle thing—
while soft as sorrow, black stars fall

unnoticed. Nothing can forestall
this subtle sense of shattering:
a pallid mask awaits us. All

precautions proved too late, too small,
too limited. Contagion sings
softly of sorrow, black stars fall

to jaundiced tatters, & we crawl
before His prophecy that brings
a pallid mask awaiting all
when, soft as sorrow, black stars fall.

Markovia

Katherine Kerestman

At first glance, the wispy cirrus clouds gliding through the deep blue sky seem almost to be in danger of getting caught on the crenellations of the crumbling, once-white stone turrets of the empty castle in ruins, the long-abandoned keep atop a dismal mountain that looms threateningly over its unkempt, craggy fellows in the Carpathian Mountains of Transylvania. An abject heap of coal-black rock, the terrible precipice is cloaked in an unwieldy mantle of thick-grown firs that extends from its jagged mountain peak and spreads as a train over the boulders at its base. Crystalline rivulets of water forge rock-strewn paths down all sides of the mountain, driving relentlessly through each clump of trees to slake the thirst of the flora that is spreading over the castle—the vegetation that is transfiguring the castle's kingly emerald fir cloak into its loathsome funereal shroud, rendering the parts of the castle that peek out from the encroaching branches, to all appearances, a windswept skull poking out from its vine-smothered grave.

Upon closer inspection, if one were foolhardy enough to get closer, one could see the black spots, the amorphous black shapes that lurk among the gnarled branches of the encroaching wood. Swaying slowly in the sylvan breeze, the sinister limbs of the strange firs sometimes give a little bounce when the unhallowed forms roosting upon them take wing and rise up to fling black stains upon the white of the wispy clouds and the blue of the end-of-summer sky, as if the white and the blue of the firmament were but fairy fabrics to be unraveled and rent.

Cold autumnal winds arrive with fury from the frozen north, and they drive tempestuous triple-decked storm clouds before them. The dark clouds bounce against one another, as if they were balls on a billiard table, pushed toward the mountain by the furious gusts of icy air. The nights grow long, as dead of winter looms, and the sun goes into hiding.

Unabashed, the cawing black crows survey the desolate castle below, noting every small thing that creeps on eight legs or slithers in the mud; and they swoop down upon each morsel of tiny life they spy, filling their bellies with death. No living thing long survives the snare of the spreading forest and its lethal flock. From every direction is heard a horrific symphony: the calling of the inky birds, a low and squawking, raspy birdsong, a grating cacophony of caws and croaks, in concert with the snare-drum percussion of the fluttering of thousands of wings, the rustling feathers whipping the wind. Foul-smelling is the forest covering the mountain, foul with the stench of decaying brush and animal corpses, dissolving into the slime, rotting toadstools and moss.

Dismal, too, is the vale, where the unruly brush sends up straggly shoots between the rib bones of cows and through the eyeless sockets of the bovine skulls that lie strewn about. Here and there uneven low stone piles mark the places of long-gone structures, obscured by the rapacious yellow and brown grasses bending in the wind. Shards of broken gray crockery and rusted iron kettles stand at odd angles, half sunken into the earth and overgrown with brambles, relics of hearths that used to warm homes. That was a very long time ago, of course, before he came.

Markovia had, long ago, been a happy place, before the final days. From the white mountaintop castle that had, in days gone by, brightened the sky with the reflected rays of the sun itself, Duke Radu and his beloved consort Elena had once administered the duchy with justice and honor, a long time ago. The farms in the valley had flourished then, surrounded by the Carpathians, which shielded them from winter storms, and from the advances of unfriendly neighbors too. Harvests were plentiful then, and on market day the town square was a bustling place, ringed around with high-piled carts of apples and cabbages and other good things to eat.

Grown-ups would barter the fruits of their labor, while children played with hoops in the street, or dodged each other, running between the wagons.

Back then, on warm summer nights when it was too nice to go inside, the villagers would rest from their labors upon the smooth-worn benches in the gravelly dust of the tavern yard. Over mugs of cider that had been chilling in the icehouse and dark ale frothing over the rims of sweating tankards, they would rehearse the stirring ballads of ancient heroes, which they all had by heart. On such occasions the good people would sometimes remark, with many a knowing nod and a wink, that most assuredly the good Lady Barbara, the beloved heiress of Duke Radu and Duchess Elena, had been blessed by the fairies.

Fair of face, lithesome of form, with thick flowing black hair that was always falling in the way of her sparkling azure eyes, Barbara was her parents' great delight. They bestowed upon her chests heavy with jewels and gowns of cloth of gold brought for her across oceans and mountains, from far-off lands at the very edge of the earth. Great wisdom, too, they lavished upon her, by means of priceless books and rare knowledge taught her by learned tutors renowned throughout the lands for the profundity of their wisdom. Gentleness and kindness of heart were the gifts conferred upon the daughter of Markovia by Nature, and her good parents found for her in their duchy worthy objects for the exercise of her own charitable inclinations. Tutors and merchants, peasants and children, and even the dogs in the market and the rabbits in the wood all felt lighter of heart whenever Barbara was near. Over the course of twenty happy years, Barbara grew in beauty and in understanding, and the citizens of the Duchy of Markovia seemed to be in very good hands for at least another half-century, lacking only a goodly consort for their Lady.

On her twentieth birthday, therefore, gentle princes from realms near and far, and goodly ladies too, came by invitation to the birthday ball for Barbara. It so chanced that the winged urchin of love drew Barbara's blue eyes in the direction of Dan, a most handsome and noble warrior and worthy statesmen, the second son of King Sigismund of the neighboring kingdom on the other side of the mountain—and drew Dan's brown eyes toward the pretty orbs of sweet Barbara. With much grace, they opened the dance, and then they waltzed again, and throughout the warm and starry night each was with great difficulty only able to bend his or her eyes from the prospect of the beloved, which they were obliged to do out of politeness for the rest of the joyful company.

Pages dressed in white embroidered with gold blew their trumpets at the top of the magnificent stone staircase as they announced the arrival of each distinguished guest. When "Vlad Dracul, Voivode of Wallachia," was announced, the Duke and Duchess and Lady Barbara made their way through the assembly to greet their illustrious visitor. The voivode took Barbara's delicate hand into his own cold palm and, bending very low, lightly placed his icy lips upon it. The prince of Wallachia then raised his eyes and paid many charming compliments to the lovely young woman. "You are most welcome to the Castle of Markovia, Your Highness," she replied. "Please enter and enjoy our fête." The duke introduced the voivoid to Prince Dan, who had now arrived to claim Barbara's promise to be his partner for the next minuet. Vlad Dracul straightened his spine, and his brow contracted; his piercing black eyes narrowed and seemed even to glare at the Prince. The voivode continued to converse with his hosts, but Barbara and Dan had forgotten all about him.

They talked at every chance they could contrive. They talked of books and fables, the lessons they had learnt in their youth. They talked of future desires, of great destinies for their nations. They talked because each loved to hear the other speak. From that wonderful day, brave Prince Dan wooed the gentle Barbara. All Markovia rejoiced in their happiness, and in the sweet promise of lasting joy in the land. That was when the sky turned black.

On that sorrowful day, Barbara and Dan had beguiled a sunny morning riding in the forest, he on his regal black stallion and she on her proud white mare. The horses' manes had been blowing in the wind, and the bells on the harnesses had been merrily tinkling, as the lovers cantered playfully along the paths, until they came to ground not cleared, where the horses needed to pick their way carefully through the brush and fallen branches, beneath the enveloping canopy of great, overspreading ancient fir trees, through which wooded ceiling the rays of the sun dared not shine. They rode for some hours, and then they dismounted and walked beneath the giant pines and beech trees. Dan picked wild violets and fashioned from them a bouquet, of which he made a pretty present to his lady-love. Barbara tucked the blossoms into the bodice of her ivory gown, which ornament pleased her more than all the cloth-of-gold of Araby. She sat down upon the mossy ground to watch the noisy blackbirds flying from limb to limb in the branches overhead. The sweethearts took some wine and bread from the saddlebags and then, being refreshed, decided to return to the castle on the mountain, where they were to dine with the duke and duchess in the great hall that night.

The wind began to blow as they were turning their horses back toward the way they had come. Soft whistling soon accompanied the blowing, and the air grew colder. Leaves rustled on the trees, their crackling noise replacing the cawing of the blackbirds as the music of the wood. The pattering of rain drops joined the ominous orchestra of whistling wind and crackling leaves. The shrill squawking of the blackbirds interjected an occasional trumpet blast. As the air grew colder, the whistling grew louder, and the pattering rain beat on the drum of the forest floor and on the pine-needle cymbals on the branches of the towering old trees.

The horses became skittish, and Dan took hold of both their reins. He dismounted to calm the animals, for he knew how to speak to horses. Barbara bent down toward the neck of her mare, to shield herself against the horse as the wind grew in strength. As a tremendous bolt of lightning struck a tree and turned it to cinders, the distraught black stallion reared on his hind legs. Dan dropped the reins of Barbara's mount and turned his attention to the terrified beast. A great gust of wind arose that forced the trees into nearly horizontal poses, and bent Dan over, as well. As he straightened up he saw a figure in a large black cloak, its billowing folds blown about by the tempest, leap onto the white mare and gallop away with Barbara, whose screams were lost in the uproar of the storm.

Dan gave pursuit. Grimly, he felt for the sword in its scabbard and patted the dagger in his vest, as he looked about him on all sides for any sign of Barbara. He urged his horse on, who needed no prodding. Through brambles they raged, leaving their blood upon the thorns. They emerged from the cursed wood into the opacity of black night. The clearing was dimly illuminated by the insipid glow of the sickly moon, whose ineffectual light was sufficient only to give boast that the dark now held the earth in thrall. Man and beast went forth into the dark.

The brave stallion bore Dan up and down the brooding mountain, maintaining his footing though the road was steep and the pebbles rolled downhill beneath his hooves. Although renowned for his prowess in the hunt, Dan was able to find neither the trail of his lady nor her abductor; neither tracks nor bent branches, nor dust disturbed did point the way. The sterile moon disappeared, smothered to oblivion beneath great piles of rising black clouds, which washed over the earth as waves upon the shore at high tide. Dan knew he could not find Barbara alone, without light, and so he blew his horn to summon aid from his men. And he dismounted to kneel in the dust for a moment in sorrow.

Within a quarter of an hour what appeared to be mystical orbs sent from heaven in answer to Dan's prayer were seen to ascend the mountain. It was the gold and silver armor of fifty mighty knights glowing and gleaming in the yellow torchlight. Gravely, the prince greeted his guard. Apprising them of the urgency of his summons, he directed his captain to order his men into every direction to rescue the Lady Barbara. He offered a prize of great value to the man who should bring her back to him safe, but no reward was needed, for each man would fain offer his own life to redeem her, so beloved was the lady by all. The troop spread out to reconnoiter the terrain, their torches and lamps little yellow lights bobbing through the trees as they searched.

As the red glow on the horizon crept into the black sky, Dan knew he would have to return to the castle to break the woeful news to the duke and duchess, Barbara's parents. Dolorously he went. He let his tears fall as they might upon his horse's neck on the journey. As he approached the drawbridge, Dan composed himself, for the sake of Radu and Elena. The parents met him at the drawbridge, for they had been watching fearfully all the night because Barbara had not come home. Elena saw at once that Dan was returned alone, whereupon such a great cry issued from her that all who were present felt that surely she must be rent apart by it. Radu stepped forward and started to ask Dan for an explanation, but the sorrow on Dan's countenance stopped his words, and the duke fell to his knees and sobbed. Dan dismounted and embraced the grieving parents. He told them of Barbara's abduction by the cloaked figure in the harrowing storm that had murdered the joyful day. Dan filled his water jugs and fed and watered the stallion, after which he and Radu departed to rejoin the knights, leaving Elena weeping on the drawbridge.

The delicate rose rays of the dawn on the horizon were pushing back the dark, and the valiant knights were still searching. Glimpsing something white among the brown needles of a lightning-stricken tree, Dan pulled on the reins to turn his horse into the brush. He halted the animal, raised himself up in his stirrups, and stretched his sword over his head to fetch down from the high branches of the dead pine tree the beautiful Barbara's pointed hat and veil. As he retrieved the relics from the grasp of the dead limbs, he saw that the hat and veil were tattered and soaked with blood. A hush fell upon the company, who crossed themselves and then resumed the search.

Month after month, as summer fell to autumn, and autumn was laid waste by winter, they looked for Barbara. Villagers formed volunteer companies to aid in the search. At last Markovia went into mourning. The castle doors and windows were draped in black silks, and the duke and duchess and all their court wore only black garments. The country grew silent; gatherings after a day's work at the tavern were solemn, rather than joyous, affairs. Children seldom played in the marketplace anymore. Families kept close.

One day a woman of the village ran up the mountain to the castle drawbridge and cried for succor of the duke. The sad parents gave orders to the chamberlain that the poor woman be admitted to the great hall and be permitted to tell them her story. Agathe, for that was the woman's name, cried, "O, great Lord and Lady, as you are good and wise sovereigns, I know you will help me. My son has vanished. He is only six years old. He was sent to bring back our black sheep from the pasture this morning, and now it is evening and he is nowhere to be found. Pray, have pity upon your humblest subjects, my Lord." The duchess clutched at the mourning stuff of the duke's sleeve. Radu called the poor woman to come to the throne, wherefrom he rose and took the woman's rough hand into his own. "Be of good hope, dear mother, for if it be the will of God my brave knights will bring your child back to you," Radu told her and bade her return home and wait for news. He ordered a search party to look for the boy.

That evening the knights returned to the castle, bearing the body of the slain child across the saddle of one of the sad company who was thinking of his own son at home. Radu met with his captain in his chamber. The captain informed Radu that the boy's throat had been ripped open, and he seemed to have been deprived of all his blood, so pale was he; that must have been the cause of his death. Radu sent one of his retainers to return the boy to his mother, and he sent word of his great sorrow and a purse to cover the poor woman's expenses and the burial of her little son.

The child's death reopened the wounds of the hearts of Elena and Radu, freshening the sorrow that had not yet diminished. Although their former joy had turned to grief, yet the worthy rulers still were endeavoring to rule their duchy with the noblesse oblige they felt was their subjects' due.

Several days later a crowd of villagers were crying outside the castle for justice from the duke. A good father and loyal subject, one of Radu's tenants, had disappeared while plowing his field. A search party found only his blood-soaked coat in the woods. Thereafter, calls upon the duke for help began to increase in frequency. An infant girl, an aged grandmother, a pregnant goodwife disappeared, and only bloodless corpses or rags of blood-drenched clothing was ever recovered.

The great King Sigismund, the royal parent of Prince Dan, sent his army—commanded by his own son—over the jagged mountain peak to aid his beset neighbor, the Duke Radu. As Prince Dan was leading the chivalrous host on the treacherous journey an earthquake split the ridge, and the raining rocks and boulders buried the knights of good King Sigismund. Dan, who rode at the head of the brave host, did keep his seat as his horse leapt over the gorge in the mountainside—even as the gap was widening under his hooves. Of the renowned army, he only survived.

As Dan and his valiant steed wended along the mountainside, they peered down upon the blighted valley below. Dan shook his head and pulled on the reins. He dismounted in dismay. He saw that the fields had been abandoned, and many of the huts had been torn down for firewood. The messengers of the duke had already brought word that many of the villagers had emigrated to other lands, and that those who stayed behind had been quarreling over food. Dan got to his knees and peered over the edge of a cliff for a better look. He removed his helmet and heard the weeping and the wailing of the people. With a great sigh he remounted.

The sky was twilit by the time Dan arrived at the castle. There was no guard at the drawbridge. Dan passed through the gate with great vigilance; with great caution he entered the courtyard. He discovered it to be abandoned. No guards nor servants did he spy. No courtiers nor tradesmen. All was still, and all was silent. Dan entered the great hall of the castle. He looked about the vast chamber, with its high stone walls and great stained-glass windows. He could just barely distinguish the tapestries hanging upon the walls, for the torches were unlit. Rats scurried along the edges of the floor, close to the walls. Webs obscured portions of the windows. Dan climbed the great staircase, scanning for movements in every direction and looking over his shoulder. He paused at the top of the stairs to look about him. Despite the increasing darkness, Dan did not light a torch, lest he make known his position to an unseen enemy. The sound of scuffling, and of furniture thrown against the wall arrested his attention. The sounds came from behind a closed door.

Dan pushed upon the hefty door that was made of great slabs of wood held together by great wrought iron hinges. It did not move. Dan moved several steps back and then pushed harder upon the door with more momentum, forcing it open. Fallen chairs lay behind the door. Clambering over the furnishings in disarray, Dan observed another door in the far wall, to which he hastened. He threw it open and gasped.

Drawing his sword, he rushed into the chamber—he rushed toward the horrific mêlée he was witnessing. Radu was being attacked by several cloaked villains. The duke lay upon the floor, struggling with the various appendages that were holding him fast, the powerful arms of the four cloaked men who were bent over him. One cloaked assailant raised his head and turned it toward Dan. Dan recognized the Wallachian voivode he had met at Barbara's birthday ball. With a hellish hiss, the deathly pale Vlad Dracul drew back his lips and bared sharp teeth that were dripping with the blood of Radu.

Brave Prince Dan cried, "I will send you to hell, you spawn of Lucifer!" as he rushed upon the vampire. He bore the steel of his sword into the gut of the monster—up to the very hilt. Alas, it had not the power to slay the undead. Dan withdrew his sword from the monstrous dead flesh and raised it over his head, preparing to slash the vampire again, when he saw Barbara, her complexion the same hue as her ivory gown, and her mouth crimson with blood.

The unholy congregation rose from the mangled corpse that was once Radu, and the now-faceless head rolled away from the body of the slain duke, leaving a trail of blood and tissue on the stone floor. The damned creatures now turned their attention to the prince, who battled most ardently, though one against four. His sword cut and pierced, but none of the enemy fell. They converged upon him, and four fanged mouths tore his flesh.

As his flesh was being ripped into pieces by the razor teeth and claws of the hellish crew—as Dan was praying to be received into paradise at this hour of his death—Elena was creeping along the wall, hugging the dirty tapestries. She was shaking from head to toe, stifling her sobs and her breaths, feeling for the door concealed behind the hangings. With trembling hands, she felt for the iron handle of the door and pulled it open as stealthily as she could—but the fiends heard the hinge creak, and they flew toward the duchess.

She ran up the narrow winding stone stairs to the door at the top and opened it. After she had attained the other side, she assayed with all her might to hold it shut against the vampires, but she was no match for their ungodly strength. As they forced the door open, Elena turned and ran to the crenellated edge of the tower. As the spawn of hell came toward her, Elena flung herself over the edge. Her body became impaled upon the branch of a decaying fir tree, which seemed to have stretched its limbs toward her for that demonic purpose.

The next day, when the few villagers who remained in Markovia made a journey to the white castle atop the mountain, in order to present to the good duke their petitions for his help in their misery, they were horrified. At the sight of the carnage and destruction, they fell upon their knees and they wept in sorrow. The grief-stricken peasants buried Radu and Elena and Prince Dan. And then they packed their wagons, and before nightfall they left Markovia utterly abandoned.

Markovia has stood deserted for nearly four centuries now. The primeval vegetation has reclaimed the mountain and the valley and has all but swallowed the castle. The predators of the dark forest are the new lords of the mountain. Rats have made a nest in the gowns in Barbara's chests. Bats and spiders hold court in the great hall. Webs have replaced the velvet tapestries that once hung upon the walls and are now disintegrated into rags. Black-cloaked figures lurk about the drawbridge and glide by the ancient well. Violent storms and earthquakes have reduced most of the castle to rocks.

The few travelers and adventurers who dare to set foot in Markovia ever live to tell of it. No one tries to resettle the land anymore. The jagged-edged mountain is obviously cursed, for all attempts to repopulate Markovia have ended in mysterious failure. Settlers have disappeared without a trace.

The inhabitants of the villages in neighboring mountains in the Carpathians, when they look toward the dreadful mountain of Markovia, often see strange red, purple, and blue lights (most notably on Walpurgis Night and the eve of the Feast of St. George). The people cross themselves and get down on their knees when that happens. Many go to the churches and light candles.

Few people speak of the mountain and the doomed lovers. Most avoid thinking about it.

Free Will vs. Love: John Collier and Brian McNaughton

David Rose

> "For Brian McNaughton seems to have mastered one of the most difficult of literary arts: to draw upon the classics of the field without losing his own voice."
>
> —S. T. Joshi, Afterword to *The Throne of Bones* (338)

> "I love what they write, unpleasant because I know I'll never be that good—Nabokov, Poe, and John Collier, to name just three . . ."
>
> —Brian McNaughton, "An Interview with World Fantasy Finalist Brian McNaughton"

> "Perhaps Clark Ashton Smith, with his delightful mixing of morbidity and humour and his evocative use of language, is the chief influence on McNaughton; but let me say bluntly that, in my humble opinion, McNaughton is a better prose writer than Smith."
>
> —S. T. Joshi, Afterword to *The Throne of Bones* (338)

I agree with S. T. Joshi on all counts. In so doing, I invariably must disagree with the late enigmatic horror writer from New Jersey. Brian McNaughton is as good and, in certain ways, surpasses many of his beloved predecessors. One of which he named.

No doubt, Smith was McNaughton's most recognizable influence as a prose stylist, but, especially in regard to McNaughton's secondary world fantasy, a number of themes explored and refined by John Collier are present, which, I submit, at a minimum equal Collier; examining deep conundrums with masterful narrative skill.

It is important to make clear that my perception of McNaughton surpassing Collier is admittedly subjective, but, more importantly, an aside when compared to the main position of this article: that both Collier and McNaughton fleshed out common themes in similar ways, the former certainly informing the latter.

One common theme is insatiability. Or perhaps better put, insatiability's consequences. In Collier's "The Lady on the Grey," we see the restless Ringwood out to seduce the local maidens, but soon seduced himself by the highest target of value. Woe to him and to his friend Bates. In McNaughton's "The Lecher of the Apothegm," Quodomass Phuonsa, a rapist and murderer, has grown tired of the usual throng of victims; he sets his eyes on an unsuspecting female ghoul, much to his misfortune.

Negative results of insatiability are also exquisitely illustrated in Collier's "Bottle Party." In this story, a big dreamer, Frank, is soon in possession of a wish-granting jinn. As we will soon examine, Frank is granted not only material excess but the woman of his dreams. Something similar occurs in McNaughton's earliest Seeluran[1] tale, "Vendriel and Vendreela." Originally appearing in *Weirdbook* #23/24 in 1988, "Vendriel and Vendreela" is the story of a powerful necromancer, fearfully referred to as Vendriel the Good. Bereft of his mother and now emotionally alone, Vendriel sets out to create the perfect woman: Lady Vendreela.

Both stories ("Bottle Party" and "Vendriel and Vendreela") beautifully and entertainingly showcase love, free will, and how, for either to exist, they must never interfere with the other.

It must be said, of course, the idea of tampering with free will/free agency at the cost of negating love is nothing new. Certainly not a rarity in many an artistic medium, and seen everywhere from silver screen hits like *Bruce Almighty* to esoteric debates over tenets of Judeo-Christianity. It is a theme well explored in conventional literature.

However, Collier's and McNaughton's use and exploration of it

---

1. Seelura is the world in which all the stories in McNaughton's award-winning *The Throne of Bones* are set. McNaughton's unfinished novelette "The Deposition of Leodiel Fand" is also set in this secondary world.

deserves added illumination—not only for the quality in which both men had written out their theses, but for both authors' stunning ability to inject a sense of pathos into tales otherwise entrenched in the macabre and unapologetically fantastic.

Collier's influence on McNaughton's "Vendriel and Vendreela" is as undeniable as it is delightful. Here we will see not only influence, but my argument that McNaughton raises the bar.

How were these dream women made? And what are they made of, and from?

Collier's brilliant "The Devil George and Rosie" seems to lay out much of the groundwork for McNaughton's coming woman. Abstract qualities are bound together, presented in human form: "She was complete in every particular, and all of the highest quality; she was a picture galley, an anthology of the poets, a precipitation of all that has ever been dreamed of love" (*Fancies and Goodnights* 166).

With regard to the creation of Lady Vendreela, observe McNaughton's own use of Collier's noted aesthetics, written in what Scott Connors referred to as his "wonderfully baroque style" (262):

> Stranger abstractions from the riches of the court were noted: she who had laughed as readily as wind-chimes grew dour: she whose hair was midnight on the sea in one light, slickenside coal in another, yet in whose blackness Polliel could smelt bronze and strike gold, went gray as a sunless fog; she whose skin was old ivory washed with honey and kissed by the shadow of a rose appeared one morning white as bone.
>
> Fancies overwrought by these real horrors might have inspired reports of less tangible thefts. The critic Ailiel Fronn wrote that certain lines from Pesquidor's *Seeluriad*, those describing the emergence of Filloweela, Goddess of Love, had gone unaccountably flat. The words were the same but the music had fled. Others professed dismay at a hitherto unseen insipidity in the erotic paintings of Omphiliard and the sensuous sculptures of Melphidor.
>
> Least credible of all, but believed to the point of general panic, was the assertion that the one perfect day of spring granted our capital city of Frothirot, when the steam of the rains has burned off

but the parching of summer not yet ignited, that this perfect day, so beloved of poets and pubescents of the randier sort, and popularly known as Filloweela's Birthday, had absented itself from the calendar for the past several years. (*The Throne of Bones* 286–89)

This undeniable enhancement of beauty is perhaps accredited to McNaughton's use and preference of second-world immersion of the Tolkien type, allowing for added description and narrative because little if any of the author's work has already been done for him. We can see further McNaughton's enhancements in his description of the Lady: "Then Lady Vendreela appeared from nowhere, and all losses seemed restored. The lines of Pesquidor, the tints of Omphiliard, the curves of Melphidor, even the lithe legs of Istreela Fand: such losses lost meaning with the emergence of the enchantress" (*The Throne of Bones* 289–90).

And thus we arrive squarely at free will. The perfect woman is made—now what? According to Collier and McNaughton; trouble:

> Unwilling to test the diagnosis, Vendriel stared at Vendreela, who stared back at him adoringly. He thought a thought and she made it flesh. He wept at her beauty and ardor. He whispered, "I love you," and he knew the truth.
>
> His first thought was to call for his apothecary to decant them both their deaths. As he was a Vendren, his second thought was to defy the gods and dupe his creature into the belief that she had a soul of her own.
>
> "You have deluded yourself!" he cried, as did she. (*The Throne of Bones* 291)

And Collier's preceding contribution? Not only a similar conclusion, but notice his description of Frank's perfect, magically provided woman:

> "Out came the most beautiful girl you can possibly imagine. Cleopatra and all that lot were hags and frumps compared with her. "Where am I?" said she. "What is this beautiful palace? What am I doing on a tiger-skin? Who is this handsome young prince?"

"It's me!" cried Frank, in a rapture. "It's me!"

. . . The jinn could say no more, but stood about the room, inflating his monstrous chest, and showing off his plump and dusky muscles. "You need not be afraid of him," said Frank. "He is only a jinn. Pay no attention to him. Tell me if you really love me."

"Of course I do," said she.

"Well, say so," said he, "Why don't you say so?"

"I have said so, "said she. "Of course I do. Isn't that saying so?"

This vague, evasive reply dimmed all Frank's happiness, as if a cloud had come over the sun. Doubt sprang up in his mind, and entirely ruined moments of exquisite bliss. (*Fancies and Goodnights* 6–7)

We have dream women incapable of loving the men who brought them into being. Additionally, we have the use of magic and a creeping sense of doom that we soon expect to fall on the heads of our misguided heroes. The distinguishing feature is simply the authors' preferences. Whereas McNaughton wallows in pain and beauty, tainted by darkness and sin, Collier enjoys using his work to mirthfully poke at the flippant and the absurd.

In "Vendriel and Vendreela" we see that magic is used by the very hand of Lord Vendriel: a dark art practiced by the man wishing for perfection and love. The hint of coming tragedy is carefully laid out in the dangers of both the character and his craft. In "Bottle Party" the magic is a jinn, and the pending tragedy of Frank, who hopes for both perfection and love as well, is hinted at by way of the jinn's rascally nature.

By carefully examining both Collier and McNaughton's use of free will and love, we are eventually brought back to their other shared treasure: insatiability. Like their creators, Lord Vendriel and Frank share something: a perfectionist's nature. Both writers seem to suggest that perfectionism and insatiability are intrinsically linked, which poses the question: does insatiability prompt perfectionism, or does perfectionism lead to insatiability? This may be a quandary both authors, as the great ones often do, left for the reader to decide.

Works Cited

Collier, John. *Fancies and Goodnights*. 1951. New York: New York Review Books, 2003.

Connors, Scott. "The Ghoul." In S. T. Joshi, ed. *Icons of Horror and the Supernatural*. Westport, CT: Greenwood Icons, 2007. 1.243–66.

Joshi, S. T. Afterword to *The Throne of Bones* by Brian McNaughton. Black River, NY: Terminal Fright, 1997. 338–41.

McNaughton, Brian. "The Deposition of Leodiel Fand." *Lore* 2, No. 1 (April 2012).

———. "An Interview with World Fantasy Finalist Brian McNaughton." Interview by Jeff VanderMeer. First published at *Nightscapes* (August 1999). Last updated August 2004, www.epberglund.com/RGttCM/nightscapes/NS11/ns11nf1.htm

———. *The Throne of Bones*. Black River, NY: Terminal Fright, 1997.

All Kings and Princes Bow Down unto Me

Darrell Schweitzer

There was a girl by the name of Anna, twelve or thereabout, of an age to be noticing boys though not yet with any serious interest, but old enough for her head to be filled with extravagant notions of romance, which she had acquired from reading and from movies. She was also certain that she was or should become an old-fashioned girl, though she wasn't entirely sure what that entailed. But it did seem fitting that a romantic, old-fashioned girl should on occasion slip out at night and dance in the moonlight.

So, having entertained *this* notion for some time, she finally put it into practice one spring night, and, well after the rest of the household was asleep, she slipped out of her bedroom window and dropped to the lawn by the side of the house. In her nightgown. Barefoot. The night was only moderately cold, and the ground beneath her feet was a little colder still, but not enough to be uncomfortable.

The full moon was up, and bright, shining through a thin haze of cloud, so that it seemed a white night, such as are more often experienced in winter, when the combination of diffused moonlight and snow on the ground makes things visible in stark, silhouetted detail at astonishing distances. Tonight, moonlight on pavement and suburban rooftops gave the same effect.

These were ideal moonlight-dancing conditions, and she swirled, with her arms out, her nightgown flapping gently in the slight breeze like a flag, or perhaps like a sheet of laundry hung out on a line. She danced to the front lawn, and then to the street, humming softly, and she admired the way her shadow was cast, huge and wide, flickering over bushes and lawn and the front of the house as she moved.

But there also seemed to be another shadow, dark and still, beside her.

Taken by surprise, a little alarmed, she fell silent, and turned once more, toward that shadow, and saw nothing.

She danced, and the shadow was beside her. She twirled in the middle of the street, down the block, half running, and she saw nothing but moonlight and her own shadow, and again she began to hum, even sing softly. It was like a dream. She was alone in a dream. Dreaming thus, she came to the end of the block and crossed an empty lot, beyond which a winding, unpaved lane gleamed like a white ribbon in the moonlight. Here the suburbs suddenly ended, and on the other side of the lane was a farmer's field, stretching to the horizon. Since it was early spring the crop, whatever it was, was barely planted, so most of the earth in that field was still bare, giving the same effect that snowy ground would on a white night in winter.

It was as she stood amid the pebbles and dirt of that unpaved lane that she noticed, far away across that field, the same black shadow she had seen before, now definitely coming toward her with long strides. It too seemed to flap around the edges, like a black cloth, a mourning cloth, a shroud, it occurred to her, somehow hung out on a laundry line. But it was clearly moving.

At this point the dream, which wasn't actually a dream, turned a bit unpleasant, and she felt a chill, not so much from the cold of the night air, but from that unpleasantness, and she stopped dancing. She turned about once more, toward home, and found herself face-to-face with a tall figure draped in ragged black. Only the face was visible. It seemed to be a man's face, but there was more than a little strange about it: as remote as the moon on a winter's night but less brilliant, just icy pale, and a little bit mottled like an old snowbank. The eyes were black pits. The face might have been a mask.

She saw, too, that the stranger bore a long staff with a curved, glinting blade on the end of it.

"Oh," she said, barely above a whisper.

"Oh," the other whispered back, mocking her.

"I shouldn't be out like this," she said.

"No, you should not."

"I'll go on home then—"

"I do not have an appointment with you yet," said the other, "for this night or for many, many nights to come. In fact, you are not yet written into my book at all." He got out a notebook and flipped through it with the thumb of one very thin, pale hand. "No, you're not there at all."

At that point she held out either side of her nightgown and curtseyed, which instinct told her was the romantic thing to do, and said, "Then I bid you good night, sir, and will be on my way."

She started to run, but he was waiting for her again at the other side of the empty lot.

And again, as she tried to make for home, he stood up between two parked cars and swept out into the street and blocked her way.

"Nevertheless," said he, "you must come along with me, for none may return from such an encounter. Those are the rules."

She twisted away and ran back into the vacant lot, but right where moonlight reflected from a muddy patch she slipped and fell face down into a puddle. She rose to her knees, sputtering, wiping her hands on what was now the wreck of her nightgown, when she felt an electrifying cold as the stranger took her by both wrists and lifted her to her feet.

"Come," he said.

She tried to scream, but somehow her voice managed no more than a faint rasp. This still seemed to be an exceptionally vivid dream as the stranger led her by one hand, back in the direction of her house, but past it. She turned her head back and saw the porch light and the front door receding behind her, forever out of reach, it seemed.

Even if this was a dream, she was not floating, as one might in dreams. There were no strange transitions. She was walking. She felt the pavement and the grass under her feet. The stranger led her across lawns, behind houses. She recognized the Ryans' house. Margaret Ryan was her best friend from school. The swing-set that creaked softly in the night breeze was for the benefit of Jerry, Margaret's kid brother, who was six.

It became more dreamlike when they passed right through the wall of a house and were standing in a dimlit room where a very old woman lay alone in bed, breathing in her sleep with great difficulty, gasping and wheezing. For just an instant a smoke-like, pale outline of the woman rose above the bed. But the dark stranger made a swishing motion with his scythe—for such it was—and then the smoky outline was gone, and Anna and her companion stood in silence for a moment in that dark room, with the old woman who was not breathing.

That was how Anna became the companion and perhaps assistant to Death. She actually assisted sometimes, at least to the extent of paging through the notebook and reading out those names that glowed in red, burning letters, or sometimes in brilliant, white ones. Yes, she knew who her companion was, having seen such a figure in illustrations in books. The Dark Angel. The Reaper. The End of All Things. There was an old song relevant to her situation, which she'd learned from her mother (who was also of a romantic disposition), and sometimes she sang it softly to herself.

They visited many houses, and open fields, and other places, even a sinking liner at sea, and her companion and master made his harvest.

Despite all this, she found him very dull company. He said little. He muttered softly while writing in his notebook with the tip of a bony finger. (He never used a pen.) When one of the names so inscribed glowed, either bright red or white, there was an appointment and a job to do. So time passed, though it seemed to her that time passed very strangely indeed. She was never quite sure if this wasn't an extension of that first night and that dreamlike encounter by moonlight, or if any time had passed at all.

When she asked about these things, she got no answer. When she asked about what became of the souls they took—for she certainly knew what was going on—he only replied, "That is a dark door beyond which I may never go." Did he know anything about the future, the nature of the universe, about God? No, he did not.

For all she had, in a sense, traveled the whole world, she grew uncomfortable, even bored. She began to complain, in a manner that children her age have long since mastered. Are girls better at it than boys? Who knows? There are no statistics on the subject. Suffice it to say that Anna had a full command of the art of getting her way.

She demanded to be allowed to go back and visit her mother. She insisted again and again, cajoled, whined, pouted. Once in a fit of temper she even tore a page out of the notebook and crumpled it up and threw it in a fire. (Whether that made the persons whose names were on that page exceptionally long-lived, or whether they all perished suddenly of a fever, is not recorded.)

So Death relented. She wore him down. It took twenty years, though she did not know that, being in her predicament insensitive to the passage of time.

Nevertheless she found herself one spring morning on the door-step of her family home, as if only a single night had passed since she'd gone out dancing in the moonlight. The door was unlocked. She turned the knob, creaked the door open, went in to the kitchen, and sat down at the table. Her mother, who was there, took one look at her, shrieked, and fell in a faint to the floor.

Anna sat there, befuddled. But it made perfect sense, of course. Twenty years had passed. From her mother's point of view, if her long-lost daughter were still alive (as she continued to hope against hope, for all the detectives investigating had turned up nothing), she would have to be a grown woman in her early thirties by now; and yet here was Anna, still a girl of twelve or so, barefoot and dirty, her nightgown little more than a rag. She could only be an apparition from beyond the grave. If she had returned with some portentous pronouncement, that would have been bad enough, but when she cheerfully said, "Hi, Mom, what's for breakfast?" it was too much and the poor woman succumbed.

Things did not get any better when her father came running down the stairs, discovered Mother, and tried to revive her. Anna noticed that Father looked different from the last time she had seen him. His hair was white now. Mother's was the same color, but dyed. There were differences in her face and figure, but Anna had not had time to notice them.

Eventually Mother did come around. She gasped. She stuttered. She pointed. But Father could not see Anna. He could not be made to believe that she had returned. He began to fear that his wife had gone insane. Indeed, she seemed quite mad as she talked to the air, as she prepared an extra breakfast of blueberry pancakes (Anna's favorite) and orange juice, and placed it in front of an empty chair. How the plate got emptied, where the pancakes went, he never did figure out, but assumed it was the sleight-of-hand of an obsessively, dangerously deranged woman. In fact, the only other member of the household who could detect Anna was the cat, who looked a bit like Mr. Cuddles, a pet Anna had had when she was genuinely twelve, and perhaps was descended from the same. But it was a different cat, and it hissed at her once, leapt out an open window, and was never seen again.

Weeks went by. The situation grew wretched. Mother wept and shuddered and tried to talk with Anna, asking her about her friends and school as if no time had passed and nothing had happened. Anna tried to comfort her. She didn't know what to say. She slept in her own room each night, which her mother had insisted on preserving exactly as she had left it. She washed and threw out the dirty nightgown and dressed in her regular clothes.

Seeing how much her mother suffered, she thought she should leave. At the same time she still desperately wanted to believe that the two of them could be again as they once were.

Besides which, she had nowhere to go. Her dark companion was nowhere to be seen.

Meanwhile Father brought strange men into the house, doctors, who examined Mother and then conversed with Father in low, grim tones. Another stranger came to the house, a tall, darkly bearded man in his mid-twenties, who, she realized, could only be her own little brother Matthew, who had been the same age as Jerry Ryan and had played with him on that set of swings. Together Matthew and the doctors conferred, and they spoke of sending Mother to some other place. The doctor recommended that they sell the house and move away, "To cut off all ties with her past."

But Mother was a step ahead. One night she poured gasoline all over her bed and herself and struck a match. Father and Matthew tried to rescue her but couldn't, though they managed to save themselves. The firemen could do nothing either; and for just a moment Anna stood before her mother amid the flames and tried to say something, but before she could even manage a lame "Goodbye," the scythe swished and Mother was gone.

Anna was left standing on the lawn in front of the smoldering ruins. There were other people gathered around, and the firemen were still working, but no one seemed to notice her, except her dark-cloaked companion, her master or mentor or whatever, who suddenly re-materialized.

"Well, that is over," was all he said. He checked off something in his notebook.

Anna wept uncontrollably for a long time, as the people wandered away and even the firemen rolled up their hoses and left. She wept for her mother, whom she loved, and for her past life, which was now indeed irretrievably cut off.

If she had not slipped out of her window into the moonlight, things might have gone differently.

If—

But it was over. She understood that.

So she put aside her grief, as suddenly as if she had flipped a page in a notebook of her own, and resorted to a kind of guile one does not expect in young girls, even a girl who has been twelve years old for the past twenty years.

She said to her companion that he was all she had left now, the closest thing she had to family, so she might as well grow up, focus, and learn the family trade, and be a genuine assistant or even become a partner. She asked to hold the scythe, so she would know how it felt. She hefted it.

Then, as if she had suddenly remembered something, she pointed at the last house at the end of the block, next to the little strip mall where the vacant lot had been twenty years ago, and said, "Didn't we forget somebody back there?"

"What?" said Death.

"Look it up in the book. Look it up."

And while he was turning the pages of the notebook, his back to her, she swung the scythe with all her might and lopped off his head.

The dark figure collapsed with a rattle of bones, into a cloud of dust. For a brief instant a voice seemed to whisper, "At last. I was so tired. Now I am free," but then there wasn't even dust, or bones, just a few bits of the cloak, which blew away like the ashes of burnt leaves.

Anna ceased to be a girl then. She became a great lady, a queen, who wore a gown as dark as the midnight sky, covered with jewels like stars. Her crown was of ice, and it glowed like the risen moon. She bore the scythe, and sometimes, out of deference to tradition, an hourglass, in addition to the notebook she carried in her pocket.

Having seen so much, having traveled through all the lands of Earth, she was beyond sorrow now. Grief and memory passed over her like smoke. She was awesomely beautiful, but dreaded by all. She was alone, utterly alone, in the dark, which was, she realized in a bitter way, very romantic.

Sometimes she danced.

Summa Oblivia

Maxwell I. Gold

In deep starry nights of my caffeinated dreams, I prayed for sleep—
the taste of the last drops from a sweet oblivion that would wash
away this copious reality from my eyes. Wandering aimlessly in
space, I found myself adrift in that City of Light, gilded with a mal-
odorous fleshy alloy as streets carved from bone and boulevards of
plastic flora snaked through the rusted viscera of the city; I wished
for relief from the shadow of forgetfulness that gripped me. My
bones were weary, ground to a fine powder under the weight of my
own sleepless musings in a society of crumpled metal. Walking
along the streets, my brain felt heavy with thoughts of dream palac-
es, waiting for solace from this horrid disease.

I had never known the pleasures of sleep or felt its embrace since
those nuclear clouds set in on the horizons, laying their hypnotic ra-
dioactivity on the world. I lay awake, with bloodshot eyes and trembling hands grasping the sheets as an insistent buzzing siren echoed
with a cacophonous mewling scratching at the very depths of my
brain. The metal shelving of my bed was cold, unwelcoming, and
gnawed at me with an icy embrace as the covers lay over my body
like a blanket of heavy ash and snow.

Memories seemed like legend, and history was a fantasy fabri-
cated from dreams as the fingers of an awful god squeezed my head.
It seemed foolish to try and remember anything before my time living as one of the infected, the forgotten. I watched the world slowly
decay in front of my eyes as colors bled into one another, rainbows
no longer holding their ancient sway over my soul; but rather a grim
lethiferous black swathe that slowly began to consume my senses.

It was then I felt reality begin to crumble, like that empyreal
City of Light, crumbling under the inexorable weight of night; every

pitiful atom screaming into the audient darkness. A sinister laughter frothed in the cyber black, clawing at me with a quickness undulating in the shadows. I tried to run, to dodge the slimy fingers that gripped my neck making every ounce of oxygen seem as precious as the last. *Dear god, someone help me!*

Then, as if it were all some surrealistic hallucination, I found myself awake in a room with thick wires obtrusively jutting forth from my body, connected to a large rusted piece of metal, like a mutilated Frankenstein that had been haphazardly taken apart and put back together and carried with it the same disgusting stench as the structures from the ruinous city. My breathing appeared to be monitored by some large metal machine, clicking and beeping in sync with my lungs as I sat up; and my heart too was under the same observation, every drop of blood and every vein under careful surveillance by an unknown thing watching, studying, and meticulously calculating my very existence down to last decaying molecule. Still, the shade of memory eluded me, the laughter of that faceless god rung presently in my thoughts, and all I wanted to do was to sleep and forget. The machine's nebulous breathing became louder as the hulking mass of decrepit metal pulled against my frail body. Within the reflection of the sparse gray fields of oxidized material, I could see its burning eyes, dripping with a molten terror that filled my soul with a banal sinistrality as I realized the true extent of my malaise and what was gazing back at me. Hazthrog, the bacterial god born from a great evil, had strangulated my mind with fungal tentacles, laced by some alien virus. I couldn't stand it any longer as my thoughts deteriorated and the world as I knew it crumbled under the unfathomable weight of an ancient force. In deep starry nights of my caffeinated dreams, I could finally sleep—the simple taste of the last drops from sweet oblivion had washed away this copious reality from my eyes.

A Matter of Belief: Further Thoughts on Lord Dunsany and Religion

Martin Wangsgaard Jürgensen

It is a cause for celebration when a new book on Lord Dunsany's fiction is published, and S. T. Joshi's study *Creator of Gods and Men*, published 2019, is unquestionably an important step forward in our understanding of the developments in Dunsany's literary production. His discussion of Dunsany's last works is particularly valuable as they in general seem, perhaps with good reason, to have garnered only limited interest within the already scarce scholarship on Dunsany. With Joshi's volume it is, however, also apparent that a number of themes in Dunsany's writing still need further exploration or discussion: and at least to my mind somewhat surprisingly, one of these themes is Dunsany's stance on religion as well as his own possible religiosity.

It is surprising because gods and religion were from the very outset part of Dunsany's fictional world, and the theme has accordingly to some extent been touched upon by nearly all his commentators. Nevertheless, a certain amount of analytical imprecision as to the role of religion in Dunsany's work is apparent, which perhaps springs from the fact that he himself said very little about it. As I am not in possession of hitherto undiscovered letters or texts, I can add no further absolute conclusions to the debate. But that being said, there is, I think, more to be uncovered, or some counterarguments to be made, concerning the generally assumed role of religion in his fiction and probably also concerning his personal beliefs, insofar as we are able to draw any conclusions on a matter about which he is otherwise silent. In this essay we will explore Dunsany's use of religion in his fiction through examples from his first publication, *The Gods of Pegāna* (1905), up to *Tales of Wonder* (1916). Based on the conclusions of this brief survey, I shall try to establish what might be called an ontology within his fiction, before the question of Dunsany's own beliefs, as they appear to me from his writing, is finally addressed.

Dunsany's commentators have more or less uniformly concluded that he was an atheist, so that all or most mention of religion in his work has been read in an oblique way, as satire, or simply as expressions of his toying with metaphysical notions for the sake of atmosphere within the narrative. All this might to a certain extent be correct, but my feeling is that we are missing important points. The first study on Dunsany, *Dunsany the Dramatist* (1917), by Edward Hale Bierstadt, is almost silent on the topic of religion, although Bierstadt has useful insights concerning the play *The Glittering Gate* of 1909, to which I shall return below. It is here noteworthy that Dunsany himself read and commented on Bierstadt's book, correcting errors and misunderstandings for the revised edition of 1919. Bierstadt was clearly reluctant to raise the question of religion, and this apparently did not displease Dunsany, who could have clarified glaringly vague passages in the book had it suited him. The explicitly voiced idea that Dunsany was an atheist, and religion an area of no great relevance to his fiction, first seems to enter the discussion after Mark Amory's biography was published in 1972. In it Amory states: "More important was the absence of religion. It had not been forced on him [Dunsany] and he had not sought it, so, without any profound spiritual struggle, he was an atheist. Nor had he been confirmed" (Amory 33). As Dunsany to my knowledge never declared himself an atheist, it is unclear whence Amory derived this information, which either came from the "literally hundreds of questions" (Amory 8) posed to Lady Dunsany, their son, and the entire household, or simply conjecture. Yet we find the conclusion repeated in almost all subsequent works on Dunsany, mostly stated as a matter of consensus in no need of further explanation.

This leads to rather curious statements, as for instance by Darrell Schweitzer in his otherwise illuminating *Pathways to Elfland* (1989), where he says, "Surely there is no religious significance, and those looking for allegorical meanings are bound to be disappointed. Dunsany was an atheist" (8). The first sentence pertains specifically to *The Gods of Pegāna*, while the second statement, again without source, must have been culled from Amory's biography. If we chronologically move forward from Schweitzer's work, we find that S. T. Joshi in a number of different publications assumes atheism, with an emphasis on Dunsany's having read Nietzsche (*Weird Tale* 46–58). Joshi, however, later moderates this in *Creator of Gods and Men* and proceeds more cautiously:

> In another way Dunsany seems very modern in spite of the jewelled archaism of language; and this is in his many traces of atheism or, at the very least, anticlericalism. [Mark] Amory states bluntly that Dunsany was an atheist, but cites no evidence for the claim; I am not entirely sure of the matter, but we have already in "Pegāna" the implications of the soul after death, so that actual atheism on Dunsany's part is likely enough. (37)

This is later in the book followed by a comment on literary scholar Colin Manlove in a footnote: "I hardly imagine that Dunsany ought to be held responsible for failing to deal with moral issues in a suitable Christian way, since by all accounts he was not a Christian" (122n5). First we have Dunsany the atheist, who then likely is an atheist and then by all accounts not a Christian. All these conclusions are fascinating, because they are at no point substantiated by anything other than the reading of Dunsany's fiction and drama, as well as what I assume to be reliance on the statement Amory made in his biography. Looking at the fiction Dunsany produced up to the First World War, I fail to find any firm expression of atheism: it is even problematic to propose, like Darrell Schweitzer, that there is no religious significance in a work such as *The Gods of Pegāna*, as I shall try to demonstrate.

When trying to locate the atheism of Lord Dunsany in his fiction, what first and foremost springs to mind is the clear distrust of institutions that prevails in his work. H. P. Lovecraft had already in 1922 noted this as occasional "touches of satire on social institutions" (106) in his charming essay on Dunsany, but it is an understatement that plays down a critical element, a stance that later was more precisely brought to light by Joshi in his chapter on Dunsany in *The Weird Tale* (50). In his two first published volumes, *The Gods of Pegāna* and *Time and the Gods* (1906), Dunsany repeatedly describes how the prayers of the priests and the sacrifices of the devout either never reach the gods or simply make no sense, because there is no direct connection between the mortal and the immortal worlds. If the gods wish, they can enter the terrestrial realm, but no true communication runs the other way and there is thus no expression of what we might call transcendence. In "The Chaunt of the Priests" it is for example said that:

> All day long to Mung cry out the Priests of Mung, and yet Mung hearkenth not. What then, shall avail the prayers of All the People?
> Rather bring gifts to the Priests, gifts to the Priests of Mung. (*TG* 546)

Give to the priests, since they have better use for gifts than the gods. Religion as a practice, then, is a purely human endeavor that does not affect the gods, even if they listen to the prayers of the priests and prophets and yearn for the attention of mortals. Priests and prophets such as the boasting visionary Yug are raised by their fellows to significance without any claims to contact with higher powers (*TG* 562). While never made explicit, it seems to be implied that it is the institution and clergy of the Christian churches that are satirized or mocked in these pages, just as we find later with the ridiculed monk in the novel *The King of Elfland's Daughter* (1924). Yet we need not read any specific existing religion into this, as in his first works to be published he basically addresses all human attempts at interaction with divine forces, no matter the creed or confession.

To say, as Schweitzer claimed, that this has no religious significance seems rather peculiar, as Dunsany certainly from the very outset of his fiction-writing career launched a pronounced challenge at organized religion; a critique that can be traced throughout his following publications. "The Idle City" from *A Dreamer's Tales* (1910) echoes the dismissive depiction in the two first books of religious practice as an almost futile endeavor, while one of the most explicit and bleak examples of this would be the short story "The Sword and the Idol," also to be found among *A Dreamer's Tales*. This story is concerned with the very creation of a religion, and the interaction between the priest, the god, and society, which at bottom is a question of power and control. Here we sense Dunsany's reluctance to accommodate institutions and persons claiming to speak with the authority of higher forces, rendered now with very little of the magic and oriental splendor he invested in his portrayal of the same sentiments in his first books.

The critique of organized religion is clearly a dominant feature in Dunsany's early fiction, and we also find a questioning attitude to the godhead as such. His Pegāna gods are petty entities, capricious and self-absorbed along the lines of the gods we know from Norse and Greek mythology. But a shift is noticeable in Dunsany's writing after the two first books, once he turned to stories placed closer to home, where the divine was treated much more carefully. Nevertheless, we do still find works openly critical of godhead. This is most pronounced in "The Doom of La Traviata" from *The Sword of Welleran and Other Stories* (1908), in which the "sinful opera" is condemned to hell by God. In vain do angels and saints try to intercede on behalf of the fragile piece of art, but God is unmoved and the short story concludes with the harsh words: "But the Lord arose with his sword, and scattered His disobedient angels as a thresher scatters chaff" (*TG* 224). The god, who can only be the biblical god, is clearly no lover of this kind of opera. We again find a somewhat disturbing portrait of an omnipotent god in "The Hashish Man" from *A Dreamer's Tales,* when the titular hashish man informs us that he has seen the secret of the universe and the creator, who sat laughing: and that all existence was a big joke.

Through such irreverent stories combined with the barbs at the religious institutions themselves, it is indeed conceivable to portray Dunsany's fiction as being carried by an anti-religious or atheistic sentiment. But these notions are only two strands within the corpus of his fiction, which throughout the first decade and a half of the twentieth century was strongly preoccupied with religion in general, and it is certainly possible to point out many more positive expressions toward belief, or rather spirituality, than the examples cited above.

First of all, it is of interest to note the words that Dunsany employs in his short stories. References to metaphysical concepts abound; the existence of the soul is a salient theme in numerous tales, and in the delightful little piece "The Kith of the Elf-Folk" (*The Sword of Welleran*) the very acquisition of a human soul for one of the elves is the crux of the narrative. However, the soul in Dunsany's fiction is not only present in humankind, but also in trees ("In the Twilight," *The Sword of Welleran*), and even cities have souls ("The Madness of Andelsprutz," *A Dreamer's Tales*), which of course should tell us that Dunsany by no means used the word in any one specific sense. Still, it seems to be a commonplace in his fiction that human beings have a soul, and Dunsany several times returns to the theme of a distinction between body and soul, a theme to which I shall return. Before that, meanwhile, we need to note the generous presence of other traditional metaphysical categories in Dunsany's work, more or less clearly embedded in a Christian worldview. The narrative in "The Ghosts" (*The Sword of Welleran*) operates from the concept of sin, which of course requires a normative moral framework guiding the right and wrong of human action, and necessarily also a concept of "grace." In "The Field" (*A Dreamer's Tales*) the houses of London are likened to buildings erected in honour of Satan. We may also note the presence of such concepts as "the good," the sacred, Satan, and hell in "The Fortress Unvanquishable, Save for Sacnoth" (*The Sword of Welleran*), while "Where the Tides Ebb and Flow" (*A Dreamer's Tales*) employs both hell and Paradise as well as a soul in the uncertain position between those otherworldly places.

This tracing of Dunsany's use of traditional, and potentially religiously loaded, words and metaphysical categories could be documented much more closely than I have done here. Indeed, much insight would probably be gained from such an exercise. What this brief mention does show is how deeply Dunsany's language is invested with religion. He builds metaphors on religious concepts and he regularly bases narrative plots on (Christian?) metaphysical concepts. What to make of this? It is not at all likely that he literally believed in the existence of Satan, ghosts, and spirits. But what then? It has almost become a platitude, when introducing Dunsany, to mention his early preoccupation with the language of the King James Bible (e.g., Schweitzer 8). We could accordingly understand his choice of wording as a legacy of this early influence. But this, I think, is unlikely and it would take away some of Dunsany's conscious artistic agency and seem wrong given his deep preoccupation with words and rhythm in his diction.

A more fruitful way of explaining his often religiously charged wording would be to state that he was a part of a culture and literature steeped in both consciously and unconsciously religious thinking. This is to say that even if Dunsany as an assumed atheist wished to express ideas of beauty and ecstasy, his writing could not escape the religious framework of his day. The strong advocate of atheism, Joseph-Pierre Proudhon, had already noted this problem in 1846, when he wrote: "We are full of Divinity, *Jovis omnia plena;* our monuments, our traditions, our laws, our ideas, our languages, and our sciences—all are infected with this indelible superstition, outside which we are not able to speak or act, and without which we simply do not think" (32). Proudhon here eloquently describes how religious vocabulary and imagery was a part of a European culture that he could not escape, although he wanted to. One may or may not follow Proudhon in this, but the phenomenon he points to is certainly not unheard of and we only need to look to Dunsany's already-mentioned disciple, the unquestionable atheist H. P. Lovecraft, to see how even he in his fiction had trouble avoiding the pitfalls of a language loaded with religious concepts. This might also have been the case with Dunsany himself, and some of his at times glib passages could hint at a more subconscious use of religious terminology. But I would still argue that there is yet more to this. There seem to be substantial metaphysical notions at play in the early work from his pen, both hinting at his understanding of what people are/amount to in the world and a spiritual interaction between them and nature.

To begin with, it is worthwhile spending a few moments on the concept of beauty in Dunsany's writing. His quest to portray and communicate to the reader a sense of beauty is a continuing effort in much of his literature, and the artistic interaction with nature clearly was his means of conveying such visions of beauty to the reader. His penchant for nature and his distaste for modern industry has frequently and noteworthily been touched upon (Joshi, "Christianity"), but before continuing into this topic, we need to dwell for a moment on his general appreciation of what we might define as religious aesthetics. The language of religion, religious art, and ritual clearly captivated Dunsany from the beginning, and he formulates the religious performance as an act vested in beauty; but he also clearly sees it as something separate from the actual intent of the religious worship. His celebrated story "Idle Days on the Yann" (*A Dreamer's Tales*) is almost an ethnographic survey of fictitious religious practices, delighting as it does in the material culture of ritual and worship. It is the sound of organ music, flickering candlelight, and evensong heard from the nave, as well as the church architecture itself, which in "The Kith of the Elf-Folk" inspires the elf of the story to long for a human soul and be part of all this. We find the same preoccupation with the outer appearance or aesthetics of religion in "The Fortress Unvanquishable, Save for Sacnoth," in which a monastery inspires the sense of beauty, while the sunrise is likened to organ music and accordingly to what we may call a liturgical experience. The most poignant passage concerning this encounter with religious beauty among Dunsany's early texts is found in the first paragraph of the "The Exiles' Club" (*The Last Book of Wonder*), which is worth quoting in extenso:

The truth (for all religions have some of it), the wisdom, the beauty, of the religions of the countries to which I travel have not the same appeal for me; for one only notices in them their tyranny and intolerance and the abject servitude that they claim from thought; but when a dynasty has been dethroned in heaven and goes forgotten and outcast even among men, one's eyes no longer dazzled by its power find something very wistful in the faces of fallen gods suppliant to be remembered, something almost tearfully beautiful, like a long warm summer twilight fading gently away after some memorable day in the story of earthly wars. (*TG* 519)

There is much to be said about a passage like this, but in our context two things stand out. First of all, we here meet again the assault on organized and institutionalized religion discussed already. The claim to established authority detracts from, or derails, what Dunsany seems to feel to be an inherent beauty in religious expression. However, this expression needs the distance of time or neglect in order to be appreciated and in order for us to close in on this quality of "truth," which he also alludes to in the passage quoted. Secondly, we here again find the close alignment of religious beauty with the discovery of nature, and, as combined by Dunsany, these ideas clearly hark back to the enlightenment ideal of the picturesque (Nicolson). Without saying so, Dunsany explores the concept of the sublime in his fiction and through his writing facilitates an impression of this to the reader, who is made to feel, for instance, a described sunrise, and even better, extend this poetic understanding of the sunrise into nature as a whole and experience it through the poet's eyes. In Dunsany's fiction the poet is often accredited with the distinct role of perceiving the world as it really is. The poet sees the ludicrous in futile endeavors (e.g., politics, organized religion), and the poet sees beauty. The poet also senses tragedy, as in "The Field" (*A Dreamer's Tales*), where a poet beholds a fair field bright with flowers and conjures a future battlefield. The poet's dealings with beauty enable him or her to channel an inner or hidden truth to the reader, a truth that often has been obscured by the dealings and industry of modern society.

In "The Lord of Cities" (*The Sword of Welleran*) Dunsany raises some interesting points. In this story "the river" and "the road" have a discussion about their purpose and their relation to mankind. The argument goes back and forth; the river clearly represents nature and beauty, while the road serves man and his artificial society. Dunsany's sympathy is mostly with the river, but the road raises an all-important objection to the self-sufficient river, as it states: "'Your beauty,' said the road, 'and the beauty of the sky, and the rhododendron blossom and of spring, live only in the mind of Man, and except in the mind of Man the mountains have no voices. Nothing is beautiful that has not been seen by Man's eye'" (*TG* 219). Nature is a closed system that cannot experience itself, but man as the outsider can see and understand what nature is. In order for nature to be fulfilled or meaningful, it needs the human gaze, and extending this, if we are to appreciate nature, we need the poet's or artist's pen or brush. Dunsany was far from the first to raise this argument of a dialectic relationship between man and nature, and of the poet as the bridge between them. It is a core idea in the early Romantic movement around 1800, which give us no small insight into Dunsany's literary endeavor (Bate).

The question of course is, if there was, to Dunsany's mind, ever a time when a union between man and nature had no need of being mediated. Without ever making this entirely clear to us, it would seem so. By portraying rural communities in pseudo-medieval, pre-mechanized, and pre-industrialized settings he was able to depict societies in balance.

> . . . of the hills, stood the village of Allathurion; and there was peace between the people of that village and all the folk who walked in the dark ways of the wood, whether they were human or of the tribes of the beasts or of the race of fairies and the elves and the little sacred spirits of trees and streams. Moreover, the village people had peace among themselves and between them and their lord . . . (*TG* 196)

The idyllic Arcadian atmosphere, here described in "The Fortress Unvanquishable, Save for Sacnoth," is of course within the narrative challenged by outside forces, but it nevertheless is an ideal utopia Dunsany formulates and we recognize the same in *The King of Elfland's Daughter*, mentioned above, in which an equally bucolic dream society ("Erl") is portrayed. Yet here again the peace is challenged, this time from the inside through the ghost of ambition among the inhabitants, a hunger for change that almost leads to the destruction of their society. Dunsany clearly was taken by the idea of a simpler world in tune with nature, but we may wonder if in fact he believed such societies were possible. The cynical streak in his fiction would seem to indicate that he was well aware that no such thing could ever have existed or could ever come to be. Nevertheless, his writing on this point does read as a conservative voice of caution, evoking a romanticized vision of a prelapsarian past, set prior to a sort of industrial fall, as a model to strive for and a goal that could bring society into harmony with its surroundings.

Dunsany then clearly integrated some or much of the Romantic movement's beliefs and aesthetic values into his fiction. Schweitzer casually remarks that Dunsany was a Romantic writer (20), but this does not lead him to further conclusions and leaves the reader hanging as to the implication of the judgment. Mark Amory more helpfully informs us that Dunsany's favorite poets were Coleridge, Shelley, and Keats (56, 233), which can come as no surprise, as it clearly was from voices such as these that Dunsany built his own literary endeavor. He thereby joined the resurgence of the literary Romantic project around 1900, a trend that gained renewed strength as a counter-voice to what was felt to be a stifling Victorian bourgeois culture and religion. From the Romantic creed as to the artists' ability to imagine and understand truth came a certainty and an urgency that resound in the fiction of Dunsany. Perhaps the most striking parallel between his use of allusion to spirituality while at the same time voicing doubt of religious institutions is found in William Blake's *The Marriage of Heaven and Hell* (1794), which utterly condemns the priesthood as well as the Church and shifts the experience of divinity to an inner condition—or, as he famously writes, "all deities reside in the human breast."

Dunsany responded to nature in ways similar to the more spiritually inclined poets, drawing inspiration from such early figures as Hölderlin and Novalis; and it is rewarding, for instance, to compare Dunsany's fiction with Carlyle's call for a new "Mythus" whose sole Bible should be what was felt in the heart (194). Again we find this reformulation of faith as an inner, personal quality that, to Carlyle, was stimulated by the encounter with the world and in particular with nature. Once again, the critique of the Christian Church as an institution is here voiced as well as the idea of transferring the agency and prerogative of formulating religious experience away from the institution and onto the individual (the poet, that is, to be precise). The nature of this experience of divinity was formulated differently among the Romantic poets around 1800, but it more often than not involved the experience of beauty. Faith was an aesthetic experience connected with the senses, not the intellect. The spiritual emphasis in this could be very different and read both like a fundamentally redefined theology, turning into what through Friedrich Schleiermacher came to be known as *Kunstreligion,* or as a secularization of the devotional experience, where the individual simply felt in tune with an inchoate and infinitely great presence that need not necessarily be supernatural (Auerochs).

I see all this as the backdrop for the early fiction of Dunsany, but there is a clear dividing line between his work and the general attitude of the Neoplatonic trend in Romantic literature, insofar as Dunsany never, to my knowledge, claims a specific experience of transcendence. He describes the world as a living thing, and spiritually charged, in what Joshi has termed an animistic response to nature ("Christianity" 32–33): but we mortals are left as spectators in all this, without any true ability to commune or interact with this spiritual dimension. This conflict was present in Dunsany's fiction from the very outset, and of course it revolves around the idea of man and nature as two distinctly separate categories in need of a middle ground in order to interact.

This finally leads us to the question of Dunsany's own beliefs. As can probably be gleaned from what has been said here, I fail to find any evidence of an expressed atheism in his early fiction. In his rather sour review of Dunsany's autobiography *Patches of Sunlight* (1938), Jorge Luis Borges writes that it is a biography that avoids confessions, and perhaps we may with Borges say the same for a large part of Dunsany's fiction as well. At least it is very difficult to reach any firm conclusions. Yet for me there can be little doubt that nature, to Dunsany, held spiritual qualities, and this came close to or was similar to an experience of divinity. At least this is a continuing theme in his fiction, but the all-important point to note in this connection is his absolute unwillingness to define this divinity or experience beyond the poetic allusion to and creation of beauty. To him there were, in other words, limits to what could or should be expressed through language or art in general. The truth in a cosmic sense was there to be recognized ("for all religions have some of it" [*TG* 519]), but art or words could not express this truth. He formulated an interesting distinction between truth and form with reference to his later stories when, on the genesis of the character Jorkens, he wrote: "And yet their background is all true; the cactus forests of Kenya are here and some of its mountains, and Egypt, Aden, the Ganges and Himalayas: *the lie is the tale itself,* worked from this material as a goldsmith will make a goddess from honest gold" (*While the Sirens Slept* 78; my emphasis).

The artifice is the lie while the natural material as such is the truth: this dictum might well be applied to the whole of Dunsany's understanding of nature or the world. Human hands could fabricate beautiful art as well as horrible machinery, but the truth is outside their grasp. This is also a clear ontological statement that I think applies to Dunsany's spirituality or religiosity in general. It is only rarely that the existence of the supernatural is rejected, but what is constantly deplored is the human attempt to formulate and control any notions about the nature of the supernatural or sacred. An example of this might be "The Unhappy Body" (*A Dreamer's Tales*). In this story we hear a dialogue between body and soul, where we as readers follow the tired and weary body while the destination of the eager and busy soul, once it leaves its carnal home, is left unspoken. A similar handling of the narrative is found in the magnificent "Where the Tides Ebb and Flow" (*A Dreamer's Tales*), in which the gruesome fate of a soul, caught somewhere between life and death, is described and we finally read of its release:

> Then when there was nothing to be heard in London but the myriad notes of the exultant song, my soul rose up from the bones in the hole in the mud and began to climb up the song heavenwards. And it seemed that a laneway opened amongst the wings of the birds, and it went up and up, and one of the smaller gates of Paradise stood ajar at the end of it. (*TG* 257–58)

But just as the soul is about to pass the gate, we learn that the narrator awakens, to the sound of chirping birds, with a hangover. It is a complete comic inversion of the grim narrative, but I would add that Dunsany here tells us two important things. The singing of birds—nature—is, first, a guide to the understanding of the afterlife, and secondly he entirely denies us any view into this promised paradise. The end of this story comes very close to the effect Dunsany sought in his first play *The Glittering Gate*, where two deceased burglars break the lock on the portal of Heaven only to find a vast, empty space on the other side and the sound of rumbling laughter. The interpretation of the play is entirely open, as Dunsany never furnished us with any help concerning the meaning behind the action, but I agree with the reading of Bierstadt, who understands the piece not as an ironic and atheistic statement concerning a non-existent afterlife, but rather as expressing the impossibility of our gaining any certainty or access to knowledge concerning any eschatological matter. As Bierstadt puts it, "The Gate of Heaven cannot be forced open with a jimmy" (25).

There is a long tradition within Protestant thinking of declining to put into words such matters outside the sphere of human understanding, and I think Dunsany himself also declined to articulate his religious sentiments or spirituality. Like quite large parts of his personality and life, they were private and no part of his public persona. His personal beliefs were simply not a thing he discussed. Writing home in 1917 to his wife Beatrice, Lady Dunsany, from one of his darkest hours in the trenches and in what could easily be understood as a goodbye letter, he ends his parting words with a "God bless you" (Amory 147). This is rather striking, in that this is a private communication between Dunsany and his wife and clearly written under severe stress. In an equally striking passage Amory recounts how Dunsany, according to his wife, in 1941 went into a cathedral to give thanks for their safe escape from Greece, managed under dire circumstances during the German advance, leading Amory to write: "His [Dunsany's] relationship with the Protestant Church was always friendly, but it certainly grew stronger" (260). What we are to make of these statements is an open question, but to me they certainly suggest the thinking neither of a staunch atheist nor of a non-Christian, but rather of a man who at least twice turned to traditional religion under stress.

I do not want to push this too far, especially an expression like "God bless you," but I find the assurance with which the research on Dunsany has defined him as an atheist and non-Christian puzzling, and from his early fiction alone I fail to see how these views can be substantiated. He certainly was very critical of religious institutions and of any religious authority speaking on behalf of a higher power, but he never, as far as I can see, denied the existence of a metaphysical dimension to life. His writing is steeped in the religion and concepts proclaimed by the Romantic writers of the early nineteenth century.

One of the problems with our understanding of Dunsany's attitude to religion is perhaps that almost all work on him has focused on the uniqueness of the content of his literature and his style, rather than trying to see where his aesthetic leanings originated. This may have created blind spots as regards his views on religion and obscured the extent to which he in fact seems to have been influenced by the critical thinking of the Romantics, which fed directly into the increasingly popular liberal theology of the late nineteenth century and thence into the individually defined theology of the twentieth century, an evolution of which Dunsany seems very much to be a representative.

What I have written here is an interpretation as much as it is a reluctance to call Dunsany an atheist, or define him religiously in any other way. Nothing is proved, and Dunsany himself certainly seems to have relished a degree of opaqueness concerning himself and his views, leading his commentators to fill in the blanks as they thought best. Lovecraft would, of course, see Dunsany's cosmic fiction as an expression of his own atheism, and no firm evidence can counter this viewpoint. However, it is my hope that this brief reflection may at least inspire a larger degree of critical thinking and caution in discussing the question of religion in connection with Dunsany as well as his fiction, and not to repeat uncritically what Mark Amory stated in 1972. I believe that there is at least as much evidence and logic against the alleged atheism as there might be for it. The road ahead lies through further in-depth discussion of Dunsany's work, and hopefully it will ultimately also lead to a broader recognition of his art.

Works Cited

Amory, Mark. *Lord Dunsany: A Biography*. London: Collins, 1972.

Auerochs, Bernd. *Die Entstehung der Kunstreligion*. Leiden: Vandenhoeck & Ruprech 2006.

Bate, Jonathan. *Romantic Ecology: Wordsworth and the Environmentalist Tradition*. London: Routledge, 1991.

Bierstadt, Edward Hale. *Dunsany the Dramatist*. Boston: Little, Brown, 1917.

Borges, Jorge Luis. "Lord Dunsany, *Patches of Sunlight.*" In *Selected Non-Fictions*. Ed. Eliot Weinberger. New York: Penguin, 2000. 187–88.

Carlyle, Thomas. *Sartor Resartus*. New York: Charles Frederick Harrold, 1937.

Dunsany, Lord. *Time and the Gods*. London: Millennium/Gollancz, 2000. [Abbreviated in the text as *TG*.]

———. *While the Sirens Slept*. London: Hutchinson, 1944.

Joshi, S. T. "Christianity and Paganism in Two Dunsany Novels." In S. T. Joshi, ed. *Critical Essays on Lord Dunsany*, Lanham, MD: Scarecrow Press, 2013. 205–14.

———. *Creator of Gods and Men: Lord Dunsany and Fantasy Fiction*. Seattle: Sarnath Press, 2019.

———. *The Weird Tale*. Austin: University of Texas Press, 1990.

Lovecraft, H. P. "Lord Dunsany and His Work." In *Miscellaneous Writings*. Ed. S. T. Joshi. Sauk City, WI: Arkham House, 1995. 104–12.

Nicolson, Marjorie Hope. *Mountain Gloom and Mountain Glory: The Development of the Aesthetics of the Infinite*. Rev. ed. Seattle: University of Washington Press, 1997.

Proudhon, Joseph-Pierre. *The Philosophy of Poverty: The System of Economic Contradictions*. Auckland: Floating Press, 2012.

Schweitzer, Darrell. *Pathways to Elfland: The Writings of Lord Dunsany*. Philadelphia: Owlswick Press, 1989.

A Grave at the End of the World

Curtis M. Lawson

Two clocks counted down, one on a ticker high above the war room reading minus eleven hours and fifty-eight minutes. The smaller clock ticked away in the corner of a computer monitor. It was at T-minus five minutes.

General Adams cursed. There was less than half a day before the extinction event if The Norns were right. They always were.

Adams watched video streaming from a test lab in another part of the facility—a place unofficially known as the Black Box. There were four men in the room—criminals he'd snatched from a military prison. Each had a number spray-painted across his bare chest. They sneered and howled from plastic cages set in each corner. Some smashed their heads against the plexiglass. Others beat upon themselves with balled fists. No humanity resided behind their eyes—only drug-induced madness.

In the middle of the lab, equidistant to each cell, stood a teenage girl named Providence. Adams had known her since she was a child, and looking upon her still chilled his blood every time. She looked mostly human, almost beautiful in fact, save for the obsidian ram horns crowning her head. Her pale skin and platinum hair glistened with sweat and her orange jumpsuit was soaked through.

A bespectacled figure with bulbous eyes and a tweed suit sat at a computer to the side of the general. Adams watched him type in a series of coded commands. None of it made sense to the general, but he pretended it did.

The man in the tweed suit, Dr. Wallach, pressed a button on the microphone by his monitor. Feedback squelched across the speakers before he spoke.

"The Norns predict that one of these men has a fixed destiny,"

Wallach said into the microphone. "One of them is supposed to die tomorrow when the event happens. We want you to kill them all right now instead. Do you understand, Providence?"

"That's not possible, Dr. Wallach. The Norns are never wrong."

General Adams winced. She was right. The artificial intelligence network that ran the facility, or The Norns as it was nicknamed, created an algorithm for predicting the future. It had never been wrong. In his time on this project, Adams had concluded that free will was a delusion.

General Adams killed the microphone.

"What's the point of lying to her?"

"I want to overtax her abilities, General. Force her to trust her instincts and go against preconceptions. She can't change the future if she doesn't learn to question it."

Dr. Wallach clicked on an icon marked "open." A siren wailed in the test lab, accompanied by flashing amber lights. The men in the cages howled and screamed. Providence closed her eyes and envisioned the night sky—a sight she had never seen with her own eyes. She floated in the cold emptiness of space, free from the sweltering concrete facility she called home. When the siren sounded again, Providence opened her eyes, centered and at peace.

The plastic cages opened, and the men charged at her with impossible speed. Providence extended her consciousness beyond her body and infiltrated the mind of the man tagged as Subject One. She could see the world through his drug-blurred eyes, could taste his foul breath, and hear his gibbering thoughts. His body was hers to command.

Providence made him tackle the man to his right—Subject Four. Four clawed and bit in response. Providence abandoned her victim's mind, leaving them to fight among themselves.

Subject Two was a wild-eyed monster with a bodybuilder's physique. He rushed at her from his corner. Even as he charged, Providence could sense the last of the prisoners coming at her from behind. She sidestepped with calm and grace, then reached out with her mind and possessed the raging giant.

Two's thoughts were as muddled as One's had been, and his senses just as dulled. His body was hard to control—cumbersome, full of drugs and hate—but she managed to charge him headfirst at the last of the men—Subject Three.

Two's shoulder caught Three under the ribs, and the girl ran them both into the wall, as fast as Two's big gorilla legs would carry them. Her consciousness snapped back into her body as the victim of her possession caved his own skull in against the steel wall.

The forceful return to her own flesh left Providence dizzy and out of sorts, but she was cognizant enough to note that Subject Three wasn't doing any better than Two. Some organ, or perhaps many, had burst inside him. Red gore drizzled from his nose and mouth. Both men slid down the wall into a lifeless heap of flesh.

"I told you this was a bad idea," General Adams said, watching from the war room. "You practically walked her down the path that The Norns predicted."

"Hush, General," Dr. Wallach said, watching the battle. "We aren't done here."

On the screen, Providence turned her attention back to One and Four. The men were still rolling on the concrete, savaging each other. They bit, punched, and gauged, each trying to dismember the other. Providence stood still and watched them, her chest heaving with each heavy breath.

"She looks spent," Adams commented. "We've been pushing her hard lately, maybe to her limits."

"Providence has no limits, General."

On the monitor they watched Subject One rip out Four's throat. He stood up, glistening with blood and turned his attention to the girl.

General Adams lit a cigar. There was no smoking in the building, but the facility, the project, Providence—none of it even officially existed, so the hell with it.

"Smoke 'em if you got 'em."

Providence was afraid of this one. Not because of his gruesome appearance or the madness in his eyes, but because the others were dead. That meant he had to be the one destined to live beyond this moment. He was the primary target—the one The Norns had decreed would live to see the end of the world. The computer had made no such assurances about her, so far as she knew.

"What is stronger than destiny?" Dr. Wallach's voice asked over the speakers in the room.

"Providence," she whispered.

Providence launched her psyche into the last of the madmen. She took his body for her own and grew dizzy in his drug-addled psyche. His pounding heart echoed in her ears. She cringed at the copper taste of blood on his tongue. His arms held more power than she had ever imagined flesh and muscle could. She took a measure of joy in that strength as she pressed his calloused thumbs against his eyes.

Providence trembled with excitement at the idea that she might actually kill this man—that she might defy The Norns' flawless algorithm. She took a deep breath, readying herself for the pain she would feel as she pressed his eyes into his skull. Using the man like a puppet, she applied pressure with his thumbs, but a feeling came over her—a forceful intuition. She stopped.

"This man . . ." The words came out in stereo from her mouth and his. "This man is supposed to die right now, not tomorrow."

The general dropped his cigar and smoke billowed from his open mouth. A wide smirk crossed Dr. Wallach's thin lips. Both men stared at the timer on the monitor. Only one minute remained until the moment The Norns had predicted the subject would die. They were almost there.

"How do you know his destiny?" Wallach asked. "Do you think you are wiser than The Norns?"

"I don't care what the computer says," Providence's voice crackled over the computer speakers. "This man is supposed to die right now, just as the others were. I can feel it."

"Very good, Providence. The Norns did say he would die right now," Dr. Wallach admitted. "Can you prove them wrong?"

Dr. Wallach's tongue darted out as he clicked another icon. Subject One fell to the ground seizing inside the test lab.

"What the hell did you do?" Adams screamed.

"Induced a heart attack."

"You what?" General Adams yelled again, pointing at the counter on the computer screen, which now read T-minus thirty seconds. "We were almost there! We almost beat the fucking computer!"

"The world's at stake, General. We need to make sure she can do this when it matters."

The shock of the heart attack pushed Providence out of Subject One's mind. She stared down at the convulsing body. She cursed and bit her lip as she reached back into his psyche and embraced his pain.

She pushed through his mental fog of toxins and trauma so that she might navigate his neurons. She slowed his breathing and relaxed his muscles. She gripped his failing heart and sang it back into rhythm.

The subject stopped seizing. His breathing regulated. He was alive, despite what the algorithm had predicted. Providence had done it. She'd proven that destiny could be shifted with the proper leverage.

"How did you know that all the four subjects were destined to perish right then?" Dr. Wallach asked. "How did you know I was lying?"

Providence looked down at her can of Pepsi, her reward for finishing the experiment. She stayed quiet for a few moments, afraid to answer. She hated most of the people in the Black Box, but not him.

She loved him, as best as she understood the concept, and she didn't want to disappoint him.

"I . . . I'm not sure. I just . . . knew."

Dr. Wallach placed a finger beneath her chin and raised her head so that she would meet his gaze.

"You just knew?"

Providence stared into his bulging, emerald eyes and felt a twinge of shame.

"Yes."

"And how did you stop his heart attack? How did you keep him alive when he'd been fated to die?"

"I, um—I took over his body and sang to his heart. I helped it find its rhythm."

"But how did you make his heart respond to your song? How did you break the hold of death?"

"I—" She couldn't explain this any more than she could explain how her heart beat or how her hair grew. "I don't know. I just willed it, I guess."

Dr. Wallach took her hand and smiled.

"That's excellent, Providence! That is what we want!"

"It is?"

"Yes, my dear!" he shouted, slapping the table.

Providence smiled then sipped her Pepsi. The sugar was nice, but it was the cold carbonation she loved. She was always so hot, always sweating and feverish, even when everyone else in the Black Box shivered and complained about the cold. The Pepsi cooled her, and the bubbles tickled her mouth.

"You have tapped into the infinite, my dear. You have the power to save the world—the power to do whatever you choose."

Providence looked into Dr. Wallach's eyes. She searched them for lies or sarcasm. She found only sincerity.

"Does this mean that I can leave now? Does this mean that I can see the stars?"

Dr. Wallach frowned, then ran his long tongue across his thin lips.

"I'm afraid not just yet. We only have eleven hours until the extinction event."

The girl stared down, past the lip of the can and into the Pepsi. The lights in the ceiling reflected off the dark surface of her drink, creating a microcosmic galaxy.

"But you said that when I mastered my talents—when I tapped into the infinite—that I would be allowed to see the stars."

"That's not what I said, Providence." Dr. Wallach frowned.

"Yes, it was!."

Tears mingled with her sweat and dropped into her cola, sending ripples through the space-time of her soft drink cosmos.

"No. Those were not my words, and I've told you the importance of speech—the importance of saying exactly what you mean."

Providence wiped away her tears, but they kept coming. How stupid had she been to think that any of her captors might be honest with her? Dr. Wallach was just another agent. He was just another man doing a job and she was just an asset. It was foolish to think otherwise.

"The event is coming. Everything changes in less than a day," Dr. Wallach said. "You decide how it changes, Providence. Not General Adams. Not The Norns. You."

"I saved one person's life! One! I'm not ready to save the world!"

"I think you're ready to do whatever you want."

"I'm not, and why would I even want to save the world? So I can rot in this hell forever? You're all liars and you're never going to let me see the stars!"

The can of Pepsi trembled on the table. Pinpricks of starlight pierced through the billowing fog that rolled out from the liquid's surface. Providence did not notice, but Dr. Wallach nodded in approval.

"I've never lied to you, Providence," Dr. Wallach said, wiping the tears from her face. "But I've guided you as far as I'm able. It's time for me to go."

The anger on the girl's face melted into panic and sorrow.

"You're leaving? No!"

The can of Pepsi burst and dark liquid spread across the table, cold fog rolling from its surface.

"You're on your own now. It's your decision if the world is saved. It's your decision if you see the stars."

"I can't do this without you," Providence said between sobs. "I can't beat that computer, and I can't stay in this hellhole with no who cares."

"The gods of fate don't rest in an algorithm. The Norns are a manmade monster. And this place is no Tartarus. It's just a grave waiting to be filled."

Providence reached out and gripped Dr. Wallach's hands. An armed guard, one of two by the door, raised his gun. Dr. Wallach glared at the man and he lowered the weapon.

"Please don't leave me."

Dr. Wallach leaned forward and pressed his forehead against Providence's hircine horns. He closed his eyes and gripped her hands.

"There's nothing else I can teach you, but if you need guidance there is one place you may look." He whispered the words. "There is a witch named Angrboda . . ."

Static squelched from a speaker in the ceiling and General Adams's voice thundered in the room.

"Lieutenant, get him out of there!"

Providence glanced at the ceiling, then all across the room. The guard raised his gun and came toward them. She didn't know why.

Dr. Wallach took her face in his hands and commanded her gaze.

"She is the weaver of destiny and the mother of tragedy." His words were rushed and intense. "Reach out into the world and find her."

One guard took hold of Providence, while the other knocked Dr. Wallach to the floor. The lieutenant aimed his rifle at Dr. Wallach and commanded him to shut his mouth.

"She will take you into the infinite and grant you all the power you need!" Dr. Wallach shouted, ignoring the guards and looking deep into Providence's eyes.

"Get him out, now!" a voice echoed over the speaker.

The guard kicked Dr. Wallach in the ribs. He groaned in pain. Providence screamed and tried to overtake the guard's mind, but she couldn't. This guard, like everyone else in The Black Box, had an Isa implant on the back of his neck—a piece of cybernetic hardware meant to neutralize her powers. A single vertical line of red light showed on the implant's display.

Unable to possess the guard, Providence broke off the tab of her Pepsi can and jumped onto his back. He flung around wildly, trying to throw her off as she jammed the small piece of aluminum into one of his eyes. Blood and tears drizzled down her fingertips.

Before she could take more than an eye from the guard, Providence heard the clicking of a stun gun from behind her. Electricity coursed through her body, sending her into convulsions. The world spun into silent darkness.

Providence awoke in a white, windowless room. Her captors called it her quarters, but she knew it was a cell. Nylon straps held her to the bed, and an IV dripped mind-numbing poison into her veins.

Sweat saturated her clothes and her sheets. Neither the drugs nor the blasting air conditioner helped much to cool her.

She glanced around, but her vision was blurred. Maybe it was the drugs, or maybe the stun gun had short-circuited something in her brain.

"You know that guard you maimed has a name."

General Adams sat on a chair beside her bed. He jabbed an accusing finger into her side. Afterimages of his hand stayed behind after each poke.

"His name is James Filmore. He has a wife and a little girl. Now he'll never be able to see them right again."

Providence looked up at the ceiling, dreaming of the stars secreted above the concrete layers of the Black Box. She imagined the absolute cold and quiet of that black place that would steal the breath from men like Adams and shut them up for good.

The general grabbed Providence by the cheeks and forced her to look at him. Anger burned in his eyes, but also desperate fear. As much as he tried to hide his terror, he couldn't. The end of the world was coming, and he wasn't ready for it. She needn't reach into his mind to know that.

"Where's Dr. Wallach?" Providence asked.

"Dr. Wallach broke the rules and has been sidelined from the project."

"Did you hurt him?"

"Not as much as I should have."

Providence wanted to reach into the general's mind and pluck out the answers she sought. If she happened to do some damage while rummaging for those answers, all the better. She couldn't of course. He was protected from her.

"So what now?" Providence asked, too weary and high to argue.

"Your little temper tantrum cost us precious time. We have less than six hours. The Norns have narrowed it down to a small list of names who might trigger the extinction event. You're going to kill them."

"I can't do that if I'm drugged up," she said looking down at the straps and the IV. "And I don't think you trust me when I'm not."

General Adams leaned in close to the girl and patted her face.

"No, I don't. But I trust my tech," he said, tapping the implant on the back of his neck. "And I get the impression you care about Dr. Wallach. If you play any games—if you don't do exactly as I say—I'll put a bullet in his face."

Tears came. Providence had learned to keep from crying after a lifetime in the Black Box, but the drugs always shattered her resolve. A whispered curse escaped her lips.

"Save that anger for the bad guys, little girl."

The general shut off the IV drip then headed toward the door. Providence glared at him, but it hurt to stare so intently. The light of the room intensified into a gleaming aura around him, and his movements left drug-induced after images burned in the air.

"Sober up," he said without looking back. "We don't have much time."

Providence closed her eyes and let the drugs coax her back into sleep. She muttered to herself as she drifted away.

"Angrboda . . ."

Providence woke up in a blanket of snow. She lay still for a moment, embracing the chill and looked to the heavens, hoping to finally see the stars, but there were none. The sky was a field of darkest blue, mottled with obsidian clouds. If alien suns did shine above her, their light was too weak to penetrate this place.

She rose, the frozen ground creaking beneath her. Cold winds blew upon her naked flesh, comforting her body and soul.

The world was tundra to the south and the west. Far to the east, the cyclopean walls of a dead, frozen city stretched high into the starless night. But it was to the north that Providence found her attention drawn—to a burial cairn on the broken cliffs that marked the end of the world.

Providence walked up the rising and narrowing cliff, her platinum hair dancing in the wind. She reached the piled stones and studied the strange, angular symbols carved into the monument. She had never seen them but she knew their meanings nonetheless. She spoke the name inscribed.

"Angrboda . . ."

The cliff trembled, knocking stones from the cairn off the cliff and into the nothingness beyond. White mist oozed from the spaces between the rocks, congealing into an incorporeal spirit, wrapped in a cloak of fog. Its face was obscured beneath the shadows of a spectral hood, but a single eye glowed in the dark recess.

"Who is this girl, to me unknown, that has called me back down this troublesome road?" the ghost asked. Its voice was hollow and husky and it spoke in a tone that might have been musical in life.

"My name is Providence and I seek Angrboda, the wisest of witches and the mother of tragedy."

"You have read the name on the rocks," the ghost spoke, "and to you I have come. What wisdom do you seek, Providence—girl who would save the world?"

"What force will destroy my world and how do I stop it?"

The ghost stood silent and studied Providence with a single glowing eye. The hungry nothingness beyond the cliff sucked at the air around them, sending Providence's hair into a wild dance, and pulling at the wispy cloak of the specter.

"I shall speak no more."

Providence leaned toward the ghost, pressing her body against the cold stones of the cairn.

"Please," she whispered. "I was told to seek you out. I was told you could guide me."

The ghost let out a disgusted huff.

"I don't know your game, but you are no girl, and your name is not as clever as you think."

Providence ran her fingers over the runes on the cairn, but the feel of the engravings did not match the sight of them. Smooth rock lay where inscriptions could be seen, and rough lines where the stone looked even.

"And you are not Angrboda," Providence said, realizing that the name she saw on the stones was an illusion. "You are a dead and jealous thing, who would see everything follow it to the grave."

The frigid nothingness sucked at the specter and its hood flew back revealing the face of an old man. His skin was marked with lines of age and lines of battle. Crimson gore stained his white beard. One eye glowed with anger and wisdom, while a black hole filled the other socket.

"Ride home, little witch. Sully no more my grave," the ghost spoke, its voice now changed. It was no longer husky or hollow, but deep, musical, and commanding. "Ride home little witch, back into the darkest pit of Hel where you belong."

Providence woke up in the sweltering confines of the Black Box. She could no longer feel the sedatives, and her head did not pound with the after-effects. A medic stood above her, removing the needle of a saline drip from her arm.

Three soldiers trained their assault rifles on her and urged her out of bed. She rose without complaint and let herself be led from her cell. The guards and the medic stayed behind Providence, their guns aimed at her back as they marched her to another part of the facility—a room nicknamed "The Pool."

Providence was sure there was something below these particular corridors. It tugged at her soul, like a hungry singularity devouring light. It called for her to burrow through the ground so that she might merge with it. The girl slowed upon this sensation, but only for a moment before the muzzle of an assault rifle urged her forward.

"What's below us?" she asked, realizing she had been too afraid to do so in all her years.

"Below us?" one of the guards answered, nudging her forward with his rifle. "The darkest pit of Hell. Now shut up and walk."

She fantasized about letting her consciousness fall back through her body, and into one of the guards. A snippet of gunfire and bloodshed played out in her mind. How easy it would be if they were not shielded by those implants. She could bounce between their minds forcing them to fire on one another, leaving each of their wives widowed and their children orphaned, all in a matter of seconds.

A few more twists and turns through the labyrinthine halls and they arrived at The Pool. The room housed a sensory deprivation tank that looked, as the name implied, like a small pool. Wires, tubes, and sensors stretched out from computer workstations where three hunched technicians monitored and controlled a number of variables.

General Adams stood by the tank. His back was straight and his face cold as stone, but his eyes were bloodshot and a day's growth of stubble marred his face. Cracks were appearing in his stoic façade.

"The Norns have identified three figures from around the world who may be responsible for the extinction event. You're going to find them, possess them, and kill them."

"How much time do we have left?" Providence asked.

"Just under four hours."

"If they're far away, in another country or on some other continent, that won't be enough time. It takes too much out of me."

General Adams put his hand on the girl's shoulder and looked deep into her icy, blue eyes.

"Wallach says you have no limits, and I don't care what it takes out of you. I don't care if it kills you. You will find these men, you will end them, and you will save the damn world."

Providence didn't argue. She disrobed, letting her orange jumpsuit fall to the floor, and walked up the plastic ladder of the sensory deprivation tank. Concentric circles rippled through the water where she breached the surface tension, and Providence sunk until she was shoulder deep. She laid back and floated upon the surface, the water filling her ears and dulling the noise of the world.

The water was frigid—salinized so that it could be kept below freezing. Providence found comfort in that cold. It was a release from the intense, enervating heat that plagued her existence.

Muffled voices spoke commands and affirmations. The medic closed the lid. For a moment all was cold and dark. These were Providence's favorite moments—the solitary emptiness just before a mission.

A video screen popped to life on the lid above her. Pictures and video clips flashed across the display. They were all of one man—an Asian dictator with the cocksure arrogance that comes from inherited power.

Providence closed her eyes and let the dark and cold carry her consciousness away. She rode upon waves of black aether and after a few moments could feel herself dissolving. Her essence thinned and she became increasingly intertwined with the void. Higher thought stretched to dissolution, and comforting oblivion set in. As a shadow, she stretched across existence, omniscient without thought, all-seeing without vision.

Some fragment of her psyche found the despot and instinctively summoned the rest of her mind. Her consciousness reformed, bits of her essence snapping back unto itself.

Providence opened her eyes to a lavish office on the other side of the world. She cursed at the bright lights from the overhead fixtures.

She looked at her hands, but they weren't hers. They were the wrong color, size, and shape. Fat, stubby fingers wiggled where she was used to seeing long, graceful digits.

Providence turned and caught her reflection in a glass door leading to a balcony. The face staring back at her, imperfectly reflected as it was, confirmed that she had found her target. She walked to the sliding doors and stepped out to the night-cloaked balcony.

The skyline of a gleaming metropolis greeted her. Skyscrapers designed with a utopian aesthetic shone in the night and stretched to the sky. To some it must have been impressive, but Providence was not moved by the urban thrall. Instead, she turned her gaze to the sky.

The stars above were blurry and dull, as they always were through another person's eyes, but there were also so few. The balcony was so high that Providence thought that she should be able to stand up on her tip-toes and run her finger across the welkin, but as close as she was, so little starlight shined. She looked out at the skyline, shining with the fire of a million electric lights, and she cursed it. Not just the city, but the very light itself—that fraudulent, manmade illumination that blocked out the gleam of the heavens.

"Someday . . ." she uttered, to the muted night sky.

Providence gripped the railing of the balcony, ready to throw herself off so that she might be done with this mission when she felt the phone in her pocket. She pulled it out and examined it. A number pad appeared on the screen and Providence ripped through her victim's mind for the code. She punched in the numbers, opening the phone's menu, then pressed a microphone icon.

"Who is Angrboda?" she asked, in the despot's voice.

Search results came up in foreign characters that she was able to comprehend after manhandling her target's psyche a bit further. Blood ran down her nose and from her ears as she scrolled past one result after another, each describing myths of a terrible giantess.

The wife of Loki.

The Bringer of Sorrows.

The mother Hel, who dwells in Jotunheim.

A mere legend . . .

Providence dropped the phone.

A Children's story . . .

She looked to the few stars in the sky.

Nonsense . . .

She heaved herself over the ledge.

Providence awoke within the cold darkness of the sensory deprivation tank. She breathed in, cherishing the few moments she might steal to herself before the lid was opened.

The monitor flashed back on, blinding her for a moment, and casting back the merciful darkness. Another series of images and videos played out across the screen above her. This time of an older man with white hair and pale skin. In the media that played across the monitor, he was most often seen standing in front of the flag that all the soldiers and officers from the facility wore on their uniforms—a series of red and white stripes beside a field of blue mottled with white stars. She had grown to dislike that flag, as she had grown to dislike most of the people in the Black Box, but she appreciated the design. Streaks of blood upon white snow, and stars shining in a dark, blue sky. It was all she wanted from life—the embrace of the cold, the freedom to paint the ground crimson with her captors' blood, and escape into the heavens themselves.

Providence licked her lips and she could taste the coppery flavor of blood. Her nose was bleeding from the exertion of the last mission, and Adams did not plan on giving her a break.

"I'm bleeding," She said. "I can't do this."

"You can and you will."

"Sir, her vitals are stressed," another voice cut in from the background. "We may lose her if we push that hard again."

The speaker cut off with a squelch. Providence let her head fall back into the water and wept. She knew that General Adams didn't care if she died. He saw her as a tool to be used until she broke.

"I can't do this without you," she muttered to Dr. Wallach, even though he wasn't there.

"You have forty minutes, girl," Adams said over the speakers.

Providence closed her eyes and let sleep overtake her as she floated in the darkness.

"Hello, Providence," Dr. Wallach said, gazing at his reflection in a pool of toilet water.

You're alive. Providence's voice echoed through Dr. Wallach's brain. She hadn't even realized that she was in his head until she heard her own words.

"For now. And how fairs my sweet Providence?"

They removed your Isa implant?

"No."

Then how am I in your head?

"How long did you think they could shackle you with trinkets of silicon and plastic? You're not a child anymore."

Providence took control of Dr. Wallach's body, more out of instinct than intent, and scanned the surroundings. He was in a cell, less hospitable than her own. Her prison at least kept up the pretense of being "private quarters." Dr. Wallach was quite plainly incarcerated.

There is no Angrboda. She's a myth. Why send me chasing ghosts?

"It was my final gift you, Providence."

How is that a gift?

Her voice bellowed through Dr. Wallach's mind, eliciting blood from his nose and ears. Providence felt his pain and was immediately ashamed for hurting her only friend. Dr. Wallach was not upset, though. He laughed, then ran his tongue up over his lip to catch a taste of the blood.

"How is it not a gift, my dear? I gave you all that you need to tap into the infinite—all you require to take the reins of fate."

You gave me nothing.

"Exactly! You sought the wisdom of a witch who doesn't exist, to save a world you do not love, from a monster that no one knows."

I don't understand!

"You will, Providence. And when you do, you *will* see the stars."

Providence tired of Dr. Wallach's riddles, or his insanity—whichever it was on display. She tore into his mind, ready to pluck out the secrets he hid, no matter how much she might hurt him. He was surprisingly strong—stronger than any mind she had invaded—and she could only grab snippets of thought.

The taste of wine and calamari—a favorite meal.

Naked men and women dancing on a snow-covered beach in the moonlight.

She dug deeper, tossing aside these unimportant bits. Dr. Wallach screamed and covered his bleeding ears.

A monstrous array of networked computers and monitors below a digital clock—The Norns.

She was getting closer. She tore deeper into Dr. Wallach's mind as he thrashed about his cell.

An ice sculpture in her image, but grown and weathered with age.

"I'm sorry, Providence," Dr. Wallach said, "but I can't let you cheapen this."

He threw himself back toward the toilet and gazed down at his reflection. Crimson streams ran from every orifice, but his eyes showed no sign of anger or fear.

"I love you, Providence."

Without hesitation, Dr. Wallach shoved his face into the water and inhaled deeply. Providence tried to stop him. She tried to force him to stand, and cough up the water, but she was evicted from his mind.

Providence awoke, gasping for breath. She could still taste the toilet water and feel it in her lungs.

"No!" she screeched, banging on the lid.

"What the hell is wrong with her now?" General Adams's voice echoed from the speakers in the sensory deprivation tank. "We don't have time for this."

Providence thrashed in the water and screamed for Dr. Wallach, knowing full well he was dead or dying. She slammed her fists against the lid, shattering the video display.

"God damn it! Sedate her, but nothing too heavy!" Adams growled through the speaker.

The lid opened and two men grabbed Providence. She thrashed against them as they dragged her from the tank. Blood dripped from her nose and between her legs.

She couldn't outmuscle them. Instead, she closed her eyes and concentrated on Adams. She conjured his terrible, gravel voice and the chemical smell of his aftershave in her mind. She imagined his stoic expression and troubled, bloodshot eyes. She thought of his cruel indifference and his threats against Dr. Wallach.

Her spirit reached out for his and her power shorted out the implant on his neck. She could feel it burning the flesh on the back of his neck and the electrical tingle that ran through his spine.

Providence allowed Adams to retain his awareness. She wanted him to experience what was about to play out. She wanted him to feel it all.

Adams was powerless as Providence forced him to pull his sidearm. She manipulated his body and put slugs into the heads of the three technicians, all in such quick succession that none of them realized what was happening. A moment later she forced him to shoot the medics who stood by her tank. Their blood contrasted beautifully with the white plastic. It reminded her of their striped flag.

A moment of confusion set over the room. Guards watched Adams, unsure what was happening or what they should do. He tried to warn them. He tried to command them to shoot him before it was too late, but no words came forth. Providence smiled with his mouth and aimed the pistol at the first guard.

She fired and a slug caught the man in the throat. Arterial spray gushed from his neck and his body slumped to the ground. The second and third guards each fired their assault rifles into the general's torso. The pain was incredible, but Providence only experienced it for a moment before jumping out of Adams's mind, leaving him alone with his suffering.

Adams collapsed and tried to utter a command for the men to kill themselves before she could take them, but only scarlet effervescence came from his mouth. Through the eyes of a guard, Providence watched him gurgle on his own blood.

The senior of the two soldiers took cautious steps toward the general, his rifle trained on him. The other, now possessed by Providence, stayed behind and fired into his comrade's back.

The possessed soldier watched his own hands bring the muzzle of the M4 assault rifle under his chin. Providence could have spared him from this fear. She could have put his consciousness to sleep and killed him with mercy, but she chose not to.

General Adams lifted his pistol, his hand trembling violently. Crimson bubbles oozed from his mouth, bursting as they rolled down his chin. Providence regarded him with a cool expression and strode across the room.

Adams tried to shoot, but Providence was in his mind again, keeping him from pulling the trigger. She knelt beside the general, unconcerned about the pool of blood around him, and plucked the gun from his hand, along with the security badge from his jacket.

"No bullets for me. No bullets for you. We both deserve to see how this ends, General."

Providence tossed the pistol away, far from Adams' reach, then left him to his final, painful moments. The door to The Pool opened as she approached. Two more guards stood on the other side, each aiming their rifles into the room. Providence reached into the minds of both men at once, frying their implants and forcing each to fire on the other.

Stepping over the dying men, she made her way to the elevator. There was still some time before the end of the world, and she wanted to see what lay in the darkest pit of Hell—that place the one-eyed ghost had told her to return to—that place at the bottom of the Black Box to which she had always felt drawn.

She swiped the security badge she had stolen from Adams over the elevator's sensor and the doors opened. She stepped inside and pushed the bottom button.

Providence made her way down, deep into the lowest reaches of the facility. The elevator stopped with a soft bounce and the doors opened to a massive laboratory. Directly across the room was a wall of networked computers and a dizzying array of monitors—the same ones she had seen in Dr. Wallach's mind. This was The Norns.

Cables ran from network hubs, all tying into a massive glass tank that stretched thirty feet to the vaulted ceiling. Entombed within the tank, floating in liquid, was a titanic figure with probes stabbed into her naked flesh—a horned giantess with Providence's face.

Two technicians lay dead on the ground, strangled with cables. Four more techs, the ones still alive, threw themselves to the ground. They kneeled and groveled as Providence stepped out of the elevator and into the lab.

"Brother Wallach said you would come," one of the men said, his forehead pressed to the floor.

"He said you would lead us into the infinite," another added.

Providence ignored the men and walked over to the giantess suspended in icy liquid. She pressed her hand against the glass and reached out for the mind of the creature that wore her face. She found only emptiness.

"She's dead," Providence whispered.

"No," a feminine voice said over speakers in the corners of the room. "Not entirely, at least."

Providence looked around the laboratory, finally focusing on the array of monitors. Three faces rendered themselves, pixel by pixel, across the screens. A girl of youth and beauty, a motherly figure, and a gray hag.

"This is Angrboda?"

"That is our mother," the youngest avatar replied.

"What happened to her?"

"Man, in his hubris, chained her and thought to steal her wisdom," the avatar in the center answered.

"But no man is not meant to wield such magic, no matter how cunning or ruthless he may be," added the crone. "It is but a recipe for their end."

Providence turned her attention back to the giantess and stroked the frigid tank. Perhaps it was arrogant, given how much they resembled one another, but she was stricken by Angrboda's beauty—the sharp angles of her features, the hypnotic spiraling of her obsidian horns, and the way her white hair billowed around her. She seemed at such peace, floating in the embrace of cold and death. Providence envied the dead witch.

"We saw this time coming," The Norns spoke in unison as the doomsday timer counted down to the end of the world. "The hour when our mother would awaken and enter the infinite."

"There's nothing inside her. She's dead," Providence responded. "Whatever there was left of Angrboda, I'm afraid it's gone."

"You're looking in the wrong place," the crone said.

Providence looked upon the face of the titanic corpse then at her vague reflection in the glass. Dr. Wallach had been right. She finally understood. She turned her back on The Norns and stepped past the groveling computer techs.

"If you'll excuse, I need to finally see the stars."

Providence stepped out from the blast doors that separated the Black Box from the outside world. The arctic air steamed against her blood-splattered flesh. She left no living soul within the facility, save for her cultists in the deepest depths of the facility, and General Adams who she hoped was still in agony. They too would soon be dead.

Providence walked out from under the concrete canopy of the Black Box, crimson footprints trailing behind her, a cold Pepsi in one hand. She looked up and let out a silent gasp. The night sky, seen through her own eyes, was as gorgeous as she had imagined. No—not as she had imagined—just as gorgeous as she remembered from another life. All the men she had possessed over the years—none could see more than a limited scope of light, and even that they viewed with weak, blurred vision. Now she looked out upon a cosmos, bathed in starlight, painted in radiation, and teeming with dark matter.

Providence opened her can of Pepsi. It made a satisfying hiss as she popped the tab. She took pleasure in the carbonation, the cold touch of the aluminum, and the sweet taste of the cola. Even now, seconds away from Armageddon, it was important to appreciate the little things.

Inside the facility, The Norns counted down the final seconds before the extinction event. Outside, Providence tossed her empty can into the snow. She ran her middle finger against her bloody sex and painted her chest with forgotten runes, now remembered. The symbols merged into one another, centering on a triangular vortex.

She spoke her own name, not the one the project had given her, but that name which was older than mankind. Her magic stripped away the atmosphere above and silence overtook the world. The snow around her melted, then boiled into gas. Providence rode the water vapor into the sky, then out into the stars.

Inside the Black Box—that grave at the end of the world—the clock had struck zero.

"The Quest of Iranon" and *Don Rodriguez:* Two Exercises in the Picaresque

Cecelia Hopkins-Drewer

This discussion will investigate the picaresque mode as exemplified in "The Quest of Iranon" by H. P. Lovecraft and *Don Rodriguez: Chronicles of Shadow Valley* by Lord Dunsany. The expectations of the genre include a rogue-like protagonist and geographic movement, and it will be demonstrated that the tales fulfill these criteria to some degree. While Dunsany's and Lovecraft's stories both appear to have elements of the picaresque, in the final examination the discussion will conclude each author has created his own permutations.

"The Quest of Iranon" will be discussed first because it is the earlier of the two tales, written in 1921 (Joshi and Schultz 77–78). This means that Lovecraft's venture into the picaresque chronologically predated Dunsany's most generally acknowledged picaresque work, first published as *The Chronicles of Rodriguez* in 1922 (see Joshi, *Lord Dunsany* 89–92). Joshi (*Subtler Magick* 72) remarks upon Lovecraft's "seeming anticipation" of Dunsanian achievement and attributes it partially to shared literary influences. Lovecraft also suggested that an "unconscious parallelism of manner . . . and independently similar cast of imagination" underpinned such coincidences (*Selected Letters* 2.95–96; see also Klein 39).

Adams notes the term picaresque is generally associated with the journey story (8–9, 54, 199) and has three essential elements. Firstly, the protagonist is lowborn or a mischievous rogue; secondly, the tale involves travel or movement; and thirdly, society is seen satirically throughout the tale. Ardila (1–18) traces a history of the picaresque from ancient times, with examples including *The Golden Ass* by Apulieus, also known as *Metamorphoses,* and the anonymous Spanish text *Lazarillo;* through European literature to *Moll Flanders* by Defoe and *Roderick Random* by Smollett; finally arriving at the American classic *Huckleberry Finn*, published in 1884. Twentieth-century "Neopicaresque" works may have shaped a new evolution of the form (Ardila 248).

Ardila deduces that the picaresque tale, especially in its Spanish form, was concerned with social mobility and the rise of the middle class (11). Comparison with Lovecraft stories, however, will often identify an inverted concern—the fall of the aristocracy and a correlated decline of the fine arts. The "Quest of Iranon" follows this theme, as Iranon claims to be the relic of the nobility of "Aira," where "my father was thy King" (249). Iranon stubbornly believes that he will be returned to nobility "and some day shall I reign over thy groves and gardens" (249). He may be deluded, as the reader learns near the end of the tale he is "a beggar's boy given to strange dreams" who "thought himself a King's son" (254).

An alternate interpretation allows for Iranon's fantasy to be true, i.e. the so-called beggar really was a dethroned king, and his son did find the magical city hidden amongst the sands. In this case, it would be the "antique shepherd" who "knew him from his birth" who was mistaken. The second interpretation is possible—but philosophically less satisfying—because it robs the tale of its picaresque satire. Emphasizing this satire allows Callaghan (72) to describe Iranon as the "Theseus myth . . . in reverse."

Traditionally, the hero of the picaresque is an outsider, a drifter, and a rogue. Iranon is certainly a drifter, as the story begins: "Into the granite city of Teloth wandered the youth" (248). Unable to find what he sought in Teloth, the wanderer moves on: "At the sunset Iranon and small Romnod went forth from Teloth, and for long wandered amidst the green hills and cool forests" (252). Iranon is also a misfit in Teloth, for the residents "liked not the colour of his tattered robe, nor the myrrh in his hair, nor his chaplet of vine-leaves" (248). His attitude leads their spokesperson to say, "Thou art a strange youth" (250).

The question as to whether Iranon is a rogue is an interesting one, and forms the pivot on which the social irony turns. The people of Teloth attempt to apprentice him to "Athok the cobbler," but Iranon has "no heart for the cobbler's trade" (250). The "archon" assures him, "All in Teloth must toil . . . for that is the law" (250), and "the gods of Teloth have said that toil is good" (250). Moreover, the industrialized philosophy of the city places the endeavors of an artist outside of the category of gainful employment.

When Iranon reaches Oonai he finds employment as a performing artist. "Often at night Iranon sang. . . . In the frescoed halls of the Monarch did he sing . . . the King bade him put away his tattered purple, and clothed him in satin and cloth-of-gold, with rings of green jade and bracelets of tinted ivory, and lodged him in a gilded and tapestried chamber" (253). The singing is regular and is recompensed with goods, transforming the activity of preference into a job. Iranon appears to have no problem with working as a performer, until his contribution is devalued by the arrival of the new novelty of "wild whirling dancers from the Liranian desert" (253).

Iranon's ability to sing for his supper makes his inclusion in the category of rogue ambiguous. If, as the shepherd says, his songs "of lands that never were, and things that never can be" and tales of "Aira" are a lie (254–55), Iranon may indeed be classed as a rogue, despite the amusement value of his efforts. But he seems to believe his own tales, which places him more in the category of prophet or wise fool, like the bard in literary tradition.

Another essential element of the picaresque tale is the motif of travel. "The Quest of Iranon" certainly includes travel. The tale begins in Teloth, a city with square buildings and "the Tower of Mlin" (248); it then moves into the countryside, where the "way was rough and obscure" and Iranon and Romnod "ate plentifully of fruit and red berries" (252). During this leg of the journey, Romnod appears to age, but Iranon does not, suggesting that there might be something magical about either Iranon or his songs (252).

Over a mountain, they find Oonai, a city of "harsh and glaring" lights, with wine and dancing (253). Romnod eventually dies in

Oonai, and Iranon moves along symbolically "[i]nto the sunset" to visit "all the cities of Cydathria and in the lands beyond the Bnazic desert" (254). Finally he reaches shepherd's cottage on "a stony slope above a quicksand marsh," where, if the resident is to be believed, Iranon was born and grew up (254). It seems that the wanderer has come full circle.

The travel motifs created by the regions Iranon visited are overlaid by mentions of the dreamlands he is seeking. These include "Aira, the city of marble and beryl" with "golden domes" (249), and places he claims to have visited such as "Narthos by the frigid Xari," "Sinara on the southern slope," "onyx-walled Jaren," where the soldiers scoffed and drove him away, "Stethelos," and even "the marsh where Sarnath once stood." Iranon claims to have also sojourned to "Thraa, Ilarnek, and Kadatheron on the winding river Ai," and lived in "Olathoë in the land of Lomar." These additional places add to the picaresque nature of the story (251).

Moreover, according to Guillén (Cappelle 18–19), the picaresque style is frequently "pseudo-autobiographical" and employs the first-person point of view. "The Quest of Iranon" is written in the third person, but the lengthy monologues create an autobiographical impression (for example, Iranon's speech [249–50]). Moving on to *Don Rodriguez: Chronicles of Shadow Valley*, a similar feature can be observed. Here the narrative is third-person, but the peculiar use of "Mine host" creates an autobiographical feel (Dunsany 1, 4–5).

Don Rodriguez: Chronicles of Shadow Valley takes a few paragraphs to get going, which is a significant proportion because each chronicle is short. At first the narrative does not appear to fit the pattern of the picaresque, because the protagonist is a young nobleman who is gifted a sword by his dying father, and not a rogue (2). Travel is involved, because Rodriguez resolves to seek out the glories of war (3). However, at the accommodation he chooses, "the Inn of the Dragon and Knight," his evil host climbs down a rope like a spider, determined to murder him. By the end of the "First Chronicle" Rodriguez kills the creature (10–11).

In the "Second Chronicle," Rodriguez has become more like the "picaro" or rogue protagonist. He sets out on the road again, accompanied by the comedic servant, Morano. Fearful of pursuit from "la Garda," Morano disguises himself as Rodriguez, and Rodriguez disguises himself as Morano (15–17). They are captured, but Rodriguez bamboozles the Garda with the help of a village priest (18–20). In the "Third Chronicle," he is rejoined by Morano, who also has ways of outsmarting the Garda (21), and the adventurers arrive at the residence of a magician (28–35). In the "Fourth Chronicle," the "professor" entertains them by showing them wonders (36–46). In the "Fifth Chronicle," they rescue a man from hanging (49–54) and deliver stolen horses to a mysterious blacksmith (60).

In the "Sixth Chronicle" Morano knocks a man out with a frying pan (62), and Rodriguez fails to attract the attention of the beautiful Serafina (66–67). In the "Seventh Chronicle," Rodriguez passes through "the Shadow Valley" (72–79). The "Eighth Chronicle" sees the travelers move on restlessly, until a boat takes them to the Pyrenees, where they camp in the rocky outdoors (90–92). In the "Ninth Chronicle" they join an army that wants to hear songs played on the mandolin (95), overpower a man, and demand his castle as ransom (97–98). However, Don Alvidar's castle is apparently lost or never existed in the first place (102–3). Subsequently, the "Tenth Chronicle" sees a return to Shadow Valley and the settlement of "Lowlight," where Serafina dwells. (109–10). The "Eleventh Chronicle" presents a romantic interlude in the garden (113–14). In the "Twelfth Chronicle" the King of Shadow Valley gives Rodriguez a castle, where he and Serafina marry and live happily ever after (126–30).

Lovecraft and Dunsany both adopt an archaic style, but there are differences. Taking the first sentence of *Don Rodriguez*, analysis shows that the subject, "the Lord of the Valleys of Arguento Harez," is followed by the verb, "called," and object, "his eldest son" (1). This is the typical Subject → Verb → Object order of the English language (Fromkin, Rodman, and Hyams 350), and while the embedded descriptive and prepositional phrases give it a slightly unusual feel, the sentence follows an anticipated pattern. Dunsany shows a preference for strong punctuation, dividing his dependent clauses with commas and semicolons, while asides are placed in parentheses. Reading through the "First Chronicle" we observe he frequently begins sentences with "And," "Now," "So," and "Nor," employing these words as prepositions and interjections rather than conjunctions. He additionally uses conjunctions for their conventional joining function within sentences. Prominent archaisms include "Thence" (3) and "Verily" (6), which are also used to commence sentences.

Analysis of the first sentence of the "The Quest of Iranon" shows that Lovecraft employs an alternate word order. The object is embedded in the prepositional phrase, "the granite city of Teloth," preceding the verb "wandered" and subject "the youth" (248). The Object → Verb → Subject sentence order is less common in English usage and has an unaccustomed feel. He could be attempting the passive voice, but the "the youth" is still the active agent, and the noun phrase carries a string of embedded adjectival phrases including "vine-crowned, his yellow hair glistening with myrrh and his purple robe torn" (250). Another accepted strategy is topicalization, where the object is moved forward in the sentence, although this technique works best with a short sentence (see Fromkin, Rodman, and Hyams 163). Lovecraft's resultant syntax tends toward the complex and oblique. It is readable, even poetic, but requires effort to understand.

Lovecraft's punctuation is meticulous but typographically lighter than Dunsany's, as he does not habitually place a comma before the first instance of a conjunction (248–50). Scanning a few pages, we find that Lovecraft occasionally begins a sentence with "And." These instances are generally associated with the character's speech and perform the more conventional continuity function (249, 250). He appears fond of specifying conditions and making exceptions using "if," "but," "or," and "nor"; and constructing rhetorical or persuasive questions, such as: "Were not death more pleasing?" (250). Some of his sentences are longer than average (for example, Iranon's travel description on 251) and contain multiple adjectives, with the occasional simile incorporated. Archaisms include "Wherefore," "Thou," "art" (verb), and "speakest" (250).

"The Quest of Iranon" makes allusions that are fantastic and exotically classical, such as "wreaths" of "vine leaves" (254); *Don Rodriguez* indulges the romantic superstitions of Catholicism. Rodriguez has been educated at the "College of San Josephus" (13) and is concerned for his "soul." His ability to speak Latin allows him to appeal to the priest for sanctuary (18–19). Having killed a monster is a "blessing for Spain" and entitles him to "absolution" for his violence (20). The "Saints of Heaven" protect him and Morano from evil spirits conjured by "the professor" (36), and the spell is broken when Morano makes "the sign of the cross" using the sword and the frying pan (45).

While the medieval motifs are presented humorously, they are also allowed to define the story, as even the ruse of Don Alvidar in claiming a "magician" vanished his castle is believed because "the child swore by the cross" (103). Perhaps, one might speculate, Dunsany was inspired by the contemporary campaign for his kinsman Archbishop Oliver Plunkett's beatification. Plunkett was declared a martyr by the Catholic Church on St. Patrick's Day 1918, and "blessed" at a ceremony in Rome at on Sunday, 23 May 1920. He was finally declared a saint in 1975 (see Saint Peter's Parish). Dunsany also enlivens his medieval episodes with a generous serving of humor and pithy dialogue.

One motif the two stories share is the food-loving side character. It is Morano in *Don Rodriguez* who constantly prepares bacon (17), and Romnod in "The Quest of Iranon" who enjoys feasting and the good life in Oonai, eventually dying "red and fattened" (253). Another commonality is that both writers have used music as a metaphor for the value of art. This theme is seen throughout Lovecraft's tale as Iranon is on a quest "to find those who would listen gladly to his songs and dreams" (254). The quest appears to have divine blessing, as indicated by Iranon's halo (249). Using the comic mode, Dunsany makes the same point by having Rodriguez fight for the "right army," selected because the men will listen to his mandolin (94–95).

In these samples, both tales qualify as picaresque, as a result of their use of the three essential elements of the genre, although neither is exactly what the reader may expect. Dunsany employs more narrative clarity than Lovecraft and makes less excessive use of adjectives. *Don Rodriguez* contains a love interest and happy ending; while "The Quest of Iranon" ends with disillusionment and death. Lovecraft tends more toward social irony, where Dunsany is humorously entertaining.

Works Cited

Adams, Percy G. *Travel Literature and the Evolution of the Novel.* 1983. Lexington: University Press of Kentucky, 2015.

Ardila, J. A. G., ed. *The Picaresque Novel in Western Literature.* Cambridge: Cambridge University Press, 2015.

Callaghan, Gavin. (2013) *H. P. Lovecraft's Dark Arcadia.* Jefferson, NC: McFarland, 2013.

Cappelle, K. "The 'New American Picaresque' at Mid-Century: An Analysis of Jack Kerouac's *On the Road* and J. D. Salinger's *The Catcher in the Rye.*" M.A. thesis: University of Ghent, 2011. Accessed online from: pdfs.semanticscholar.org/324b/4fb119bd4b49b9509e1dfc3b3a9425f95f88.pdf

Dunsany, Lord. *Don Rodriguez: Chronicles of Shadow Valley.* 1922. n.p.: Createspace, 2017.

Fromkin, Victoria; Rodman, Robert; and Hyams, Nina. *An Introduction to Language.* 7th ed. Boston: Thompson Heinle, 2003.

Joshi, S. T. *Lord Dunsany: Master of the Anglo-Irish Imagination.* Westport, CT: Greenwood Press, 1995.

———. *A Subtler Magick: The Writings and Philosophy of H. P. Lovecraft.* Mercer Island, WA: Borgo Press, 1996.

————, and David E. Schultz. *An H. P. Lovecraft Encyclopedia.* New York: Hippocampus Press, 2004.

Klein, T. E. D. *Providence After Dark and Other Writings.* New York: Hippocampus Press, 2019.

Lovecraft, H. P. "The Quest of Iranon." In *Collected Fiction: A Variorum Edition.* Ed. S. T. Joshi. New York: Hippocampus Press, 2015–19. 1.248–55.

———— *Selected Letters.* Ed. August Derleth, Donald Wandrei, and James Turner. Sauk City, WI: Arkham House, 1965–76. 5 vols.

Saint Peter's Parish, Drogheda. *The Canonisation of St. Oliver Plunkett.* 2015. Accessed 1 January 2021 from www.saintoliverplunkett.com/pdf/Book_3__The_Canonisation_of_St._Oliver_Plunkett.pdf

Like Vultures

Scott J. Couturier

Above, the metal fan blades circle like vultures.

I have no idea why I'm here.

They grabbed me off the street during my morning run. A big black van, with round tinted windows, the decal of some indecipherable rune stuck on each door panel. I had my headphones in, didn't hear as they threw open the doors, crept up, and seized me from behind. Then—chloroform, or some stinking chemical, pressed over my mouth, half-senseless body dragged into the van's hot, dim interior. As consciousness faded they tied a blindfold over my eyes, double-darkness falling to obliterate.

I woke in some damp and lightless cellar space, surrounded by others. I could hear their moans, their groans, their pitiable whines and screams, though in the pitch-darkness none of us could see the others. Perhaps I still wore the blindfold? Perhaps they'd gouged out my eyes, and I would never see again? I didn't know.

In the distance we could all hear chanting. Low, murmurous, and sinister, at first reminiscent of Catholic masses remembered from my childhood. This led to other, more evil memories, Father Morgan sliding his hands beneath the hem of my altar boy's robe. . . . The groans around me amplified, becoming almost frantic, and I joined my misery to the chorus. When in hell, and all.

The darkness never broke, not for untold hours, though the distant chanting grew nearer and stranger. We all writhed together in that restless sepulcher, like maggots dreading an impending exhumation. I knew—we all knew—they were coming for us. At last, the ambient black exploded with the vibration of ritual cries, torches flaring to fill up that cavernous hole of sorrow.

I still had my eyes. I saw my fellows in captivity, chained along the uneven, moisture-slick rock wall. Some were naked, bruised and bloodied, showing signs of long occupation in the hole. Others were fresh, like me—still wearing their clothes from outside, eyes bright with a feverish fear and panic where others shone dull with accumulated suffering, numbed by dread.

I thrashed myself against the stone as the torchbearers came to unchain me from the wall. Who they were, what was their purpose . . . All I could see were hideously tall figures swathed from crown to foot in black robes, faces obscured by silver masks filigreed with obscene designs, dull gems inset in the bright-polished metal. It reflected the torches, so their faces seem to glow, to burn . . .

Resistance is token where agency is nil. I was unchained from the wall, another cloth strip wound over my eyes. I gagged at the stench, bits of withered skin clinging to the sheet—it was a grave binding, unwound from a corpse long-putrefied! Limbs shivering, voice raised in pointless pleading and demands, I felt myself ushered out of that benighted cell on a tide of silver-masked worshippers, whose voices were raised in a vile cacophony of unctuous, atonal chanting. Drums, timbrels, flutes, and ill-tuned lyres maintained a morbid air as I was marched down, down, down, through successive cycles of humid cave and catacomb. Things crunched, scuttled, or squelched under my feet. Reaching out at intervals to steady myself, I felt the walls thick with a mucous-like secretion, bubbled with jellyish growths that trembled when I touched them. And always the chanting, diabolic and strange, intoxicating and sickening, rank with devotion to something so foul its essence permeated their wordless rhythms. Or rather—*were* they words, just such words as no human mouth could properly pronounce?

I felt blasts of sticky, stinking air, currents of musky tomb-cool relief. At intervals we passed open passages in the walls; others were with me, taken from my own cell or from elsewhere. Who knows how many such holes they have, holding however many prisoners, honeycombing the bedrock with pits of sightless suffering? And yet,

I wished they'd left me behind, chained to the wall in the noisome dark. Better that than this forced march ever downwards, to some untold, unspeakable fate. At intervals I heard the scream of others as they were hauled off down adjoining passages, right or left; but I continued my descent, manhandled by my captors, the dull flare of their torchlight barely filtering through the festered black cloth binding my eyes.

At last, when my harried footsteps began to stumble, we emerged into a subterranean vault. I could tell because the sound of their chanting, never-ceasing, swelled to fill the vast space. Others, it seemed to me, must be there, more wearers of the black robes and the silver masks, more singers of that endless, nameless, wordless intonation. We were herded forward with prods from what felt like spears, or halberd-tips: I reached up to claw the blindfold from my eyes, but heavy hands savagely gripped my wrists and twisted them behind my back, binding them with rope. Finally I unleashed the scream that had been building up in me like pressure in a teakettle, only to have those same heavy hands strike a blow to my temple. I swooned and slipped into half-unconsciousness, felt the scrape of stone as my body was dragged toward some unknowable destination.

Stirring awhile later, I heard the neat slice of knives on flesh, coupled to agonized screams cut short by gurgles and wheezes. Slit throats, punctured lungs—I felt a flash from the world *before*, when I was just a medical student out jogging in the early morning, thinking about that afternoon's autopsy. I heard the flow of blood, trickling—*gushing*—into a chasm, only the faintest patter as it struck some abyssal bottom below. It reminded me of the sinks on the morgue tables, where all the posthumous fluids flow. Blood, bile, pus, digestive and spinal admixture, all swirling together in a homologous soup. Then down the drain, twirling clockwise, the corpse staring and silent, tag on its toe hanging unerringly still.

This is a different world. Here, corpses rise and move, thrive and feed. At least, that's what I think I heard down in the depths. A mass shambling, faint groans, the lapping of tongues as rivers of blood coursed like hot slop into a trough. I felt bile rising in my throat, started to vomit; one of the chanters grabbed me by the neck and positioned me over the chasm, my sick raining down alongside effluence of the sacrificed to nourish whatever feasted unseen in the darkness below.

A knife was set at my throat, then over my heart, each lung, my groin. The chanting beat in my ears like a constant of nature, rising and falling with rhythmic perfection only marred by the hideous atonality of its progression. I smelt burning flesh, heard that most unmistakable of sounds: intestines being sloppily unspooled from the body cavity. Gore sloughed into the pit as I trembled in the grip of wicked hands, knife continuing to trace a languid, sharp, sensuous path. At last it stopped to hover just over my hamstrings, and finally! the expected pain. Two quick slits made, two hisses between my teeth. Spurts of blood as my feet folded limp against the stone, useless.

They took to working on me then. Cutting into me with multiple blades, carving out signs unseen but intimately felt, on soul as well as flesh. Then, skin a script of sigils, they dragged my mutilated husk back up from those nether deeps, from which I never thought to return. Back to the black room for a spell, chained to the wall, where I joined my groans and screams to the throng in wholehearted degradation. My body marred, my mind sick and reeling, fever starting to set in from the cuts . . . God knows what I rolled in, on the edge of that chasm wherein unliving things flourish and feed.

After an aeon of dream-stupor, they came for me again. Not with chanting this time, but low murmurous mantras, as if in the presence of something blessed. With uncommon gentleness they unchained me from the wall, and a drink—liquid, but not water—was pressed to my lips, sipped from a vessel that felt like bone. The runes scored into my hide seared as if rubbed with salt, and I felt something stir in me, entering through each cut to invigorate my ailing being. Upwards they dragged me this time, toward the sun: the sun! Like a memory from another world. My head felt full of restless chanting now, wordless sounds on tongues writhing like crypt-worms in throats ill-suited to enunciation. I opened my mouth and tried to join them, finding the phrases came with an uncommon ease. The cuts burned more brightly, though still my eyes were bound.

At last they left me in this room, blindfold torn from my eyes at the last instant; a blear of black-cloaked figures before the door slammed shut. Above, the insectile hum of fluorescent lighting, so foreign now, different from the crack and billow of torches, dipped (so I now know) in tallow of corpse-fat. I look around to see nothing but blank white walls. Before me a black altar-stone, empty. Above, the metal fan blades circle like vultures.

I have no idea why I'm here.

Basilisk Eye

Leigh Blackmore

From blue morning sundance to dim twilight dream
The Basilisk broods by the rippling stream.
The bright light gleams forth from its green-golden scales
The warrior hunts it, beholds it, and pales.

Through cycles of aeons this grim serpent king
Has ravaged and plundered; the people still sing
Of how from a rooster it hatched from an egg
And grew to be monstrous. The village folk beg

For an end to its slaughter. It slays with a glance
With its Basilisk eye and the warrior's lance
Is no weapon against it, its poisonous breath
So noxious and fatal that mortals meet death.

Its curves are alluring; the people fall prey,
Drawn in by deception. Its camouflage gay
Is blindingly bright. The good townsfolk are led
To regard it with caution lest they should fall dead.

The warrior rides, plated over with mail
That in battle protects him; he cannot now fail.
But *his* weapon is different. The Basilisk turns
And snarls at the man, as with courage he burns.

This man has been clever—'tis done in a trice!
He holds up a mirror! Another! And thrice,
He circles the monster. And three times at least
The Basilisk's gaze rebounds on the beast!

The serpent is conquered—it falls on its knees.
The warrior triumphs! He drinks to the lees
The sweet cup of victory. The serpent is dead!
No more need the people abide with their dread!

Alchemical powder of Basilisk skin
Is ground up for use by the alchemist's kin.
No longer the villagers live at dire risk
Of death from the monster—the feared Basilisk!

A Mysterious House

Algernon Blackwood

[The following story was first published in *Belgravia* 69 (July 1889): 98–107. So far as is known, it is his first published short story.]

Explanations are usually very tedious, and so without any introduction or preambulation I will plunge right into the midst of this uncanny story I am about to tell. . . . When, some fifteen years before the time of which I write, I was a schoolboy at Eton I made close friends with a fellow above me in the school, named Pellham. We were very great chums, and later on we went to Cambridge together, where my friend spent money and time in wasting both, while I read for holy orders, though I never actually entered the Church. Since that time I had completely lost sight of him and he of me, and, with the exception of seeing his marriage in the papers, had no news at all of his whereabouts. One morning, however, towards the close of September 1857, I received a letter from him, short, precise, and evidently written in a great hurry, asking me to go down and see him at his family seat just outside Norwich. I packed my bag and went that very same evening. He met me himself at the station and drove me home. We hardly recognised each other at first sight, so much had we changed in appearance, both being on the dark side of thirty-five, but our individual characters had remained much the same and we were still to all appearances the best of friends. My friend was not very talkatively disposed, and I kept up a fire of questions until we drew up at the park gates. Going up the drive to the house he brightened up considerably, and gave me plenty of information about himself and family. He was quite alone, I was surprised to hear, his wife and two daughters with an uncle of his having left for the Continent two days previous. After dinner he seemed quite the old "Cambridge Undergrad" again, and once settled round the old-fashioned hearth, with cheroots and coffee, we talked on over the days spent at Eton and Cambridge. We were just discussing our third edition of tobacco, when Pellham suddenly changed the subject, and said he would tell me now why he had written so shortly to me to pay him this unexpected visit. His face grew grave as he began by asking me if I was still a sceptic as regards ghostly manifestations.

"Indeed I am," was my answer; "I have had no reason to change my views on the subject, and think exactly as I used to at Cambridge, when we so strongly differed; but I remember you then saying that, if ever in after years you should come across an opportunity of proving to me your ideas on the subject, you would write to me at once, and I also recollect giving my word that, if possible, I would come. But during the fifteen years that have since passed by I have bestowed little, if any, thought on the subject."

"Exactly," answered Pellham, with a grave smile that did not please me; "but now I have at last heard of a case which will satisfy us both, I think, so I wrote to you to come down and fulfil your old promise by investigating it."

"Well let me hear all about it first," I said cautiously. I certainly was not overjoyed to hear this news, for, though a sceptic to all intents and purposes, still "ghosts" was a subject for which I had a certain fear, and the highest ambition of my life was not to investigate haunted houses and the like just because I had years ago promised I would should a chance occur. But I repressed my feelings and tried to look interested, which I was, and delighted, which I certainly was not. Pellham then gave me a long account—thrilling enough too it was—of the case, which I have somewhat condensed in the following form. Some three or four years before, my friend had bought up a house which stood on the moorland about eight miles off. One morning before breakfast the tenant of the house, a Mr. Sherleigh (who was there with his family), suddenly burst into my friend's study without any ceremony, and, in great heat and excitement, shouted out the following words:

"You shall suffer for it, Lord Pellham, my wife mad, and the little boy killed with fright, because you didn't choose to warn us of the room next the drawing-room, but you shall—." Here the footman entered, and at a sign from his master led the excited and evidently cracked old man from the room, but not before he had crashed down some gold pieces on the table, with: "That's the last rent you'll get for that house, as sure as I am the last tenant."

"Well," continued my friend, "that very day, now two years ago, I rode over there myself and the house was empty. The Sherleighs had left it, and since that day I have never been able to let it to anyone. Mr. Sherleigh, who was quite mad, poor fellow, threw himself before a train, and was cut to pieces, and Mrs. Sherleigh spread a report that it was haunted, and now no one will take it or even go near it, though it stands high and is in a very healthy position. Two nights ago," he went on gravely, "I was riding past the road which leads up to it, and through the trees I could see light in one of the upper rooms, and figures, or rather shadows, of a woman's figure, with something in her arms, kept crossing to and fro before the window-blind. I determined to go in and see what on earth it was, and tying my horse just outside I went in. In a minute or two I was close underneath the window where the light was still visible, and the shadow still moving to and fro with a horrible regularity. As I stood there, undecided, a feeling within warned me not to enter the house, so vivid, it was almost a soft voice that whispered in my ear. I heard no noise inside, the night air was moaning gently through the fir trees which surrounded the house on one side and nearly obscured the upper part of the window from view. I stooped down and picked up a large stone—it was a sharp-edged flint—and without any hesitation hurled it with all my might at the window pane, some eight or ten feet from the ground. The stone went straight and struck the window on one of the wooden partitions, smashing the whole framework, glass and all, into a thousand splinters, many of which struck me where I stood. The result was awful and unexpected. The moment the stone touched the glass the lights quite disappeared, and in the blackness in which I was shrouded, the next minute, I could see hiding behind the broken corners of glass a dark face and form for a short instant, and then it went and all was pitch dark again. There I was among those gloomy pine trees hardly knowing which way to turn. The face I had caught a momentary glimpse of was the face of Mr. Sherleigh, whom I knew to be dead! My knees trembled. I tried to grope my way out of the wood, and stumbled from tree to tree, often striking my head against the low branches. In vain. With the weird light in the window as a guide, I had taken but a few minutes to come, but now all was dark and I could not find my way back again. I felt as if the dismal tree trunks were living things, which seemed to move. Suddenly I heard a noise on my left. I stopped and listened. Horror! I was still close to the window, and what I heard was a cracking and splintering of broken glass, as if some one from inside were slowly forcing their way out through the hole made by my stone! Was it he? The fir tree next me suddenly shook violently, as if agitated by a powerful gust of wind, and then in a gleam of weird light I saw a long dark body hanging half-way out of the window, with black hair streaming down the shoulders. It raised one arm and slammed down something at my feet which fell with a rattle, and then hissed out: 'There's the last rent you'll ever have for this house.' I stood literally stupefied with horror, then a cold, numb sensation came over me and I fell fainting on my face, but not until I had heard my horse give a prolonged neigh and then his footsteps dying away in the distance on the hard moorland road. . . . . When I recovered consciousness it was broad daylight. I was cold and damp; all night I had lain where I fell. I rose and limped, stiff and tired, to the place where I had tied my horse the night before, but no horse was there. And the horrible sound of his hoofs echoing away in the distance came back to me, and I shuddered as I thought of what I had seen. After a terrible trudge of three hours I reached home. A tremendous search had been made for me, of course, but no one dreamt of looking for me where I really was. The horse had found his way home, and I have never found out what frightened him so."

My friend's account was over. He lit his cigar, which had gone out during the narrative, and settling himself comfortably in his chair, said, "Well, old boy, that's a case I don't feel at all inclined to investigate by myself, but I'll do it with your aid. You know, a genuine sceptic is a great addition in such things, so we'll get to the bottom of it somehow."

My feelings at that moment were not difficult to describe. I disliked the whole affair, and wanted heartily to get out of it; and yet something urged me to go through with it and show my friend that the house was all right, that imagination did it all, that the horse may have taken fright at anything, and that very possibly there really was someone in the house all the time, and imagination had done the rest. Such were the somewhat mixed thoughts in my mind at the time. However, in a few moments all was settled and we had agreed to go the following night, search the house first, and then sit up all night in the room next the drawing-room. Then we both went to our separate bed-rooms to think the matter over and get a long sleep, as we neither expected to get any the following night.

Next morning at breakfast we both talked cheerfully about the coming night and how best to meet its requirements as regards food, etc. We agreed to take pistols for weapons, horses as a means of conveyance, and abundant food wherewith to fortify ourselves against a possible attack of ghosts.

The day drew on towards its close. It was very hot and sultry weather, and not a breath of wind stirred the murky atmosphere, as at 4.30 P.M. we bestrode our horses and made off in the direction of the "White House." A long gravel road, lonely in the extreme, led us across the wild uncultivated moorland for six or seven miles, then we saw a copse of fir trees which, my friend informed me, were the trees which sheltered one side of the house. In a few minutes we had passed through the front garden gate and were among the dark fir trees, and then as we turned a sharp corner the house burst full upon us. It was square and ugly. Great staring windows in regular rows met our eyes and conveyed an unpleasant impression to the brain—

at least, they did to mine. From the very moment we had passed the front gate till I left the house next morning, I felt a nasty sick sensation creep over me, a feeling of numbness and torpor which seemed to make the blood run thick and sluggish in my veins. The events of that night have remained engraven on my brain as with fire, and, though they happened years ago, I can see them now as vividly as then. Only an eye-witness can possibly describe them, should he wish to do justice to them, and so my feeble pen shall make the attempt.

It was about 6.30, and we had settled our horses in a barn outside for the night. There were only two walls to keep the barn in position, and these were simply a row of rotten posts, half-decayed in places, so we securely tied the horses and, with a good supply of hay, left them for the night. We then approached the door and, after fumbling in the lock for some time, Pellham succeeded in opening it. A sickly, musty odour pervaded the hall, and the first thing we did after a thorough search, which revealed nothing, was to open all the doors and windows all over the house, so as to let in what little air there was. Then we went upstairs into the little room next the drawing-room, where, according to Sherleigh, strange things had occurred. But the window was in pieces, and hardly an entire pane of glass was left, and we were forced to select another room on the same floor (i.e. the second) and looking out on the same copse of pine trees, whose branches almost touched the glass, so close were they. It was a very ordinary room; a fire-place, no furniture but a rickety table and three chairs, one of which was broken. The only disagreeable feature we noticed about the room was its gloominess; it was so very dark. The trees outside, as I have already said, were so close that the slightest breath of wind rustled their twigs against the window. We soon had six candles fixed and burning in different parts of the little room, and the blaze of light was still further increased by a roaring fire, on which a kettle was singing for tea, and eggs boiling in a saucepan, and at half-past seven we were in the middle of our first tea in a haunted house. It was, indeed, less luxurious than the dinners I had been used to lately, but otherwise there was nothing to find fault with, and a little later the tea things were cleared away in a heap in a corner (where, by-the-by, they are to this day), and we were sitting round an empty table, smoking in silence. The door out into the passage was fast shut, but the window was wide open. The sun had sunk out of sight in a beautiful sky of wonderful colouring. Small fleecy clouds floating about caught the soft after-glow and looked unearthly as seen through the thick fir branches. The faint red hue of the western sky looked like the reflection of some huge and distant conflagration, growing dimmer and fainter as the dark engines of the night played upon it, extinguishing the leaping flames and suffusing the sky with a red reflected glow. Not a breath of air stirred the trees. My friend had left the window and was poking and arranging the fire, with his back turned towards me. I was standing close to the window, looking at the fast-fading colours, when it seemed to me that the window sash was moving. I looked closer. Yes! I was not mistaken. The lower half was gradually sinking; gradually and very quietly it went down. At first I thought the weight had slipped and gone wrong, and the window was slipping down of its own accord; but when I saw the bolt pulled across and fastened as by an invisible hand, I thought differently. My first impulse was to immediately undo the bolt again and open the window, but on trying to move—good heavens! I found I had lost all power of motion and could not move a muscle of my body. I was literally rooted to the ground. Neither could I move the muscles of my tongue or mouth; I could not speak or utter a sound. Pellham was still doing something to the fire, and I could hear him muttering to himself, though I could not distinguish any words. Suddenly, then, I felt the power of motion returning to me; my muscles were relaxing, and turning, though not without a considerable effort, I walked to the fire-place. Pellham, then, for the first time noticed that the window was shut, and he made a remark about the closeness of the night, asking me why I had closed it.

"Hulloa," he went on, before I had time to answer, "by the gods above! what is happening to that window? Look—why it's moving!"

I turned. *The window was slowly being opened again.*

Yes, sure enough it was. Slowly and steadily it moved or was pushed up.

We could but believe our eyes; in half a minute the window was wide open again. I turned and looked at Pellham and he looked at me, and in dead silence we stared at one another, neither knowing what to say or wishing to break the silence. But at length my friend spoke.

"I wish I were a sceptic, old man, like you are; sceptics are always safer in a place like this."

"Yes," I said, as cheerfully as I could, "I feel safe enough, and what's more, I am convinced that the window was opened by human agency from outside."

Pellham smiled, he knew as well as I that no human fingers could have fastened the bolt from outside. "Well," he said briskly, "perhaps you are right; come, let's examine the window."

We rose and approached it, and my friend put his head and shoulders out into the air. It was very dark, and a strange oppressive stillness reigned outside, only broken by the gentle moaning sound of the night wind as it rustled through the trees and swept their branches like the strings of a lyre. I followed my friend's example, and together we peered out into the night. Soon my eyes rested on the ground below us, and at the base of one of the nearer pines I thought I could distinguish a black form, clinging, as it seemed, to the tree. I pointed it out to Pellham, who failed to see anything, or at least said so; anyhow, I was glad to believe that my excited imagination was the real cause. We were still leaning out of the window in silence, when several of the trees, especially the one where I imagined I had seen the shape, were most violently agitated, as though by a mighty wind; but we felt not the slightest breath on our faces. At the same instant we heard a subdued shuffling sound in the room behind us, which seemed to come from the direction of the chimney. But neither of us referred to it as we slowly walked back to the fire and took up our places on either side on the two chairs, which were at the best very rickety.

"It isn't wise to leave the window open," said my friend, suddenly, "for if there really is anyone outside, they can see all and everything we do; while we, for our part, can see absolutely nothing of what goes on outside."

I agreed, and walked up to the window, shutting it with a bang and firmly drawing the bolt.

"I've brought a book," he went on, "which I thought we might read out aloud in turn to relieve the dulness and the silence."

He stopped speaking and looked at me, and at the same moment I raised my eyes to his face. To my intense horror and surprise I noticed for the first time a long smear of blood, wet and crimson, across his forehead. My horror was so great that for some seconds I could not find my tongue, and sat stupidly staring at him. At last I gasped out:

"My dear fellow, what has happened to you, have you cut yourself?"

"Where? what do you mean?" he replied, looking round him with surprise.

For answer I took out my handkerchief, and wiping his brow, showed him the red stains. But as I stood there showing him this proof and as he was expressing his utter astonishment, I distinctly saw something that for the moment made the blood rush from the extremities and crowd into my head. Something seemed to tighten round my heart. I saw a large, gleaming knife and hand disappear into the air in the direction of the window. It was too much; my nerves failed me, and I dropped fainting to the floor.

When I came to myself I was lying where I fell by the fireplace. Pellham was sitting beside me.

"I thought you were dead," he said, "you've been unconscious for over an hour." He said this in such a queer manner and laughed so fiendishly that I wondered what had happened to him during the interval. Had he seen something awful and gone mad? There was a strange light in his dark eyes and a leer on his lip. Just then he took up his book quite naturally and began to read aloud, every now and then he made a comment on what he was reading, quite sensibly too, and soon I began to think, as I sipped my brandy out of our flask, that I must have had a frightful dream. But there at my feet lay the blood-stained handkerchief, and I could not get over that. I glanced at his face; the smear had disappeared, and no scratch or wound was visible.

Pellham had not been reading long, perhaps some five or ten minutes, when we heard a strange noise outside among the trees, just audible above the death-like stillness of the autumn night. It was a confused voice like the low whispering of several persons, and as I listened, still weak from the last shock, the blood stood still in my veins. Pellham went on reading as usual. This struck me as very curious, for he must have heard the noise plainly; but I said nothing, and glancing at him I saw the same light in his eyes and the evil leer on his mouth, looking ugly in the flickering glare of the candles and firelight.

Suddenly we heard a tremendous noise outside, altogether drowning the Erst. The horses had broken loose and were tearing wildly past the house. Long and wild neighs rang out and died away, and we knew our horses were gone. Pellham was still reading, and as I looked at him a sudden and horrid thought flashed through my brain. It was this: Had he anything to do with this? Was it possible? Before I had time to answer my question Pellham threw down the book and made for the door, locked it, drew out the key, and opening the window threw it far away among the trees. I then recognised the awful fact that I was alone with a madman. I glanced at my watch, it was a quarter to one. Instead of one hour I must have been unconscious two at least. This was terrible in the extreme. He was a man of far more powerful physique than I. What was to be done? Pellham strode grinning up to the fire, went down on both knees and commenced blowing between the bars with all his might. I saw my chance, and quietly walking to the window, without a word I climbed out, and letting myself as far down as my arms would allow I then let go and dropped. It was a distance of four or five feet, but in the darkness I tumbled forward on my face. As I rose, uninjured, I distinctly heard the sound of running feet close to me, but in my bewilderment I could not make out clearly in which direction they were going; they only lasted a moment or two. But what a terrific sight met my gaze as I turned the corner of the house, and saw volumes of smoke pouring steadily out of the windows and roof of the back portion of the house. Now and again a long flame, too, shot up to heaven.

"Good God!" I cried, "the house is on fire."

No wonder the horses had taken flight. But my poor friend, what could I do for him? The window was too high for me to climb in again, and the doors were locked. In a few minutes the flames would spread to this side of the house and the poor fellow would be burnt to death unless he had enough sense left to jump out of the window.

I hurried back to the spot where I had let myself down from the window, just in time to see the last scene of the most ghastly experience I have ever witnessed. Pellham was standing at the window. In his hand was a red-hot poker, and it was pointed at his throat, but the strain was too great for my nervous system and with a violent start *I woke up!*

After our heavy tea we had both fallen asleep, just as we were in our chairs. Pellham was still snoring opposite me, and the light was stealing in through the window. It was morning, about half-past six. All the candles had burnt themselves out, and it was a wonder they had not set fire to the dry wood near them.

Twenty minutes later we had re-lit the fire and were discussing the remnant of eggs and coffee. Half an hour later we were riding home in the bright, crisp, morning air, and an hour and a half later we were in the middle of a second and far superior breakfast, during which I did *not* tell my dream, but during which we *did* agree that it had been the dullest and most uncomfortable night we had ever spent away from home.

Icy Portents of Doom:
Clark Ashton Smith's Hyperborean Cycle and the Polar Myth

Ian Fetters

Introduction

> "Unseen and untrodden under their spotless mantel of ice the rigid polar regions slept the profound sleep of death from the earliest dawn of time."—Fridjtof Nansen, *Farthest North* (3)

Thus is how Fridtjof Nansen, the nineteenth-century Arctic explorer, begins his account of the harrowing fifteen-month-long journey to reach the North Pole, a feat that no Westerner had accomplished up to that point in history.[1] In 1893, the year Nansen set sail on his voyage to Arctic, the pole remained in the Western imagination an unknowable and inaccessible place, the merest mention of the region conjuring up images from the Viking age of Norse gods and Thule to the oldest and most bizarre tales to come from ancient Greece of a mythic northern land where a race of super-humans communed with the gods. And though Nansen and his crew did not reach the pole—traveling more than a hundred miles farther than any previous expedition or known account of the far north—he brought back with him a startling tale of survival, adventure, and awe at having crossed one of Earth's last remaining thresholds between the known, inhabited world and the mythical far north of legend.

However, Nansen's account of the very real and unforgiving polar landscape did little to dispel the myths that had circulated around the region since the beginning of recorded history. In fact, Nansen,

1. Work on this essay was made possible through the generous support of the Donald Sidney-Fryer Research Fellowship.

well respected as a shrewd and rational observer of natural phenomena, paints the Arctic region with a touch of the supernatural at times. Perceived encounters with apparitions and mirages on the ice are commonplace among explorer accounts of the long, dark polar winters. Extreme isolation and climate conditions, it is obvious, has a tendency to drive clear-headed individuals to madness—but the Arctic region's storied past involving recurring themes of mythological beings, supernatural phenomenon, and speculative geographies has stood the test of time and stubbornly refused to yield in face of modernity.

The myths of rumored Thule and Hyperborea have found even more purchase in Gothic literature: supernatural themes abound in eighteenth- and nineteenth-century novels and stories set in the Arctic. There is a longstanding literary tradition of representing the strange and the supernatural in polar space—here referred to as the Polar Gothic, an all-encompassing modality for the exploration of supernatural themes and mythopoetic musings set in and around the far north, and the Arctic's mighty southern cousin, the Antarctic continent. Shelley, Poe, and even Coleridge's proto-Gothic mariner, who encounters the physical manifestation of Death in Antarctic waters, belong to this school of polar fiction.

The twentieth century sees writers, like H. P. Lovecraft in his exemplary short novel, *At the Mountains of Madness, weird* the Polar Gothic—reorienting the literature of the poles away from the more typical Gothic inner explorations of outer spaces and toward a perspective of the polar setting as an ideal threshold for incursions of cosmic weirdness into reality. This *weirding* of the polar space comes about at a time when techno-scientific advances in geology present a more complete picture of the prehuman history of the Earth and its poles, but the legends of old polar specters and myths, even older still, lurk in the psyche of man, in defiance of the modern age. Taken together, a coalescence of myth, science, and prehuman pseudo-history prove to be a fertile, yet icy ground for the Weird to flourish.

Clark Ashton Smith, the California poet and weird fantasist, wrote "The Tale of Satampra Zeiros" in 1929, the first of the Hyperborean Cycle tales, initiating his participation in this "weird turn" of the Polar Gothic tradition. The cycle is a thematic collection of prose tales taking place on and around the northernmost continent of Earth in the earliest days of mankind—Hyperborea, a kind of proto-Arctic, mythic space that was said to have flourished during the Miocene era approximately fifteen million years in the past. The tales that comprise the cycle, of which there are thirteen in all, are spread across eras in Hyperborea's fictional history. Some are set during the temperate Miocene, when human civilization flourished across the continent from jungle-covered Commoriom to Mhu Thulan, whose location corresponds approximately with modern-day Greenland in the Arctic circle (Behrends 61). Others still are set epochs later in the Pleistocene (beginning two and a half million years ago), amid the desolation of the continent's ice age and the seemingly perpetual encroachment of glaciers upon formerly verdant landscapes.

The tone of the stories in the cycle varies: Smith scholars tend toward the consensus that the Hyperborean set tales are at best a mixed bag of sardonic and horrific prose that is more amusing than vital. Steven Tompkins describes Hyperborea as "a flyover on the nonstop trillion-year flight to Zothique" (260), while Smith biographer Steve Behrends claims that the mock pretension and irony that flow freely from Smith's pen across almost all the tales serve to diminish their vitality and impact, ultimately lessening their distinctiveness among the writer's prolific catalogue of fiction (63). Yet this unfortunate diagnosis fails to account for the richness of setting that the Hyperborean tales celebrate—which is, in my estimation, the true critical focal point for the cycle. The Arctic setting of the Hyperborean continent is crucial to a broader understanding of the cycle's importance not only in Smith oeuvre, but also in twentieth-century weird fiction. And beyond setting, the cycle's "Arctic-ness," the collective sense of space, temporality, and historical and mythological context of the far North, has the potential to illuminate that greater significance for the cycle. By delving into the Hyperborean cycle's relation to Arctic history and its engagement with the "Polar Myth"—defined here as the foundational and apocryphal mythos of the Arctic region since the dawn of recorded history—the cycle is reimagined as a vital contribution to the observable Weird Turn in the Polar Gothic, earning Smith the title of poet laureate of the mythic Far North.

The following textual analysis of select Hyperborean Cycle tales demonstrates Smith's engagement with Arctic-ness, the myth and real-world history of the far northern polar region. One story in particular, "The White Sybil," draws on the Greek Hyperborean myth for inspiration, while at the same time evoking real incidents of Victorian mesmerism involving British-led Arctic exploration in the nineteenth century. In a similar vein, "The Coming of the White Worm" stands out in contrast to the Greek-Hyperborean myth: outer gods comingle with humans, resulting in disastrous consequences, further portraying Hyperborea as a liminal space in which the Outside comes In. Finally, texts such as "The Ice-Demon" serve to characterize the iconic glaciers and icy wastes of the Hyperborean landscape as a post-historic entity whose origins lie not in earth-bound history but in the cosmic space "beyond the pole." In the end, the texts all focus on bringing the Outside to Hyperborea via the their varying degrees of engagement with Arctic-ness (myth and history) as well as Smith's highly developed weird fantasy praxis, which serve to elevate the Hyperborean Cycle both in his own oeuvre and in the polar Gothic-weird literary tradition.

"The White Sybil" and Arctic Mesmerism

The origins of the Greek myth of Hyperborea are shrouded in mystery. According to Lin Carter's *Eldritch Dark* article on the origins of the Hyperborea myth, though Homer never makes mention of the Hyperborean continent or its superhuman inhabitants in his texts, the historians Herodotus and Hesiod do. The poet Pindar features the mythic northern land in his tenth Pythian ode. The Greek characterization of Hyperborea—at least as it is portrayed in the few surviving texts that make mention of it—is of a continent whose strange peoples live in rapturous bliss, unbothered by the woes and struggles of the terrestrial world to the south of them. The Greeks envision such a place as

> an idyllic paradise—an Eden of the pagans. They [the Greeks] had many stories about Hyperborea—Hercules visited it; Perseus cut off the Gorgon's head there; it was the birthplace of Apollo's grandfather. The best yarn of them all was about the globe-trotting Hyperborean wizard-priest named Abaris who visited Greece, studied magic under Pythagoras, and stopped a plague from destroying Sparta before returning home. (Carter)

A common thread tying together nearly all surviving depictions of the Grecian Hyperborean myth is that the continent acts as a stage for the extraordinary interactions between gods, demigods, and a host of otherworldly beings, including the Hyperboreans themselves who were considered to be more than human, a race of super-human beings. The Hyperborea of ancient Greek tradition is a major locus for the supernatural: a space for confluence between outer forces (the gods) and those more liminal beings (the Hyperboreans) who exist between the human and the divine in the surreal taxonomy of myth.

Smith's imagined Hyperborea is built on this same foundation of liminality and confluence with the weird. In a 1931 letter to H. P. Lovecraft, Smith pitches Hyperborea as such a place: "This primal continent seems to have been particularly subject to incursions of 'outsideness'—more so, in fact, than any of the other continents and terrene realms that lie behind us in the time stream" (*Dawnward Spire* 304–5). Though the characters, beings, and dooms of the Hyperborean cycle are very much a product of Smith's *sui generis* thinking, one cannot help but draw a specific parallel, an unmistakable connection, to the foundational Greek myth of the far north here:

the ancient Greeks saw Hyperborea as a prime setting where the other-worlds of divinity meet with the mundane, and Smith's Hyperborea is no different, where divinity becomes "outsideness," or weirdness.

This vital connection to the foundational Hyperborean myth is exemplified in "The White Sybil." In this short tale, the narrator recounts the fate of Tortha, a poet "with strange austral songs in his heart," who wanders idly about in his native Cerngoth (a city in the Hyperborean province of Mhu Thulan) "in the quest for that alien beauty which had fled always before him like the horizon" (*CF* 4.43). The poet looks aimlessly to and fro for poetic inspiration to no avail—that is, until he spots in the middle of the town square the White Sybil of Polarion, a semi-mythical being in Smith's Hyperborean lore who is said to be either a "goddess or ghost or woman" with a penchant for prophesying doom. This description of the White Sybil as a liminal being—neither wholly human nor totally phantasmic—recalls the supernatural incident of Hyperborean spirits at the defense of the oracle of Apollo at Delphi in historical times. A surviving ancient Greek tale tells of two Hyperborean prophets, pilgrims to Greece from the northern land, returning to Greece as phantoms after hundreds of years when the temple is under attack by the Gauls. According to the legend, the supposed spirits of these prophets—neither wholly corporeal nor totally phantasmic in description—rout the Gauls and save the temple from being razed to the ground ("Legendary Realms: Hyperborea"). Like the White Sybil in Smith's tale, these Hyperborean-Greek entities (prophets and divinators of the future also like the Sybil) appear both to influence real-world events and to exist in the realm of the spirit—existing in liminal space between the supernatural and the real.

In "The White Sybil," the title entity is said to drift between places, descending spirit-like from the icy mountains of Cerngoth, whilst "appearing more often in cities remote from the ice-bound waste of Polarion" (*CF* 4.44). The tale's narrator makes it clear that the Sybil's travels cannot be accomplished by an earthbound person alone: "Truly," the narrator proclaims, "she was no mortal being, for she had been seen on the same day in places hundreds of miles apart" (*CF* 4.45). Parallels between the otherworldly movements of the Sybil and the apparition-entities of the Hyperborean prophets become clear: both entities of the fictional Hyperborea and the Hyperborean-Greek myth utilize supernatural means for travels to, from, and around the far northern mythical continent.

Even more than supernaturalism in terms of space and movement, both the White Sybil and her ancient Hyperborean-Greek forebears belong to a Weird Arctic temporality, where the past, present, and future coalesce and the distinction between mythic time and historical time blurs together. The phantom prophets of Hyperborea in the Greek myth come down across vast plains of space and time to exact vengeance on the real-world Gauls invading Apollo's temple—setting the precedent for Smith to distort time and reality to his design in the fictionalized Hyperborea. The Tortha, the poet-protagonist of "The White Sybil," is mesmerized by the Sybil's otherworldly beauty, and as she escapes from view after his initial encounter with her in Cerngoth's city square, he returns home, vowing to set eyes on her again (*CF* 4.43). It seems that the poet has found the inspiration he so desperately craves in the form of a strange, ethereal woman who is known to "utter weird prophecies and cryptic tidings of doom" of icy apocalyptic events that have yet to befall the inhabitants of Hyperborea at this point in the fictional continent's history (*CF* 4.44). The White Sybil brings divinations of the impending ice age to the human inhabitants of Mhu Thulan, a doom that still seems to them eons away as the glaciers from the North creep inconspicuously, yet inexorably, on the land.

The Sybil's prophecies seem out-of-joint with the reality of the Hyperborean continent, and yet, on a metatextual level, readers know that this particularly icy doom has already befallen Mhu Thulan. Though both "The White Sybil" and "The Ice-Demon," a Hyperborean cycle tale set eons after the glaciers take the Hyperborean continent, were written by Smith in July 1932, "The Ice-Demon" saw publication first in the April 1933 issue of *Weird Tales*, while "The White Sybil"—whose events precede those in "The Ice-Demon"—did not see publication until 1934 in *The White Sybil and The Men of Avalon* (see Joshi et al. 111, 139). Though contemporary readers may encounter both of these tales in a different order from that of their initial publication, the original effect is one that destabilizes time in the fictional world of Hyperborea. In other words, the Sybil's icy portents of doom ring out backwards and forwards across different epochs, at once accurately divining Mhu Thulan and Commoriom's apocalypse while always seeming to echo from the distant past.

In terms of Arctic-ness, this out-of-joint temporality is a feature rather than a glitch: the coming of the ice to the fictional Hyperborean continent as well as the real-world Arctic space represent a stalemate in the forward progress of time, which is in itself a defining characteristic of the far north. John McCannon, in his introduction to *A History of the Arctic,* summarizes the prevailing attitudes toward the Northern polar region and its relationship to time:

> Throughout recorded history, wilderness in many forms has served to symbolize elemental vastness and permanence. The forest primeval. The earth-rooted mountain. Boundless steppes and limitless seas. That said, perhaps no landscape has stood out in the modern mind as so quintessentially timeless as the Arctic. In the Western imagination, the polar world has featured as a realm of crystalline purity, as a grey kingdom of frozen death, and in other guises besides, but is most often seen as eternal and unchanging. (1)

Eternal and unchanging: these words recall Fridjtof Nansen's proclamation that the Arctic has "slept the profound sleep of death since the earliest dawn of time" (1). The White Sybil's whispered words of doom echo in these modern descriptions of the Arctic as a place where the ice has quite literally frozen time and human perceptions of the passage of time. Taken with the context of the Greek-Hyperborean tales and their semi-mythic, apocryphal phantoms wreaking vengeance on the Gauls from across centuries, the distortion and "icing over" of Arctic history—blurring what were once distinct categories of myth, history, and fiction—serves to place Smith's own polar apocalyptic prophet as a Hyperborean oracle of " outsideness."

We travel now from the ancient Greek divinators and their apocryphal Hyperborean allies to the Victorian age of Arctic exploration. The accounts of British expeditions to the Arctic during the nineteenth century, as well as the cultural artifacts to come out of that exploratory period, are rife with supernatural occurrences and encounters with non-human, otherworldly agencies. There is, in this period of intense polar interest, a general sense that the Arctic is a region particularly saturated by the uncanny, echoing Smith's assertion that his own mythopoetic Arctic continent, Hyperborea, is marked especially by "incursions of outsideness." For nineteenth-century British explorers the feeling of piercing through the misty white veil of Arctic fog into icy waters was one of "crossing an ontological boundary into a non-historical realm [. . . causing] the explorer to express his experiences in terms of dreams, visions, and castles in the air" (McCorristine 151). As a realm existing out-of-joint with time, being situated right up against the edges of mapped lands, and generating epochs worth of apocryphal myth and legend, it is no wonder that the Arctic region is at this point in history such a locus for real-world manifestations of weirdness, or outsideness.

But what of those left behind in England? Did the families, friends, and public experience the Arctic's uncanny attraction just as the explorers did? Dreams of the weird polar wastelands at the edge of the known world did not belong to explorers alone, nor were they solely the province of men. The phenomenon of Arctic mesmerism—the practice of mediums contacting or communing with lost or dead explorers and their Arctic environs—represents one of the stranger moments in Arctic-adjacent history. The most notable example of this mesmeric practice involves the surviving families and friends of the doomed Franklin expedition (1845). In a bid to break through the ice and locate a Northwest Passage through the Arctic, Sir John Franklin sail set to the far north in what was, at the time, one of the largest exploratory undertakings in polar history—and one whose failures were highly publicized in England and across the British empire.

Typically, in Victorian-era mesmerism—and the transatlantic variant strains of spiritualism that made their way to the British isles from America—it was rare for mediums, usually young women, actually to speak with the dead or visit a spirit realm outside of their bodies. However, according to Arctic scholar Shane McCorristine, the doom visited upon the Franklin expedition and the subsequent collective cultural spiraling into anxiety and speculation as to the expedition's whereabouts occasioned a whole new element of Arctic-focused mesmeric practice to take hold among the surviving families and acquaintances of the expedition crews, as well as complete strangers. McCorristine draws attention to the widespread nature of these mesmeric incidents:

> Contemporary newspaper reports reveal the existence of dozens of clairvoyants (mostly young women) in Ireland, Britain, India, and Australia who, on being put in a mesmeric trance, described visiting Franklin in the Arctic [. . .] it seemed that the clairvoyant was a highly sensitive person capable of collapsing the distance between the explorers and those searching for them through disembodied travelling during her mesmeric séances. She could [often] name locations for audiences, bring back news, and "perform" Arctic experiences, such as cold and hardship. (152–53)

Such performances linked to the Franklin expedition were used by both believers and skeptics to prove or disprove the validity of the strange spiritual connections to the polar region and to the men believed to be dead or alive, depending on the source. National tragedy in the Arctic set the stage for an outpouring of supernatural claims coming in from across all corners of the empire.

Despite the highly contested and contestable nature of these mesmeric practices and the new spirituality from which they arose, all incidents of this so-called Arctic mesmerism hold in common a mythical and fictional resonance: the young women proclaiming and performing clairvoyant miracles do so less to bring words of hope ("Sir J. was readg [*sic*] prayers to the crew, who knelt in a circle, with their faces upward" [Spufford 133]), but more often to deliver portents of cold, lonesome death for the crew of the Franklin expedition. These female Victorian mediums seem to be inheriting the White Sybil's role as a conduits for "outsideness" to manifest itself and prophetesses of icy doom for those who set foot in the Arctic realm (though the White Sybil herself does not appear in fiction until nearly one hundred years later).

When Tortha, the poet-protagonist of "The White Sybil," finally tracks down the object of his misplaced affections amidst the bleak ravines and crags of Cerngoth, on the borders of Polarion, he observes a distinct change in the scenery and in the environmental atmosphere around him. As he lays eyes on the ethereal form of the Sybil, a portentous change overtakes the scene: "Amid the supernal ardor of his ascent, the poet was aware of a sudden chill that had touched the noontide. The rays of the sun had grown dull and heatless; the shadows were like the depth of ice-hewn Arctic tombs" (*CF* 4.47). Tortha follows the Sybil farther into the high gorges of this winter-touched place, until the space shifts entirely into a different realm, one that is imbued with the strangeness of the Sybil herself:

> He stood in a valley that might have been the inmost heart of some boreal paradise—a valley that was surely no part of waste Polarion. About him, the summer turf was piled with flowers that had the frail and pallid hues of a lunar rainbow. They were not the flowers that bloomed around Cerngoth: their delicate forms were those of the blossoms of snow and frost [. . .] The sky above the valley was not the low-arching, tender turquoise heaven of Mhu Thulan, but was vague, dream-like, remote, and full of an infinite violescence, like the welkin of a world beyond time and space. Everywhere there was light; but Tortha saw no sun in the cloudless vault. It was as if the sun, the moon, the stars, had been mol-

ten together ages ago and had dissolved into some ultimate, eternal luminescence. (*CF* 4.48)

It is clear that Tortha has been "transported" to some even more distant polar region than that of Mhu Thulan at the tip of the Hyperborean continent, one that is distant in both space and time, especially given the radical transformation of the summer season into a wintry, otherworldly dusk.

Similarly, the participants in mesmeric séances of the nineteenth century were transported to the Arctic world—that is, a weird impression of the Arctic space. According to Francis Spufford in his book on the Arctic and the English imagination, Lady Franklin—wife of the lost and feared dead leader of the 1845 Franklin expedition—received a letter detailing the writer's experiences of a séance conducted by a female child with the intention of locating the Franklin expedition. The letter supposedly recounted a macabre scene wherein three children communed with the spirit of young woman and sister of the three (shortly after her death) as she laid out before them an unusual scene: "so far as your [Lady Franklin's] interest is concerned the deceased speaks to her sister Anne by some chance the question was put is Sir J. Franklin Alive when to the surprise of Anne, the room they were in appeared to be filled with Ice some Channels and a Ship in one narrow creek or harbour between two Mountains of Snow and Ice" (134–35).

This recorded incident may stand in stark contrast in terms of poetic impact to the narrator's recollection in "The White Sybil," but the effect remains the same: the supernatural transport to and transformation of an Arctic space beyond that which is thought possible, due to some potential otherworldly influence. In the case of the deceased young Victorian woman, she acts as a supernatural conduit, a direct transportive link to the Arctic and, allegedly, to the lost Franklin expedition; and the Sybil, who is not entirely corporeal herself, draws Tortha into her liminal realm between the real crags and gorges of upper Cerngoth and some distant (spatially and temporally) polar land where the "secret of her essence" and her divinity belong to that which lies beyond the pole—a cold strangeness that is "real beyond all that men deem reality" (*CF* 4.49).

Lady Franklin, on hearing the news that the mesmeric conduit between the deceased and the living (all strangers, and before recently unfamiliar to her and her husband's estate) had possibly located the expedition, was said to have channeled her own supernatural force out of sheer joy or hope or love or some other kind of ineffability. According to Reverend J. Henry Skews's written account of witnessing Lady Franklin's reading of the letter, she was supposed to have cried, "It is true! It is true!" and then "Light, as from an invisible world, now permeated her whole being. She was, as by seraphic force, raised to a plateau far above all the heights of human measurement" (quoted in Spufford 135–36). Of course, given the source of the recollection (a reverend of the Christian faith) and the language therein ("Light," "seraphic force"), the spiritual incident could be a religious embellishment of a particularly triumphant moment celebrated by Lady Franklin—a cause for hope eliciting an ecstatic response from an individual for whom all had seemed lost before that moment. Regardless of the reality on the ground, the image of a trance-like floating "above all the heights of human measurement," that is to say beyond human capacity for representation, resonates with the final moments of lucidity in Tortha's physical experience of the Sybil's traumatic degeneration while in his arms. After the Sybil's transformation first into a horrific frozen corpse, then a "dark corruption," and finally evaporated nothingness, he finds himself thrust, as if by some great, inhuman force, into the air:

> He was plunging into some deep gulf together with that illimitable chaos of driven snows. Gradually, as he fell, the air grew clear about him, and he appeared to hang suspended [. . .] He was alone in a still, funereal, starless heaven, like the catafalque of some dying world; and below, at an awesome and giddying distance he saw dimly glittering reaches of a land sheathed with glacial ice from horizon to far-curved horizon. (*CF* 4.49–50)

These instances, both engaging to a greater and lesser degree in a "fictionalized" Arctic mesmeric experience, further reinforce the transportive element of the polar weird—whether via a spectral link from Victorian England to the pole thousands of miles away, or the journey from mythical Hyperborea to a weirder trans-arctic clime that is the ultimately province of the "Outside."

In just this one tale of the Hyperborean cycle, readers see the expansive nature of Smith's weird fantasy worldbuilding, as the Arctic context—the region's mythological resonances, historical points of reference to nineteenth-century spiritualism, and temporal manipulation of the Arctic space—serves to bridge the gaps between reality and fiction on the mythical Hyperborean continent. Whether Smith was cognizant of the Arctic-ness with which his Hyperborea is imbued is of little concern to the overall impact of the tales in the cycle, "The White Sybil" especially. In other words, Hyperborea serves as a locus for the Outside to come Inside, to invade reality. Though fictional, Smith's far northern mythopoetic continent exemplifies liminality, the blurring, as well as the bridging, of the mythical and historical that the Arctic and its accompanying polar myths have always already epitomized since the dawn of recorded history.

Doom from Beyond the Pole

While "The White Sybil" illustrates the Hyperborean cycle's emphatic theme of outsideness breaking through into the real-world Arctic space, the weirdness at the core of that tale still takes on a somewhat "human" guise, featuring an entity whose arresting, if incorporeal, beauty takes on a decidedly anthropomorphic form, and whose prophecies of doom are whispered to those foolish enough to embrace her. But what of the mythic North's more radically nonhuman outside forces, those entities that come down from "beyond the pole" to Hyperborea? Even the most weirdly fantastical moments in the cycle are linked to the polar myth and to the history of the Arctic. "The Coming of the White Worm," whose titular antagonist is possibly the strangest being in all the cycle tales, is a highly mediated account (via Eibon the sorceror) of the triad between humans, Hyperboreans, and Outer Gods—a symbolic tripartite relationship also found at the center of the Greek-Hyperborean discourse and myth surrounding the far north. However, Smith warps this mythological resonance to serve his own Hyperborean design, reinforcing the theme that the outside always already brings doom with it.

In a similar vein, the ice itself is a representative from the outside and a weird agent in "The Ice-Demon." It is a tale of vengeance and the inexorability of glacial, time-halting doom upon the first continent of mankind, serving to spotlight a crucial variation on the theme of the icy sublime as it appears in explorer accounts of the polar regions. The sense of Arctic-ness that results from these connections to (and deviations from) polar myth and real-world Arctic chronicles imbues the Hyperborean continent's Ice Age history with liminality, placing Smith's weird fantasy worldbuilding even more at the threshold between the real and the imaginary.

We return to ancient Greece to revisit their contribution to the polar myth: Hyperborea, an intermediary space and stage for the interactions between divinity and mortality. Among the key "players" in the myth, only the Hyperboreans claim the continent as their home, while humans are barred from entry; and the gods, as it were, are only sometimes visitors to the elusive "Eden of the pagans," as Lin Carter calls it. Athanasios Votsis, in his semiotic analysis of the Greek-Hyperborea myth, claims that there exists a tripartite relationship in literature between the three groups: humankind (the Greeks), Hyperboreans (the more-than-human inhabitants of the far northern continent), and gods (48). This relationship, according to Votsis, is founded on "the relatively harmonious placement of the Greeks and their gods in one unified schema, with Hyperboreans as an interesting mediator. Greeks and gods indeed exist in the Hyperborean myth and play a crucial role in the construction of the meaning of Hyperborea itself" (50). Of key importance to the analysis here is the notion of a "harmonious" relationship between the three groups: that harmony plays out particularly in the aforementioned legend of the defense of the Delphic temple from the barbarian Gauls, when Hyperborean spirits—no doubt in league with the gods—come down from across the centuries and the threshold of the afterlife to assist the real-world Grecian defenders. An additional legend suggests that Zeus directed Hercules to find "a tree to shade all people and a crown to honor the victors of the Olympic Games," where the mortals compete in athletic events; Hercules located such a horticultural prize, the olive tree, in Hyperborea and persuaded the native Hyperboreans to allow him to take it back to Greece—a true testament to the cooperative interactivity between mortals, more-than-mortals, and the gods themselves in the myth (Votsis 45).

In Smith's Hyperborea, we see a similar triad emerge from the interactions between non-mortal presences (the outside), the Hyperborean natives (who exist in a liminal space), and mortals; however, the relationship looks slightly different, and perhaps a bit darker as well. "The Coming of the White Worm" represents a crucial moment and story in the fictitious Hyperborean history, of such importance that the human sorceror, Eibon, dedicates the entire ninth chapter of his tome, the Book of Eibon, to its recitation. In the tale, the Hyperborean wizard Evagh is conscripted into servitude aboard a massive floating iceberg to serve his new otherwordly master: Rlim Shaikorth, a massive white worm and supernatural entity bent on visiting doom across all Hyperborea. There on Yikilith, Evagh learns from other captive wizards of the terrible, new hierarchy to which he belongs:

> "We serve the One whose coming was foretold by the prophet Lith [. . .] From spaces beyond the limits of the north he hath come in his floating citadel, the ice-mountain Yikilith, to voyage the mundane oceans and to blast with a chill splendor the puny people of humankind. He hath spared us alone amid the inhabit-

ants of the broad isle of Thulask, and hath taken us to go with him in his sea-faring upon Yikilith. He hath tempered our flesh to the rigor of his abode, and hath made respirable for us the air to which no mortal may draw breath [. . .] Hail, O Evagh, whom we know for a great wizard by this token: since only the mightiest of warlocks are thus chosen and exempted." (*CF* 5.44)

In no uncertain terms, Rlim Shaikorth's regime is recited to the mortified Evagh. In this passage alone the grim new Hyperborean triad is formed: mortals, the "puny people" of the continent, are relegated to the role of causalities in Rlim Shaikorth's icy reign of terror, while those wizards deemed strong enough (the superhuman Hyperboreans, now made immortal via supernatural means) serve him as mediators in his doom-bringing; finally, Rlim Shaikorth, a godlike being not from this Earth, rounds out the tripartite structure. Given the violence with which the white worm is to accomplish his objective, the relationships herein can hardly be called harmonious, as with the Greek-Hyperborean myth. However, as far as the myth structure goes, the Greek model is reflected: the besieged Hyperborean coastline forms the stage upon which this particular drama in Smith's pseudo-myth plays out, like the mythical Arctic coast of the Greek-Hyperborea.

There is, in Eibon's account of Evagh's defeat of Rlim Shaikorth and the melting of the great glacier-fortress Yikilith, a notable distortion to the tripartite Grecian-inspired myth structure. Given the interwoven temporality of the tales in the cycle, spanning across eons of the time, readers know that despite the failure of the white worm's regime to "bring eternal frost on [mankind's] gardens," the frost does indeed come for those selfsame gardens eons into the future. In other words, the ice-borne doom that Rlim Shaikorth initiated did not end with him. In "The Ice-Demon," the Hyperborean continent is no longer a verdant realm of wonders, but a long-forsaken icy wasteland, given to the inexorable crawl of the glaciers upon the land. Rlim Shaikorth himself amounts to no more than a weird prophet of what is still to come—granted, a prophetic being from outside who wreaked harm all across the coast of Mhu Thulan. Unfortunately, this means that Evagh, one of the only true "hero" characters across the Hyperborean cycle tales, dies only to exchange one doom for another down the line; his sacrifice is ultimately meaningless in the context of the inevitable end of humanity's reign on the continent, if it ever had the right to the proto-Arctic space at all. After all, Hyperborea's liminality extends to possession as well: as the threshold between "incursions of outsideness" and the realm of man's first civilization on Earth, no being, neither the white worm nor humanity, can claim the continent. Hyperborea has always already existed outside of such confines, belonging only to the glaciers and colder spaces beyond the pole.

Eons after the events in "The Coming of the White Worm," Smith returns to Mhu Thulan, now abandoned and desolate, a more familiar Arctic landscape dominated solely by the encroachment of massive glaciers on what was once fertile soil— a doom foretold by the White Sybil and initiated by Rlim Shaikorth. "The Ice-Demon" tells the tale of a doomed grave robbery in the ice: Quanga, the barbarian, and his dubious colleagues face only death in their pursuit of riches in King Haalor's frozen tomb, his undecaying corpse encased in the very ice that killed him and his army in an age past. The tale follows a more typical fantasy adventure format, featuring a climax in which the grave robbers are destroyed for having disturbed the tomb of a great Hyperborean ruler; however, Smith warps this typical plot to make for a true "incursion of outsideness" into the story. Here, the ice itself—the glacial tomb of King Haalor—is the antagonist of the tale, an example of the outside imbued into the Hyperborean space.

In the Western imagination—both now and in the nineteenth century, the heroic age of polar exploration—the qualities of polar outsideness are manifestations of the sublime, of the struggle of nature reflecting back in the human. What is the difference between the outside and the sublime in polar symbolism? It comes down to a question of agency. Francis Spufford shows just how English explorers to the poles viewed the agency of the ice. In regard to an iconic glacier photograph, taken during Scott's Antarctic expedition, he makes the following claim:

> The picture dramatizes a struggle which will be based upon differ-
> ence of size between [the men in the photo] and landscape [. . .]
> The glacier is already sublime, sublime in and of itself. Like a per-
> petual flood, upreared and then frozen into place, the glacier as-
> serts a huge, swallowing indifference to the efforts of the travelers
> [. . .] Its sublime authority could not be gainsaid; and the explorers
> responded by identifying themselves with its sublimity, glorying in
> the place even as it thwarted or even hurt them. [. . . The ice] was
> a worthily impersonal adversary, whose force could be acknowl-
> edged without the shattering effect of submission to a human ri-
> val. (37–38)

For the English explorers, the ice represents a sublime, overwhelming force, but one that ultimately reflects back to them their own
participation in the "struggle" against cosmic forces. In other words,
the glacier is less an entity and more of a mirror for peering into the
human; the ice possesses authority, but the truth of its agency, for
the explorers, lies not in its non-humanness, rather in its implacabil-
ity (i.e., its being both obstacle and worthy opponent). In this sense,
there is a certain comfort taken in the fact of the non-human, for
the glacier is no man and cannot claim victory over the hubristic explorers as a human being can. It can only stand in the way, noble
and enduring—qualities such as the explorers see in themselves.

Far from being a major obstacle or "worthy adversary," the non-
human Ice-Demon in Smith's Hyperborean tale is terrifying in its
sublimity, its agency belonging to outer forces beyond the pole—
that is to say, beyond the intruders' capability for understanding.
Even before the tomb raiders set foot inside the glacial resting place
(or not so restful, one supposes) of the ancient king, the landscape
seems to take on a shifting appearance, as if time and space warp on
the fields of ice before the doomed men: "The sun appeared to grow
pale and chill, and to recede behind the adventurers; and a wind
blew upon them from the ice, like a breath from abysses beyond the

pole" (*CF* 4.55). Already, the ice exerts its agency upon the doomed men, not presenting itself as an enduring obstacle, but as an overwhelming supernatural force capable of shaping the very world around the doomed adventures to its own design. The focus is on the strangeness of the moment rather than the efforts of the humans to adapt or overcome the circumstances.

We see this again in the climactic struggle between human and ice cavern, which transforms gradually from landscape into malign entity: "Quanga, as he climbed, was considering the monstrous alterations of the cave, which he could not aline with his wide and various experience of the phenomena of nature. [. . . He] found himself confronted by a thing that outraged his reason; a thing that distorted the known face of the world with unearthly, hideous madness" (*CF* 4.58). Perhaps Smith's narrator goes too far here in prescribing the theme of outsideness in this moment, but the effect remains: though voiced by a human narrator, the focus again is solely on the Ice-Demon's supernatural capabilities, its outsideness as imbued by the forces beyond the pole. Readers are not necessarily meant to sympathize or relate to the human characters in this moment; their emotions and stakes are neglected in favor of Smith's narrator foregrounding the Arctic space's predatory, otherworldly nature. In the end, none of the tomb raiders survive the ordeal and Haalor's rubies are reclaimed, eventually, by the ever-creeping glaciers. An important final note here on the subject of the ice's supernatural agency is that while the stolen rubies belong to long-dead Haalor, it is not the king's spirit of vengeance that is the origin of the tomb intruders' doom. Rather, it is solely the glacial ice that brings doom upon the human characters. The Sybil may whisper portents of this doom across the ages, and the white worm plays his part in commencing the apocalyptic reign of the glaciers; but it is the ice that exacts vengeance on humanity.

The narrative focus on the non-human represents an important moment of praxis for Smith, who theorizes on the role of the outside in fantasy literature. In his essay "The Tale of Macrocosmic

Horror," first published as an editorial response to a reader in *Strange Tales*, January 1933, Smith outlines what he thinks should be the focal point of a weird tale:

> In a tale of highest imaginative horror, the main object is the creation of a supernatural, extra-human atmosphere; the real actors are the terrible arcanic forces, the esoteric cosmic malignities; and the element of human character, if one is to achieve the highest, most objective artistry, is properly somewhat subordinated [. . .] One is depicting things, powers and conditions that are beyond humanity; therefore, artistically speaking, the main accent is on these things, powers and conditions. (*Planets and Dimensions* 18)

Smith revels in speaking in absolutes here on the topic of artistry and craft, but the theory espoused at the core of the essay is one that echoes throughout the Hyperborean cycle tales, especially in "The Ice-Demon," where the most the radically non-human agent in the tale, the glacial ice, exemplifies the condition of existing as a "esoteric cosmic malignity," or stated here more often, a true "incursion of outsideness." While the Western imagination has characterized the polar ice as a awe-inspiring source of sublime inspiration, via real-world accounts of exploration into unknown polar spaces, Smith's created Hyperborean ice turns the Arctic sublime on its head, prioritizing the outside instead.

The ice plays a crucial role in the characterization of the Hyperborean space and its tendency for ruptures of the outside into reality. In exploration history, the ice is a sublime force, one to be reckoned with, but also one deemed respectable in its overwhelming display of natural power and obstacle. Smith's Hyperborean ice plays out as a dark variation on this theme, where the human is relegated to the background as the icy domain, as both entity and agency, traumatically overtakes the story. Though the personification of the Arctic ice is not a radically new theme in the Polar Gothic or in polar literature on the whole, the way in which the titular Ice-Demon is portrayed in the tale—its Arctic-ness—simultaneously resonates with and shifts away from real-world Arctic accounts of the sublime qualities of the ice. Smith's characterization of the ice as vengeful entity, a dark noumenon, ultimately serves to reinforce the quality of outsideness that the liminal space of the Hyperborean Ice Age possesses, "like some frozen world of the outer void" made manifest in the interstices between the real and the imagined far north (*CF* 4.55).

He Whose Coming Even the Gods May Not Oppose

Hyperborea is often cast off in Smith scholarship as a lesser cycle in the writer's prolific catalogue. Even Smith admits—in the same letter in which he praises Hyperborea's propensity for attracting weirdness no less—that the far northern continent's impact and interest does not exceed that of the far-future Zothique cycle, a collection of what is arguably some of Smith's best and most sinister prose. Yet what truly attracts one to Hyperborea is not the sardonic characterization nor the strangeness and miscellany of the tales therein: it is the place itself. Smith's Hyperborean cycle is a triumph of *sui generis* worldbuilding, and its contributions to Lovecraft's Cthulhu Mythos are, indeed, a standout feature of the collection; but Hyperborea is so much more than that. Far from being the "unseen" and "untrodden" far northern land that has "slept the profound sleep of death from the earliest dawn of time" that Fridtjof Nansen suggests in his narrative of polar discovery, the Arctic—mythic and real Hyperborea—is a space that has lived many lives across countless ages, the once thrilling prospect of a legendary land whose vitality is so strange it vexes us to this day. The Ice Age and its subsequent domination of the Arctic landscape by glaciers, ice fields, and frozen horizons is how most readers know the polar regions of the world; it forms a bleak image in the mind, one that is both terribly cold and lifeless—if there was any life to the place to begin with.

But Smith saw more than just the Arctic ice; he sees what lies beneath, frozen in deep time and across vast spaces and memories of man. And deeper than that, beyond the ice and the incomprehensible vastness of those glaciers, he recognizes the far north's potential as an exemplary site for the weird fantasist to run amok with generating one's own myth-cycle, blurring the lines between legend and apocrypha of past civilizations and strange stories hinted at in obscure tomes—some circulating in the deep cultural consciousness up until today. But even the writer has his doubts. In a modest letter to H. P. Lovecraft on the completion of his first Hyperborean tale, "The Tale of the Satampra Zeiros," Smith remarks to his weird fiction colleague the fact of his strict propensity for the unreal over actuality. He says, "I, too, am capable of observation; but I am far happier when I can create *everything* in a story, including the milieu. This is why I do best in work like 'Satampra Zeiros.' Maybe I haven't seen enough love for, or interest in, real places, to invest them with the atmosphere that I achieve in something purely imaginary" (*Dawnward Spire* 197). And he does, indeed, create most everything in his stories—as stated before, his *sui generis* thinking and artistry that brings the outside into the human accounts for much of the writer's appeal in a modern world seemingly so focused on the interiority of personhood. His is an art existing for and of its own essential outsideness: outside convention, outside the canon, and outside life itself.

However, the polar myth—that collection of apocryphal and historical Arctic-ness that is pervaded with the strange and liminal—stretches out across vast distances and temporalities, echoing to the poet on frosted breath, whether Smith knows it or not. On dim polar shores, the Hyperborea of the past and present—both real and imagined—collides and fuses with each other like so much water freezing into ice, trapping the continent's strange past in parallel with the glaciated now. We see traces of Smith acknowledging this Arctic liminality clashing and eventually melding with the mythopoetic in his work that predates the Hyperborean cycle and much of his prose writing. In an undated poetic fragment discovered among the miscellany of the Smith papers at the Bancroft Library in Berkeley, California, Smith writes of the mythic Arctic as a literal and metaphoric threshold for the artist. The final stanza of "Ultima

Thule" reads: "Borne by the dusk and occult tides of fate, / When unto us will that shore line appear? Ah much I marvel what will there await, / Whether the lost things that we held most dear, / Our loves and hopes just as they were before, / Or—darkness and oblivion evermore."[2] Love, hope, darkness, and doom—all coexisting in the mind of the young poet in Ultima Thule, the farthest north region on this earthly plain, and beyond it. The Arctic and its strange history is a space for the artist to inscribe those emotions into the ice, preserving them always already in the ice. Smith's Hyperborea may transcend Arctic-ness with the originality of his own mythos deftly woven into the Earth's deep past, but it does not escape its own Arctic resonances; he cannot evade the eons-old "baggage" of setting foot into a realm so fraught with outsideness both imagined and, as we have seen, so often quite real.

Works Cited

Behrends, Steve. *Clark Ashton Smith: A Critical Guide to the Man and His Work,* 2nd ed. San Bernardino, CA: Borgo Press, 2013.

Carter, Lin. "Behind the North Wind." *The Eldritch Dark: The Sanctum of Clark Ashton Smith,* www.eldritchdark.com/articles/biographies/46/behind-the-north-wind.

"Hyperborea." *Theoi Greek Mythology,* www.theoi.com/Phylos/Hyperborea.html.

Joshi, S. T.; Schultz, David E.; and Connors, Scott. *Clark Ashton Smith: A Comprehensive Bibliography.* New York: Hippocampus Press, 2020.

Lovecraft, H. P., and Clark Ashton Smith. *Dawnward Spire, Lonely Hill: The Letters of H. P. Lovecraft and Clark Ashton Smith.* Ed. David E. Schultz and S. T. Joshi. New York: Hippocampus Press, 2017.

McCannon, John. *A History of the Arctic: Nature, Exploration and Exploitation.* London: Reaktion Books, 2012.

2. Located in box 5 of the Clark Ashton Smith Collection at the Bancroft Library, University of California Berkeley. BANC MSS 2004/158c.

McCorristine, Shane. "Mesmerism and Victorian Arctic Exploration." In Eleanor R. Barraclough, Danielle M. Cudmore, and Stefan D. Donecker, ed. *Imagining the Supernatural North*. Edmonton: University of Alberta Press, 2016. 149–64.

Nansen, Fridtjof. *Farthest North: The Incredible Three Year Voyage to the Frozen Latitudes of the North*. Ed. Jon Krakauer. New York: Modern Library, 1999.

Smith, Clark Ashton. *The Collected Fantasies of Clark Ashton Smith*. Ed. Scott Connors and Ronald S. Hilger. San Francisco: Night Shade Books, 2006–10. 5 vols. [Abbreviated in the text as *CF*.]

———. *Planets and Dimensions: Collected Essays of Clark Ashton Smith*. Ed. Charles K. Wolfe. Baltimore: Mirage Press, 1973.

Spufford, Francis. *I May Be Some Time: Ice and the English Imagination*. New York: St. Martin's Press, 1997.

Tompkins, Steven. "Coming In from the Cold: Incursions of 'Outsideness' in Hyperborea." In Scott Connors, ed. *The Freedom of Fantastic Things: Selected Criticism on Clark Ashton Smith*. New York: Hippocampus Press, 2006. 259–76.

Votsis, Athanasios. "The Ancient Greek Myth of Hyperborea." In Eleanor R. Barraclough, Danielle M. Cudmore, and Stefan D. Donecker, ed. *Imagining the Supernatural North*. Edmonton: University of Alberta Press, 2016. 39–52.

The Holiday Transmission

Scott Bradfield

The first time Arnold Simonson heard from his dead father he was sitting in his poorly furnished one-bedroom apartment holding a mug of instant hot chocolate in his lap and watching a random "classic" Christmas movie on his first-generation Kindle—which kept freezing every twenty seconds or so on account of the landlord's crummy broadband. Then, just as it hit Arnold's favorite scene ("We're your worst nightmare: elves with *attitude*—"), the small smudged screen went black, flashed bleakly several times, and Arnold found himself staring into the wild-eyed face of his extremely dead father, Arnold Simonson, Sr., former CEO and controlling stockholder of Mega-Security Corp., Prisons 'R' Us, Big Pharma-Con., and its overarching media conglomerate, Dark Info Fukkyu-com, Inc., which boasted more than a dozen undisclosed corporate offices worldwide.

He's been dead six months, Arnold thought, and wouldn't you know it? He looks better than ever.

"Hey there, kiddo, you arrogant little do-gooder you. It's me, your horrible daddy, who was apparently so horrible that you never called or wrote when I was alive and couldn't even say anything remotely cordial at my funeral. Well, have I got news for *you!* As a result of my well-earned riches, I bought my way into Grand Imperial Estates, where wealthy souls enjoy eternity while the rest of you losers shovel shit in the Holy Basement. And get this: every day's a party in Grand Imperial Estates, where they serve icy buckets of pink champagne, gleaming silver platters loaded with fresh shrimp, slabs of filet mignon as big as dinner plates, and vistas of strawberry-covered cheesecake. We got beautiful young girls dancing on tabletops up here, kid, and full symphony orchestras playing celestial music from the likes of Enya, Yanni, George Benson—and did I mention the beautiful girls? These chicks'll do anything we ask, and believe me—I do a lot of asking. Which reminds me: I've got a bridge tournament in fifteen minutes, and most of the Angelic Choir haven't given me my afternoon blowjob yet. So take care, kiddo, and keep doing all those do-gooder things you do down there at Tree Huggers Anonymous, or Save the Children from Evil, or whatever the hell it is that you do-gooders do. Because I gotta fly—and I mean that, of course, both literally *and* metaphorically."

Then, like a ghost who had found itself crashing the wrong visitation, Arnold's father devolved into a froth of staticky bubbles. The rainbow disc re-emerged on the smudgy screen, buffered, buffered, and abruptly Tim Allen's florid fat Santa face returned and said, "So maybe just once around the block?"

At which point the Kindle expired in Arnold's hands with a tiny click, and something oily slithered from the audio jack.

It smelled like sulfur and roses.

"Well, that certainly *sounds* like your father," his mother told him later on a Skype call from Rio, where she was coordinating a teacher's strike for the local Workers Party. "He only cared about one thing, and that was enjoying a better life than everybody else. He had to have the best car, the best wife, the best house, and whenever one of them got old or unfashionable, he dumped it and bought another. But anyway, I don't have time to piss on your father's grave, hon, as much as I'd like to. Let's look at the bright side. At least he called, which is something he never did when he was alive. And while he may be dead, he's still your father. You guys should get together. Something noncommittal, like dinner or a movie."

Over the next few days and nights, Arnold tried to recall his relationship with Arnold Simonson, Sr. As a child Arnold had looked up to his father, who always knew what coat to wear with which slacks, drove a sportier car than other dads, and annually presented Arnold with a $1000 birthday-bill in a crisp white envelope, stapled to a typed set of recommendations for stocks, T-bills, and foreign currencies.

"Some people spend their lives waiting for government bailouts," Arnold Simonson, Sr. told his son at every such birthday "celebration"—which ritually consisted of a cake baked by Arnold's nanny, Consuela, and a chimichanga cooked by his nanny, Consuela, and a big bear hug from his nanny, Consuela. But Arnold's favorite part was sitting on his father's lap at the computer and deciding how to invest his birthday present. With his father's firm hand on his shoulder, he scrolled through quotes for Uber, Apple, and Berkshire Hathaway back when they were just gleams in a stockbroker's eye. He opened his first IRA before he hit puberty, and his first tax-exempt college fund while still doing his best schoolwork in Crayola. And everything Arnold's father told him to buy paid off in huge dividends, even while emotional investments in his father never did.

"Sorry, I don't *do* school concerts, kid," Arnold Simonson, Sr. often told him. And: "Parent-teacher conferences are for losers." And, inevitably: "Of course we'll still see each other, sport. But when my lawyer's finished with your mother's lawyer, you'll have trouble scraping up bus fare to meet me downtown for lunch. Anyway, my evenings are pretty busy, on account of all the women. But even while you may not see much of me over the next few years, never doubt how much I love you. And every time you look through that *muy excellente* stock portfolio we've assembled, my love for you should never be in doubt."

"I never had anything *against* your mom," Arnold's father explained the next evening, after erupting from a GIF on Arnold's Facebook feed. He was wearing a black tuxedo and stood in a room filled with other men in black tuxedos, many of whom Arnold recognized from the obituary pages of the *Financial Times*. "Being angry at your mom wouldn't make sense, financially speaking. I saw your mom simply as a threat to my reputation; and when anybody threatens *my* reputation, I shut them down. I strip their assets. I feed their entrails to my stooges. It wasn't personal; it was business. There's only one principle to living a good life, son, and that's to enjoy your privileges while you're alive. Otherwise, how can you know which privileges to *continue* enjoying after you're dead? Think about it. Even if you don't like me, you have to admit that I make a lot of sense."

Dad's image was slowly disassembling into a foam of white tele-visual static, reforming, and then slowly disassembling again. It was like trying to stream movies during a thunderstorm.

Finally Arnold said, "Dad, I have a question. But I don't know how to ask."

Dad was half-turned from the screen, accepting a tall sparkling glass of champagne from a silver tray. He seemed to find the glass a lot more interesting than he found Arnold.

"Go head, kid," he told the glass. "Shoot."

"Let's say that you and your old friends are living the same hap-pily exorbitant life you lived when you were alive. My question is this: what about everybody else? What about all the *normal* people like Grandpa and Granddad, or even Consuela, who fixed me din-ner every night, all the people who may not have been rich, but who worked hard all their lives, did the best they could, and died? Where do *those* people go in the after-life, Dad? Not a big deal or anything. Asking for a friend."

Arnold's dad had finished his champagne. His eyes were closed. He breathed slowly and exhaled. Then, without opening his eyes, he handed his empty glass to a tuxedoed waiter who arrived just in time to take it.

Turning his hard blue eyes to the camera (or to his MacBook Pro, or to whatever celestial photo-imaging app they had up there in the afterlife), he said:

"Don't waste time worrying about what happens to losers like your granddad and Consuela, kid. Just make sure that the *next* loser isn't *you*."

Arnold called in sick at work and powered down all his devices, in-cluding his smartphone and his desktop. He bought several books on Zen and signed up for a watercolor class at Adult Ed. He sprouted several seeds of automatic-flowering White Widow in a hanging pot outside his bedroom window, repainted his apartment in neutral colors, such as Filmy Green and Blue Diamond, and practiced deep-breathing exercises in the bathtub, sometimes with either a mug of Lapsang Souchong cradled against his chest, or a small glass of bourbon.

"You need to get his voice out of your head," advised his ex-girlfriend, Philomena Rodriguez, who had moved to Philadelphia to work part-time at Trader Joe's. "Your dad is like all your negative energies rolled into this one big cloud of self-hate. These negative energies eat away at your insides. They turn your chakra inside-out. When we were together, Arnold, I could feel you channeling these negative energies all the time, and while I truly hope you can escape your dad's horrible influence, I'd prefer not to hear from you again. You're a big fat drain on my karma. You're a walking metaphysical bummer. I've only been talking to you for like five minutes and the poinsettia on my dining room table is starting to wither. That was a perfectly healthy poinsettia five minutes ago, and now it doesn't look like it'll last through Christmas."

For several days Arnold behaved as unproductively as possible. He took long walks on Avila Beach. He read paperback mystery novels purchased from thrift stores and avoided any publications related to the material world. And instead of trying to resuscitate his rapidly dwindling house plants, he dumped them in the steel trash bins behind his apartment. It was best to cut yourself off from all forms of organic life, he reflected. Otherwise, you might get lured into affections for the world that produced them.

But as much as Arnold tried, there didn't seem to be any way of avoiding his dead father. Arnold blamed it on the prevalence of interactive social media, which required people to maintain contact with people long after they shouldn't maintain contact with them.

"He left a message," his co-worker at the Arroyo Grande Center for Political Justice, Alice Locklear-Jones, told Arnold when he arrived at the office on Christmas Eve. "And it's long. Should I read it?"

"I'd prefer you didn't."

Arnold sat in a faded leather swivel chair next to Alice at the otherwise empty switchboard. All their sensible co-workers had left for the holidays, but Arnold and Alice had volunteered for the Christmas Eve shift, since Arnold's mom was off canoeing for democracy and none of Alice's family talked to her.

Alice held the pinkish *You've Got A Message* slip in both hands as if preparing to read a legal judgment in court.

"'You can't hide from family, son,'" she read stiffly in a flat, unaccented fake-male voice that sounded like HAL from *2001: A Space Odyssey.* "'I've tried communicating through your iPad; and I've tried communicating through your cell phone; but it's like you're avoiding me. So here's what we're gonna do. Later tonight, you're going to be visited by one ghost—*me!* And I'm not leaving until you've learned how to improve your life through capitalism. Seriously, there's not a university on this planet that can teach you what I can about making money, screwing over everybody who *doesn't* make money, and sending your soul on the path to Everlasting Happiness and Reward. I should write a book on the subject, but I was never very good at punctuation. So enjoy your last few hours of barely-existing and eating your frozen turkey dinners and so forth. Those days are coming to an end *hard.* Oh, and is that Alice What's-her-face taking down this message? We were just discussing her at yesterday's Executive Board Meeting. On New Year's Eve, she will choke on her own vomit and spend eternity washing our floors and cleaning our toilets. Remember, kid: heaven doesn't make excuses for losers. And later tonight, that's the *first* thing I'm gonna teach you.'"

When Alice finished, her eyes were filled with sadness for everyone in the world except Arnold.

"What's most disturbing about your dead dad, Arnold," she said, "is that he actually makes sense. You *can't* turn your back on family. Now, if you don't mind, it looks like I've gotta see a lawyer about my will."

*   *   *

When Arnold drove home that night on Highway 101, it didn't seem like Christmas Eve. The skies were bright and clear, littered with hard bright stars; attractive young people in tank tops drove past in open convertibles, playing their dashboard sound systems full blast. With intermittent splutters, Dad's voice erupted from each dashboard speaker that passed by:

> "I'll be home for Christmas!"
> "You can plan on me!"
> "I'll be home for Christmas!"
> "If only in my dreams!"

"You can't shut me out of your life forever, son! We're both the same person deep inside!"

"Ho ho ho!"

"Fa la la!"

"Reprise! Reprise!"

"If only in my dreeeeeeeams!"

By the time Arnold pulled into his concrete carport, he felt sweaty, dried out, and exhausted, like a dead leaf. His apartment was filled with the day's accumulated heat, as heavy and profound as bad news, and his potted fir sapling had spilled an array of spiny brown needles across the thin carpet. Not another Christmas, Arnold thought sadly. Not another Christmas like the last one.

Out of spite, Arnold heated a saucer of eggnog on the stove, spiked it with a generous splash of generic rum, and filled two matching Santa mugs purchased two years previously from Oxfam. Then he laid out two small plates of Christmas biscuits on a fold-out plastic card table, plugged his television into the wall, and took the remote control to his stuffed chair as if preparing to comfort a small pet.

It was the same blocky bottle-glass-colored Panasonic analog television with the cracked channel dial that Arnold inherited when his mom moved away. Even connected to the cable through a converter box, the wobbly picture was streaked with rainbows. The transistors warmed with a slow, vibratory thrum, like the engine of a broken microwave oven.

"Jesus Rice Crispies," Dad said, squeezing through the blurry screen head-first like a well-dressed POW emerging from the mouth of an escape tunnel. The effervescent static came blowing in around him, settling on the carpet and furniture like pale confetti. "You could do serious damage to a guy with a crappy TV like that. The first thing we do is get you a flat-screen so I can drop by any-time I want and I don't damage the suit. Now look, let's spruce our-selves up"—at which point Arnold Simonson, Sr. slapped the flaky white and green snow from his chest and shoulders—"and find some trashy lap-dancing establishment that's open Christmas Eve. Which, as I seem to recall, is probably all of them." He looked un-naturally smooth, as if he had just been shellacked.

It had taken Arnold several decades to develop an imperfect comprehension of his father. Initially he considered him a check-book Santa who dropped by each year to deliver an envelope. Then, for several years, he was an absent Santa, remarried to a Guatemalan model named Fabiella and living in a series of tax havens that Ar-nold couldn't even pronounce. Finally he was dead Santa, preserved in all his rage in the North Pole somewhere, surrounded by bitter, recalcitrant elves. All my life, Arnold reflected, Dad was either bare-ly here, or not here, or never going to be here. Until he died and re-fused to go away. Go figure.

"Where you going, son? Come back here! We need to drop by an ATM for a stack of C-notes! You can't get a decent blowjob on Christmas Eve without a stack of C-notes. I been there, kid, and I know!"

The only item from his father that Arnold took home after the funeral was a set of 24-karat gold-plated Honma Five Stars golf clubs that now stood in his bedroom closet, shrouded in old sweaters and jackets. His mom used to say, "If you want to get close to your father, hon, you should disguise yourself as one of those damned golf clubs. He loves those golf clubs. He sits up late at night stroking and talking to those golf clubs. I've never been concerned about the women he sneaks around with; the only thing that concerns me is his relationship with those golf clubs." It was the only time Arnold remembered his mother using the word "damned." That's because his mom wasn't a "damned" sort of person. She was more a "forgive-and-forget" sort of person, and Arnold had spent his life trying to be more like his mom than his dad.

But that didn't mean he had been successful.

"What the hell, son!" his father shouted joyfully when Arnold returned to the living room. "Is that my old nine-iron? I've been looking all over for that little piece of hand-tooled beauty. I thought they'd sell them in the Hereafter, but no such luck."

Sometimes, Arnold decided, you needed to accept the worst aspects of yourself just as confidently as you accepted the best ones. Sometimes the worst aspects were more useful.

(Such as the part that *never* forgave and forgot.)

"Hey, kid! What're you doing? Are you kidding? You can't hurt me with that thing! I'm already dead! And anyway, at the first sign of trouble, all I gotta do is dive back through this television into the eternal glory of my luxurious posthumous life. Unless, of course, what you're really trying to do is—*no!* Son! Please! Not *that!*"

Arnold had never learned the proper way to wield a driver—certainly not one as well-balanced as this one. He suspected that you probably shouldn't hold it (as he was holding it now) like a sledgehammer and swing it (as he was swinging it now) as hard as you could.

At which point, Arnold smashed the blocky Sony Panasonic into a hundred tiny pieces.

It was the best damned Christmas present he had ever given himself.

* * *

If life is funny, Arnold reflected over the next few weeks and months, then death is even funnier. Especially when it happens to somebody who isn't you.

For the first few days, Arnold's dad howled the way forlorn Irish ghosts were supposed to howl in tarn-locked gothic castles. "Oh, *nooooo!*" he howled. "What did you do to the goddamn tee*veeeeee!* Oh, *nooooo!* What do you mean you donated your broken Kindle to Unicef and you don't even have a transistor radio? Oh, *noooooo, oh, nooooo!*" It was as if Arnold's dad—like the vast majority of American teenagers—couldn't survive for two minutes without digital interface.

"I guess you're just stuck with me, Dad," Arnold enjoyed reminding his father every evening when he came home from work with either a veggie-supreme gluten-free pizza from the Community Co-Op or materials for a rocket and vinaigrette salad. "But that's not so bad, is it? I mean, this allows us to do a lot of catching up. For example, you probably didn't know I sold my investment portfolio back in high school and donated what felt like ill-gotten-gain to a series of charities, such as Brand-New Congress and the International Red Cross. Which is why we can't afford to move out of this crummy one-bedroom, where I'm afraid you'll have to keep sleeping on that wobbly couch. Also, since I'm a longstanding member of the Young Socialists Alliance and we have our meetings here on alternate Tuesdays, you should get used to lots of beards and braids stopping by—but don't expect any smartphones or tablets. We've banned any electronic devices that could collect data on the various plots we're hatching against the government. And I'm not talking about just *our* government, Dad. I'm talking about *all* of them."

As Dad's howling diminished, his enthusiasm for elaborating Arnold's failures diminished with it. Day after day and week after week, he sat in his slowly fading, rumpled tuxedo gazing desultorily down at whatever herbal tea he had procured from Arnold's minimally provisioned kitchenette, nibbling loosely at rice cakes and falafel-bread, and slowly losing focus in the candlelight. (Arnold had installed a dozen candles in old wine bottles around the apartment after the electricity was cut off.)

"At this rate," Arnold often thought out loud, "we'll be living on the street by next Christmas."

A premonition that always inspired Arnold's face to break into a smile.

Sad Steps Beneath the Silent Moon

Frank Coffman

"With how sad steps, O Moon, thou climb'st the skies
How silently, and with how wan a face . . ."
—Sir Philip Sidney, *Astrophil & Stella* 31

Those nights the silent moon in fullness slips
Just past, or scuds along the flying clouds,
Or grimly dimmed when welkin dark enshrouds,
Through Summer's haze or when cold Winter grips—
All seasons through the sun's elliptical trips—
Whether through Autumn's spare branches, or when crowds
Of Springtime foliage dim the moon's stark floods—
An Evil lurks abroad with slavering lips.

Those are the nights the cursed ones change their skin!
And prey upon the rest of humankind.
A bite survived means a horrid life begins
When next the round moon shines. A shape defined
Against that bright orb, cresting on the hill—
A ghastly man-wolf stalking it's next kill.

Hodgson, *The Night Land,* and William Morris

Lee Weinstein

The Night Land (1912), often considered to be William Hope Hodgson's *magnum opus,* was originally subtitled "A Love Tale," an apt description. It can also be categorized as science fiction, supernatural horror, and not least, as a heroic fantasy.

Briefly, *The Night Land* is the story of an unnamed man (X)[1] of what is generally assumed to be the seventeenth century,[2] whose beloved wife, Lady Mirdath, has died. In dreams he wakes in the remote future—a future in which the sun has long since burned out and the surviving millions of humanity live within the protection of a great pyramidal structure with hundreds of levels, each of which is a city. Outside is the Night Land, occupied by dangerous and dimly understood creatures and malign forces. The future incarnation of X telepathically receives distress calls from a young woman named Naani, who is the future incarnation of Mirdath, and lives in a second, smaller pyramid. The power that sustains the second pyramid is failing and she is about to fall prey to the sinister forces that lie in wait outside.

Despite its setting many millions of years in our future, in a world of darkness and monsters, the mainspring of the novel is a heroic quest, bearing more than a passing resemblance to a medieval romance. X is, in essence, a knight in futuristic armor on a mission to rescue a maiden in distress. In his first-person narrative he de-

---

1. Hodgson's heavily edited 20,000-word version of *The Night Land* was first published as "The Rescued Fragments of The Dream of X" (New York: R. H. Paget, 1912).
2. Nothing in Hodgson's text states the time period in which the first chapter is set.

scribes his surroundings in language appropriate to his own past era; thus he calls the huge metal pyramid in which he resides the Last Redoubt. He calls the telescopic device used to observe the surrounding landscape "The Great Spy-glass," and his telepathic ability, "Night- Hearing."

The Redoubt is an immense structure eight miles high and four miles square at ground level. It has 1,320 levels above ground, each of which is a city, and extends 100 miles deep below ground with 306 fields for farming. The power comes from "Earth-Current" tapped from the ground. This aspect of the novel is pure speculative fiction. But Davidson refers to it metaphorically as a castle and calls it "the key to understanding the depth and resonance of the meanings in the story" (122). From this "castle," a knight of the distant future battles demonic creatures to rescue a fair damsel.

It is a unique, visionary work, seemingly *sui generis,* although, because of the lack of available information, critics have had to speculate on what Hodgson's influences might have been.

Primary source material about Hodgson's reading habits is scarce. It is known that when he decided to become a writer, he became a voracious reader. "Hope had to teach himself to type; read every book he could lay his hands on how to write and also on the supernatural, the occult, spiritualism, and contemporary phantasy and horror authors—not many of course" (Everts 13). Davidson says, "it is not possible without access to his notes to determine exactly what Hodgson read and what influenced him . . . However it is possible to know what was 'in the air' at the time" (138).

It is generally agreed that he was familiar with Poe, Machen, Blackwood and Conan Doyle. Based on internal evidence in *The House on the Borderland* (1908) and *The Night Land,* critics believe that he was familiar with *The Time Machine* (1895). It is known that he actually met H. G. Wells through his membership in the Society of Authors (Moskowitz 28). *Omega: The End of the World* (1894) by Camille Flammarion has also been cited as a very probable influence (Bleiler 425). According to Stableford, "The imaginative groundwork for the more elaborate terminal imagery contained in such works as ... *The Time Machine* ... William Hope Hodgson's *The House on the Borderland* and *The Night Land* ... was first laid by Flammarion" (139). Davidson (125) suggests that the architecture and society of the Last Redoubt may have been inspired by the 1662 philosophical work *The City of the Sun* by Tomasso Campanella. But if Hodgson was inspired by such ideas, he extrapolated from them in extremely creative ways.

In a letter, Hodgson says about his novel *The Boats of the "Glen Carrig"* (1907): "I've tried hard to be commonplace in it; but, I'm afraid, with but poor success. I cannot ride above that failing of mine which urges me to write original stuff" (Gafford 13). The remote future of *The Night Land* may have been suggested in part by the very brief scene near the end of *The Time Machine* where the Time Traveller travels ahead to the final days of earth. Another source is very likely the end days of the earth described in *Omega*. Davidson (124) suggests that Hodgson may have been partially inspired by Poe's "Colloquy of Monos and Una," a philosophical dialogue on the nature of death by the spirits of two former lovers. But it seems more likely that the telepathic link between X and Naani echoes a scene toward the end of *Omega*. The earth of the remote future is dying. Two people, a man, Omegar, and a young woman, Eva, are the sole survivors. They are quite physically remote from each other. But Eva contacts Omegar telepathically, first as an image in a dream and then as a request to join her. He responds and travels to Ceylon via electric airship to be with her (255–57). And so Hodgson has seemingly transmogrified a few short scenes in *The Time Machine* and *Omega* and woven them into a much larger and original tapestry.

These partially explain some of the science fictional roots of Hodgson's vision of the remote future. But why did he couch it as a tale told from the viewpoint of a man from centuries earlier? The inspiration for the oft-criticized archaic language, and the romantic quest across the dark, Boschian landscape to rescue Naani, must have come from elsewhere.

Hodgson would have been familiar with retellings of medieval romances such as tales of King Arthur and his Knights of the Round Table. But one very popular book in Hodgson's time may well have served as at least an inspiration for his novel, if not as a template or backbone. Rather than a group of related stories, like the Arthurian tales, it is a long quest novel set in an invented world, of about the same length as the *Night Land* and published not terribly long before it.

The book in question is *The Well at the World's End* (1896) by William Morris. Morris was a pre-Raphaelite, a Romantic, and an avid medievalist. He "saw himself as a knight on a charger, roaming the woods in quest of adventure and enlightenment, aiming to set the world to rights" (Mathews 4). "He read widely . . . in the stories of the Younger and Elder Eddas; in the Arthurian legends . . . Eventually, he read and translated early epic romance materials from southern France to, most notably, Iceland" (Pfeiffer 300). Toward the end of his life, Morris wrote a number of pioneering secondary-world fantasy novels or romances, set in imaginary versions of medieval Europe. "No writer gave more that is valuable to a twentieth-century literature of epic fantasy than William Morris" (Pfeiffer 299). *Well* has been called "the longest and most popular of [his] fantasies" (Pfeiffer 303).

Hodgson, an avid reader, was likely to be familiar with it. As Fussell puts it, "Morris's most popular romance was *The Well at the World's End*. . . . There was hardly a literate man who fought between 1914 and 1918 who hadn't read it and been powerfully excited by it in his youth" (135). Hodgson, who fought and died in World War I, was such a literate man. The book would have particularly appealed to Hodgson, who had been a rebellious youth and who ran away from home several times and joined the merchant marine at age fourteen by lying about his age (Frank 14). Ralph of Upmeads, the protagonist of *Well*, and a son of the king, is also a rebellious youth and runs away from his home, the High House of Upmeads, at the beginning, to seek adventure.

Davidson, in discussing sources for *The Night Land*, mentions Morris's novels only in passing. "His fantasy novels, such as *Well* . . . idealize the medieval period and chivalric adventure using a deliberately archaic prose style" (126), a description that could almost apply to *The Night Land* as well. However, Davidson's concern is more with both Hodgson's and Morris's opposition to the contemporary social order.

The two novels at first glance are quite different. As with Morris's other late novels, *Well* is set in an imaginary medieval Europe populated with kings, knights, maidens, castles, villages, and woods. The plot is rambling and picaresque. Ralph only decides to seek the titular Well after hearing of it from several people in his wanderings. The dangers he faces are entirely human in nature. His "call to adventure," as Joseph Campbell would later call it, comes from within himself.

The Night Land's setting, by contrast, is the remote future and the plot is a quite straightforward quest: there and back again. X meets no people on his outbound journey; the book contains virtually no dialogue. The dangers are described in the book as "Monsters and Ab-human creatures . . . certain dreadful forces to have the power to affect the life of the human spirit." X's call to adventure comes from without, from a distress call.

Landow notes that while Morris makes "progressive use of the fantasy, Hodgson uses it to embody reactionary social and sexual belief" (136). He describes Morris's female character, Ursula, as a "strong active figure who . . . shapes her own destiny" (136) Hodgson's character of Naani, on the other hand, is quite the opposite. She is submissive, dependent, and occasionally foolhardy. Both characters subvert the idea of chivalry, but in different ways.

It has been argued that *Well*, with its quest for magical water, is replete with spiritual symbolism involving water and Mother Earth that can be summarized as "how to make the waste land bloom again and how to make a house a home" (Mathews 43). The spiritual aspects of *The Night Land*, on the other hand, are overt rather than symbolic. The Watchers, the House of Silence, and the other evils abroad are avatars of extra-dimensional forces, and likewise the forces of good that come into play at the end.

But the similarities cannot be ignored. Both works are structured on the lines of the classic "hero's journey." Common sources, such as Arthurian legendry, can be argued for only some of this. Both are novels of more than 200,000 words in which a lone protagonist sets out, despite initial opposition, on a long quest, meets a young woman, and returns with her to his home. *The Night Land* was begun less than a decade after the publication of *Well* in 1896. Letters from Hodgson, discovered in 1991, suggest that *The Night Land*, although it was the last of his four novels to be published (1912), was actually written, or at least started, possibly as early as 1903 (Gafford). Hodgson wrote in an inscription to a young friend in a copy of the novel, "to . . . that impudent maiden to whom I first told the ever shaping tale of The Night Land" (Frank 26). It was, like *The Lord of the Rings*, a tale that grew with the telling.

Both are written in antiquated English. Although *The Night Land* has often been criticized for its stilted, artificial language, Landow describes it as being told in an "archaic, almost Morrisian diction" (136). Hodgson was attempting to tell the tale through the eyes of a man in a past century who experiences the far future through a series of dreams. Morris, who also wrote his novels in an archaic, if somewhat different style, was attempting to imitate medieval romances. Brown has argued that Hodgson was attempting to use a biblical style. Hodgson, if not attempting to imitate Morris directly, at least may have been inspired by Morris to tell his tale in an archaic dialect.

X wishes to attempt a solo rescue mission, after the group of 500 youths who precedes him comes to a bad end. He, against the wishes of his mentor, the Master Monstruwacan,[3] wants to brave the nightmarish outside world to find and rescue Naani, whom he knew and loved in a previous life as the Lady Mirdath. His mentor reluctantly relents and equips him with armor, a kind of electrical spinning sword called a Diskos, and a scrip containing food pellets and a source of water for the journey.

Similarly, after his older brothers are given leave by their father to leave home and seek their fortunes, Ralph goes against his parents' wishes and sneaks away from his home in Upmeads to seek his own adventures. Armored and armed, he first encounters his neighbor Dame Katherine, who likewise provides him with some food in a scrip and a protective talisman and tells him of the titular Well, which promises to provide the drinker with immortality.

X, after facing and defeating or avoiding numerous malign forces, eventually attains his goal and finds Naani, precisely at the halfway point of the novel. She is at first hidden in the shrubbery, and although they have never before seen each other, they are able to recognize each other through the telepathic link they share. They then begin the arduous return journey together, retracing X's outbound journey.

Similarly, in *Well*, Ralph meets his future mate, Ursula, halfway through the novel. She is disguised in a suit of armor at first, and he initially takes her for a man. When she removes her helmet and reveals herself, he realizes that he has unknowingly met her previously. Just as X had previously known Naani as Mirdath, Ralph had met Ursula briefly on two occasions near the beginning of his journey, and had had a dream later on in which she told him her name was Dorothea.

They find the Well after braving numerous dangers, and both drink from it. The remaining quarter of the book recounts their triumphant return to Upmeads, passing the places Ralph encountered on the way there.

---

3. The Monstruwacans are the scientists who keep watch on the bizarre phenomena outside of the Redoubt.

Both books describe much of the geography that the respective heroes traverse. In *Well*, although Ralph passes through oddly named places areas such as the Wood Perilous, the Dry Tree, and the Thirsty Desert, the dangers he encounters are human villains. In *The Night Land*, X passes such areas as the Country of Silence, the Plain of Blue Fire, and the Red Pit, and the dangers he faces are inhuman or, to use Hodgson's term, "ab-human."

As a final piece of evidence, the following passage from *Well* describes a desolation that might have suggested to Hodgson the dark landscape he details in his own book. This is from chapter nine of Book Four, where Ralph and Ursula are on the return journey from the Well with a sage as their guide and they enter upon a place called the Rock Sea:

> But on the next day as they went, the aspect of the rock-sea about them changed: for the rocks were not so smooth and shining and orderly, but rose up in confused heaps all clotted together by the burning, like to clinkers out of some monstrous forge of the earth-giants, so that their way was naught so clear as it had been, but was rather a maze of jagged stone . . . Night fell, and as it grew dark they saw the glaring of the earth-fires again; and when they were rested, and had done their meat, the Sage said:
>
> "Come now with me, for hard by is there a place as it were a stair that goeth to the top of a great rock, let us climb it and look about us."
>
> So did they, and the head of the rock was higher than the main face of the rock-sea, so that they could see afar. Thence they looked north and beheld afar off a very pillar of fire rising up from a ness of the mountain wall, and seeming as if it bore up a black roof of smoke; and the huge wall gleamed grey, because of its light, and it cast a ray of light across the rock-sea as the moon doth over the waters of the deep. (2.39–40)

Compare this to Hodgson's passage in chapter seven, in which X has left the Redoubt and is beginning his treacherous journey:

> And in this part of my journey did I come to The Place Where The Silent Ones Kill, as it was named in the Maps. And I observed a very wondrous caution, and went away from it a little, unto the North, where I did see at a distance the shinings of fire-holes; the which did promise me warmth through my slumber.
>
> And here you must know that the Place Where The Silent Ones Kill was an utter bare place, where all did seem of rock, and no bush did seem to grow thereon; so that a man might not come to any hiding; though, in truth, there might be some hole here or there . . . ; neither did there seem to be any such to me, as I did creep there among the moss-bushes to the Northward of the Place, and look constant and fearful towards it; so that I should see quickly whether any Silent One did move across all the grey quiet of that rocky plain.

The similarities are obvious. The utterly barren rocky terrain in both, with Morris's earth-fires or Hodgson's fire-holes glowing against the darkness. And quite specifically, compare Morris's "pillar of fire" in the above passage, and Hodgson's "Great Gas Fountain" described later in chapter 15: "the background of the night was made to lose somewhat of the intensity of its darkness, as with constant shudders of light; and this to be surely the far away dance of the flame of the Great Gas Fountain."

Just as the brief episode of the telepathic union between Omegar and Eva at the end of *Omega* might have suggested the basic driving premise of Naani's call for help to Hodgson, the fire-lit desolation in this short episode of *Well* might have suggested the similar grim landscape of *The Night Land*.

The accumulated evidence suggests that Hodgson was very likely to have read and related to *Well*. It may well have inspired, at least in part, *The Night Land*, which seems to have been his earliest attempt at a novel. He took the trope of the medieval quest, transplanted it to a future age (while retaining its basic elements), and couched it in the idiom of a long-bygone age. The overall effect is to tell a story that is indeed timeless.

Pfeiffer states, "C. S. Lewis, J. R. R. Tolkien, Andrew Lang, Lord Dunsany, James Branch Cabell, W. B. Yeats, Lloyd Alexander, George Bernard Shaw, and H. G. Wells have acknowledged debts to Morris for their own mythic narratives" (299). Perhaps William Hope Hodgson should be added to that list.

Works Cited

Bleiler, E. F. "William Hope Hodgson." In E. F. Bleiler, ed. *Supernatural Fiction Writers*. New York: Charles Scribner's Sons, 1985. 421–28.

Brown, Nigel "The Word Current: An Apology for the Linguistic Architecture of *The Night Land*." nightland.website/index.php/background/essays/nigel-brown-s-night-land-essays/175-the-word-current.

Campbell, Joseph. *The Hero with a Thousand Faces*. Princeton: Princeton University Press, 1968.

Davidson, Brett. "Terminal Eden: The Last Redoubt and the Closure of History." *Sargasso* 1, No. 3 (2014): 122–49.

Everts, R. Alain. *Some Facts in the Case of William Hope Hodgson: Master of Fantasy*. 1974. Toronto: Soft Books, 1987.

Flammarion, Camille. *Omega: The Last Days of the World* (1894). archive.org/details/omegalastdaysofw00flamrich/page/n7/mode/2up

Frank, Jane. "Under his Skin: A Profile of William Hope Hodgson." *Sargasso* No. 2 (2014): 10–27.

Fussell, Paul. *The Great War and Modern Memory*. New York: Oxford University Press, 1975.

Gafford, Sam. "Writing Backwards: The Novels of William Hope Hodgson." *Studies in Weird Fiction* No. 11 (1992): 12–15.

Hodgson, William Hope. *The Night Land*. Auckland, NZ: Floating Press, 2009. e-Book collection (EBSCOhost).

Landow, George P. "And the World Become Strange: Realms of Literary Fantasy." In Roger C. Schlobin, ed. *The Aesthetics of*

Fantasy Literature and Art. Notre Dame, IN: University of Notre Dame Press, 1982. 105–42.

Mathews, Richard. *Worlds Beyond the World: The Fantastic Vision of William Morris.* San Bernardino, CA: Borgo Press. 1978.

Morris, William. *The Well at the World's End.* New York: Ballantine Books, 1970. 2 vols.

Moskowitz, Sam. "William Hope Hodgson: The Early Years." In Hodgson's *Out of the Storm: Uncollected Fantasies.* Ed. Sam Moskowitz. West Kingston, RI: Donald M. Grant, 1975.

Pfeiffer, John R. "William Morris." In E. F. Bleiler, ed. *Supernatural Fiction Writers.* New York: Charles Scribner's Sons, 1985. 299–306.

Stableford, Brian. *Heterocosms.* Holicong, PA: Wildside Press, 2007.

Notes on Contributors

Manuel Arenas is a writer of verse and prose in the Gothic horror tradition. His work has appeared in *Spectral Realms* and *Penumbra* as well as in various genre anthologies, including (most recently) *Knock Knock: Wyrd Folks and Wives' Tales* from Frisson Comics. He currently resides in Phoenix, Arizona, where he pens his dark ditties sheltered behind heavy curtains, as he shuns the oppressive orb which glares down on him from the cloudless, dust-filled sky.

Leigh Blackmore's horror fiction has appeared in more than sixty magazines from *Avatar* to *Strange Detective Stories*. He has reviewed for journals including *Lovecraft Annual, Shoggoth, Skinned Alive,* and *Dead Reckonings*. His critical essays appear in volumes including Benjamin Szumskyj's *The Man Who Collected Psychos: Critical Essays on Robert Bloch,* Gary William Crawford's *Ramsey Campbell: Critical Essays on the Modern Master of Horror,* Danel Olson's *21st Century Gothic,* and elsewhere. New weird verse has appeared in *Penumbra* and other journals.

Adam Bolivar is a Romantic poet specializing in the composition of folkloric balladry in traditional rhyme and meter. He also carves marionettes out of wood, tailors clothes for them, and compels them to perform in fiendish plays of his own authorship. Born and bred in Boston, Adam Bolivar currently resides in the gloomy dreamland of Portland, Oregon, with his beloved wife and golden-haired son.

Scott Bradfield is the author of *The History of Luminous Motion, Good Girl Wants It Bad,* and several collections of short stories, including the latest, *The Millennial's Guide to Death*. He reviews regularly for the *Los Angeles Times,* the *Los Angeles Review of Books,* the *Spectator,* and the *New Republic*. He lives in his native state of California with his wife, his dog, and his parakeet.

Ramsey Campbell was born in Liverpool in 1946 and now lives in Wallasey. The *Oxford Companion to English Literature* describes him as "Britain's most respected living horror writer." He has received the Grand Master Award of the World Horror Convention, the Lifetime Achievement Award of the Horror Writers Association, the Living Legend Award of the International Horror Guild and the World Fantasy Lifetime Achievement Award. In 2015 he was made an Honorary Fellow of Liverpool John Moores University for outstanding services to literature. PS Publishing recently brought out *Phantasmagorical Stories*, a sixty-year retrospective of his short fiction. His latest novel is *Somebody's Voice* from Flame Tree Press, who are in the process of publishing his Brichester Mythos trilogy.

Frank Coffman is a retired professor of English and Creative Writing. He has published speculative poetry and short fiction in a variety of magazines, anthologies, and collections. His three collections of poetry are: *The Coven's Hornbook and Other Poems* (2019), *Black Flames and Gleaming Shadows* (2020), and *Eclipse of the Moon* (2021). His collection of seven occult detective mysteries, *Three against the Dark*, will be released this year.

Scott J. Couturier is a poet and prose writer of the weird, liminal, and darkly fantastic. His work has appeared in numerous venues, including *The Audient Void, Spectral Realms, Eye to the Telescope, The Dark Corner Zine, Space and Time Magazine,* and *Weirdbook.* Currently he works as an editor for Mission Point Press, living an obscure reverie in the wilds of northern Michigan with his partner/live-in editor & two cats.

Ian Fetters is a researcher of the weird and the hauntological. He is the 2017 recipient of the S. T. Joshi Endowed Research Fellowship for the project "Lovecraft's Dark Continent." He is also the first recipient of the Donald Sidney-Fryer Research Fellowship in 2018. His research on Lovecraft has been published in *Lovecraftian Proceedings* and the edited volume *Lovecraft in the 21st Century: Dead,*

But Still Dreaming, forthcoming from Routledge. Ian lives in San Luis Obispo, California.

Wade German is the author of the poetry collections *Dreams from a Black Nebula* (Hippocampus Press), *The Ladies of the Everlasting Lichen and Other Relics* (Mount Abraxas Press), the verse drama *Children of Hypnos,* and two slim volumes of verse in Portuguese translation, *Incantations* and *Apparitions* (Raphus Press).

James Goho is a writer and researcher who lives in Winnipeg, Canada. His most recent short story, "Calls from Home," appeared in the literary magazine *Fiction #64.* His book, *Caitlín R. Kiernan: A Critical Study of Her Dark Fiction,* was published by McFarland in 2020.

Maxwell I. Gold is a Rhysling Award–nominated author of weird fiction, writing short stories and prose that center around his profane Cyber Gods Mythos. His work has appeared in numerous publications including *The Audient Void, Space and Time, Weirdbook,* and many others.

Cecelia Hopkins-Drewer lives in Adelaide, South Australia. She has written a Master's thesis on H. P. Lovecraft, and an M.Lett. dissertation on fairy tale motifs in nineteenth-century English novels. Her poetry has been published in *Spectral Realms* and *PS: It's Poetry,* compiled by the Poetry Soup community. Micro-fictions have appeared in the "Dark Drabbles" series published by Black Hare Press, and the "Scary Snippets" series produced by Nocturnal Sirens. Her research interests include Gothic horror, fantasy, and popular culture, including film and television.

Martin Wangsgaard Jürgensen lives in Copenhagen with his family. He is employed as a researcher at the Danish National Museum and specializes in the intersection of art and the history of emotions. He has published numerous articles and volumes in Danish and English as well as five novels. He is currently finishing a large study on fantasy fiction and the first volume on H. P. Lovecraft in Danish.

S. T. Joshi is a widely published literary and cultural critic and the author of *The Weird Tale* (1990), *I Am Providence: The Life and Times of H. P. Lovecraft* (2010), *Unutterable Horror: A History of Supernatural Fiction* (2012), and many other volumes. He has edited the work of H. P. Lovecraft, Ambrose Bierce, Lord Dunsany, H. L. Mencken, Leslie Stephen, and other writers.

Katherine Kerestman has a B.A. from John Carroll University and an M.A. from Case Western Reserve University. She is the author of *Creepy Cat's Macabre Travels: Prowling around Haunted Towers, Crumbling Castles, and Ghoulish Graveyards* (WordCrafts Press, 2020) and is a member of the Jane Austen Society of North America, the Horror Writers Association, and the Dracula Society, and a *Dark Shadows* fan. You can find her frolicking in the cemeteries of Salem most Halloween nights.

Curtis M. Lawson is an author of unapologetically weird fiction. His work ranges from technicolor pulp adventures to bleak cosmic horror and includes *Black Heart Boys' Choir, The Devoured,* and *Those Who Go Forth into the Empty Place of Gods.* Curtis hosts the Wyrd Transmissions Podcast. He lives in Salem, Massachusetts, with his wife and their son.

Ngo Binh Anh Khoa is a teacher of English in Ho Chi Minh City, Vietnam. In his free time, he enjoys daydreaming, reading, and occasionally writing poetry for personal entertainment. His speculative poems have appeared in NewMyths.com, *Heroic Fantasy Quarterly, The Audient Void,* and other venues.

Shawn Phelps received an M.A. in Anthropology from the University of Chicago. After leading a series of expeditions in the Amazon, he was elected to be a member of the Explorer's Club. Currently he works as an outreach RN in the Downtown Eastside neighborhood of Vancouver, B.C. He has been a lifelong enthusiast of weird fiction. This is his first publication.

Geoffrey Reiter is Associate Professor and Coordinator of Literature at Lancaster Bible College. He is also an Associate Editor at the website Christ and Pop Culture, where he frequently writes about weird horror and dark fantasy. As a scholar of weird fiction, Reiter has published academic articles on such authors as Arthur Machen, Bram Stoker, Clark Ashton Smith, and William Peter Blatty. His poetry has previously appeared in *Spectral Realms*.

David Rose is an avid fan and reader of weird fiction. Along with being a self-proclaimed McNaughton scholar, he is the author of such works as *Amden Bog: A Novel in Stories*. His newest release is the short story collection *The Scrolls of Sin*. He lives in Orlando, Florida, with a noisy fish tank.

Mark Samuels lives in Kings Langley, England. He is the author of six short story collections and of three novels, the latest of which is *Witch-Cult Abbey* (Zagava Books, 2020). Zagava is now in the process of reprinting all his earlier work in deluxe limited editions throughout this year and the next. In 2020 Hippocampus Press published a selection of his best horror stories under the title *The Age of Decayed Futurity*.

Ann K. Schwader lives and writes in Colorado. Her newest collection, *Unquiet Stars*, is now out from Weird House Press. Two of her earlier collections, *Wild Hunt of the Stars* (Sam's Dot, 2010) and *Dark Energies* (P'rea Press, 2015), were Bram Stoker Award Finalists. In 2018, she received the Science Fiction & Fantasy Poetry Association's Grand Master award. She is also a two-time Rhysling Award winner.

Darrell Schweitzer is a former editor of *Weird Tales* and a poet, short story writer, novelist, critic, and anthologist. PS Publishing recently issued a two-volume retrospective of his work, *The Mysteries of the Faceless King* and *The Last Heretic.* Fedogan & Bremer issued a collection of his Lovecraftian stories, *Awaiting Strange Gods* (2015). His major verse collections are *Groping toward the Light* and *Ghosts of Past and Future.* He is overdue for another one.

John C. Tibbetts is Professor Emeritus at the University of Kansas in Film and Media studies. His books include *The Furies of Marjorie Bowen* (McFarland, 2019), *The Gothic Worlds of Peter Straub* (McFarland, 2016), *Those Who Made It: Conversations with the Legends of Hollywood* (Palgrave Macmillan, 2015), *Peter Weir: Interviews* (University of Mississippi Press, 2014), and *The Gothic Imagination* (Palgrave Macmillan, 2012). John has researched, written, produced, and narrated two radio series, *The World of Robert Schumann* (broadcast worldwide on the WFMT Radio Network) and *Piano Portraits* (broadcast on Kansas Public Radio). He was awarded in 2008 the Kansas Governor's Arts in Education Award, presented by Governor Kathleen Sebelius.

Kyla Lee Ward is a Sydney-based creative who works in many modes, which have garnered her Australian Shadows and Aurealis awards. She has placed in the Rhyslings and received Stoker and Ditmar nominations. *The Macabre Modern and Other Morbidities* is her second collection of dark and fantastic fiction and poetry after *The Land of Bad Dreams* (2011). Reviewers have accused her of being "gothic and esoteric," "weird and exhilarating," and of "giving me a nightmare."

Lee Weinstein is a retired Philadelphia librarian with a lifelong interest in science fiction, fantasy, and horror. He has edited a collection of Edward Lucas White's horror stories, and his essays have appeared in *Studies in Weird Fiction, Supernatural Fiction Writers,* the *New York Review of Science Fiction,* and elsewhere. He was a contributor to *Horror Fiction through History* and is an ongoing contributor to the online third edition of the *Encyclopedia of Science Fiction.*